LOVE AMID *the* ASHES

MESU ANDREWS

a Novel

Revell

a division of Baker Publishing Group
Grand Rapids, Michigan

Published by Revell
a division of Baker Publishing Group
P.O. Box 6287, Grand Rapids, MI 49516-6287
www.revellbooks.com

Printed in the United States of America

Library of Congress Cataloging-in-Publication Data
Andrews, Mesu, 1963–
    Love amid the ashes : a novel / Mesu Andrews.
      p.   cm.
    Includes bibliographical references.
    ISBN 978-0-8007-3407-7 (pbk.)
    1. Title.
PS3601.N55274L68 2011
813′.6—dc22
                                  2010037855

12   13   14   15   16   17   7   6   5   4   3   2

To my beloved husband, Roy, and my daughters, Trina and Emily. Your love and encouragement throughout my own "Job suffering" helped me realize God's calling to write. You swept away the guilt and self-pity of chronic illness, and you continually cheer me on to hope and strength. This book is yours. My heart is yours.

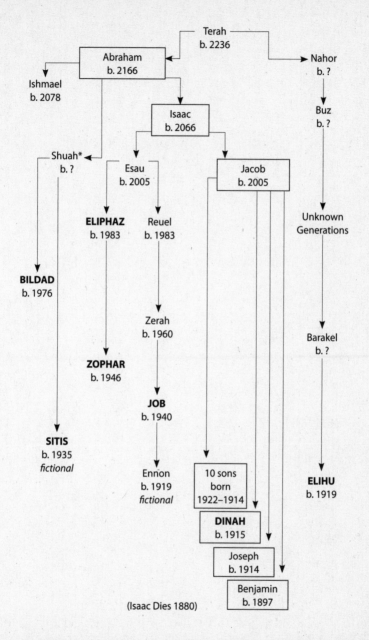

Terah
b. 2236

Nahor
b. ?

Abraham
b. 2166

Ishmael
b. 2078

Isaac
b. 2066

Buz
b. ?

Shuah*
b. ?

Esau
b. 2005

Jacob
b. 2005

ELIPHAZ
b. 1983

Reuel
b. 1983

Unknown
Generations

BILDAD
b. 1976

Zerah
b. 1960

Barakel
b. ?

ZOPHAR
b. 1946

JOB
b. 1940

SITIS
b. 1935
fictional

Ennon
b. 1919
fictional

10 sons
born
1922–1914

ELIHU
b. 1919

DINAH
b. 1915

Joseph
b. 1914

Benjamin
b. 1897

(Isaac Dies 1880)

Dates are approximate and dependent on the author's best interpretation of scholars' commentary. All dates are BC. **BOLD/ALL CAPS** names are major characters in the novel. All characters listed above can be found in Scripture unless designated *fictional*. **SAYYID**, **ABAN**, and **NADA** are fictional characters of unspecified Ishmaelite lineage. An additional fictional character, **NOGAHLA**, descended from a mixed Egyptian and Cushite (today's Ethiopia) lineage. Bela, son of Beor, is of an unknown Edomite lineage.

Boxes denote the line of inheritance for God's covenant promise to Abraham.

*Denotes Abraham's son Shuah was adopted by Ishmael (adoption fictional).

PROLOGUE

~Job 1:6, 8–11~

One day the angels came to present themselves before the LORD, and Satan also came with them. . . . The LORD said to Satan, "Have you considered my servant Job? There is no one on earth like him; he is blameless and upright, a man who fears God and shuns evil." . . . Satan replied, "Have you not put a hedge around him and his household and everything he has? You have blessed the work of his hands. . . . But stretch out your hand and strike everything he has, and he will surely curse you to your face." The LORD said to Satan, "Very well, then, everything he has is in your hands, but on the man himself do not lay a finger." Then Satan went out from the presence of the LORD.

PART I

1

~Genesis 35:28–29~

*Isaac lived a hundred and eighty years. Then he
breathed his last and died and was gathered to
his people, old and full of years. And his sons
Esau and Jacob buried him.*

Dinah's leaden feet left no print in the sun-baked soil
of Grandfather Isaac's Hebron camp. He had fought
death's pale rider for many days, but his aging lungs finally
lost the battle for breath. He was gone. Her sun and moon
and stars, the only man who had seen beyond Dinah's shame
and loved her after Shechem. Her heart felt as desolate as the
dwindling wadi, where she knelt to rinse the rags with which
she'd washed and anointed Grandfather's body.

"Mistress."

A small voice rippled over Dinah's shoulder, barely louder
than the water's flow. Startled from her contemplations, she
dropped the cloths into the running waters. "Oh no!" she

cried, crawling along the bank to retrieve the myrrh-scented rags. Rocks scraped her knees, and the muddy waters churned with each attempt to snag the cloths.

An agile, dark form jumped in front of her, rescuing the floating treasures. "I've got them, mistress!" A young servant girl from Grandfather's camp stood in ankle-deep water, hand lifted victoriously above her head, raining drops onto her mossy, short-cropped hair. Her rich black skin and angular cheekbones bespoke a Cushite heritage. Dinah had noticed her among the camp's servants, but the long hours at Grandfather's side kept Dinah sequestered in the family tents.

"Why do you call me mistress?" Dinah asked, reaching for the dingy, dripping rags. "We've never even spoken before, child, and I'm no better than a servant myself." She squeezed out the cloths and laid them in the basket slung over her arm.

"Master Job told me that I was now your handmaid—since you'll be marrying his son."

Standing to full height, Dinah towered over the girl and mimicked Abba Jacob's thunderous declaration of the past week. "Just because Job is the greatest man in the East, doesn't mean he can walk into Grandfather Isaac's camp and start shouting orders."

The girl's countenance drooped like the drought-weary grasses of Hebron's plains.

Regretting her harshness, Dinah placed a comforting arm across the girl's shoulders and began the short trek toward the tents. "It's just that I'm not a part of Master Job's household yet." She paused, her heart wrung out like the rags in her basket. "I'm not really a part of any household," she whispered, staring at the tents ahead. They walked a few more steps in silence. "Job shouldn't promise things that Abba might not fulfill." Glancing down at the girl beside her, she saw disappointment mirrored on her face. Dinah wished she could offer reassurance, but how could she comfort another when she felt lost and alone? Besides, this little Cushite was Grandfather's serving maid. The way Abba Jacob and Uncle Esau were fighting over Grandfather's possessions, who knew how the inheritance and servants would be divided?

"I'm sorry, mistress." The girl sounded rather distracted. Dinah noticed she had begun a little game, taking giant leaps and tiny steps to avoid the cracks in the dry earth. "But may I pretend to be your handmaid until your abba says differently?" She hopped to the next small patch of smooth dirt, balancing precariously on one foot.

Dinah steadied her with a hand on her shoulder. "Only if you stop calling me mistress." With an arched brow, she waited for the girl's nod before resuming their journey toward camp.

The girl fell in step beside her, a full span shorter than Dinah, and continued to chatter. "Abraham was a great prince among his people, and your Grandfather Isaac as well. So should I call you princess?"

"Ha!" The bitter laugh broke through the stone wall of grief, surprising even Dinah. But the smile that lingered for this wide-eyed, innocent girl was heartfelt. "No one has ever called me a princess, little Cushite. You may simply call me Dinah."

Just then the high-pitched keening of mourners began, and Dinah searched the path over the horizon between the poplars. As suspected, she saw Grandfather Isaac's wrapped body jostling in a cart on its way to the burial cave at Mamre, north of Hebron. His sons, Jacob and Esau, followed the cart, their hatred sparking like flint stones. Jacob's eleven sons walked behind stoically. But from Esau's bountiful clan, only two paid homage to the patriarch. Esau's great-grandson, Job, mourned as if his own abba lay in the burial cart, and Esau's firstborn, Eliphaz, comforted him. The numerous other Edomites had been rumored to worship Canaanite gods and had little respect for Isaac, the son of Abraham, Yahweh's covenant bearer.

"Come." Dinah swallowed hard, holding back the wave of sadness threatening to drown her. "What should I call you, little one?"

"I am Nogahla." Her lilting voice almost obscured the mourners' wails.

"Come, Nogahla. I have no need of a handmaid, but I would appreciate your help packing my supplies for the journey to Uz." An amiable agreement. No more words. The air was too full of grief, uncertainty, and the mourners' echoes.

They reached Grandfather's camp, arranged in circular tent rows around a large central fire and ovens. Paths like spokes in a wheel joined the tents of family members to servants. The tents closest to the fire identified the highly esteemed guests and relatives, while the servants occupied the outlying dwellings. Dinah and Nogahla moved past the outer realms and family tents, shooing stray herding dogs and nodding greetings to servants. They arrived at the central ovens, where busy hands baked bread for Esau's soon-departing caravans and for the relatives and servants who would remain in Hebron.

Three tents were always at the center of camp. Grandfather Isaac's was closest to the fire, Abba Jacob's on its west side, and Uncle Esau's on the east. Dinah stopped, eyeing the dwellings. Grandfather Isaac's massive black tent lay empty now, fronted by a great canopy. It had once been a busy gathering place for visiting merchants and dignitaries who sought an audience with the great son of Abraham. Abba Jacob's tent stood austere, functional, and precise—much like her abba, the calculating twin son of Isaac. Uncle Esau's dwelling was crudely fashioned from various animal skins and rough-hewn wood.

The twins' tents were as opposite as the brothers themselves—a constant battle between conniver and hunter. Though almost one hundred years had passed since Abba Jacob bought Esau's birthright with a bowl of soup, and nearly fifty years since Abba stole Esau's covenant blessing, the brothers' rivalry had grown stronger with each passing year. Thankfully, they seldom visited Grandfather Isaac at the same time. Abba Jacob spent most of his time pasturing flocks and herds in Beersheba, while Uncle Esau tended his large clan in the Seir Mountains.

Passing under Grandfather's canopy, Dinah ducked through the tethered flap on her own little tent. Her prominent location at the center of camp had been a source of contention when she'd arrived fifteen years ago, but Grandfather had settled the matter, citing his need for immediate access to medical care. Dinah knew it was simply one of the ways he chose to honor her.

Nogahla entered the dimly lit enclosure, and Dinah heard her soft gasp. "Mistress! You are a physician of great wisdom."

Determined not to chafe at the unearned adulation, Dinah tried to imagine her little home through Nogahla's eyes. The myriad vials of herbs and potions, perched on her rough-hewn cedar shelves, stung the nostrils with heady scents of coriander, aloe, and myrrh. Abba Jacob's speckled and spotted wool rugs graced the floor with only a center aisle of dirt separating her sleeping area from living space. She owned two robes, four tunics, and three head coverings, which probably seemed extravagant to a Cushite servant. The rest of her tent was filled with herbs, unguents, and potions in every form and fashion.

Dinah's needs were basic and her lifestyle simple. She seldom left the confines of the central fire and small area between her tent and Grandfather Isaac's. This was her world, her home. But no more.

For fifteen years she'd felt secure, capable, and useful as she cared for Grandfather Isaac. Now she wondered what truly belonged to her and what greedy Uncle Esau would seize for himself. When the men returned from the burial cave, she would be expected to obey Isaac's command—to marry Job's son.

"Why would you say such a thing?" Dinah whispered to the grandfather who had loved her.

"I just thought you must be a fine physician to have so many medicines." Nogahla's bright eyes shone even in the low light of the tent, undoubtedly believing Dinah had spoken to her.

Suddenly reeling with regret, Dinah wished she were alone. She needed time to consider Grandfather's shocking command. He'd given no inkling of his wishes to see her married at this late stage in her life. Thirty-five was well past "honey and cream" and dangerously close to "curdled milk." *And why would he condemn me to marry a man in Esau's clan?* But she knew the answer to that question. Because Dinah was Jacob's daughter, Grandfather had said her womb would be the "garden of promise" in which Esau's descendants could share in the covenant blessing Jacob had deceitfully stolen.

"Ha!" A bitter laugh escaped, but this time Nogahla seemed to realize Dinah wasn't pondering herbs. "Men do not look at me as a 'garden of promise,' Nogahla. Men see me as dirt."

The girl patted her shoulder gently. "Master Job does not look at you as dirt."

Dinah shrugged off her hand and reached for a myrrh pot and piece of fleece to wrap it. "Master Job only offered his son because Uncle Esau refused any other Edomite—even when Grandfather was drawing his last breath." Tears clouded her vision. "So Job, the jewel in Esau's crown, the golden man of the East, stepped forward to do the righteous thing. He offered his firstborn, Ennon, to marry me, Jacob's tainted daughter."

"Master Job's eyes are clear and good." Nogahla's head was bowed, her voice barely a whisper. "I don't believe he would have offered his son if he thought it would harm either of you."

Oh, what innocence, Dinah thought. *All men eventually harm you.* She needed to blame someone for her fate, and she refused to blame Grandfather. He had loved her too well for too long. She wanted to hate Job. She tried to think his wealth and success made him prideful and pompous. But Nogahla's hope—though utterly unthinkable—seemed well placed. Job had been kind and compassionate, tenderly caring for Grandfather in his dying days, gaining nothing for himself. The best one to blame would be Uncle Esau. That hairy red mountain of a man had always been the target of Abba Jacob's hatred, and he seemed well fitted for the offering.

"Mistress, I'm sorry about Master Isaac." Nogahla's voice was as soothing as balm to Dinah's heart. "I know you loved him."

A single tear wet Dinah's cheek. She wiped it quickly. "Let's get started packing. I don't know which supplies will travel with me to Uz and which will go to my abba and Uncle Esau, but we must wrap each vial carefully." Emotions knotted her thoughts and more tears threatened, but she refused to release them. "I wonder if the blossoms look the same in the mountains of Edom?" She reached for a second pot of myrrh and a scrap of fleece to cradle it.

A gentle hand halted her restless arm, dismantling the thin veil of control. "I listen well, mistress."

"Evidently you don't listen well, or you wouldn't be calling me mistress!" Words and emotion tumbled out. "My future has been sealed like a worthless mule sent to market, and Grandfather Isaac is gone!" Dinah hurled the myrrh pot at the center tent post, and the pungent scent of the broken pot filled the air, causing her head to swim slightly. Just one more sign that the sleepless days and nights had left her physically and emotionally spent. Examining the shards of pottery on the rug, she met Nogahla's shocked gaze. "Just like my broken life."

The girl reached out, leading her by the hand to a pile of speckled and spotted rugs. Dinah sat numbly. "You're right, mis—Dinah. Your life *is* like that beautiful, shattered pot. It has just been broken open, and the lovely scent that's been locked inside your heart is about to be shared with Master Job's son."

Nogahla paused, her eyes begging for a response. When none came, she picked up the pieces of pottery and retrieved a chipped clay vial from a shelf. Wrapping both the shards and the vial in old sackcloth, she said, "Let's say this little pot is my life. Something tells me that if we pack our lives together, they'll turn out better." A tentative smile lifted her cheeks. "Rest your head, mistress. I'll pack your things. You must rest before the men return from the burial cave."

2

~Genesis 34:1–4~

*Now Dinah, the daughter Leah had borne to
Jacob, went out to visit the women of the land.
When Shechem son of Hamor the Hivite, the
ruler of that area, saw her, he took her and
violated her. His heart was drawn to Dinah . . .
and he loved the girl and spoke tenderly to her.
And Shechem said to his father Hamor, "Get me
this girl as my wife."*

Dinah watched the young Cushite bundling each piece
of pottery and plant, every herb and vial. Nestling
down on the rug and gathering a blanket beneath her head,
Dinah's eyelids drooped, lulled by the rhythmic sounds of
the Hebron camp at work. Wooden spoons clanged on brass
cooking pots. Lambs *mahhhed* for the ewes. Children's laughter floated on the spring breeze. But a new sound joined the

chorus. Nogahla's gentle hum sent a soothing vibration deep into Dinah's soul, and sleep carried her away.

❄ ❄ ❄ ❄ ❄

The dream was as vivid as the first time Dinah lived it. She was fifteen again, and the heavy morning dew soaked her robe as she moved quietly through her abba's flocks, careful not to disturb the ewes with their lambs, lest their bleating wake her surly brothers. Her thighs ached as she climbed the steep limestone terraces covered with wheat fields, olive groves, and vineyards. Brilliant purple and orange hues glowed in the eastern sky, casting an alabaster glow on her high-stepping march through the golden heads of wheat.

The morning sun burst over the high walls of Shechem, and the prince bearing the city's name stood at the gate. Dinah was transfixed by the outline of his muscular frame, the backdrop of the glowing sunrise making him appear more god than man. Shechem bowed as if she were royalty and he the shepherd's child. "Good morning, beauty of Jacob."

Dinah felt her cheeks grow warm at his words, and she returned his bow, keeping her gaze downcast. Never had a man spoken to her in such a way. He reached out for her hand, and she instinctively drew back. He gently touched her chin, and she looked into his eyes for the first time. "I will never force you to do anything against your will, lovely Dinah."

Her breath caught. "How do you know my name?" she asked.

The brightness of his smile on that sun-kissed face matched the dawn. "When your abba bought the land from my brothers and me, we were mere children, but I noted how beautiful you were, and I asked your name. Now I am twenty, and you are marriageable age, are you not?"

Dinah dropped her gaze immediately. She couldn't breathe or think or reason. Had this handsome prince just asked her to marry him? Impossible. "Yes, I am of age," she heard herself say.

"Well, I have been waiting to make you my wife. My father has only one wife, and I plan to follow his example. You are my choice, Dinah." He held out his hand once again. Dinah studied it, knowing her future hung in the balance. His hand was large and tanned and gentle as it folded around hers.

She could feel his pulse racing through her hand, its rhythm turning her thoughts into a jumbled torrent of words. "But Ima Rachel's silver!" She blurted out the words, startling poor Shechem. "She is a midwife, and I'm her assistant. I promised to retrieve her payment from Nebal the merchant and then return home. Abba and Ima Leah don't even know I've gone into the city alone. They'll be worried if I don't return soon." She hated that her voice sounded desperate and childish, but if she went home without Ima Rachel's silver . . .

Home. Would she be returning home? Her head snapped up and she searched Shechem's face. Kind eyes and a gentle expression.

She became lost in him. What was this aching in her chest? This glorious desire to sing, to run, to melt into his arms—all in the same moment?

Shechem gently squeezed her hand and winked, a wide grin stretching across his broad face. "Your ima Rachel will have her silver. I'll see to it," he said. "Nebal told me you were coming today. It's why I'm here." He reached out to trace her jaw with one finger.

His touch broke the spell, and Dinah dropped her gaze.

She peered at the passing merchants, her head bowed shamefully. Suddenly conscious of the stares, she regretted allowing Shechem to show his affection in public. If her abba heard, there could be trouble.

Shechem must have realized her discomfort because his next words came with a chuckle, and his hands fell to his sides. "Tell me, Jacob's daughter, would you like to stand here at the city gate and discuss our wedding, or shall we go to the palace for the remainder of our conversation?"

"Wedding?" Dinah breathed, her heart beating so hard and fast, she was certain her woolen robe danced without her permission. She giggled, her cheeks on fire, and then leaned in close. "Am I to spend the rest of my life with a flushed face, Prince Shechem?" she whispered. Her first attempt at teasing was met with his delighted laughter, and before she could object, he hoisted her into his arms and carried her through the city streets.

"What are you doing?" She tugged frantically to cover her exposed ankles.

Her question was met with princely strides in the direction of the palace towers. "I am carrying my wife through her city," he said, his eyes so full of her that Dinah could see her reflection in the warm brown pools. "Tell me, daughter of Jacob, how do you feel about being a queen someday? What do you think of our city?"

Dinah didn't know whether to be embarrassed at being carried like an injured lamb, or honored or frightened or suspicious. After all, she didn't really *know* Prince Shechem. He was widely renowned as the most honored and respected of all King Hamor's sons, but was he an honorable man? Did he have many women? Was he deceiving her? All she knew at this moment was that he was handsome and charming, and he had just asked her a question she was supposed to answer.

"I'm sorry, what did you just ask me?"

His laughter boomed and his eyes sparkled—not a glimmer of impatience or frustration. "I asked what you think of our city." His grin and arched eyebrows said that he would wait in silence for her appraisal.

Though Dinah had visited Shechem dozens of times with Ima Rachel, she'd never roamed freely through the market-place. And even if she'd seen the market a thousand times, the view from Prince Shechem's arms was certainly different. Vendors shouted from their crowded booths. Animals of all shapes and sizes were traded for labor and sold for meat. Children scampered from merchant to merchant, some begging bread and others tucking items into the tiny folds of their robes. A man holding a heavy metal chain led ten women wearing iron collars. Each woman wore a costume from a different land, though two of them wore nothing at all. City life was a completely different world to Dinah, and when she returned her attention to the prince, his eyes were clouded with worry.

"What do you think of your new home?" he asked. "Can you ever be happy surrounded by high stone walls and noisy people after living on quiet hillsides in neat tent rows?"

Dinah saw true concern on Shechem's features, and she was awed by his tenderness. She couldn't remember ever being asked her opinion or having anyone show concern for her happiness. Tears threatened, and she couldn't let him think she was such a child, so she answered with her mischievous side. "I confess I prefer the smell of shepherds' fields and sheep dung to rotted food and smelly old men in the city streets, Prince Shechem—but *you* are far more appealing than my ugly brothers." Holding his gaze, she tilted her head and lifted an eyebrow, letting only one side of her mouth show its pleasure.

His response was better than she hoped, more pleasing than she expected. He smiled, stopped in the middle of the street, and kissed her deeply. Those bustling around them stopped to applaud, and when he pulled away, Dinah was breathless. "I'm glad you find me appealing," he said, mischief of his own dancing in his eyes. "Ha!" He resumed his march toward the palace, and she nestled her head against his shoulder, finding it comfortable enough to satisfy her for the rest of her life.

When they arrived in the large limestone structure, Dinah was surprised that they didn't stop in the main hall. Instead, Shechem continued carrying her through a maze of winding hallways, past several doorways and wondering servants. He climbed a narrow stairway and finally entered a room grandly furnished with extravagant rugs and plush furniture. Dinah was awestruck. She remembered Ima Rachel's instructions for when they tended the wealthy births in Shechem, and tried to keep her gaping mouth closed. The prince gently set her feet on the floor, but she rushed from one beautiful hanging tapestry to the next.

"It's all so elegant," she said, forgetting her soon-to-be bridegroom at the door. When she finally remembered where she was, and what—or who—had brought her there, she was once again humiliated by her childishness. "Please forgive me, Your Majesty." Her cheeks were aflame, and she bowed to Prince Shechem. In her subservient posture, she noted that she had stopped directly beside the large veiled bed in the middle of the room. She tried to swallow, but her mouth had gone as dry as the Eastern Desert.

In less than a heartbeat, Prince Shechem stood before her,

one hand lifting her chin, the other securely around her waist. "So it's 'Your Majesty' now, is it?" he said with a sly grin.

She saw hunger in his eyes and looked away, not knowing how to respond. Why had she allowed him to carry her to his bedchamber?

"I said I would never force you to do anything against your will, Dinah." His eyes searched every corner of her soul. This time she couldn't turn away no matter how hard she tried. But did she even wish to try? He'd captured her in less than a moment's breath, not in body but in heart.

"What do you ask of me?" Dinah whispered the words. She knew what he was asking, but would he say it? Could she do it?

"I ask you to be my wife. Today. Now."

"Your wife? Now?" Panic clawed at her. "But what about your family? Isn't there some ceremony we must follow?"

"Dinah, I am the prince of Shechem. I marry whom I wish, when I wish it. I have waited many years to have you. You are the one I want, Dinah—the only one I want."

"But my father . . . he is the son of Isaac, the son of Abraham. We worship Yahweh and—"

"My father and I will offer a bride-price for you, my beautiful Dinah, that is beyond anything ever paid for a daughter in Canaan. Your father will be overjoyed at our happiness." Before Dinah could say more, Shechem covered her mouth with his kiss. The bliss of physical union united their souls—a wedding day of the heart, unknown and unapproved by Abba Jacob.

⁂

Dinah's dream faded, and she lingered between two realities. Her tent felt empty. She opened one eye to find three neatly stacked baskets against one wall, filled with fleece-wrapped jars and tight rolls of dried herbs. Activity in the camp grew louder, but the ecstasy of Shechem's kisses drew her back to the land of dreams. She vaguely recalled her present reality. Grandfather Isaac was dead. He'd commanded her to marry a new husband, and she should be packing her things for her departure to Uz. But Dinah's dream returned her to the rapture of her wedding day with Shechem. Every color, sound, and scent of that day came back in a flood of sweet surrender.

❦ ❦ ❦ ❦ ❦

The next morning, Shechem and Dinah emerged from his chamber, and King Hamor performed a simple Shechemite ceremony, making official the marriage of their hearts. "I'll return before tonight's wedding feast," Shechem said confidently, as he and the king left the palace to negotiate her bride-price with Abba Jacob.

That's when her dream turned to a nightmare—as it always did. Now she tried to wake, but couldn't. Dinah had waited at the palace with King Hamor's wife, and they were among the women who cried out against the sons of Jacob when they demanded all the men of Shechem undergo circumcision so that Dinah could remain Prince Shechem's wife.

"No, my love," Dinah said. "Please, put me away. Take a Shechemite woman and forget about me." But the night before his cutting had been the tenderest night of Dinah's short life, and the love he'd shown her was beyond anything she'd ever known. Surely, no man had ever loved a wife like Shechem loved her—not even Abba's love for Ima Rachel could compare.

On the second day after his cutting, the prince said, "You see, my love, this will all be over soon." Dinah had pampered and spoiled her beloved every moment of his recovery. He caressed her cheek as she slipped into bed beside him that night. "Someday we will laugh and tell our grandchildren the story." The love in his expression pierced Dinah's heart. Never before had she known such selflessness.

"Perhaps we should have children before we start talking about grandchildren," she said, kissing his cheek, his neck, his shoulder.

He smiled and kissed her forehead. "Perhaps we should turn out the lamp and go to sleep so I can heal quickly." Dinah giggled and snuffed out the oil lamps, taking her place in the bend of her husband's arm until their breathing became slow and deep and steady.

And then came the wailing.

Dinah tried to wake but was captured in a semiconsciousness of horror and dread. Shechem's face lay before her. His eyes empty. His lovely mouth twisted in death's last plea. Her arms were warm, wet, sticky with her husband's blood. "Simeon, Levi, no!"

Her brothers stood over her, their swords dripping.

"This Shechemite dog will never defile another man's sister." Simeon spat the words as he reached for Dinah's arm.

"No! He did not defile me! We are married!"

"Not according to Abba, you're not!" Simeon lunged at her, and she recoiled, trapped between the bloody shell of the man she loved and the animal brethren who had killed him.

"Get away from me! He did not rape me! Shechem loved me!"

※ ※ ※ ※ ※

"Dinah." It was a man's voice. "Dinah." She felt a hand shaking her arm. "Dinah, wake up, we must leave." It was the voice of Simeon—no, it was Levi!

28

Dinah screamed, terror gripping her anew. She clawed at the copper hair and beard before her. "No! Get away from Shechem. No, Levi! He loves me! He didn't rape me! Don't hurt him, Simeon! He loves me!" She flailed and kicked at the man trying to restrain her.

"Dinah, it's me, Job. Dinah! Shh. Dinah, stop." Strong arms subdued her. She couldn't struggle free. Her screams turned to sobs, and Dinah's body went limp.

"Dinah, shh." Gentle arms rocked her. "It's me, Job. Shh. It's all right, Dinah."

She gazed up into deep brown eyes, the color of her ima's dark bread.

"You're coming home with me, Dinah. You'll be safe with my son."

Dinah finally awakened fully, and for a moment—just a moment—she longed to melt into the strong, loving arms of the man who held her. He sat on the rug, cradling her, stroking her hair. But this man was to be her father-in-law!

Humiliation and shame tightened their hold on her. She wrested herself from his arms, huddling near the stacked baskets like a wounded animal. They had barely ever spoken, and now he had seen her deepest wound exposed. A low, guttural moan escaped. "Go," she said, turning her face away. He tried to help her stand, but she crouched lower still. "No, please. Just go."

He stood over her, offering his hand once more. "Dinah." Silence hung in the tent like the thick burial odor of the shattered pot of myrrh. "Are you all right?" The mourners' wails echoed in the camp with Job's sigh. "Your abba has returned with Great-Abba Esau from the burial cave. Esau wants to leave for Mount Seir right away and asked that my caravan accompany him to the south." Job paused again and spoke softly. "I'll tell him I'm not prepared to leave so soon, nor can I afford the extended travel route. Can you be ready by dawn to leave for Uz?"

Dinah nodded, her throat too tight to reply. She heard the tent flap fall closed, and when she looked up, Job was gone.

Her breaths came in short, quick gasps. She hugged her knees to her chest, hoping to still her violent trembling. *I must not join the mourners' wailing*, she thought. *For if I begin, I may never stop.* Rocking back and forth, she moved in tempo with the keening. What if her nightmares worsened? What if she screamed and flailed in the arms of her new husband? Would he be as understanding as Job had been? Dinah's heart pounded, and she rocked faster.

A tiny shadow flitted past the narrow ray of sunlight peeking through the tent flap. Dinah stopped rocking. There it was again. And then a sweet chirrup broke through the mourners' wails. A pink-and-black-crested hoopoe bird landed just outside. The little creature peered in and then proceeded to enjoy its late afternoon dust bath. *Oop-oop-oop* came its lovely song, slicing through Dinah's pain.

"Oh, little bird," she whispered, "we are too much alike, you and me. Grandfather Isaac said you were one of Yahweh's most lovely creatures, but He has judged you as unclean." Tears streamed down her cheeks. "Men have said I am lovely too, but must they all judge me as unclean?"

In the frenzied activity of the camp, a servant rushed by and frightened the hoopoe into flight, and loneliness gripped Dinah's heart anew. "Oh, how I wish I had wings and could fly away to a new home of my own making. A home where my past was forgotten and my future unfettered."

3

~*Genesis 9:26–27*~

[Noah] said, "Blessed be the LORD, *the God of Shem! May Canaan be the slave of Shem. . . . May Japheth live in the tents of Shem, and may Canaan be his slave."*

Job stood beside Dinah's tent, hearing only her mumbled whimpers. He ached with the need to comfort her but trembled with frustration at her refusal. Dinah had endured more tragedy than any young woman should bear. When he had reached out to wake her, she cried out to protect Shechem—the man reported to have raped her. Why? There was obviously more to the story than rumors disclosed. If she was to marry one of his sons, he had the right to know exactly what had happened in Shechem.

Job could easily locate Uncle Jacob. Just listen for the constant bickering in the camp, and the sons of Isaac were at its source. He stepped away from Dinah's tent, crossed under

Grandfather Isaac's canopy, and came upon the hotheaded brothers.

"Every speckled, spotted, or dark-colored sheep and goat is mine!" Jacob railed. "I slaved for Uncle Laban twenty years to earn those flocks and herds, and you'll not lay a hand on them."

"You can keep your moldy-looking animals, but I'm taking everything else." Esau was red from head to toe, eyes bloodshot and bulging.

"You can have everything, you big red dog," Jacob cried, "but Abba anointed me with Abraham's covenant promise, and that includes the land of Canaan. So you can have all the worthless possessions, but leave the Promised Land to me."

"Ha! It is you who holds the worthless piece, brother! Elohim may have promised Canaan to Abraham, but He forgot to inform the Canaanites. It is you who's been swindled this time."

Jacob gritted his teeth and rose up on his toes to spit the words in Esau's face. "I am not as easily swindled as my dimwitted brother."

When the mighty red mountain raised his hand to strike Jacob, Job cried out, "Great-Abba, no!" Esau seemed startled by the intrusion and was distracted just long enough for Jacob to dive at his midsection and tumble his massive brother to the ground.

Job's fury peaked at these selfish old fools whose abba's dead body was barely cold in the grave before they pawed at the inheritance and brawled like children. He promptly walked over to the ridiculous, rolling elders and kicked dust in their faces.

When they separated and stood up sputtering, Job began his rebuke. "You should both be ashamed of yourselves, tussling like Hittites in Isaac's camp. You're old men with brittle bones!" He knew such an argument didn't hold much sway with the great hunter, Esau, and the able-bodied shepherd, Jacob. Both men were almost as strong at age 125 as Job was at age sixty.

Jacob raised an accusing finger. "If he wasn't so greedy, trying to take all the inheritance instead of just the firstborn's two-thirds, we would have no problem."

Esau started to bluster, but Job raised his hand and spoke through clenched teeth. "Look at the servants around you! Look at them!" The sons of Isaac glanced about sheepishly. The servants, who had been working feverishly to prepare for the journey, had halted their work and were staring at the spectacle. With the brothers' gaze upon them, however, they hurried back to work, humming and whistling shepherds' songs.

Job kept his voice low. "How dare you defile Grandfather Isaac's memory by acting so shamefully in front of all these servants? Now, please, let's go into Uncle Jacob's tent. I have important matters to discuss." Job marched right past the two men, who at that moment looked like pouting children.

In the time it took the tent flap to close, Esau had regained his bluster. "Job, our caravan will leave immediately following the evening meal. We'll travel in the cool of the night by torchlight to avoid the sun's heat by day."

Job smiled kindly but shook his head. "I'm sorry, Great-Abba, but I cannot be ready to leave so quickly. My servants will require more time to prepare my caravan to Uz."

Esau's eyes narrowed, and Job watched the wheels of his great-abba's mind spin, gathering the truth of Job's delay. "Because of that *woman*." Esau spat the word as though it were a curse. "I saw you coming from her tent. She thinks she can steal away the valuable herbs and treasures in her tent and you'll just blindly load it onto your caravan. Well, she owns only the clothes on her back and—"

"Great-Abba," Job interrupted, "you know that I respect you, and I always honor and obey you whenever it does not conflict with El Shaddai's teachings." Esau started to protest, but Job's fury silenced him. "Dinah will take only the possessions that belong to her. You can be sure of it, but we will *not* leave with your caravan tonight! Furthermore, I *request* that you leave twenty of your servants to accompany me to Uz." Job turned his attention to Uncle Jacob. "I'll need the extra men to carry the dowry I'm sure you'll wish to offer for your beautiful daughter."

"Dowry? My abba didn't command me to give her a dowry." Uncle Jacob's protest silenced every clang and clatter in the camp outside. "And you've offered me no bride-price. Why should I pay a dowry for a woman who has already been defiled?" Esau's bawdy laughter chilled Job's blood and stoked Jacob's anger. "I'll not pay one silver kesitah for her dowry! She's been in our abba's house for fifteen years. If there's a dowry to be paid, let my brother—who now holds the wealth of Isaac's household—give Dinah her dowry."

Esau stopped laughing. "I would not claim such a daughter, and I will not pay her dowry!" he screamed. The two brothers spiraled into a new fit of rage, and Job dragged his fingers through his hair, letting his head fall back in frustration. *El Shaddai, how do You endure such selfishness on this earth?* "Enough!" Job shouted above the noise, and both men turned to him in surprise.

Esau's eyes narrowed once again. "Listen here, son of Zerah. Even though you are my favorite great-grandson, I will not endure your bossy tongue."

Job smiled in spite of his irritation and reached up to place his hand on Esau's muscled shoulder. "And even though you are my great-abba, I will not endure you speaking unkindly of my soon-to-be daughter-in-law." Job held Esau's gaze until the big man grunted a truce and stomped out of the tent.

When Job turned to Uncle Jacob, the elder man's mouth was agape. "I've never seen anyone quiet my brother the way you just did, Job. How did you come to have such a hold over that devil Esau?"

Job's heart squeezed a little at the hate encompassed in Jacob's question. "Well, Uncle," Job replied, "I suppose Great-Abba's respect for me began on the night I was smuggled away in the hunting party meant to kill you." Uncle Jacob's face registered the shock Job had hoped for. "Are you truly interested in hearing the story?"

A suspicious smile spread across Jacob's face. "What are you asking as payment for your story? I have no intention of paying Dinah's dowry, no matter how well you tell a story."

Job shook his head, weary of the pettiness in his family. "No payment is required, Uncle, and I'll even be happy to pay a bride-price for Dinah. She is a pearl of great price."

Suspicion creased Uncle Jacob's brow. Job placed his arm around the older man's shoulders and guided him to one of the legendary rugs of Jacob's tribe. The speckled and spotted sheep and goats produced a uniquely woven cloth that had become quite coveted throughout Canaan.

"I simply ask that you tell me a story in return." Job smiled and waited for his reply.

"I suspect there is more to the agreement, but my curiosity about your relationship with the impenetrable Esau forces me to agree," Jacob said.

Job lifted an eyebrow and motioned to the lamb's wool rug, and Jacob nodded his permission for them to sit together. "I was thirteen years old," Job began, "but I remember it like it was yesterday. It was seven days after you'd deceived Grandfather Isaac into thinking you were his eldest son. When he conferred the covenant blessing on your head, you realized the soon-coming wrath of Esau and fled in fear for your life, hoping to reach Uncle Laban's home in Haran."

Jacob raised his chin, his usual defense at the ready. "I may have deceived my abba to receive the touch of blessing, but El Shaddai knew who would best protect Yahweh's truth and fulfill the covenant of Abraham. Esau refused to sit under the great teachers of the House of Shem. He didn't deserve the blessing."

Job nodded but refused to condone his uncle's deception. "Great-Abba Esau called a meeting of all the men in his clan. He commissioned Eliphaz to lead what he deemed 'an important hunt.' Esau called on his other four sons to choose one more from each of their families. They were to follow at a distance until you crossed the Jordan River, and then his secondborn—my grandfather Reuel, the greatest archer of the Edomites—was ordered to send an arrow into your thigh." Job paused. "They wanted to wound you first, to instill fear before the others encircled you and killed you, Uncle."

Jacob's face lost all color.

"Upon your death, Esau believed he would be free to reclaim Abraham's covenant blessing at the touch of Isaac's hand."

Apparently too agitated to remain seated, Jacob rose and began to pace. "Is there a point to your story, Job? I thought you were going to tell me why you could lead my brother on a leash like a pet lamb. What does all this nonsense have to do with your power over Esau?"

"Oh, this is not nonsense, Uncle. It is the reason you are alive." Jacob stopped his pacing, and Job motioned for his uncle to resume his place on the rug beside him. "Please, won't you sit down for the end of the story?"

Jacob growled and lowered himself onto the rug while Job waited patiently to continue. "You know that Eliphaz would rather fall on his own sword than harm a single hair on your head, since you two were disciples together in the House of Shem. Uncle Eliphaz looked like day-old ashes when Great-Abba Esau called on him to lead the so-called *hunt*."

"As it should have been. The whole idea of hunting a man is barbaric."

Jacob's self-righteous attitude set Job's teeth on edge, but he refused to digress from the story. "When Reuel chose his secondborn son—my abba, Zerah—for the hunt, the look on Abba's face matched Uncle Eliphaz's."

Jacob looked awestruck. "Why would Reuel choose another disciple of Shem among the hunters? He knew I taught your abba in the House of Shem. He knew that the three of us—Eliphaz, Zerah, and I—were the only three of Isaac's seed who were joined by El Shaddai's teachings. Why would he choose to place my two allies in the hunt?"

"Esau chose Eliphaz for the same reason Reuel chose my abba. Each hoped that by forcing your allies to choose duty over devotion, they would become stronger—as Esau defines strength. You see, both Great-Abba Esau and Grandfather Reuel perceived priestly skills as weakness and valued only the abilities of a hunter and warrior."

Jacob closed his eyes. "El Shaddai, help us." Looking at

Job, he asked, "How did one as kind and gentle as you come from a bloodthirsty tribe like Esau's?"

Job ignored his question and continued with the story, knowing that his next words would be answer enough. "I waited for my abba just outside the Tent of Meeting to congratulate him on his appointment. When he didn't come, I peeked inside again and heard him and Uncle Eliphaz planning to take me on the hunt. At first I was excited—just as bloodthirsty as the rest of Esau's clan, Uncle." Job saw the look of horror on Jacob's face. "And then I became furious. They weren't going to let me fight at all. Uncle Eliphaz planned to assert his firstborn authority to protect you from his brothers' swords. He planned only to let them rob you of the secret gifts Grandmother Rebekah sent along to buy Uncle Laban's favor."

"And they stole everything!" Jacob said with venom. "Esau is the reason I arrived at Uncle Laban's household without a single kernel of grain to offer as a bride-price for my beloved Rachel!"

The fury Job had tamped down bubbled up. "Yes, they robbed your silver, grain, and spices, Uncle, but at least you're alive, and you returned from Padan Aram twenty years later with four wives, eleven sons, and a beautiful daughter."

Jacob hushed in the face of Job's anger.

Regaining his composure, Job remembered his greater purpose and spoke softly. "When our hunting party released you, Uncle Eliphaz continued the journey northward with me to the House of Shem. Our nine kinsmen returned to Esau's camp with your treasure, but it wasn't enough to assuage Great-Abba's anger. Once again, Grandfather Reuel challenged my abba to overcome his weakness, and he forced my abba to explain the failed hunt to Esau. When my great-abba heard the report, he struck my abba to the ground. His head crashed against a rock, and his lifeblood spilled out."

Jacob raised his chin once again, as though grief and remorse would slide off his hard exterior like water off a bird's wings. "So you're saying that Esau's guilt over Zerah's death makes him bow to you like a pauper to a prince?" Jacob waved his hand. "Pshht. I don't believe it. I've known that red beast too long. Esau has no conscience. His guilt doesn't make him bow to you."

"No, Uncle," Job said. "Great-Abba Esau doesn't bow to me at all." Job examined every line and furrow on Jacob's weathered face. "Esau respects me, Uncle Jacob, because I have forgiven him and loved him even when he wronged me."

Jacob's eyes flashed. "Then you are a fool."

Job allowed the silence to echo his uncle's words before he spoke again. "Now it's your turn to tell me a story." Without blinking, without any emotion or accusation, Job finally asked the question that had burned on his heart since the moment he'd heard Dinah's pained cries. "Did your sons kill Prince Shechem with righteous cause, or has your own unforgiveness infected your whole household with hatred?"

Jacob began to tremble, and his face flushed as red as his twin's. "Get out! Get out of my tent!"

"I will leave," Job said calmly, rising to his feet, "but I will take Dinah with me and teach her the ways of El Shaddai as I was taught in the House of Shem—as she should have been taught in your household." Before he lifted the tent flap, he offered one final word. "I pray that someday, Uncle, you will find the freedom that comes with forgiveness."

"Get out!" Jacob's angry voice accompanied sounds of breaking pottery as Job walked away from his uncle's tent. He could only hope that in the days to come, Jacob would remember some of his words and the seeds Job had planted would grow and bear fruit.

❦❦❦❦❦

"Thank you for asking Uncle Esau to allow us to travel separately." Finally, on this third night of their journey, Dinah could move beyond her embarrassment and voice her gratitude. Her camel plodded beside Job's. A canopy of stars sparkled above as torchbearers lit the way below. "And thank you for not being angry when I wasn't ready to travel at dawn the next day. I hope waiting on a woman did not shame you in front of the servants."

Job chuckled. "Dinah, those who think me weak for waiting on a woman would certainly find something to criticize, if not that. I am not shamed by what others think. My shame or innocence is settled between me and El Elyon." He furrowed his brow and tilted his head in a distant stare.

Dinah fell silent, studying him. Tall and muscular, he was the epitome of Edomite strength. Yet this tender man was as different from Esau as the sun from the moon. In the throes of her nightmare, his copper hair and raspy voice had reminded her of her brothers, but his kind and gentle character had wiped away any resemblance to the men of Jacob's tribe. The few silver strands in his wavy mane caught the glimmer of torchlight, and when Job turned to look at her, his dark eyes penetrated her soul.

"Thank you for agreeing to marry my son. You will make a beautiful bride."

Dinah's heart leapt into her throat. She searched his face for signs of ridicule—there were none. "Of course, I would never think of disobeying Grandfather." Focusing on the caravan ahead, her cheeks felt as if they might burst into flames.

"The customs of Abraham's daughters give you the right of refusal. Yet you didn't refuse." He paused.

Her heart raced. Did he wish she had refused?

"I'm glad you'll be a part of my household now." Job's voice sounded like warm, honeyed wine. Dinah slowly turned and found herself lost in his brown eyes.

He thinks I'm beautiful, and he's glad I'll be a part of his household . . . Had any man been so kind to her since . . . ?

Wait!

Wasn't this the same trap that had ensnared her at Shechem? Was every man a betrayer? Dinah shook her head as if waking from a dream. For twenty years, merchants and shepherds had recounted the story of Jacob's sons slaughtering innocent Shechemites, and most had blamed *her* for going to the city that day. Abba Jacob told the tale that Prince Shechem brought the trouble on his city by raping his daughter, defiling her without the proper marriage traditions of Yahweh. No matter which story Job had chosen to believe, she would never allow him—or any man—to deceive and betray her again.

Snapping her eyes forward, she said, "I'm anxious to meet your son." Her words were clipped, her hands tight on the reins. Just ahead she noticed the night's camp coming into view. "Just in time," she whispered.

"You must be tired," he said, pointing to a group of rocks amid the beautiful red cliffs surrounding them. "A warm fire awaits." Job nodded graciously and prodded his camel on, speaking with the guide and greeting the rest of the caravan.

Again tonight, he'd sent a few servants ahead to prepare the camp for all the weary travelers.

Nogahla waited patiently for Dinah to dismount. Abba Jacob had given the little Cushite handmaid as Dinah's lone dowry. No traditional gifts to ensure her safe return if Job's son refused her. No wedding gown or headpiece of coins and jewels to wear. Job had been gracious and offered Abba a bride-price, but preserving a measure of dignity, Abba had refused.

"Good evening, mistress," the Cushite girl said, ushering Dinah into their tent as though she were the queen of the Nile. Were it not for Nogahla's white teeth and sparkling eyes, she might have disappeared into the night.

Dinah reached for her hands, trying to settle her emotions yet still press her wishes. "Please, Nogahla, as I told you last night and the night before, there's no need to bow to me. I am no better than a servant myself."

The girl looked utterly stricken.

"Would it surprise you to know that one of my abba's wives was a Cushite?" Dinah asked, tenderly brushing her cheek.

Nogahla's eyes grew round, and she nodded. Dinah chuckled. The little maid could carry on an entire conversation without speaking a word—her expressions seemed a perfect reflection of her heart and mind.

"My ima Rachel's serving maid, Bilhah, was just as dark-skinned as you are," Dinah said, "and one day Rachel gave Bilhah to Abba as his wife."

Studying her timid Cushite maid, Dinah tried to imagine how Bilhah must have felt entering into the intimate act of marriage as a servant, not a real wife. An adult sorrow gripped Dinah, a sadness of which children were blissfully ignorant. She remembered grinding grain and baking bread with her third ima Bilhah's careful instruction. Her fourth ima, Zilpah, loved to weave and spin, but she had no patience for teaching Dinah the fine artistry of cloth and thread. Zilpah had been given to Jacob as a slave wife too—the handmaid of Leah—but Zilpah never regained her smile as Bilhah had.

"My mother was taken as a slave from our homeland in Cush when she was very young," the girl said, interrupting Dinah's memories. "I am the daughter of her master. My father was a wealthy Egyptian soldier, and my mother was a slave in his household. Though he had a wife, my father loved my mother and would sometimes let me ride with him on his fine horses."

Dinah searched Nogahla's expression for regret or sadness. There was none. The girl knew only a servant's life. She spoke of her heritage as though it were a list for the market. "How old are you, Nogahla?"

"I'm not certain," she said, tapping her chin with a graceful finger. "But just before I was taken from my mother, she told me I was five years old, and I helped prepare ten annual feasts in Master Isaac's camp."

Dinah's heart broke at the girl's sparse recollections and recalled the women led by chains and iron collars in the streets of Shechem. "Nogahla, I can't keep you as my servant."

The girl's full, pink lips began to tremble. "Mistress, please. If you put me away, do you know what others will do with a girl my age?" Tears leapt over her bottom lashes. "If I have offended you, I'm sorry. I'll—"

"No, you have not offended me." Dinah sighed and reached for the girl's hand. "I simply think it's wrong to make you my servant. I have never needed a servant."

"But I need a mistress," the girl whispered, squeezing

Dinah's hand. "And my mistress needs a friend. Can we not take care of each other?"

"Excuse me." Job's voice was soft and tentative outside the tent. "Dinah, are you still awake?"

Nogahla pulled away, and Dinah hurried to the tent opening. "Is there something wrong?"

Job's face was—well, indiscernible. She didn't know this man well enough to interpret the subtle furrow of his brow or the way the right side of his mouth tilted up just a little.

"Will you follow me to the fire?" he said and then looked at the Cushite. "Alone." Nogahla's gaze fell to her feet and she backed into the tent as Dinah stepped into the night.

Dread twisted Dinah's stomach. "What is it?" She gazed around the camp. All the servants were in their tents. She was standing in the moonlight alone with Job. *No! El Shaddai, no, not again.* The last time a man was kind and led her to a place alone like this . . .

"Dinah, don't be frightened." Job gently placed his hand at the small of her back and nudged her forward. "I simply want to talk with you. Will you sit with me by the fire?"

He had laid two rugs side by side. Dinah began shaking her head. "No, please. I can't. I won't. You've promised me to your son!" She turned and started to run into the darkness, anything to escape the betrayal of another man.

"Dinah, listen to me." He captured her in his strong grasp, but when she fought him, he released her immediately. "I won't hold you, but you can't run into the desert at night."

Trembling so violently she could barely stand, Dinah wrapped her arms tightly around her body and stared at the rocky, red soil. *No tears, El Shaddai. Please, I don't want to shed more tears.*

Job stepped toward her and reached out his hand, but she drew back like a frightened child. "I simply want to sit by the fire and talk to you about El Shaddai before we arrive in Uz." His eyes were tender. Clear, as Nogahla had mentioned before. "I won't hurt you. Look at me, Dinah."

But how could she ever look at him again? Their first encounter had been her hysterical nightmare, and now she had accused him of planning a despicable act with his soon-to-be daughter-in-law. Why wouldn't he pack her things and send her back to Abba Jacob's camp right now? Suddenly she realized she and Nogahla were very much the same. They both lived in terror of being rejected by their masters.

Stiffly, Dinah moved to the fire and sat near the flames. She would listen to Job. She would even speak if required. But she could not look at him.

Job's patience unnerved her. The fire popped and cracked. Several sparks flew heavenward before he finally broke the silence. "Tell me about Prince Shechem, Dinah. Did you love him?"

Her breath caught. She blinked hard, breathed fast, fought the emotion. No one had ever asked her—not even her imas had cared to know. She threw a piece of dried dung on the fire. Maybe he'd ask a different question.

"Dinah, please. I saw the way you cared for Grandfather Isaac in his last days. I know you have a heart full of love. You were so young when Simeon and Levi rescued you. Did you believe you were married when Prince Shechem took you to his bed?"

"How dare you ask me such intimate questions!" Her outburst startled even her. "Not even my abba spoke of such things!" Dinah balled her fists, willing their trembling to cease.

Job waited, but she couldn't restrain her tears much longer. Panicked, she tried to scurry to her feet, but Job's strong hand held her fast. "Stop running, Dinah. Stop hiding. Tell me what happened at Shechem." His eyes pierced her. "I visited Grandfather Isaac at harvesttime and shearing every year, but I never knew you were in his camp until last week. Why did you hide for fifteen years, Dinah?"

"They made me hide because they were ashamed of me!" Her tortured scream echoed in the desert sky, racking her body with sobs. Job released her arm as if she were leprous. Was it revulsion on his face? Shock? Horror? Bowing her head, she let the tears flow quietly, too spent to care.

A screech owl called out in the distance. Job moved closer. "Dinah, listen to me." He touched her shoulder, and she flinched. "I'm sorry," he said, releasing a sigh. "Please, Dinah. Did you love Shechem?"

"Yes, yes, I loved him," she cried, "and he loved me." Dinah glared at the man who would determine her future. Replacing the shield of pain and bitterness around her heart, she wiped her cheeks. "He loved me, Job. Is that so hard to believe? Why can't anyone believe a man could love me?"

Job placed one arm around Dinah's shoulders, and she felt his tenderness but no passion. The simple act dismantled her fragile defenses. She hugged her knees tightly, burying her face in a private world of release.

Job let her cry, let the silence do its healing work. Then, when her tears had slowed, he said softly, "Dinah, I must ask you another hard question. It is not to judge you or chastise you but to ultimately free you from the pain you're feeling right now." He laid his cheek on the top of her head like a caring father with a small child. "Did you know it was wrong to submit to Prince Shechem before receiving your abba's and El Shaddai's blessing?"

Dinah closed her eyes and pulled away from his embrace. She started to stand and go back to her tent when Job grasped her arm. "Answer me, Dinah."

She pulled away roughly and wiped the tears. "Will you at least send a guard to accompany me back to my abba's household?" Laughing bitterly, she added, "Or do I deserve whatever a bandit gives me?"

Job reached for her again, rising to his knees, and this time he grasped her hands gently. "Please answer, Dinah. It's important that you say the words aloud."

"Yes. I knew!" she said, ripping her hands away from him. "I knew that lying with Shechem before receiving Abba's blessing was wrong, but I did it anyway." Tears came again. "This may be impossible for someone like you to under-stand—someone who has lived a blessed life without pain or struggle. But Shechem was the first person who ever loved me, Job, and I simply couldn't say no."

Job drew out a knife from his belt. A rush of fear coursed through her, and Dinah instinctively tensed to run. But just as suddenly, resignation settled like a shroud. It was the fate she should have shared with her husband twenty years ago. She closed her eyes and waited for the blow.

Instead, she heard Job rise to his feet and walk away. She watched him retrieve a lamb that had been tethered to his tent. He led the perfect little creature back to where she stood by the fire.

"Dinah, we all sin—every one of us—and sin brings death.

But El Shaddai taught Adam and Noah and Abraham the way to atone for our sins through blood." He knelt by the lamb, looked up at Dinah, and then slit the lamb's throat.

"No!" She fell to her knees. "What are you doing? Why did you kill this helpless creature?" She began to shake, anger welling up as the lamb's blood poured out. "I thought you were kind and gentle, but you're as ruthless and uncaring as all men." She had heard of Abba Jacob's and Grandfather's blood sacrifices, but as a woman, she had never been allowed to witness their offerings.

"The lamb died, Dinah, so you could live." Job's steady, calm voice broke through her bitterness. "This is El Shaddai's way of freeing us from the weight of our sin. As the priest of my family, I make regular offerings for my children just in case they've cursed God in their hearts." Job touched her hand, and the lamb's blood smeared on her wrist. "You are soon to become my daughter-in-law. I make this offering for you," he said. "Now you must release your shame."

She stared at him in disbelief. "How can you give me to your son now, knowing the shame that hangs on me like filthy rags?"

"I will offer this lamb to El Shaddai as a burnt offering, Dinah. By morning, nothing will be left of it." Job stood and helped Dinah to her feet. "What shame?" he asked. "I see no filthy rags on you." Turning away, he began the priestly work of preparing the animal for offering. Dinah watched in silent wonder for a few moments before returning to her tent.

Nogahla met her with wide, questioning eyes, but Dinah was too numb to explain. "We will speak of it in the morning," she promised, and then drifted to sleep with the sweet aroma of roasted lamb in her dreams.

4

~Genesis 3:1, 4–5~

*Now the serpent was more crafty than any of
the wild animals the* LORD *God had made. . . .
"You will not surely die," the serpent said to the
woman. "For God knows that when you eat of
[the forbidden fruit] your eyes will be opened,
and you will be like God, knowing good and
evil."*

The public dining hall of Sitis's cliff-hewn palace buzzed
with midday activity. Beggars, widows, and orphans
filled every table in the large, square room with its high ceilings and private courtyard. She gazed into the sea of hungry
faces seated on the benches and chairs, while more of the
needy waited outside to partake of Job's daily provision.
Household guards stood at each table to keep order, and the
mingling odors of dirty bodies and barley gruel saturated the

49

air. Sitis waved away a fly from her face and wondered if her husband ever dreamed they'd feed this many people each day.

Everyone in the house was busy serving, even Sitis's old nursemaid. "Nada, put your tray down and hurry over to Ennon's house." Sitis, her own hands full, motioned with her head for one of the other servants to take Nada's tray. "Tell his lazy wife to come help us." Sitis took a quick inventory of her other children and counted all three daughters serving, as well as her other five daughters-in-law. Her seventh son had never settled down long enough to marry. "Tell Ennon's lounging princess that if she refuses to dish up gruel, she'll not wear my son's gold."

Nada was already pressing her wide body through the narrow aisles, fists balled on hips, marching off to deliver the ultimatum to the prodigal in-law. Sitis watched her go and mumbled, "Job should have let *me* pick Ennon's wife. I would have chosen Bela's daughter. At least that girl knows how to work." A little wicked delight teased Sitis's heart as she imagined Nada's stormy reprimand to Ennon's wife.

But the reality of toothless beggars, dirty children, and sickly women closed in around her. Did Job think his household could save the world?

Pressing on a smile like a potter working half-dried clay, Sitis tightened her grip on her serving bowl and ladle. She dabbed her forehead with the back of her hand and bent down to serve. "Widow Orma, would you like more barley broth?"

The old woman's eyes were cloudy but perceptive as she rose from the widows' table. "Mistress, why don't you allow me to serve your guests today? Your husband has been gone for nearly a full moon, and you've been working too hard." A little mischief played on the old woman's wiry gray brows.

"Have you had your motherly talk with Uzahmah before her betrothal banquet?"

Sitis's baked-on smile broke into genuine pleasure. Widow Orma was her favorite of all the widows who regularly came for provisions. She almost made this degrading charade worthwhile. "No, Orma. I've had little time to do anything but keep up with household duties."

The widow gently relieved Sitis of ladle and serving bowl. "Go, dear. Every day this household serves those of us who have no food. Let me serve today, and you rest."

Though Sitis perceived no judgment in Orma's words, a twinge of guilt shadowed her heart. She didn't really despise serving the needy—at least, not as much as she used to. It was just that she had so many preparations for Uzahmah and Elihu's betrothal banquet. "Thank you, Orma. Job and Elihu should both be arriving in three days, and I want to have everything ready to surprise them."

The widow smiled her good-bye and began serving. Sitis watched for a moment—the way the old woman leaned close, spoke quietly, touched a shoulder, listened well. *I suppose if you had nothing or no one else, you could spend your days listening and serving as if you hadn't a care in the world.*

Sitis hurried past the sweaty bodies and emerged through the heavy red-gold tapestry into the small, dark hallway. Oil lamps sputtered on shelves niched into the rock walls, and Sitis closed her eyes, breathing deeply. Crushed cloves and dried mint bathed her battered senses. The relief of this place was like water to a parched desert soul.

Would she ever grow accustomed to the foulness of the poor? As Ishmael's granddaughter, Sitis had grown up in the most luxurious desert tents and thought Job's ideas of charity a coarse knot to untangle. She chuckled to herself. In forty years of marriage, serving maid was only one of many masks she wore to maintain their relationship—a small price to pay for ten beautiful children and the prospect of grandchildren someday.

Taking a long, cleansing breath of the sweet-smelling spices, Sitis proceeded to the private banquet hall, where the gifts and decorations for Uzahmah's betrothal banquet lay spread out on tables. Her fingers brushed lightly over the shiny silver cups she'd purchased from Aramean merchants yesterday. She lifted a bronze plate and checked her image in its shiny reflection. *Hmm, more fine lines under your eyes, Sitis.* Her black hair was streaked with a few gray strands, and the rosy cheeks of youth were gone.

"Yes, Sitis-girl, you're as beautiful as when we were thirteen."

The deep, resonant voice made Sitis jump, and she nearly dropped the plate. "Sayyid! What are you doing sneaking into my house? You'll give me more gray hair!"

Her childhood friend walked toward her confidently, regally, as befitted a wealthy grain merchant. With mischief in his voice, he bowed and said, "I've come to ask the mistress of the house if she'll require more grain for the grand occasion of her youngest daughter's betrothal banquet."

"Oh, stand up." Sitis waved away his antics like flies in the beggars' hall, but she couldn't wave away the smile that always came with his presence. "You know we have more than enough grain. You've been generous as always, my friend."

Sayyid's eyes lost their playful glint, and his usual gentle gaze captured Sitis's heart. "I've brought something special for Uzahmah." He glanced around the empty banquet room as if ensuring they were alone. Reaching into the folds of his robe, he produced a leather pouch that appeared heavy with its contents. "Just as I gave you the gift of Ishmaelite wisdom so long ago, so I wish to grant life to your daughter." He loosened the string and let three perfectly crafted Ishmaelite goddesses fall into his hand: Al-Uzza, Al-Lat, and Manat.

Sitis gasped. "Oh, Sayyid, they're exactly like the ones you gave me, when . . ." Tears welled up, and her throat tightened with emotion. "When Job's God had forgotten me, you gave me the goddesses, and I never miscarried again." She couldn't meet his gaze. This wasn't something a woman talked about with a man, but Sayyid wasn't just any man. His family had been tenant farmers in her father's camp, and Sayyid had loved her once—many years ago. "My daughters were a gift from our Ishmaelite deities." She finally looked up and was startled at the ferocity of his expression.

"Job almost killed you, expecting you to bear sons like the herds of Edom. No woman can bear three sets of twins in six years and survive." Sayyid's anger at Job still burned after all these years, but Sitis had learned to keep the men apart—though the two remained close in her heart.

"It wasn't Job who mistreated me, Sayyid," she said, reaching out to stroke his cheek. "My husband loves me. It was Job's *God*, El Shaddai, who forgot me." Letting her hand fall again to her side, she felt the familiar hardness overshadow her at the mention of Yahweh. "It was just as you've always told me, Sayyid. El Shaddai is a man's God and doesn't hear the pleas of a woman longing for a child." She gently placed each of the three images on the table in front of them. "I told Job that our daughters' names proclaimed their Ishmaelite heritage, but their names were truly reminders of my fertility goddesses." She transferred a kiss from her finger to the head of each of the goddesses. "Alathah was named for Al-Lat, Manathah for Manat, and Uzahmah for the almighty goddess Al-Uzza." Turning to Sayyid, she smiled tenderly and kissed his cheek. "And of course, they always remind me of my childhood friend, who rescues me whenever I need him."

❀❀❀❀❀

The ground shook, and shouting pierced the first rays of dawn. Chaos exploded in Job's camp. Dinah saw an ox run past her tent, a herdsman in pursuit. She threw off the heavy furs that had warmed her through her first dreamless sleep since childhood, and she shot straight up on her goatskin rug. The aroma of sacrificial lamb had completely faded.

Nogahla was huddled in her arms before Dinah was fully awake. "Nogahla," Dinah whispered, "go hide under that mound of blankets. They mustn't find you." Marauders often came just before dawn, and if Job's caravan was indeed under attack, raiders would soon burst into their tent.

"But mistress, where will you hide?" The girl's voice trembled as she scrambled toward the blankets.

Nogahla pulled her last fingertip under the woolen mound, and Dinah listened to the sounds around her. Instead of the clomping of camels' gallops, she heard the pounding thunder of horses' hooves. Now Job's servants were crying out more in confusion than fear.

"What is going on out there?" Dinah said. Gathering her courage, she moved toward the slender shaft of sunrise cutting through the front of their tent. She peered through, watching Job and a portly Sabean sheik walk calmly toward the fire, while the rest of the camp continued to stir. She couldn't quite make out the other man's features in the pre-dawn glow.

"That's odd," Dinah whispered. "There's something familiar about that sheik."

When the confusion began to settle, Nogahla peeked from beneath the blankets and asked, "Is everybody dead?"

Casting a chastising glance at the girl, Dinah reached for her head covering and cautiously opened the tent flap. She bowed to exit, and when she straightened to full height, she met the gaze of the Sabean sheik seated by Job—a man she'd indeed met before. His hatred burned her cheeks like hot coals. Dinah recoiled blindly into the tent, nearly knocking the center post to the ground. *Elohim, not him, not now.*

"Mistress, are you all right?" Nogahla had emerged from her woolen fortress and caught Dinah as she stumbled backward. Fear clouded her features when she glimpsed Dinah's expression. "Have they harmed Master Job?"

"No, Nogahla," Dinah whispered, regaining her balance more readily than her composure. "Master Job is well." She glanced around frantically, trying to discern what they could pack quickly into small bags. "We must hurry and pack a few things. Master Job will be sending us back to my abba's camp any moment now." Who knew if Job would allow them to take a camel or donkey—or if they would be cast out of the camp to find their way on foot.

❄❄❄❄❄

Job's guards had been taken unawares, and the lead guide was now before Job on his knees. "Master, forgive us. The horses approached more swiftly and quietly than camels." This man knew every desert and mountain trail like the back of his two-fingered hand. He was rugged, capable, and not known for making excuses. "Who would expect a troop of horses this far from Egypt?" the guide added, twisting his two fingers fiercely, awaiting the reprimand of a master whose camp had been turned upside down with fright.

"I understand," Job said, placing a calming hand on the guide's shoulder. "But because we're near a port city, my friend, you can never know when my spice-trading cousin Zophar will turn up."

The guide issued a scathing glance at the rotund, red-haired sheik on the lead horse, who was now laughing hysterically. Job could see his guide's anger building, but he had bigger problems than the man's wounded pride.

"All is forgiven," Job said, "but my oxen seem to be headed toward the cliff." Job pointed toward the jagged granite bluffs a few hundred paces away, and the man leapt to his feet, shouting commands at his herdsmen.

"Must you always make a grand entrance, Zophar?" Job shouted above the confusion as he approached Zophar's sleek black stallion.

Zophar ambled off the beast and hurried over, slapping Job on the back. "My ships arrived yesterday in Elath, and some merchants brought word that you were camped in these hills above the city. I know I should have sent messengers announcing my arrival, but I wanted to surprise you."

"Well, you almost received the surprise welcome of my javelin," Job said good-naturedly, guiding his cousin to the camp's fire.

"You were always quite skilled with the javelin, cousin," Zophar said, impishly checking his shoulder muscle. Job nudged his hand away and the two tussled like boys at play.

The chill of the desert still lingered, but the warmth of shared lives erased years of separation.

"I had forgotten Grandfather Esau took special pride in your weaponry training as a youth," Zophar said with a final shove.

"Just as Great-Abba took special interest in your trading skills." Job chuckled and nodded at the horses behind them. "So tell me, my ambitious cousin. What sort of bargain have you struck with Egypt to gain such stallions?"

"Well, cousin, to trade in horses, one must be prepared to give Pharaoh what he wants—cinnamon." Zophar leaned close so he could be heard over the continuing state of confusion. "But between you and me, camels are much better suited to carry my mighty physique." He patted his ample middle and showcased it proudly before lowering himself awkwardly onto a rug by the fire.

Job delighted in hearing Zophar's latest venture, envying just a little his ability to live life with such abandon, such zeal. Soon after their days together in the House of Shem, Esau had arranged a marriage for Zophar to the daughter of a wealthy Sabean spice merchant. Zophar traveled to southern Arabia to help spread the teachings of the Most High to the Ishmaelites, and at the same time to learn every detail of the lucrative spice trade. Within a short time Zophar married a second wife, gaining access to the ancient Sabean secrets of water channeling and sailing through his second father-in-law—a sailor by trade. Now he was the wealthiest spice trader in the East, and the teachings of the Most High had become the responsibility of another disciple of Shem, Sitis's brother, Bildad.

"I see you have new rings, Zophar." Job lifted one eyebrow

as he crossed his legs and lowered himself easily onto a rug beside his cousin.

Zophar inspected his chubby fingers, heavy with gold and gemstone-covered rings. "Perhaps I do have a new trinket or two since I saw you last, but—"

"No, cousin. I mean those dark circles under your eyes that tell me you've been working too hard and sleeping too little." Job felt like a nagging wife, but Zophar looked tired and un-kempt—unusual for this fastidiously fashionable merchant. Zophar waved off his concern, but Job probed further. "Tell me, cousin, is this the first you've returned to Edom since your trade journey to Saba two years ago?"

Zophar closed his eyes, inhaled deeply, and expelled what seemed to be the exhaustion of two full years. "Finally, I am on my way home, Job. I was delayed because a large group of Sabeans booked passage on my spice ship." Ducking his head conspiratorially, Zophar nodded at the eleven horse-men who'd accompanied him. "Those Sabeans and their friends tested my patience to the limit, asking for more time to gather provisions for their new settlement in Moab. What was I to do? They'd already paid a handsome price for their passage—much of which purchased my trade cargo for this voyage."

Job glanced again at Zophar's Sabean escort, and indeed they appeared to be a surly group. The gemstone hilts on their curved jambiyas glinted in the morning sun. Worn at the center of their belts, the double-edged daggers were a bold warning that quickly defined a Sabean's tribe.

Job glanced at Zophar's belt. No jambiya. Testimony that Zophar was still torn between the varied traditions he called home. He had lived in Saba only ten years before returning to Canaan with his wives and children to establish his trade routes through Edom, Arabia, and Egypt. But still Zophar dressed in Ishmaelite robes and wore the all-white ghutrah of a Sabean sheik instead of the black-and-white keffiyeh of his Canaanite neighbors. When asked why he refused the unique wool blend of Canaan's head scarf, Zophar joked that the Sabean ghutrah accentuated his rugged good looks, but Job knew the real reason for his refusal. The keffiyehs were woven from the speckled and spotted wool of Uncle Jacob's flocks, and Zophar had long ago rejected anything from Uncle Jacob.

"Anyway, I waited for that Sabean group and their Egyptian horses," Zophar whispered, cocking his thumb at his rough-looking escort, "and we finally set sail four moons ago." Zophar glanced around distractedly, finally settling on Job's guide. "Whatever possessed you to hire a caravan guide missing three fingers?"

Job chuckled. "My servant Atif recommended him highly. Now, don't change the subject." He backhanded Zophar's chest. "How did you ever make it through the Gulf of Aqaba in the winter? Wasn't it monsoon season?"

Zophar dissolved into yet another fit of laughter, and the sound warmed Job's heart like the camp's fire chasing away the morning chill. "Only by the hand of El Shaddai and the secrets of Sabean seafaring did we sail through the headwinds of Aqaba in the winter." Zophar slapped his knee, continued his story, and scanned the remainder of Job's camp. "It was not a pleasant trip with one hundred Sabean ruffians and fifty Egyptian horses!"

Job listened in utter delight and laughed quietly, more amused by Zophar's inability to concentrate than by his storytelling abilities. As a boy in the House of Shem, Zo-

59

phar had found it nearly impossible to sit still and learn the teachings of the Most High. But give him a topic to debate, and even the finest teachers couldn't refute his quick and agile mind.

Wrapped in fond memories, Job was startled when Zophar's easy banter ceased and his features turned to stone. Eyes flaming, Zophar jumped to his feet, his chubby hands balled into fists and trembling. "What is *she* doing here?"

"What? Who?" Job stood beside him, looking in the direction of his cousin's gaze, but he couldn't imagine what would have turned Zophar's mood so quickly.

"That murderess of Shechem!"

Job immediately glanced at Dinah's tent.

"Yes, *her!*" Zophar screamed. "How could you allow her to defile your camp?"

At first, shock seized Job's throat. How did Zophar even recognize Dinah? "Zophar, be quiet. She'll hear you." He glimpsed Dinah's retreating form and saw the rest of his caravan standing like statues. *Everyone heard him.* Anger flared in Job, but when he turned to Zophar, he saw the man's anger fall away like a snake shedding skin in the desert. *Is that fear I see in you, Zophar?*

Baffled, Job sighed deeply and said, "Tell me why you suddenly look frightened."

"Because she's like a disease, Job. She'll infect your household—like leprosy!"

Job reached out and tried to calm Zophar, but he backed away. "This is ridiculous," Job said, trying to keep his tone even. "Tell me how you know Dinah."

Zophar's eyes bulged, the veins in his forehead and neck straining with the force of his voice. "Everyone *knows* her,

Job! From the Nile to the Euphrates, men have heard of her treachery against the Shechemites."

"*You*, Zophar!" Job grabbed the front of Zophar's robe, squeezing the fine linen between white knuckles. "I asked how *you* know Dinah. I don't want the retelling of shepherds' tales and traders' gossip."

Zophar slapped away Job's hand and smoothed the front of his robe, his face pinched like a sun-dried fig. "When I returned from Saba with my wives to establish my household in Naamah, the Canaanites hated me because Uncle Jacob had poisoned them against Esau's descendants. But King Hamor of Shechem was generous and kind and spoke on my behalf, saying Edomite trade routes would benefit generations to come. Prince Shechem was the best of Hamor's sons—the most honorable young man I'd ever met. They were my friends, Job." Stabbing his finger toward Dinah's tent, he said, "*That woman* seduced the prince so her brothers could murder and loot the town to fill Jacob's tents with gold. I was on the road between Shechem and Bethel when Uncle Jacob's caravan passed by. I saw her dressed in the bloody rags of royalty, sitting on top of a cart full of Shechemite plunder."

"Enough!" Job's defenses rose to fury. "You know nothing about Dinah or the *real* story or the pain she has borne all these years! This young woman is responsible for her sin alone. Not her brothers' or Jacob's." Job continued relentlessly, as if Dinah's battle had somehow become his own. "I have made the proper sacrifices for her sin—whatever small part she might have played in the awful tragedy. She stands forgiven before El Shaddai."

The shock on Zophar's face was palpable. "How can you say she is forgiven, Job? Her treachery continues long past

Shechem. During my trade visits to Isaac's Hebron camp, I watched her coddle and cajole our grandfather. She is as conniving as her abba, trying to ensure her future by—"

"Stop right there, Zophar!" Job warned. "She is part of my household now."

Zophar's face was as white as his ghutrah. He grabbed Job's shoulders and shook him. "A part of your household? No, Job! Tell me you have not betrayed your vow to Sitis and taken *that woman* as your wife!"

Job measured Zophar's question. "If you can take a second wife, Zophar, why can't I?" he said with icy calm.

"Because you promised!" He shoved Job's chest, knocking him back. "You promised Sitis that she would be your only wife—as Rebekah was to Grandfather Isaac. No, Job, you didn't. Tell me you didn't!"

Job stood his ground and stared at Zophar defiantly, his heart pounding in his ears. Of course he would never break his vow to Sitis, but for the first time in his life, he refused to explain himself. He and Zophar had disagreed many times, but somehow this felt different. A chasm had formed between them that no words could bridge.

"I am taking her home to marry Ennon," he said, expressionless. "But regardless, she is forgiven, Zophar. She is forgiven by El Shaddai—even though you and Uncle Jacob and Great-Abba Esau have seemingly forgotten how to forgive."

Zophar's face turned scarlet with rage. "She has cast her seductive spell on you—just like she did on Prince Shechem. She'll ruin your household. Mark my words."

"I am under no spell, Zophar. And Dinah is no longer under the weight of her shame." Job shook his head, feeling the weariness of his travels and this futile argument. "If you would just talk with her, you would see the great love she had for Grandfather Isaac, and you would understand his dying wish that she marry Ennon."

Shock drained all of Zophar's anger, and his eyes welled with tears. The sudden silence stole Job's breath. How cruel to tell Zophar of Grandfather's death in such a thoughtless way.

"Forgive me, cousin." Job hung his head. "Grandfather Isaac finally rests with Father Abraham."

No one spoke. The camp noise swelled, the oxen finally corralled for travel, tents falling to be packed and loaded.

Finally, Zophar spoke into the dying fire. "I didn't know Grandfather as you knew him, Job. I passed through Isaac's camp only occasionally on my trade routes. I didn't study the teachings with him as you did."

Job turned to Zophar, waiting for him to meet his gaze. He wouldn't. "Zophar, my cousin-brother, Grandfather Isaac commanded that Ennon marry Dinah because their offspring is the only hope of bringing Abraham's covenant blessing into Esau's clan."

Zophar's head snapped up. "So Grandfather Isaac forced you to take Dinah?" He gave a sardonic smile. "Uncle Jacob must have finally persuaded him to rid *his* clan of that woman's shame."

Job felt as if he'd swallowed white-hot embers. "Don't ever speak of my daughter-in-law that way again, Zophar. Dinah is a beautiful woman who has been wrongfully accused and shamefully treated all her life."

Fury returned to Zophar's features. "How can you be so blind?" He picked up a handful of dust and flung it at Job's chest.

"That's enough," a woman's quiet voice said from behind them. Dinah's features were a detached facade that hid her pain beautifully. Nogahla stood beside her, poised as if she might dart back to their tent at any moment.

Turning to Job, Dinah asked, "Will you provide a guide for Nogahla and me to return to Abba Jacob's household?" Job saw triumph on Zophar's face and deadness in Dinah's eyes. "Now that you've heard Zophar's recounting, I'm sure you've changed your mind about me."

Job's heart broke at the old shame hanging anew on Dinah this morning. Last night's lamb would be worthless ashes if Dinah returned to Jacob's bitterness. "No, I will not hire a guide for you and Nogahla to return."

Dinah squeezed her eyes shut and turned. Grasping Nogahla's hand, she started down the path to Elath, each woman carrying two small packs.

Before Job could call Dinah back, Zophar laughed and said, "Come back here. Even *you* don't deserve what a bandit would do to you on the way back to Hebron. You can travel with one of my spice caravans along the coastal mountains. They'll find your thieving abba somewhere between Beersheba and Hebron, I'm sure."

Dinah stopped but didn't turn, and Nogahla simply looked up at her mistress. Waiting.

"No, Zophar," Job shouted loudly enough for Dinah and Nogahla to hear. "I refuse to release her to Jacob's household. Grandfather Isaac promised Dinah to my son Ennon, and I will not give her safe passage unless he refuses her."

"Why?" Dinah dropped Nogahla's hand and rushed at the two men, all pretense gone. "Why not send me back now and be done with it? You know your son will hold the same opinion of me as this—this—" She motioned to Zophar, her tone laced with disgust.

"Be careful, Dinah," Job said quietly amid her storm of words. "I would not allow him to accuse you unjustly, nor will I allow you to dishonor Zophar in my presence."

"How can you say he accuses me unjustly?" Tears threatened to overflow her beautiful long lashes, but she swiped at both eyes with the back of her hand. "You know what I've done! Send me back! Don't make me wait for the humiliation of your son's refusal." More tears threatened, but she valiantly guarded her veil of dignity.

"Send her back, Job." Zophar gripped Job's arm, pleading. "If you force Ennon to marry her, he will become a laughingstock in Edom."

Job gently covered Zophar's iron grip. "And what of El Shaddai's forgiveness? What of Isaac's wish? What of Abraham's blessing to Esau's clan? Do none of these mean anything to you, my cousin-brother? Does a woman's heart and soul mean so little?"

Zophar jerked his hand away. "Take caution, cousin. This woman will destroy your household." He looked at Dinah and spit on the ground at her feet. "I don't care if Grandfather Isaac believed you carry Abraham's covenant blessing in your womb. Your abba is a liar and a thief, and your brothers are murderers. You're no better."

Dinah turned and grabbed Nogahla's hand on her way back to their tent. Zophar marched to his horse without another word and disappeared with his Sabean escort in a cloud of red dust.

Job stood quietly, turning slowly in a full circle, amazed that his servants had dismantled his camp in the short time it had taken for him and Zophar to dismantle a lifelong kinship. Nearly everything was ready for travel into the port town of

Elath, where they would trade livestock for gifts and gather supplies for the final three days of their journey to Uz. Only Dinah's tent was still standing, but he wasn't yet prepared for the confrontation sure to come. He decided instead to walk toward a beautiful outcropping of rocks about a hundred paces toward the sun, overlooking the city below. He needed some time with El Shaddai.

Many mornings during the past five years, on his journeys home from Grandfather Isaac's camp, Job had found a comfortable cleft in the rocks and rested his back against the rough red stone until the whisper of El Elyon's truth resonated in his soul. Of course, God Most High had never spoken to him. Such a miracle was reserved only for those who possessed the covenant blessing, but perhaps someday one of Ennon's sons would hear the voice of El Shaddai.

What would it be like to hear You speak, El Elyon? Would a man ever be the same?

5

~*Job 1:1–3*~

*In the land of Uz there lived a man whose
name was Job. . . . He had seven sons and three
daughters. . . . He was the greatest man among
all the people of the East.*

"Nogahla, stop gaping out the tent flap and help me
pack." Dinah was too angry and humiliated to let
the girl's curiosity slow her busy hands. "If Job is determined
to have his son reject me in front of the entire town of Uz,
then we must be ready to leave with the rest of his caravan."
Tears still threatened, but she refused to let them spill over.

Nogahla gently took the sleeping mat from Dinah's hand.
"Let me roll it, mistress. Change your robe and tend your
hair. Ready yourself to go into Elath today."

Dinah's hands shook. Images of Zophar's angry red face
flashed before her. She just wanted peace—the peace she'd
had after last night's sacrifice.

"Mistress, are you all right?" Nogahla placed a tender hand on Dinah's arm.

A loud hand clap signaled a visitor outside their tent, and every muscle in Dinah's body tensed.

"I need to speak with you for a moment, Dinah." It was Job.

"We're almost finished packing," Dinah said, answering Nogahla's silent questions with a shrug. "We're working as quickly as we—"

Job's face appeared at the tent opening. "I have a request," he said, his expression kind but firm. He straightened, and his presence filled the women's small tent. "Dinah, I would like to have your jars of herbs and medicines, please. The ones Grandfather Isaac gave you."

Dinah waited for him to explain, but his silence was as empty as his expression. "Why?" she asked finally.

"After you marry my son, you'll have little time for midwifery. I can offer your herbs to the midwives in Uz, and then everyone—both in my household and in our town—will benefit. Don't worry, Dinah. I know what's best." His smile was genuine, but some strange emotion niggled at the corner of his mouth.

Dinah lingered between despair and indignation. Of course she should be willing to share her herbs with others, but these jars were gifts from Grandfather Isaac. Shouldn't *she* be able to decide who used them, since she knew the healing power of each one? Besides, she'd not only issued new life through these potions, they'd resurrected her own dead soul.

"I'm sorry," she said, keeping her gaze downcast. "I can't give them to you."

"You must." His voice remained kind but insistent.

Dinah looked up, searching Job's eyes for a soul she knew existed. "How can you ask this of me?" Her voice broke a little, and she hated her weakness. "When you know how much I treasure them?"

Job inclined his head and spoke gently as though explaining to a reluctant child. "I have made this decision for everyone's good, Dinah. I'm asking you to set aside your selfish desires and think of others."

Job's words pierced her like a red-hot spear. He thought she was selfish? Maybe he was right. He was the honorable one, after all, the greatest man in the East. Who was she to question Job? She was nothing.

Stepping toward the woven baskets and leather bags containing her herbal treasures, she reached out to grasp the handles, but something deep within cried out against his demands. "I won't!" she shouted. "Grandfather Isaac gave them to me, and *I* will share them when and with whom I choose." She stepped toward him, and he stepped back as if considering a swift exit. "Why do people think they can just take whatever is mine? No! Not this time, Job."

Dinah braced herself. Would he strike her? Wasn't that what angry men did to women of their household who spoke so disrespectfully?

Silence hung like a wet wineskin, invaded only by Nogahla's soft whimpers and Dinah's heavy breathing. Finally, Job smiled. "Why didn't you defend the gift of forgiveness as fiercely as you defended your herbs?"

Dinah could only blink, allowing the words to penetrate her anger.

"As surely as Grandfather Isaac gave you those pots of healing, Dinah, El Elyon healed your soul with the blood of the lamb. But when Zophar tried to steal your gift of forgiveness, you gave it up to his reproach."

Dinah stared at him, breathless. She had no words. And Job's eyes were once again warm pools.

He reached for her hand, and she allowed him to cradle it. "You are a strong and beautiful woman, Dinah," he said. "The journey ahead of us is harsh. Both the mountains we'll travel and the people you'll meet can be dangerous and unforgiving." He gave an almost imperceptible squeeze of her hand. "But neither the mountains nor the people can rob you of the forgiveness God has given—unless you let them." Then he turned and stooped to exit her tent, calling over his shoulder, "I'll send one of the servants to tear down your tent. Make sure you're not in it!" His laughter rang out.

Dinah stood like a statue. The warmth of his touch still tingled on her outstretched hand.

"Mistress," Nogahla said, her voice a hushed whisper. Even a young servant girl realized the moment was too holy to speak in ordinary tones. Dinah grinned and remained silent, savoring the moment.

"Mistress, we must hurry."

Dinah finally let both hands fall to her sides but still moved as though lost in a dream—a lovely dream in which a good man continued to prove faithful to his word and his God.

✿ ✿ ✿ ✿ ✿

Sitis gazed into the ocean of night sky from her bedchamber balcony and thought of Job. Was he counting the same myriad stars, staring at the same half moon? Pulling her woolen robe tight around her neck, she leaned over her balcony railing to see their children's houses just beyond the canyon below. Nine of them owned homes of their own—eight married and one son as unfettered as a wild ox. Uzahmah, the youngest, slept snugly in her chamber down the hall but was all too anxious to marry Elihu, Job's star pupil.

Sitis squeezed the bridge of her nose and released a weary sigh. Her youngest girl had always been a bit impetuous—like her mother. As Job's caravan had left the city gates one full moon ago, he had promised Uzahmah the betrothal proceedings could begin as soon as he returned. A smile creased Sitis's face. *She did just what I would have done.* Uzahmah interpreted her father's promise as permission to schedule the betrothal banquet for the moment his caravan returned through the gates of Uz. The girl had pestered Sitis to send scouts and messengers, timing Elihu's arrival with Job's caravan. If her scouts were reliable, Elihu would arrive with a Chaldean trading caravan from the north. And Job's caravan from Hebron would enter the city gates from the south—both about sunset tomorrow.

Placing her elbows on the railing, Sitis massaged her temples and wondered if indulging her daughter's impatience would drive a deeper wedge into her marriage relationship. Would Job be angry that she had planned the banquet and made all the arrangements without asking him? Would this be just another argument to widen the distance between them?

She bent down and tipped the tiny pitcher of olive oil over the heads of her three Ishmaelite goddesses. After the yearlong betrothal, Uzahmah would have her own home to manage, and Sitis would be alone with Job in their cliff-hewn palace. What would they talk about? It seemed they could no longer say two words without arguing. She inhaled the crisp night air, and this time her sigh quivered a little. The emotions were getting harder to press down.

"Oh, ladies of life, hear my prayer," she said, massaging

the oil into each image. "May I soon hear the happy cries of grandchildren in my home, the gentle patter of little feet in these hallways." Al-Uzza, the almighty goddess covered with a multitude of breasts, stood stately in the center of the low ivory table. Golden Al-Lat was on her right, perched on a camel, her morning-star necklace glistening with oil. Holy mother-in-law, Manat, on the left, had become Sitis's favorite in recent years. The headless idol was seated, legs extending only to the thighs—a golden lap awaiting grandchildren. Her arms were crossed, holding up bare breasts as an altar on which pungent spices testified to her strength.

"Why haven't you blessed my household with grandchildren?" she asked the goddesses. "My offerings helped rebuild your temple for the Ishmaelites in Chaldea after Job and his men destroyed it. What more do you require of me?" Clouds shrouded the moonlight, making the idols' silence even darker. *Gods never answer*, she thought, straightening again at the balcony railing.

Looking into the black night, she remembered when she had believed Yahweh created all things. "Not so long ago," she whispered. "But a lifetime ago."

She was the daughter of Shuah, Abraham's son through his concubine, Keturah. Ishmael married Keturah after Abraham's death and adopted Shuah, making Sitis and her brother, Bildad, grandchildren of both Abraham and Ishmael—double royalty, doubly devoted to Yahweh, according to Bildad. Sitis's brother had been Ishmael's representative at the House of Shem. He had demanded Sitis's devotion to Yahweh, even when their parents died and she grew up alone. She was a princess among servants. Bildad had arranged her marriage to Job—and then Job demanded her devotion to Yahweh, even when her babies died. She'd been a mother with full breasts and empty arms.

"Creator of all." She laughed bitterly. "I don't think so."

The cool night air lifted her dark curls from her neck, the desert chill prickling her skin. She let her robe fall around her shoulders. Her third-story balcony was nestled in the western red cliffs of a private canyon in the refined second sector of Uz. Only one other home shared the canyon—Sayyid's. It was a smaller palace directly across the canyon, carved into the eastern cliffs. But it was late. No one would see her. The lamps in Sayyid's household had long been dark, and tonight's stillness was her last chance at freedom until Job's next journey. She let her robe fall to the stone floor, the frigid wind ravaging her body, making her feel alive before she resumed her living death.

Tomorrow Job would return with his shrouds of expectations. Sitis would again choose her words carefully and speak politely, avoiding her husband's gaze. She would endure the loneliness because she loved her home, her children, her status as Job's wife—the greatest man in the East. She glanced down at the oily glow of the golden goddesses in the moonlight. Tonight she would tuck them away safely so Job would never suspect their presence in his home.

She glanced across the canyon at Sayyid's dark balconies and windows. Would Job suspect that Sayyid had been present in their home? She'd said a tearful good-bye to her friend tonight, apologizing again that she couldn't see him until the next time Job traveled or they had a chance meeting in the city market. Tears sprang up unbidden. "Why must I choose between my husband and my best friend?" she whispered to the night. She knew the answer. Job still blamed Sayyid for her refusal to worship El Shaddai.

When Job had discovered Sayyid delivering Sitis's offerings to the Chaldean temple on the day of Ennon's wedding, Job ordered the temple destroyed and Sayyid banished forever from their home. *But you cannot banish him from my heart.*

She braced herself against the railing and let her tears flow freely. Why couldn't Job understand that Sayyid was like a brother? Closer than her own brother who had betrayed her heart. Sayyid always listened, really listened, when she was afraid or hurting—more than any other man in her life.

Sitis knelt to retrieve her robe and placed a kiss on each of the goddesses. Carefully, reverently, she wrapped each image in fleece and placed it in the sacred stone cube. She slid the cover into place and stood, pulling her warm woolen robe tightly around her body.

"We are all wrapped in some sort of shroud, I suppose," she whispered, thinking of the golden images in their fleece-lined home. She glanced up at Sayyid's eastern cliffs, dark yet alive with his presence. "Perhaps someday I'll break out of my tomb and worship freely, speak freely, live freely." Lifting the sacred cube, she turned toward her bedchamber. "Until then, I have a beautiful daughter to pamper and a betrothal banquet to prepare."

✠✠✠✠✠

After trading all the animals for merchandise at Elath, the caravan traveled much more quickly. Still, the heavily loaded camels and the few donkeys carrying servants meant frequent water stops as they climbed to higher elevations. Though the drought had diminished the flow of natural mountain springs, the caravan guide was adept at finding every drop of clear, cold refreshment. The sun's rays peeked over the western sandstone cliffs, but the mountain heights also meant falling temperatures, and Dinah's teeth chattered to the sway of her camel. Her speckled woolen robe would soon be no match for the chilly winds. Looking ahead, she saw a forest of trees and scrub covering a plateau and prayed the guide would find water there. Searching the back of the caravan for Nogahla's white donkey, she found the girl, shoulders crouched and shivering, bouncing atop her little beast of burden along the mountain ridge road.

"This looks like a good place to rest," Job shouted ahead to the guide. "If there's water, we'll stop."

Dinah sighed with relief and noted Job's kind smile. Had he noticed her discomfort?

"But Master Job, Uz is around the bend at the next plateau. Why stop now?" The guide turned and met Dinah's gaze. She tried to still her chattering teeth but couldn't. The man made no pretense of hiding his frustration, but upon reaching the forest and bubbling spring, he reined his camel to a stop.

By the time Dinah halted her weary camel, Job had dismounted and was waiting with blankets in hand. "A little colder than you'd expect in the desert, isn't it?"

Dinah's cantankerous camel spit and squawked its protest all the way to its knees and belly. Talking to the beast gently, she patted its neck and stepped free from her four-legged throne.

Job laughed. "You seem to enjoy travel far more than my wife and daughters." He placed a blanket on her shoulders and walked toward Nogahla's donkey with another blanket. "Sitis hates the smell of camels," he said over his shoulder, "and our daughters think 'sleeping under the stars' means a tent, three layers of fleece for a bed, and servants fanning them with ostrich plumes."

Dinah was two steps behind Job when Nogahla nearly leapt off her donkey. "M-m-mistress, I'm c-c-c-cold!" Job's laughter echoed between the mountain peaks. He wrapped the second blanket around the girl's shoulders, and she cuddled in its warmth.

"Thank you," Dinah said, awed at his thoughtfulness. Job nodded, waving away her gratitude as if unnecessary.

Pointing the way toward a cozy campfire, Job had taken only a few steps when Dinah saw two fingers claw at Job's shoulder. "We cannot waste time here. If we are to reach Uz before sunset, we must be on our way within the hour." The guide stalked away, leaving Job gawking. Dinah silently marveled that a hired man would speak to his master with such disrespect.

"He's up to something, Master Job. He's no good." Nogahla spoke offhandedly, as if anyone could have seen the truth had they been watching. "He's had sneaky eyes since we left Elath."

Dinah was unsettled by Nogahla's candor. "Nogahla, Master Job chose his guide with much care, and he trusts him implicitly." Watching Job's expression, she hoped for some sign of confidence. None came.

"Actually, the man came highly recommended by my house steward, Atif." Job glanced at the impatient guide, who was shouting orders at the camel drivers. "Atif and I have a long history of differing opinions. I'll never take his advice on such a matter again." Job effectively closed the subject by smiling and extending his hand toward the crackling flames. "Why don't we sit by the fire so you two can warm up?"

Dinah and Nogahla fell in step beside him.

"Would you mind telling me about the rest of our journey

to Uz?" Dinah asked. She and Job had spoken little during their last three days of travel. They'd enjoyed shopping for gifts and herbs in Elath and the short camaraderie of evening prayers before retiring to their tents. But Dinah had hoped Job would volunteer information about Ennon during the long days of travel. He'd been strangely silent. She was battling worry and losing the war.

"We'll travel the ridge road," Job said, pointing to the narrow watershed, "skirting the eastern side of the cliffs, and we should arrive at sunset." He poked at the flaming dung chips with a stick. "Would you like to ask me what's really on your mind?"

Dinah's cheeks suddenly warmed, and it wasn't because of the fire. Did this man read everyone's mind, or just hers? She would start with something simple. "How old is your son?" Her heart was pounding. She tried not to cringe, but she'd been dreading this answer for days.

"Ennon is thirty-nine."

Oh! He's a child! Dinah consciously slowed her breathing. How could a man only four years older look at her with love? She was an old goat compared to the young brides he could have married.

But wait . . . A thought occurred to her for the first time.

Dinah turned, but Job continued to study the flames. "I heard you tell Zophar that you promised to marry only one woman." She paused. "Have your sons made a similar promise, or is Ennon already married?"

Job remained silent, awkwardly so. His expression lost all signs of joy, and her heart sank at the words he didn't speak.

"Is he at least an honorable man, like his abba?" she asked quietly.

"You will be Ennon's second wife, Dinah, but I believe you will win his heart," Job said. "My first son is not unkind."

"But he is not honorable," she said, defeat and resignation lacing her tone.

"Ennon is still finding his place in the world." Job was almost apologetic. Then, as if grasping at some hope, he said, "He is respected among his peers." More silence. They continued staring into the fire. "But I fear his peers set the standard too low."

Dinah slowly turned to Job in disbelief. "Why would you tell me this? I am merely a woman. He is your son and soon to be my husband. I am supposed to honor and obey him without question."

A small smile worked at one corner of Job's mouth. "I tell you this because I saw your love and compassion for Grandfather Isaac. Your tenacity with Zophar. You are not *merely* a woman, Dinah, and I doubt that you could ever obey without question." He chuckled then and turned to meet her gaze. "Ennon has no children. Perhaps a child—a seed of promise—will strengthen his faith. Perhaps the love of a woman like you can teach him that a worthy woman is worthy of an honorable man."

Dinah felt herself blush to the roots of her blonde hair, but if Job was willing to speak plainly, she would find no better time to ask her questions than now. "What about your other children? Do your other sons have wives? Do you have grandchildren?"

"I have seven sons and three daughters," he said. "Six of my sons are married, but El Shaddai has not yet blessed my household with grandchildren."

Job started to explain further, but Dinah interrupted. "Why is it that you don't offer me to your unmarried son?"

Job's answer came quickly, and he was seemingly unperturbed by her boldness. "My youngest is barely thirty and not yet ready for marriage. Though the men of Esau's clan are expected to marry at age twenty—so the Edomite tribes grow quickly—I ask *my* sons to wait until they are thirty so I can teach them the ways of the Most High. I believe they should rule their hearts before they rule their households." He looked at her, lingering as if he wanted to say more, but then shook his head. "I ask my daughters to wait beyond marriageable age as well—until they are twenty—before I find a suitable husband for them, in order that they too can learn Yahweh's teachings."

"Your daughters learn the ways of the Most High? I didn't know women were allowed to see the sacred writings." Dinah almost shouted her amazement.

Job lifted an eyebrow, measuring her before he answered. "I don't actually possess the covenant writings. Those belong to your abba—the bearer of the covenant blessing—but I have the knowledge of El Elyon's teachings from my days in the House of Shem. I teach young men from many tribes. In fact, one of my pupils from the tribe of Nahor, Abraham's brother, will soon marry our youngest daughter."

A shadow of sadness swept over Job's face. Smoke rose from the fire, and he waved it away. "Great-Abba Esau doesn't really care who learns El Shaddai's ways. He is angry, however, that my family's delayed marriages slow down the growth of his Edomite clan." A little mischief dawned on Job's expression. "But he doesn't complain about my children's education as long as the other Edomites marry young and produce offspring like desert rabbits." Job chuckled.

Dinah nearly bit off her tongue to keep from cursing hateful

Uncle Esau, but one bright spot suddenly glimmered in her dreary thoughts. "Could I learn the ways of the Most High with your daughters?" As soon as the words slipped out of her mouth, she wondered if she'd gone too far. Job's eyes sparked, and his expression was a puzzle.

"Yes!" Job shouted, raising a victorious fist in the air. "I was hoping you would. Oh, Dinah, when you know El Shaddai's ways, you always have hope, always have answers to your questions."

Had such a wonderful opportunity ever been laid before her? Dinah could most certainly live as the second wife of a husband who was "not unkind" in order to learn more of El Shaddai.

"Thank you, Job." Her heart was as full as the baskets of herbs he'd purchased for her in Elath. "And thank you for the generous gift of medicines and spices. You have been too kind to me already."

Oop-oop-oop. Dinah glanced in every direction to find the source of the now familiar hoopoe bird's song. *Oop-oop-oop.* Fluttering near a fissure on the cliff face, a pink-and-black-crested hoopoe tucked in pieces of scrub to soften its rocky nesting place.

Job must have followed her gaze. "Ah, we've been blessed with good fortune for the last leg of our journey."

Dinah's furrowed brow voiced her question.

"My mother said the hoopoe is carved into Egyptian tombs as a symbol of joy and affection." Nogahla nodded her head as if she'd offered the definitive word on the subject.

Job and Dinah exchanged amused grins before Job offered another bit of lore. "And Zophar says the traders of the Far East think the little bird brings good luck."

Dinah turned to study the little creature, whose flight resembled a moth more than a bird. "But Job, I heard you and Grandfather Isaac say El Shaddai considers the hoopoe unclean." She looked into the strong features of the man who would become her father-in-law. An honest man who knew Yahweh's teachings. "How can something unclean bring joy or luck?" Looking into the dying embers, she swallowed back emotions, regained control. "How can something unclean gain anyone's affection?"

Job spoke quietly but without hesitation. "El Elyon judges acts and animals unclean in order to protect His people. We were created in the image of our Creator and are never irrevocably unclean or unredeemable." He paused. In the lingering silence, she looked up and found him awaiting her gaze. "Yahweh loves you more than He loves the hoopoe, Dinah."

A mighty gust of wind swirled dust and rocks around them, and she covered her face with the blanket.

"Master Job!" the guide shouted. "We must leave now! A storm is coming in!"

✿✿✿✿✿

Job felt strangely unsettled. Dinah's fears, the sudden storm . . . but most of all he wondered why his guide seemed in such a hurry to reach Uz tonight.

The strange storm raged. Wind and lightning, but no rain. "Let's get going," he said to Dinah. "This storm is coming in fast." Job wiped his hand over his face. Feeling a fine layer of grit, he covered his face with his red and white shmagh, leaving only a small slit for his eyes.

Both women ran toward the animals, and Job kicked dust onto the embers of dung chips. His heart was pounding like the hooves of Zophar's Sabean horses. Had the storm quickened his pulse, or was it his concern about the guide? Job hurried toward the camels and helped Dinah step into her saddle.

"I've invited Nogahla to ride with me," she said, offering the servant girl a firm support as she climbed onto the spitting beast. "The view from atop my camel is much better." Dinah quickly shouted instructions at one of the servants to tie Nogahla's donkey to her camel's hind harness.

Job grinned beneath his shmagh and marveled at the woman soon to be his daughter-in-law. What other mistress would be so considerate of her maid? He'd seen the fear on Nogahla's face when the storm began, but he would never have dreamed a mistress would share her saddle with a maid. "Will you both fit in the same saddle?" he shouted, moving toward his own camel.

Dinah feigned offense, raising her voice above the storm. "Well, Master Job, are you saying that Nogahla and I have been eating too many candied dates?" Her sapphire blue eyes sparkled, the only part of her visible beneath Jacob's uniquely woven head cloth.

"Yes, Mistress Dinah. You and your girl are as fat as oxen," Job said as he climbed aboard his own mount, dodging a corded bracelet Dinah flung at him. It was carried away on the violent wind.

"Oh!" Dinah growled, and the little serving maid let out her own huff. Dinah leaned down to whisper something to the girl, whose white smile escaped between the folds of her head scarf.

The guide was waving wildly to get under way, and this time Job agreed—they must hurry home. But even as the thought crossed his mind, the weight of it pierced his heart. Would Sitis welcome him, or would they resume their argument about Sayyid where they'd left off? And how would Ennon receive Dinah? Would he see beyond her reputation and appreciate the beautiful woman beneath the rumors?

The darkening sky split with jagged bolts of lightning. Servants feverishly tried to light torches, but the wind licked away the flames before the fire could ignite.

"We can't wait!" the guide shouted.

Job nodded and waved the caravan forward. Their final approach was under blackening skies along the mountain ridge road. Relying solely on the camel's sure-footed instincts, riders wrapped their faces against blowing debris. *El Shaddai, help us.* On a road that could normally be traveled three camels abreast, single file was necessary as the sky grew darker, the sun completely hidden behind the steep sandstone cliffs and slate gray clouds.

Job followed closely behind the guide, Dinah and Nogahla on the third camel, with the rest of the caravan following as close as was safe in the raging wind. He kept a watchful eye on Dinah and Nogahla. The women moved gracefully as one, wrapped in a blanket to shield against the cold wind and flying dust.

No rain, only wind and lightning, he marveled. *An odd storm indeed.*

When the caravan finally reached Uz's city gates, Job's sense of dread deepened. The market was empty, the merchants' stalls deserted. At this time of day, the city was usually buzzing with activity—last-minute haggling, merchants closing their booths, children hurrying home with full water jars. But tonight the natural plateau on which the city's first

83

sector sat resembled a graveyard. Small stones rolled by like desert scrub.

"Come on. Let's get into the siq!" Job's guide shouted above the distant thunder, leading the caravan toward the narrow split in the high red cliffs. "Single file! Leave plenty of space between the animals." The guide shouted his instructions but waited for no one. He disappeared into the narrow cleft between two towering walls of rock.

Job turned and saw terror in both women's eyes. Dinah began shaking her head. "No!" she cried. "This can't be Uz!" The rest of the caravan arrived on the plateau and entered the city gates, anxious to continue home. But Dinah's fear halted them. "What are those caves carved into the mountainside? Where are the houses?" She pointed at the tattered curtains flapping at the entrance of the beggars' dwellings and then spotted the empty merchants' booths. "Where are all the people, Job? I'm not going into that . . . that . . . siq until you tell me what's beyond it. I don't even think my camel will fit between those rock walls!"

Job tried to imagine Dinah's first impression of his city—a deserted market, a violent storm, and troglodyte dwellings dotting the mountain's face. He guided his camel toward Dinah and Nogahla, trying to calm them before panic spread. "Dinah, look at me!" Job shouted above the storm. "I promise your camel will fit through those walls. A new life awaits you beyond that siq." Both women seemed to calm some. "Now listen. There is a slight descent as we enter the siq. Lean all the way back on your saddle. The camel knows the way, and its footing is sure. Close your eyes if you're frightened."

The little serving maid nodded readily, but Dinah didn't look as quick to trust.

"Dinah," Job said, "if you can't trust me, at least believe that El Shaddai has brought you here for His purpose. Can you do that?"

Dinah paused. Job was learning that her answers were never impulsive or halfhearted. "I trust you and El Shaddai for whatever lies beyond the siq," she said.

In the courage he saw in her misty blue eyes, Job too believed he could trust El Shaddai for what lay ahead.

6

~Job 1:13–14~

*One day when Job's sons and daughters
were feasting and drinking wine at the oldest
brother's house, a messenger came to Job.*

Dust and debris stung Dinah's face as the desert wind continued its fury. "Mistress, I'm scared." Nogahla leaned back into Dinah's chest, and she could feel the girl's whole body trembling.

Job's camel slowly made its way into the narrow siq, stepping down and skidding on the red sandstone grade. Dinah watched as he followed his own instructions, leaning back on his saddle, his broad shoulders resting against his Bactrian's second hump. Dinah's camel languidly chewed its cud from side to side and then began its descent without prodding when Job's beast cleared the path.

Nogahla cried out above the noisy wind gusts. "Miss . . . nah! I . . . scared!"

"No crying!" Dinah sounded braver than she felt, but she had to maintain some level of composure or dissolve into another fit of hysteria. Grasping the reins with white knuckles, she squeezed her eyes shut as Job suggested. Trying to think of anything but tumbling into oblivion, Dinah began reliving her most recent humiliating display. Fear had overwhelmed her when she saw Uz. She was a seasoned traveler with Abba Jacob's camp through many terrains in all kinds of weather. But these red Edomite mountains were as imposing as Uncle Esau himself, and the eerie caves and deserted market sent dread racing through her. An unspoken voice had warned her of unseen danger.

"Good, Dinah! You've almost reached level ground," Job shouted, giving Dinah courage to open her eyes.

Noting the lessening incline, she poked Nogahla's side. "Look above us!" The red cliffs of Edom surrounded them, and below she could see a sandy gravel path running parallel to a wadi full of water. Warm, damp air fused the dirt and sand to their scarves. The muscles in Dinah's stomach ached from leaning back so long, but her heart was growing lighter.

As the path leveled and widened, Dinah saw no more caves. Instead, stunning homes carved into the mountainside lined both sides. Each home boasted beautiful courtyards and gardens—yes, gardens—with leeks and garlic and figs and date palms. Amid the protection of the siq's high walls, the wind's fierce breath faded to a whisper. Torch flames danced gently, illuminating a lifestyle as luxurious as that of Shechem's merchants.

"Nogahla, have you ever seen such a beautiful place? Do you see?"

"Yes, mistress. I see a miracle in the desert." Nogahla

pointed to a large fountain where the siq spilled into a long, level plain stretching north and south between two mountain ranges. Several modest tents, battered by the intensifying storm, formed a meandering village following the wadi through the plain. Small flocks and herds stirred nervously, and children ran to their mothers' arms for shelter.

The caravan traveled southwest through the plain, wind and dust punishing Dinah's eyes mercilessly. She'd never before wished to be a camel, but a protective second eyelid would have been helpful while she took in the sights of Uz. Farther south, clustered around private fountains and standing nobly against the storm, were exquisite house tents, made of a design she'd never seen before. Each home was constructed with red stone walls as tall as a man. A goat's-hair weave stretched to a peak over large wooden beams was joined to the walls by large posts a cubit tall. The resulting structure appeared as a red cube with a black tent hovering on stilts above it, allowing sunlight and breezes to enter the home from every side.

Job began pointing wildly at one elegantly built house tent, its cut red stones and tall roof standing like a soldier in the storm. "Ennon! Ennon!" he shouted above the noisy wind. Dinah's heart nearly leapt from her chest when she realized Job was pointing to her new home.

All too quickly, their guide veered south into a private canyon surrounded on three sides by majestic cliffs and rock-hewn facades. The camel drivers and servants hurried forward, and soon the animals halted.

"Mistress, the whole western cliff is a palace!" Nogahla's neck stretched to its limit, searching the heights of Job's impressive four-story fortress.

"Come, ladies!" Job was already off his camel and prodding Dinah's camel to its knees. "I'll give you the full tour tomorrow after the storm blows over." A streak of lightning split the darkening sky. "It appears we've made it just in time," he said, guiding Dinah and Nogahla toward a canopied courtyard.

An elderly Ishmaelite steward welcomed Job just outside an ornately carved wooden door. "Greetings, Master Job," he said, "we thank Al-Uz—we're thankful you've arrived safely."

Dinah saw Job's face cloud over like the darkened sky, and Dinah noted the Ishmaelite steward's near mention of his god. She wondered if this was part of Job's "history of differing opinions" with his steward.

"I see you've brought more servants of Yahweh to distribute goods to the poor." The steward stared condescendingly at Dinah, and she glanced down at her dust-covered robe of Jacob's tribe. Why would he immediately assume both she and Nogahla were servants?

But one more glimpse of Job's stormy expression, and Dinah realized the servant's venom had little to do with her and everything to do with her God. "No, Atif," Job said calmly, his jaw flexing. "I've brought home a new wife." He paused, engaged in a silent battle with his Ishmaelite steward.

Atif gulped and seemed to swallow his arrogance. For some reason, Job's threat of a second wife dashed cold water on the old steward's fire.

"A wife for Ennon," Job added, after reminding the steward who was master.

Dinah stifled a grin and reached for Nogahla's hand. Though the mountains of Edom were strange and new, it seemed the tensions of a household ran deep even here. She had no idea why a servant would care that his master took a second wife. And why would Job allow such insolence from a pagan steward? She squeezed Nogahla's hand. *Thank You, El Shaddai, for my Cushite friend's determination to stay with me.*

Job took a step inside his front door, and Atif moved with him like a dance, blocking the way. Holding Atif's gaze, Job held out his hand to Dinah and said, "Come, dear. I want you to meet my wife." The old Ishmaelite stared daggers at Job but stepped back, allowing Dinah and Nogahla to follow into an ornately decorated hallway.

Dinah's mouth was suddenly as dry as the desert. Job's wife would be the first family member she would face—but not the last. Would her new mother-in-law know her by reputation? Would Job reveal her secrets?

The hallway curved, and Nogahla gasped. "Mistress, look!" Dinah remembered Ima Rachel's long-ago warnings to remain placid in the presence of splendor. But Ima Rachel had never seen Job's home. Bronze lamps in wall niches cast sparkling light on golden threads in the tapestries lining the way. Abba Jacob's lamb's-wool rugs silenced their sandaled feet, and the sandstone bench running the length of the hallway was embedded with gemstones, reflections dancing in the lamplight. This hallway was a living thing—a dreamland in which Dinah floated amid shimmering lights above and billowy softness below.

Suddenly, abruptly, the dream ended in a large square dining area. Thirty or forty starkly built tables stood empty, and two stunningly elegant people stood alone. Job staggered back as if he'd been struck in battle. When Dinah saw the regal man and woman turn in surprise, she knew the war had begun long before this night.

⁂⁂⁂⁂⁂

Job blinked twice, three times. Had Sayyid been touching Sitis's face? The two of them stepped apart quickly, and Job searched his wife's expression. Was it guilt he saw there, or something else?

"Job, you're home!" Sitis hurried across the room, arms outstretched, tears forming. "I was worried about your travel in this storm." Sayyid sneered at Job and then watched Sitis—every step, every sway, every curve—as she moved toward her husband. Job said nothing, trying to remember how to breathe.

His teary-eyed wife slowed as she noted Job's silence. She stopped dead when she saw Dinah. "And who is this woman, Job, with her little Cushite handmaid?" Her voice had become shrill and accusing.

Job let his gaze wander from the defiant Ishmaelite to his demanding wife. "I will speak of it when the bread merchant leaves." His words escaped through clenched teeth.

Deep puddles formed in Sitis's eyes. "But Sayyid just came to warn me about the storm, that it might delay—"

Job grabbed her arm, leaned in close, trying without success to keep the venom from his voice. "When will you see him, Sitis? Truly *see* him for who he is?" Not waiting for her answer, he stepped around his wife and toward his adversary. "Sayyid, I thought I made myself clear. I don't ever want you in my home again. Not when I am present nor when I am absent." Job stepped aside and lifted his hand, directing Sayyid to the door. "I will remind *all* my servants of this, not just the Edomite servants loyal to me, but also the Ishmaelite servants loyal to Sitis."

Job turned and eyed Atif, who watched from the shadows.

The old steward studied his brown feet. Job returned his attention to the arrogant merchant in his dining hall. "You are not welcome anywhere on my property or the properties of my children, Sayyid. Leave now." Job bowed slightly, waiting for his response.

Sayyid didn't move.

Every bone, muscle, and sinew in Job's body screamed for revenge. This man had deceived his wife into idolatry, teased his sons with greed, and undermined his authority as a city elder. *Please, El Shaddai, let me spill this man's blood.* But years of studying God's ways reminded Job that vengeance was Yahweh's alone. Job would not use the skills Esau had taught him to inflict harm on another human being.

"Atif!" Job shouted, and everyone in the room jumped—except Sayyid. The man's hand moved to his belt, under his outer robe, where Job saw the glint of a dagger.

The steward's words snapped the tension. "Yes, Master Job?"

"You will escort Sayyid out of my home for the *last* time." Job held Atif's gaze. "Do you understand?"

Before the steward could answer, Sayyid stormed past him and through the hallway. Atif bowed and said quietly, "If I may be excused, I'll be sure Master Sayyid finds his way out." And the old man was gone.

"Job, it's not what you think." Sitis clutched the front of Job's robe, her voice trembling. "Sayyid came to warn me—"

Job placed a quieting finger on Sitis's lips and embraced her, hoping his arms would quiet her words and her heart. He saw Dinah standing near the wall with Nogahla, both looking as if they wished they could melt into the cold stone. Their welcome had been anything but planned or proper, but perhaps the struggles they'd seen would assure them that everyone needed El Shaddai's grace.

Job too was trembling. His unspent anger and the desire to whisk his beautiful wife to safety were overwhelming.

When he drew Sitis away, he kissed the tears from her cheeks. "We will speak more of this later, but right now I must introduce you to your new daughter-in-law and her maid."

Sitis straightened and wiped her cheeks. Understandably embarrassed, she approached Dinah timidly and introduced herself. *Always the prince's daughter*, Job marveled.

"Please forgive me for this misunderstanding, my dear," Sitis said. "I certainly would have wished for a better welcome for you. Please don't judge us too harshly by what you've seen."

Job extended his hand, inviting Dinah to join him and his wife. "Dinah knows that circumstances aren't always what they seem at first glance, Sitis."

Dinah offered a gracious bow.

"So, your name is Dinah," Sitis said, studying her new daughter-in-law in the lamplight. "Job, isn't that the name of Great-Abba Esau's niece, who—"

"Yes, my love," Job interrupted before Sitis made any regrettable remarks about Dinah's reputation. Lifting one eyebrow, he tried to communicate discretion to his wife. "This is Uncle Jacob's daughter, Dinah."

Shock. Accusation. Questions. All in Sitis's reflexive glance at the recognition of Dinah's name. Zophar had known her by sight, but the rest of Job's family would identify her only by name—and by rumor.

Dinah looked stricken, her face gray, but she bowed again, hiding her reborn discomfort admirably. "It is a great honor to meet you, mistress." Lifting her gaze, she resembled a prisoner awaiting a verdict.

Sitis's expression softened, and she grasped Dinah's hands. "Which of my sons will be blessed to call you his wife?" Job watched Dinah's tortured features relax under the caress of Sitis's approving words—but was his wife sincere?

Before he could study Sitis further, he heard the rustling of a robe in the hallway, running footsteps, heavy breathing. Had Sayyid returned, planning vengeance? His attention fixed on the entry, Job reached for the dagger strapped to his calf.

"I'm here, Ima Sitis!" Elihu's tall, wiry frame came bounding into the room, nearly knocking Nogahla to the floor. "Oh, I'm sorry, who are you?" He stopped abruptly, mouth agape, his eyes as big as ostrich eggs. "Abba Job! You're home." His gaze darted toward Dinah, his cheeks coloring three shades of crimson. "Forgive me, I didn't know you were entertaining women—a woman—I mean . . . guests."

Job chuckled. Though Elihu rivaled any man in the memorization of sacred texts, when it came to social graces, he was as awkward at thirty as he'd been at twelve. "Elihu, my favorite student! What are you doing here? I thought you were studying with Uncle Eliphaz in Teman."

Elihu drew a breath to answer, but Sitis interrupted. "Job, it's the spring of Uzahmah's twentieth year. You promised Elihu's betrothal proceedings would begin upon your return, remember?" The left side of her smile twitched, as it always did when she was nervous. She hurried over to take Elihu's hand, leading him to Job. "Come sit down, Elihu. Job has just arrived, and I haven't had time to tell him about the betrothal banquet. The children are all at Ennon's house celebrating."

Dinah seemed to snap to attention at the mention of her husband-to-be.

Sitis blurted out the rest of the information as if releasing the hot handle of a cooking pot. "I sent Nada to tell the children we would join them as soon as you both arrived."

"Now? You expect us to attend a betrothal banquet now?" Job heard the censure in his voice but couldn't contain it.

Living statues filled the room as Job contemplated his response. The courtyard doors clattered behind him, raging wind and lightning invading their silent world.

That's when they heard it.

A single voice with low-pitched, tortured howls drew nearer. Every eye turned toward the courtyard entry.

"Nooo!" A herdsman burst through the doorway, the wind slamming the oaken slabs hard against the sandstone walls. Robes bloodstained and torn, Job's chief herdsman ran across the dining hall and fell at his feet. "Master Job, they're all dead!" Weeping shook his shoulders.

Job motioned Elihu to gather the women aside, and then he bent down and lifted the bloodied herdsman to his feet. "Shobal, are you hurt? Is this your blood?"

"No, Master Job. I hid in a dry wadi when the Sabeans attacked. They took away all your plowing oxen and the donkeys that were grazing nearby. They put all the servants to the sword. As soon as the Sabeans rode away on their horses, I tried to help the other servants. I tried, Master Job, but I'm the only one who has escaped alive to tell you!"

Job's mind reeled. He had almost seven hundred servants tending his five hundred yoked oxen and five hundred donkeys. How could they *all* be dead?

"Shobal, are you sure—" Job's heart leapt to his throat.

He couldn't swallow. *It can't be.* "Did you say Sabeans? On horses?"

Job glanced up and saw Dinah's horrified expression. She too must have made the connection between Zophar's Sabean escort at Elath and the Sabean attack. Panic stabbed Job like a bronze-tipped arrow. He shook the bloodied herdsman. "Shobal, did they have any prisoners with them? Did you see a caravan in the distance?" His angry parting with Zophar replayed mercilessly in his mind.

But before the herdsman could form his reply, another voice sounded in the distance and a second servant stumbled through the courtyard entrance. It was Lotan, Job's chief shepherd, and he collapsed beside his friend Shobal. His clothes were singed, his face, arms, and hands blistered with burns. "Master Job, the lightning! It was so horrible."

Job bent to inspect his wounds. "Lotan, what happened to you?" Noting the charred skin on the man's hands, he glanced at Dinah and called her over. "Listen, my friend. I have someone here who can tend to your wounds."

"No, Master Job. The flocks, the servants." He gulped for air, delirious, disoriented.

Job looked up at Sitis, her beautiful black eyes wide with fear, her whole body trembling. She stepped sideways without looking. Feeling her way to a bench, she sat down hard. Dread seemed to strangle everyone in the room.

Only Job uttered a whisper. "What about the flocks and servants, Lotan?"

The man's face twisted into a mask of agony. "The fire of God fell from the sky, Master Job. It burned up all the sheep and every servant tending them." Sobs garbled his words, but Job understood the last phrase, repeated again and again. "I'm the only one left . . . the only one left."

The shepherd clutched Job's robe, Job cradling him. Dinah knelt a few paces away, evidently perceiving Lotan needed compassion more than medicine right now.

"I'm just glad you're safe, my friend," Job said.

Dinah turned away, tears rolling down her cheeks. Job saw that Elihu was comforting Sitis, as much like a son as the children of her womb. The young man would make a fine husband to their daughter, but what kind of dowry could he offer for Uzahmah now? Three-quarters of Job's wealth had been swallowed up in a few moments. Worse than that, over a thousand of his servants had died tonight—mothers, fathers, sons, and daughters. And how would they bury all the dead?

Lightning flashed again, and Lotan bolted from Job's arms, terror-stricken. At the same moment, bloodcurdling screams echoed through the canyon outside the courtyard. Job exchanged horrified glances with the men in the room, and all seemed to realize that some sort of attack was under way.

"Elihu, get the weapons!" Job shouted. "Shobal, can you fight?"

"Yes, Master Job!" The herdsman ran to barricade the courtyard door.

"Lotan, you stay here with—" Job's instructions were cut short by Sitis's scream. He saw Atif, his defiant steward, stumble from the hallway, hands on his belly and blood on his hands.

"Atif, my dear Atif." Sitis was instantly on her feet and at her servant's side.

Elihu, who had been on his way to the weaponry closet, grabbed Atif under the arms and dragged him toward a table. Job, Shobal, and Lotan helped Elihu lift the old man onto a table, while Nogahla retrieved Atif's keffiyeh from the floor.

Job saw the steward's gaping wound and stood paralyzed by fear.

Dinah grabbed the black-and-white keffiyeh from Nogahla and pressed it against the wound. "Push the cloth firmly here to help stop the bleeding."

Atif groaned, and Sitis shoved Dinah away. "Stop! You're hurting him." She hovered over the old man. "It's all right, Atif. You're going to be all right."

Job watched Dinah back away, Nogahla's arms waiting to console her, but he didn't have time to assuage hurt feelings now. He could still hear a battle just outside his doors. "Atif, who did this?" he said, uncertain if his steward could even comprehend the question. "Atif, can you hear me?"

"Master Job . . ." His voice sounded raspy, like spit in a flute. "Chaldeans, master. Three raiding parties. Taking camels. Killing the servants."

"Chaldeans?" Elihu gasped. Job looked into the young man's pale face, and Elihu looked at Sitis. "When Ima sent word to Eliphaz in Teman, I joined a large caravan of Chaldeans that brought me to Uz tonight. I left them just moments ago. They seemed like common merchants." Job watched the dawning horror on Elihu's features. "How could the people I've ridden with for days be the same raiders that murdered your servants?"

"It was your guide, Master Job." Atif clutched at Job's collar. "Your guide sent word to the Chaldeans that you would arrive tonight at sunset." The old man cringed in agony. "I'm sorry, Master Job. You hired the guide on my word." His eyes closed and he seemed to lose consciousness.

"No!" Sitis cried. "Atif, don't leave me!" She buried her head in his chest, mumbling her grief. "I have no father but you, no brother but you. Please, don't leave me."

The old man's eyes fluttered and his hand moved weakly to stroke Sitis's cheek. In a whisper barely audible, he said, "You'll be all right, child. Nada will care for you." Turning to Job, he stilled his hand. "The camels are gone, servants gone—all gone." Atif's eyes froze in death's stare, and he expelled the final rattling breath from his lungs.

"Atif?" Sitis clutched wildly at his robe. "Atif! Atif!"

Job stroked his wife's back as she lay across the lifeless body of her lifetime friend and guardian.

"Whom do I have but you and Nada?" She poured out the loneliness of her childhood, and her wailing crescendoed beyond bearable.

But wait . . . Another keening voice, the same tone and pitch, emanated from the curved hallway and created an eerie duet.

"Nada?" Job breathed the name, identifying with horror Sitis's portly nursemaid, who emerged from the hall covered in fine red dust.

Nada's cries changed to shrieks, her eyes wild at the sight of Atif's blood now covering Job and Sitis. "My mistress, not you too! I cannot bear to lose you too!" She ran to Sitis, lifting her mistress's chin, her arms, inspecting her for injuries.

Job tried to gather the hysterical woman in his arms. "Nada, calm down. What's happened? What do you mean—"

"No!" Elihu grabbed the maid's arm with such ferocity and strength that Job stood gaping. "Nada, where is Uzahmah?" Elihu raved. "I saw you walking to Ennon's house as I entered the city." The old woman buried her face in her hands, shaking with sobs, unable—or unwilling—to speak.

"No," Sitis said, her voice a menacing growl, head wagging side to side.

Nada let her hands fall to her sides, her expression pleading. "Mistress, I tried to help them."

"No! Nada! It's not true. Tell me right now that my children are safe!" Sitis screamed, trembling violently. "Tell me the babes you caught on birthing stones are alive and drinking wine at my oldest son's home."

Job suddenly felt as though he were inside a narrow hallway. Sounds became distant. He grabbed Sitis, clinging to her. Was this real or a terrible nightmare?

"Nada," he said, struggling for breath, "tell us clearly what happened." He was vaguely aware of others in the room, but he couldn't recall their names or why they were present. He could see only Nada, hear only her voice.

"I went to Ennon's house to tell the children you had arrived home and Elihu would be here shortly." Nada gasped, the rest of her words coming out in a cry. "Then the wind came. A mighty desert wind struck the four corners of the house as I walked out of the courtyard. The stone walls gave way, and the tented ceilings and beams came down on top of them."

"Nooo!" Sitis collapsed into Job's arms, but this time he had no strength to hold her. They both tumbled to the floor, lost together in private agony. Sitis continued her wailing, groping on the floor. Someone cradled her, tried to comfort her, but Job couldn't think about Sitis. He had to know about the children.

Like a madman, Job was back on his feet. He grabbed Nada's head between his hands and drew her face so close, he could smell the sweet wine she'd been drinking. "The children, Nada," Job shouted above Sitis's cries. "Did you see them? Did you see any of the servants? Could they have escaped somehow?"

The old woman's arms began to flail. "No!" she screamed. "The children, the servants—everyone. They're all dead! I saw them begging me to help them, their hands held out to me among the red rocks and broken beams!" She called out the children's names, slapping herself in the face, smashing her fists into the unyielding stone wall until her knuckles were bloody.

Job tried to restrain her, but she shoved him away with surprising strength. He watched helplessly as hysteria entered their midst, its grip like the leviathan's jaws.

Elihu ran from the room, screaming, "Uzahmah, no! Uzahmah!" Job called after him but realized the boy was beyond reason.

Sitis clutched at Dinah's robes, her hair, her face, as though grief were quicksand and Dinah the lone rope. Then, just as quickly, Sitis rebuffed Dinah's embrace and struck her violently. Dinah tried to quiet her, tried to restrain her, but the grief fueled his wife's strength, and Dinah moved away, giving wide berth to Sitis's frenzy. The inconsolable mother pulled out handfuls of her long, ebony hair and clawed at her own face, leaving deep gouges.

"No, not my children! El Shaddai, Al-Uzza, by the gods, not my babies!"

"Come, wife," Job said with a sudden and unexplained calm. He grasped Sitis's shoulders, lifting her gently to her feet, restraining her tenderly but firmly. "Only one God can help us."

"No!" Sitis screamed. "This is your fault! You and your God!" She broke away from his guiding hands.

"Sitis. Stop this. Please, let me help you."

"Like you helped me by destroying the Chaldean temple?"

Sitis's words cut Job like a blade, and he doubled over, bracing his hands on his knees. But she didn't stop—perhaps she couldn't stop. "The Chaldeans killed my Atif and the other servants. They took our camels—all as vengeance, Job. Why did you have to destroy their temple? Why couldn't you allow Sayyid to take my offerings to Al-Uzza's temple? Who did it hurt?"

"Me!" Job sprung from his stance like an arrow from a bow. "You hurt me!" He beat his chest. "You deceived me, and you betrayed El Shaddai!"

Sitis didn't recoil. A mere handbreadth apart, they stood locked in a silent battle.

Job finally spoke—softly, patiently. "It is no coincidence that the Sabeans and Chaldeans, traveling from opposite ends of the earth, raided our livestock on the same day, at the same moment, Sitis. And it is not by chance that fire from heaven burned up our sheep, and a desert wind swept away . . . " His lips quaked. "Took away our precious lambs." He calmly rested his hands on Sitis's shoulders, but when she shrugged them off, his patience was spent. "Sitis, I destroyed the Chaldean temple nine years ago. Why did they wait until today to attack? You can't blame man for one tragedy and El Shaddai for the others, when *all* things—blessings and trials—come from the Almighty."

Her expression became as hard as flint. "Fine, I am content to curse El Shaddai for all my pain," she said with deadly calm. "And if you embrace El Shaddai, I curse you too."

7

~*Job 1:20–21*~

*At this, Job got up and tore his robe and shaved
his head. Then he fell to the ground in worship
and said: "Naked I came from my mother's
womb, and naked I will depart. The LORD gave
and the LORD has taken away; may the name of
the LORD be praised."*

Dinah stared in utter horror as Sitis's words echoed
off the high red walls surrounding them. The silence
that followed screamed rebellion, lifting the hair on Dinah's
arms and the back of her neck. Lightning flashed outside
the courtyard door, and she winced, wondering if the fire of
Yahweh would reach into Job's dining hall and consume his
belligerent wife. Nogahla grasped Dinah's hand and looked
up. Dinah saw her own disbelief and sorrow reflected in the
girl's midnight pools.

"Nada, we're going to my chamber," Sitis said flatly. "I

have nothing else to say to this man." Job flinched as if she had slapped him. Stirring the tension with a hurried swish of her robe, Sitis grabbed Nada's arm and fled the dining hall. Her purple robe disappeared behind a tapestry curtain covering a connecting hallway.

Dinah stared after her, wondering how anyone could rebuild after such devastation. She wanted to console Job, to say something comforting, the way he had eased her years of pain and grief. But what could she say or do? Family and faith united them, but in reality she barely knew the man. He glanced in her direction, but his eyes looked through her. He buried his face in his hands and wept bitterly. Dinah turned away, unable to bear the agony of his strong silhouette shaken with grief.

Instead, she gave her attention to the herdsman Shobal, who had found some cloth and was tearing it into bandages to wrap his friend's burns. Hoping to busy herself, she tugged lightly on Nogahla's hand, moving in the direction of the two servants.

Shobal offered Dinah a weak smile but returned his attention to his friend. "Sit down, Lotan, so we can dress your wounds." He shouldered the man's weight, and Nogahla supported his left side, helping the injured shepherd to a nearby bench. Lotan's burns weren't as serious as Dinah had originally feared, but they covered a significant portion of his face, hands, and arms. She had just torn the last narrow strip of cloth when a cry jolted her.

"No, Abba!" Dinah turned as Elihu shrieked and leapt toward Job—at precisely the same moment she saw Job raise his dagger to his throat. "Abba Job, you can't. You mustn't. It's against the teachings." Job lay motionless on the stone tiles, gazing into Elihu's tortured face.

At a time that should have been rife with tension, Job's unnatural calm startled Dinah. With all her restraint, she held back an inappropriate giggle at the sight of Elihu—a tall, skinny broom tree—tackling the muscular, sinewy Job. Elihu lay on top of Job, panting. The younger trapped the elder's arms to the floor. The dagger lay sprawled on Job's relaxed palm, the atmosphere writhing with unasked questions.

Tentatively, Dinah walked toward them and plucked the dagger from Job's hand. Elihu met her gaze and nodded, seemingly satisfied that she had joined his efforts to protect Job. When she stepped back, the two men stood. Neither one spoke or looked at the other. Dinah looked up to meet Job's gaze and then offered the knife back to him.

Elihu shoved her. "What are you doing?" He grabbed for the weapon, but it was already firmly planted in Job's hand. The two men locked eyes in challenge, each measuring the other, student testing teacher, would-be son protecting surrogate abba.

"Elihu, you are mistaken." Job's voice fell into tortured silence. Dinah saw sadness in him but not despair. She trusted this man—even now, when his life lay in ruins.

Elihu turned on her, raging. "His blood is on your hands . . . woman!"

Dinah suddenly realized that this young man didn't even know her name. His anger wasn't aimed at the usual Dinah of Shechem but at a nameless woman he feared had endangered his beloved abba-teacher.

"Elihu, I—" But her explanation halted when Job abruptly turned, dagger in hand, and walked toward the same tapestry through which Sitis had disappeared.

"Abba, wait!" Elihu followed, and with sick dread, Dinah fell in step behind them, wondering if she'd mistakenly returned a weapon to a desperate man. Nogahla, Shobal, and even the injured Lotan trailed through a dimly lit hall, into the kitchen and servants' quarters, and finally to an exterior courtyard. Job walked as if in a trance to the farthest corner of the yard. Passing kitchen scraps and garden waste, he trudged into a pile of ash collected from household braziers that was as tall as a small child. Job turned toward his followers and fell to his knees, sinking into the fine gray ash.

The surrounding torches illumined Job's tears, sparkling diamonds streaming into his coppery beard. With one hand, he ripped the neckline of his robe and released a feral cry. The dagger in his other hand returned to his throat. For one terrible moment, Dinah feared his death, but in the next, she marveled at his life.

One swipe up, and Job's flint blade razed the first swatch of beard. Another swipe, and Dinah was mesmerized. Nogahla, Elihu, and both herdsmen joined in hushed reverence as Job's coppery tresses fell into the ashes. He shaved his head and face without a mirror, each nick of skin mingling his blood with tears.

When at last he was cleanly shaven, Job lifted his grief to heaven in worship. "Naked I came from my mother's womb, and naked I will depart. Yahweh gave and Yahweh has taken away; may the name of Yahweh be praised."

In his home's waste yard, the symbol of all that was used up and broken, Job released his torrent of anguish in a desperate sacrifice of praise. He had held his grief amid the tragedies. He had controlled his rage during Sitis's attack. But in El Shaddai's presence, his emotion poured out as an offering. He rocked and prayed, throwing ash toward heaven, allowing the fine dust to fall over him like Yahweh's healing balm.

The sudden unsheathing of a dagger startled Dinah. She'd been so consumed by Job's faithfulness, she hadn't noticed when Elihu removed his keffiyeh. He approached Job and knelt beside his mentor and would-be abba. Without hesitation, Shobal and Lotan followed, and soon all three men began the tremulous task of shaving their heads and beards.

"Naked I came from my mother's womb," Elihu began, his scraggly beard and wispy brown hair lying in the ashes beside him. The herdsman and shepherd joined the refrain, emulating the life lesson of their righteous master. They too had lost their livelihood tonight. They too had lost friends and family in the tragedies of this household.

Dinah felt her throat tighten with emotion, swept away in the presence of such devotion. A man devoted to his God, student to his teacher, servants to their master. Her heart squeezed like olives in a press. *Could I be so devoted? Or would I have rebelled like Sitis—bitter and angry?*

Job worshiped El Shaddai, though he admitted freely Yahweh's responsibility for the devastation. Still Job trusted El Elyon's perfect understanding and perfect ways. How could anyone live this way—with such faith, such unwavering trust?

Dinah felt a slight tug on her robe and looked down into Nogahla's wide, questioning eyes. She hugged the girl so tightly, they almost toppled over.

"Mistress Dinah," Nogahla whispered, "please, I want to leave here."

Dinah cupped the girl's cheeks in her hands. "Nogahla, where can we go?" The moment the words escaped her lips, the deeper truth of Dinah's circumstance seemed real for the first time.

The shimmer of moonlight in Nogahla's tears intensified her pleading. "Mistress Dinah, I'm afraid to go, but I'm afraid to stay."

Fear steered Dinah's thoughts down an awful path of possibilities. Job's son was gone, and her future had died with him. Dinah couldn't ask Job to spend his depleted resources for her return to Jacob's tents, but how could she and Nogahla survive on their own?

El Shaddai, what will we do? She had marveled at Job's faithfulness and trust in God when all was lost, but now realized she faced the same uncertainty. *How will I provide for Nogahla?*

Her gaze was once again drawn to Job, who just a few nights ago had taught her the love and forgiveness of El Shaddai. Tonight he showed her the sovereignty of Yahweh and that a person's response must always be trust and praise. She wasn't sure that she could accept God's will without question, but she would try to follow Job's example.

Dinah hugged Nogahla resolutely before releasing the girl and turning her back to the men. She grasped the neckline of her undergarment, and with a strong pull, the woven fabric gave way. "We didn't know those who died," she whispered to Nogahla, "but our dreams have died tonight too. Our grief is just as real, our future just as unsure." Careful to cover the torn tunic beneath her robe, she slowly faced the men on the ash heap once more.

Dinah didn't need to intrude on the men's ash pile. She didn't need to shave her hair in order to speak to the Creator who had given her ima Leah's wheat-colored tresses. Dropping to her knees beside dinner scraps and garden waste, she recited Job's words. "Naked I came from my mother's womb, and naked I will depart. Yahweh gave and Yahweh has taken away; may the name of Yahweh be praised."

As she began to formulate her own words of praise, she sensed Nogahla turn, and heard her garment rip and her sweet voice repeat the now familiar refrain.

✵✵✵✵✵

Sayyid listened contentedly as Uz regained its quaint still-ness. Taking a long, slow drink of his sweet wine, he glanced over his cup at his Edomite friend. Bela, son of Beor, was a short, squat gem merchant whose girth covered the full width of Sayyid's courtyard bench.

Swallowing the sweet nectar, Sayyid tried to calm his nervous friend. "Take a deep breath, Bela. My guards will soon return with the final report on our substantial gains."

The man's little eyes darted back and forth over rounded cheeks like two horseflies jumping over gourds. "Why is it taking so long?" he whispered. "The screaming stopped long ago." Bela smoothed his mustache, his fingers rounding his mouth and tugging at his long, red beard.

Did all the men of Esau have that hideous copper coloring? Bela was pompous and repulsive, but Sayyid forgave his faults because he was the second-wealthiest man in Uz. And after the Chaldeans raided Job's camels, Bela would be the wealthiest.

"You need not whisper." Sayyid soothed him in liquid tones. "Every servant in my home is loyal and would not dare betray me." He clasped the wrist of a young serving girl as she offered olives and cheese. His grip tightened, and he felt her immediate submission. Head bowed, body trembling, she set the tray aside and fell to her knees. Sayyid tipped her chin with one finger and tilted her face toward Bela for approval. "You see, my fine Edomite friend, my home is a sanctuary, and every servant knows my desire before I speak it." Sayyid eyed her hungrily. *Perhaps I will choose you to help me celebrate my victory over Job tonight*, he thought as she glanced warily between the merchants.

"How can you think of women at a time like this, Sayyid?" Disgust laced Bela's tone. "And tell me this. Why do all your slave girls look the same? Dark hair, dark eyes, full lips and curves. All the same height and weight—just differing ages of the same woman. Where did you even find so many who look alike?"

Sayyid laughed to hide his discomfort. No one had openly posed the question before. "I decided a long time ago to start a collection of perfect women." Sayyid released the girl and waved his hand, explaining his obsession as a silly game. "It's the reason I've never married, Bela. Why buy one cow when you can drink milk from a thousand herds?"

Bela's chuckles caused dizzying ripples across his ample middle. Sayyid was relieved to divert the man's attention from the corps of Sitis look-alikes he'd purchased over the last forty years.

The sudden sound of marching halted Bela's laughter and sped Sayyid's heartbeat. "Now we'll have our report on the Chaldeans' raid, my friend. We will be rich men and Job's camel caravans ruined."

As if summoned by the words, the captain of Sayyid's household guard appeared at the gate, followed by a small detachment of men. The massive captain, Aban, in his black robes and keffiyeh, almost disappeared into the night until he smiled. The brilliant white teeth in his chiseled jaw glowed as brightly as the torches lighting his way across the pebbled path.

"Master, all three Chaldean raiding parties completed their objectives," he said. "Job's camels are being driven to Damascus for sale and his servants are dead. Job's Hebron guide, who helped coordinate the Chaldeans' arrival, has been—" Aban paused, glancing at Bela. Sayyid nodded his permission to continue. "The guide has been *silenced* and is no longer a threat to expose your plan." The captain lifted one eyebrow and pursed his lips.

Sayyid recognized immediately the telling signs that his young captain had suppressed further details—perhaps something displeasing. He rose from his chair, standing eye level to Aban's chest, and with a menacing whisper still commanded enough respect to back his captain onto his heels. "Tell me what you hesitate to say."

Aban swallowed hard, and Sayyid watched the lump bob up and down in his throat. "Master Sayyid," he began, "Job's old house steward, Atif, was mortally wounded in the attack. I'm sorry, master. I know he's been a friend since you and Mistress Sitis were children."

Sayyid released the breath he was holding and waved away Aban's concern. "It can't be helped. I was afraid you were going to report something awful—like some of Job's camels survived the raid."

The lump in his captain's throat bobbed again. "The Chaldeans took all of Job's *corralled* camels, Master Sayyid. However, the few camels and supplies from his Hebron caravan were sheltered in his household stable and were overlooked by the Chaldeans."

"Overlooked? You're telling me Job still has camels *and* goods to trade?" Sayyid heard the shrillness of his voice and hated it.

"Sayyid, calm down." Bela's voice melded into Sayyid's building fury. "What are a few camels and some baubles compared to the three thousand camels Job lost to our Chaldean raiders?"

Before Sayyid could berate his fat little Edomite friend, Aban interrupted again. "Job has lost much more than camels tonight, my lord. I believe the gods have smiled on both Master Sayyid and Master Bela this evening."

The sudden anticipation on his captain's face calmed Sayyid's fears more than words. Aban wouldn't have offered Sayyid hope if he couldn't deliver. Master and captain knew each other implicitly. Not only had Sayyid trained the boy with bow, sword, and spear since his mother had served as Sayyid's concubine, but he'd seen Aban's warrior instincts develop at a young age. Aban was the youngest captain in Uz, the most relentless, and loyal beyond question.

"Tell me," Sayyid said, soothed by Aban's confidence. "Slowly, so I can relish each detail."

The captain's left eyebrow rose again, this time drawing up the left side of his mouth. "Sabeans have stolen Job's five hundred yoke of oxen and his five hundred donkeys, and they killed every servant." Sayyid laughed so loud, Bela jumped, rippling his belly again. Aban bowed to the delighted lords before continuing. "It seems even the gods have joined in your quest to ruin the man. Lightning fell from the sky and burned up every sheep and servant in Job's fields, and desert winds collapsed the four corners of Ennon's home, killing every child of Sitis's womb."

Sayyid's laughter stopped. "Sitis's children are dead?" he said, stumbling back, feeling blindly for the ivory chair he called his throne.

Bela scooted to the edge of the bench beside Sayyid, his

feet almost touching the ground. His fuzzy red hair and beard matched his now bloodshot eyes. "I never dreamed Job would lose everything," he said. "I simply wanted to set myself above Job for the day when Great-Abba Esau appoints his successor to rule Edom." Shaking his head, he pressed his thumb and forefinger to weepy eyes. "I didn't want to ruin Job. We are Edomite kinsmen, after all."

A white-hot ember of panic rose inside Sayyid's chest. He couldn't afford Bela's remorse or sudden attack of conscience. "Your kinsman?" he said, placing a firm hand on Bela's arm.

Bela looked up, startled by Sayyid's grasp.

"You don't owe Job loyalty just because your grandfathers descended from Esau's loins!" Sayyid released Bela's arm and slammed his hand on his ivory throne. "Was he acting as your *kinsman* when he spoke against your appointment as city judge, saying you were too young and inexperienced? Was he your *kinsman* when he renounced your worship of Kaus, the Edomite mountain god?" Sayyid rose from his perch, and with each question stepped closer, dug deeper into Bela's emotional wounds. "We did not ruin Job, my friend. It was the gods who have ruined your *kinsman*, and it is your duty as a city elder to protect the rest of Uz from further retribution."

The little Edomite stood, his tears for Job's misfortune dried amid the bitter wind of accusation. Bela's expression changed from concern to outright fear. "What do you mean, 'further retribution,' Sayyid? Do you think the gods would exact their vengeance on Job by striking others in Uz?"

Sayyid offered a meager shrug. "Perhaps if others in Uz will distance themselves from the man, they may be safe from the gods' vengeance." A sorrowful sigh punctuated his perfor-mance. "But who could be sure? Perhaps the gods will turn on Job's *kinsman* next." Sayyid glanced at Bela to be sure the short, squat Edomite grasped his insinuation.

"I will speak to the city elders in the morning," Bela said, a determined set to his jowls. "Job should be revoked as chief judge, and another respected citizen should be named elder in his place."

"Very wise, Bela." Sayyid wrapped the man's shoulders with a friendly embrace and walked him toward the courtyard gate. "I believe you should go home to your lovely wife and consider who should replace Job on the city council."

Bela smiled slyly. "Of course you know who I'll suggest." The Edomite clasped Sayyid's shoulders and pressed his bristly, bearded right cheek against Sayyid's trimmed and oiled beard. "Peace and prosperity to you, my friend."

Taking a deep breath, Sayyid suffered through the scratchy farewell. "And to you, Bela." He watched the gem merchant's guards escort the man's donkey out of the canyon. Bela would no doubt return to his home in the northern plain of the second sector, sleeping little and eating much, impatiently awaiting the dawn.

When the Edomite's escort was well out of sight, Sayyid turned to Aban, who stood beaming with unspoken satisfaction. "Wipe that silly grin off your face!" Sayyid said. "Our work has just begun." He marched through the courtyard, the pebbles of red rock crunching beneath his feet. He had planned only the Chaldean raid, but it seemed the gods had truly been at work to ruin Job. Finally, Sitis, in her poverty and grief, would run willingly into Sayyid's arms. "Dismiss your men and follow me to my chamber," he called out over his shoulder, making his way to the grand hall and toward the winding stairs. "Grab a torch on your way!"

He could hear Aban's hurried commands and scuffling sandals on the tiles behind him. Soon torchlight illumined the curving stairway. Sayyid smiled. He had trained his captain well.

When the two reached Sayyid's fourth-story bedchamber, a serving girl waited in the sitting area with a pitcher of wine and two cups. She stood beside the bed, an ostrich plume fan in her hand to stir the night breeze. Sayyid eyed her briefly but walked beyond the main chamber onto his balcony, his sanctuary of rest and peace. Aban holstered the torch on the bedchamber wall and followed Sayyid to the balcony.

"Aban, my boy, we must move quickly," he said, squinting through the settling dust on the canyon floor.

Aban's bushy, black brows knit together. "I'm not sure I know what you mean, my lord."

"We must strike Job while he is at his weakest, totally destroy any resources he could use to rebuild his wealth. And we must do it before he requests help from Esau or Sitis's brother, Bildad."

"What do you ask of me, my lord?" Aban said, focused so intently on Sayyid's words that he missed the lithe, slender form on the balcony across the canyon.

"Go back into my chamber and snuff out every lamp and torch," Sayyid said calmly.

The big man followed Sayyid's gaze across the canyon, finally noticing the woman's figure on her balcony. "Yes, my lord." He bowed and retreated into the chamber. Darkness came slowly, in stages, with each snuffing out of lights. Sayyid wondered if Job felt the same tonight when each loss was reported—a little more darkness, a little more death, until finally the blackness consumed the night.

Gazing across the canyon at Sitis's shadowy form, Sayyid thanked Al-Uzza that Sitis had maintained her nightly ritual. He feared the tragedies would have thrown her household into such turmoil that she might have neglected her visit to the balcony, their nightly hideaway.

After snuffing the last of the lamps, Aban rejoined his master on the balcony but kept his gaze respectfully lowered. "Do you ever tire of watching her, master?" Aban spoke in barely a whisper.

Sayyid would have cut the throat of any other man who asked such a question, but—he chuckled at the thought—no one else knew of his nightly perch. "I'll answer with a question for you, Aban. Do you ever tire of seeing the sunset or a desert flower growing between two rocks?"

"I suppose that kind of beauty is tireless." Aban's reply seemed hesitant. Perhaps he was simply cautious commenting on the master's most prized treasure. And rightly so.

Sayyid squeezed the captain's strong shoulder, a stiff but amiable show of camaraderie. His captain understood him well. Sayyid had settled for the second best location in Uz—the cliffs directly across from Job's great palace. A fair arrangement, since the mountain city of Uz was Sitis's dowry from her brother. Considering Sayyid's heart twisted each time he saw Sitis in Job's arms, he had earned every moment's pleasure of his fourth-story view of her third-story balcony.

"Why aren't you in Job's arms tonight, Sitis-girl?" Wicked satisfaction creased his lips. "Perhaps Princess Sitis has already decided a poor man with no property isn't worth her time."

All too quickly, the old hag Nada wrapped a blanket around her mistress and hurried her inside. Sayyid's heart plummeted, his mood darkening like clouds obscuring the moon. Glancing at Aban, he spoke in measured tones. "As I said, we need to be sure Job has no way to rebuild his wealth. Send some men into the desert to find the Nameless Ones."

The moonlight revealed streaks of dread on Aban's features. "Master, I don't trust them. I don't even know if we can find them. They live in dry streambeds, underbrush, and holes in the ground. Most of them are more animal than human."

"You will find them, Aban," he said as if speaking to a child, "because you'll carry with you the cook's choice lamb and quail, and they'll find *you*. Then you will trade them food for folly. They'll enjoy stripping clean the rest of Job's possessions. And tell their leader *someone* will pay handsomely for it."

"What is their leader's name?"

Sayyid squinted, working hard to remember if he'd ever heard a name given to any of the desert dwellers. They were like apparitions, ghosts, waiting for night to enter the city to steal, kill, and destroy. "The leader is known only as the Nameless One, but his authority is tenuous at best, and he leads with reins no sturdier than a spider's web."

Aban's intense dark eyes were hooded by his black garments, his voice like the low rumble of a storm. "I will find this Nameless One, master, but they may not stop at thievery. They take women for sport and kill men for pleasure."

His captain had never been so talkative, and Sayyid's patience grew thin. "You will stop them, Aban!" he said, letting his frustration show. "I will become Sitis's protector, and Job will remain unharmed." He turned away, examining the empty balcony across the canyon. "I want Job to suffer when Sitis runs into my arms."

✠✠✠✠✠

The sound of Job's worship mingled with Dinah's hushed whispers as she spoke the names of Yahweh she'd learned from Grandfather Isaac: El Shaddai, God Almighty; El Elyon, God Most High; El Roi, the God who sees; Jehovah Jireh, the God who provides. Time had no meaning. Sound became a distant echo. She was aware only of an unfamiliar warmth and peace.

"Dinah."

Her breath caught, and she was afraid to open her eyes. Had Yahweh spoken her name?

"Dinah," the voice said, this time louder, more urgent. Her heart was racing. She gathered her courage and slowly opened one eye. A man stood before her, barely recognizable, his head and face shaven, streaked with blood and ashes. Was she disappointed or relieved?

"Dinah, come," Job said. "I'll take you and Nogahla to a room where you can get some rest." Nogahla was curled up beside her, sound asleep, and the other men were gone. Dinah realized it must be quite late. All but one of the torches was completely burned out.

"Nogahla and I can sleep here in the courtyard," she said, amazed and humbled that Job would consider their comfort in the midst of his grief.

"Please, Dinah, follow me."

She woke Nogahla from exhausted slumber, and Job lifted the torch from its mounting and began the long winding walk through the dimly lit stone palace. Gathering golden lamps from wall niches, Job handed one to Dinah and another to Nogahla, blowing out the remaining lamps as he walked past. Their silent march wound through lovely mint-scented corridors and reception halls, servants' stark dwellings, and musky work spaces.

Climbing a maze of stairs, they finally reached their destination on the third floor. Job drew back beautiful azure drapes fluttering in the breeze. Dinah's dim flame revealed a lovely anteroom furnished with an elegantly cushioned couch, tapestries, and rugs.

Job led them directly to a finely carved door but stopped before entering. "Please forgive me," he said, his expression lifeless. "I'll let you and Nogahla find your way from here." Job bowed and was gone.

"Is he mad at us?" Nogahla's voice was gravelly from sleep, and she rubbed her face.

"No, my friend," Dinah said. "Though Master Job is a strong and faithful man, he's still human. He's tired, and he needs time to reflect on all he's lost today." She reached for the bronze handle and opened the heavy oaken door.

"Oh, mistress!" Nogahla was suddenly wide-awake in view of the splendor that awaited them. An ornate, canopied bed stood in the center of the room, and an attached balcony revealed a cluster of moonlit clouds just beyond a curtained door frame.

Nogahla ran to the balcony and gazed over the railing. "It's a long way down!" Her voice echoed into the dark, still night.

Dinah chuckled despite her weariness. "Shh, Nogahla. I'm sure at least part of the town is trying to sleep." Dinah joined her on the balcony for a few moments, taking in the majestic sandstone cliffs of Uz, wishing she and Nogahla could stay. "Come, we must try to sleep. We have no idea what tomorrow brings."

With heavy hearts, the two walked back into the chamber and shed their outer robes. Nogahla shuffled toward the door. "I'll be in the anteroom on the couch if you need me, mistress."

"You will not." Dinah smiled at the girl. Nogahla glanced back, arched eyebrows coupled with a hopeful grin. "Come on." Dinah climbed onto the mattress, sinking down in its wool-stuffed softness. "I'm not sleeping in this big bed all by myself."

8

~Job 1:22~

In all this, Job did not sin by charging God with wrongdoing.

Job walked through the dimly lit hallway, considering each doorway he passed. The third floor had been reserved for the women in his home. Once a lively haven for his wife, his daughters, and their guests, the red-hewn walls now mocked his solitude. On the way to his fourth-floor bedchamber, Job paused at the door marked by fourteen sheer linen curtains. Sitis loved fine linen, and he loved Sitis.

Each time Job traveled or his merchant cousin Zophar visited Uz, Job bought more linen for his wife. He remembered the first linen scarf he'd presented her at their wedding, its color reflected in her glistening ebony eyes. His grieving bride had learned to love him with each new scarf, and each day her heart grew more tender toward him. She had learned to let go of whatever—or whoever—bound her to the Ishmaelite village of her youth, and soon the scarves became the emblem of their love.

As he rubbed the gauzy fabric between his fingers, Job thrilled at the memory of the night she gave her heart and body willingly. The years that followed had been the happiest of Job's life. His chest tightened, ached, remembering the day he'd destroyed the Chaldean temple. Something between them had died that day, something linen scarves couldn't revive.

Pulling aside the drapes, he reached for the silver handles on the first set of double doors leading to Sitis's antechamber. He paused. Perhaps he should wait until morning. *No. I've waited long enough*, he thought. He pushed open the doors, and Nada rose from an elaborate couch, eyes bleary from sleep. She must have decided to stay in Sitis's guest foyer for the night.

"Master Job," she said, "what are you doing here?"

"Go back to sleep, Nada. I've come to talk to my wife."

The old woman was on her feet, hands on hips, a formidable barrier to the second set of doors to Sitis's bedchamber. "The mistress is asleep, my lord. Come back in the morning."

Job normally dismissed Nada's protective nature as endearing; however, tonight his tolerance was spent. "You will move aside, old woman, or find yourself in the stable with the camels." Shock showed only briefly before obedience overtook her. The woman stepped aside, issuing a loathing glance as Job passed.

Walking into his wife's chamber was like swimming in a sea of fine linen. Long ribbons of sheer cloth hung like willows, catching the slightest breeze, diffusing light. A silent testimony of the love they once shared.

Job could see her empty bed. She was on the balcony, her

sanctuary. He paused for a moment by the bed in the exact spot where they'd parted with such bitter words before he left for Hebron. They'd quarreled about Sayyid. She'd broken her promise and allowed him into their home again. To his knowledge, it was the first time in nine years. On that day, he'd left his responsibilities at the city gate early and found Sayyid and Sitis in the scroll room. Sayyid's arms were coiled around her, and Sitis was struggling to escape his embrace. *But would she have remained in his arms had I not intruded?* The lingering doubt ate at his heart like maggots feasting on carrion.

Sitis's quick gasp interrupted his thoughts. "Oh, Job. Your face." She stood in the doorway of her balcony, the soft glow of moonlight revealing the lovely curves beneath her linen gown. She covered her mouth to stifle more cries.

Moving closer, Job saw in the dim lamplight that her grieving had been ceaseless, her eyes swollen, cheeks mottled pink. He moved to embrace her, but she stepped back, signaling the hesitation they both felt. He wondered again about the wisdom of seeing her tonight. Should he turn and go?

Their long years of marriage permitted the silence. Searching the windows of their souls, neither one flinched at the other's probing gaze. *It's why I love you so*, Job thought, *your strength, your fire, your will. But it also infuriates me.* He felt his anger rise at the memory of her outburst—and then he smiled slightly at the resurgence of ever-present love. He would stay.

She tilted her head with a frustrated, puzzled expression. "What can you possibly smile about tonight?" she asked, her words clipped, her voice tight.

"You." He stepped forward again and traced her jawline

with one finger. She didn't pull away this time. It was a start. But what now? She tried to appear strong, but instead she looked vulnerable and frightened. He wanted to hold her, but her defenses built an impenetrable wall. He wanted to resolve their anger, but as long as she defended Sayyid and condemned El Shaddai, they remained at an impasse. *El Shaddai, show me how to begin.*

Perhaps tonight, if he was cautious, Sitis would welcome her husband's comforting embrace. Job took a step closer, and his wife did not retreat. He held her gaze before trying to hold her hand. Offering a weak smile, he rubbed his bald head and said, "I suppose I don't look like myself with no hair and all this dirt on my face?" He tried to use his sleeve to wipe the ashen streaks away but suddenly felt her hands and a linen scarf on his skin.

Mopping the ashes from his face, Sitis said, "No, you don't look like my husband at all right now." She took his hand and led him to her bed, gently pressing his shoulders down so that he sat on the edge. She moistened her scarf in the copper water basin on the bedside table and reached up to wipe his forehead.

But he grasped her arm, halting her ministrations. "Close your eyes," he whispered. Never one to submit blindly, she hesitated—but obeyed after playfully lifting an eyebrow.

"Is this your husband's voice?" he asked softly.

"Yes," she said, relaxing as Job placed her arm at her side.

"Keep your eyes closed," he said. Then he stood, pressing his body against hers, steadying her. He could see tears starting to form beneath her thick, dark lashes. Job leaned down to kiss her gently. "Was that your husband's kiss?"

A tenuous smile formed where his lips had been. "Yes."

"And precious wife of my youth," he said, sliding his hands around her waist, "is this your husband's embrace?"

"Oh, Job." Her defenses crumbled, and Sitis abandoned herself into his arms.

He held her tightly and buried his face in that tender spot of her neck that knew his kisses well. *Thank You, El Shaddai,* Job cried inwardly, *for this respite from cold indifference and heated anger.* Tonight's loss of wealth had been difficult. The loss of his children, beyond what he thought he could bear. But when his precious wife cursed El Shaddai, he feared the loss of himself—for he believed God's teaching that he and Sitis were one flesh. He breathed in her scent, brushed her soft curves, heard her quiet weeping, and was suddenly overcome by gratitude for this most precious gift from Yahweh.

Job began to sway rhythmically from side to side, and his wife's tension fled. When she lifted her head, tears flowed into the small channels of fine creases made by years of smiles. "Job, I love you." She had said the words a thousand times before, but tonight a new urgency swelled their meaning. Her eyes were pleading, digging deeply into his soul.

"Sitis," he whispered, "I love you too." She seemed desperate to hear him say it. Why? He studied her gaze. Perhaps the words were purer tonight, truer after so much of their lives had been stripped away. But as he examined her angled brow, full lips, and almond-shaped eyes, he saw fear in his beloved's expression. "What is it, Sitis? What makes you question my love?"

She buried her head again and held him so tightly, he could barely breathe. Her weeping became as tormented as it had been during the calamities. "Job, hold me. You're all I have. Without the children, I am nothing." She was panting, struggling for breath. "Our home is empty. Our stables are empty. My womb is empty." Her panic grew. He bent to lift her into his arms, and she curled around him like a child.

When her crying eased, she lifted her face, the longing evident. "We are the only two on earth who know this pain, who understand this grief. Please, Job, please love me. Fill my womb again."

Job kissed her, overwhelmed by the need in her eyes. Oh, how he longed to love her thoroughly, to enjoy the well-ripened fruit of their lifelong union. His three-week journey had left him parched for his wife's body, and somehow the raw grief sweetened the passion. But with every fiber of strength, he pulled away.

"Sitis, we must mourn seven days for our children and servants," he said breathlessly. "The teachings of Shem say El Shaddai forbids marital relations during that time, my love."

She pushed against his chest so violently, he nearly dropped her. "Your God forbids! Your God destroys! Your God hates! And I hate your God!" She ran to the balcony and clutched the railing, her shoulders heaving with sobs.

Job doubled over, stumbling to his knees as if he'd taken a physical blow. "Ahhhh!" He screamed long and loud, feeling as if he might retch. Covering his face in frustration and shame, he lifted his head toward heaven. *El Shaddai, how can I live with a woman who hates You?* Job waited for the thunder of God's voice, for lightning to strike her down, for some kind of punishment or condemnation for Sitis's blasphemy. Instead, he heard only the desperate weeping of the woman he'd loved for forty years. Still on his knees, he watched Sitis, alone on her balcony. And the broken pieces of his heart shattered smaller still.

Even before today's tragedies, she had perceived El Shaddai as unjust. Did his refusal of tonight's intimacy inflict yet another wound—bludgeoning her with the commands of God while he tried to live as a man of God? *El Shaddai, how do I love her and still obey You?* Confused and disheartened, Job gathered the woolen blanket from Sitis's bed. Scattering pillows across the floor, he began a slow walk toward the balcony.

Sitis turned when she heard his approach. Trembling, she cupped her hands over her mouth and stumbled backward. "You hate me, don't you? You're going to put me away—judge and disgrace me at the city gate." Her fear grew as Job moved toward her. He was afraid she would fall over the railing.

"No, my love. I would never—" He made a desperate grab for her and drew her securely to his chest.

Her arms curled between them, resisting his love, but at the same time she leaned into him, seeming desperate for his assurance.

He wrapped his arms around her, kissed the top of her head, and stroked her raven-black hair. "Do you know so little of my love?" he whispered. "Shh. Have you heard nothing I've said in our long marriage, my precious Ishmaelite princess? I adore you. I will never reject you." All the while, his heart cried out to El Shaddai, fearing for his wife's soul and her sanity. *El Shaddai, how do I convince her of both Your love and mine?*

Sitis slowly relaxed, allowing her arms to fall limp at her sides. Job maintained his reassuring embrace as he retrieved the blanket from the tiled floor. The couple stood, cocooned together against the night chill, until Sitis's despair found its voice. "Why does El Shaddai make such meaningless demands?" she asked. "Why does He take away everything I love?" Her voice was void of emotion, empty now.

Job squeezed his eyes shut. Her pain was unbearable. He tightened his arms around her and rested his cheek on top of her head. "When I discovered Sayyid was taking your secret offerings to the priests at Chaldea, I destroyed that temple in an impetuous rage, Sitis. I acted in the name of El Elyon's judgment, but I also acted out of my own anger."

Sitis kept silent, as had become her custom during the nine years since the incident.

Job continued, not knowing if she comprehended his words. "Tonight, even though I knew God's good plan for mourning, I drew you to passion because of my own selfish desires." He lifted his face to heaven and drew in a ragged breath. "Now, my precious wife, because I have allowed my human failings to stain God's ways, you perceive El Shaddai as unjust and uncaring."

"No," she said as though observing from a distance. "I perceive El Shaddai as unjust and uncaring because He killed my children."

This time it was Job who remained silent. His face twisted in uncontrolled sorrow, sobs escaping even as his wife stood lifeless in his arms. Their love, their marriage, had been so rich in every way—except the most important. *El Shaddai, please open her heart. I don't know what else to say.* Finally, Job gently grasped her shoulders and leaned down to meet her gaze. For the first time, she looked away.

"Please, Sitis." He cupped her face in his hands, and she turned to him, her stare as black and cold as polished obsidian. "I don't know why our children are gone, our wealth destroyed, but I know El Shaddai's commands are not meaningless. His ways are the ways of an all-knowing, righteous God. Just because we do not understand them does not mean they do not have merit. Just because we do not understand *Him* does not mean we cannot worship Him."

Seemingly without her permission, her hard exterior cracked. Her eyes of black ice thawed, and tears trickled down. "I love you so much, Job," she said, swiping at her tears. "But I don't want your God." Her head began shaking. "What will I do without my children—my daughters? They were my life."

She collapsed into his arms, and Job carried her to the balcony couch, rocking her like a child. "Our babies are gone, my love," he said through his own tears, "but we can still love each other well." Job wiped a salty drop from Sitis's cheek and listened to the stillness of Uz.

Oop-oop-oop. A pink-and-black-crested hoopoe fluttered to rest on the balcony railing, and Job's heart warmed. *Oop-oop-oop.* Sitis jumped when the little bird took flight less than three cubits from where they sat. The hoopoe hovered near a hole in the cliff face just outside Sitis's bedchamber.

"Oh! That bird will make a mess of my balcony," she said, momentarily distracted from her misery.

Job leaned back on the cushioned couch and pulled her closer. "I believe that little bird was sent by Yahweh at this precise moment to encourage us, my love." Sitis shook her head in disbelief and her tears returned, but Job continued. "I have studied these beautiful little birds in my travels, and they fascinate me. The male and female are true to one another for life." He lifted her chin and gazed into her deep wells of sadness. "And the mother hoopoe cares well for her young."

Job leaned down to place a gentle kiss on her lips, but they were interrupted by the trilling sound. *Oop-oop-oop.* When he lifted his head, Sitis's expression was almost peaceful.

She spoke in a reverent whisper. "Do you remember how Ennon put mud on Letush's cheek so he could tell the difference between his new twin brothers?" She chuckled quietly and looked up, her eyes glistening and swollen, her cheeks rounded in a soft smile.

Job marveled at the beauty their life had etched into her features. The resplendent royalty of his Ishmaelite bride, the weary glow after each birth, the doting grin of a proud ima watching ten children grow into esteemed adults. "You've never been more beautiful than you are at this moment," he said, stroking her tawny cheek.

Another gentle kiss prodded Sitis to recite a fond memory of Uzahmah. An evening of terror transformed like healing balm into a night of remembrance. Tears mingled as husband and wife lovingly mourned one night's torturous events by speaking of life's joyous memories.

While his wife recounted another story, Job glanced at the hoopoe and offered a silent prayer. *Thank You, El Shaddai, for uniting us in memories and for teaching me to love without knowing all the answers.*

The night grew long, and the couple returned to Sitis's chamber. Job slept atop the woolen blanket, Sitis beneath her linen sheets, her head pillowed in the bend of his arm.

✾ ✾ ✾ ✾ ✾

Dinah woke with a start. The red hues of a pre-dawn glow stained the sandstone walls of her chamber, and she instinctively checked her hands for her husband's blood. At almost every waking, she still relived Shechem's horror. *El*

Shaddai, will I ever forget that moment in time? Nogahla's deep, steady breathing stole Dinah's attention. She wondered if last night's bloody herdsman and the burned shepherd would live as vividly in the little Cushite's memory. Oh, how she grieved this young girl's tainted tomorrows, stained by yesterday's ghastly scenes and sounds.

Voices in the hallway interrupted her brooding. Nogahla stirred, and Dinah slipped out of bed, wrapping her robe around her shoulders. Her toes tingled on the cold tiles as she crept toward the door. "What's happening?" Nogahla whispered. Dinah motioned for the girl's silence as she opened the door slightly, listening. The hall was too dimly lit to see faces, but she distinguished two male figures.

"I'll meet you at the sacred altar before the sun rises." Job's voice. "Have Shobal and Lotan bring a torch and stack the wood."

Another male voice. "We found only one goat last night in the courtyard behind the kitchen. Shouldn't we save it for milk?"

There was a slight pause, and then Job said, "Jehovah-Jireh, Elihu. Yahweh provides. He can give us milk from any goat, but we can give Him our single goat only once."

Dinah heard fading footsteps and closed her door. "Nogahla, hurry and get dressed. We should be ready for the first caravan leaving Uz when—" A quiet knock on their door curtailed her instruction, and the sleepy Cushite maid bolted upright and was on her feet, her robe thrown hastily around her shoulders.

"Yes, who is it?" Dinah called out and took one of the lamps from the wall niche.

"Dinah, I'm sorry if I woke you." Job's voice was low and urgent. "May I speak with you?"

As Dinah opened the door, she noted Job's swollen, grieving eyes and the nicks on his head and face from the flint knife. "You didn't wake us. May we help you with something?"

"I'm going to make a sacrifice to El Shaddai. Would you and Nogahla like to join us?"

Dinah was honored, stunned. Abba Jacob had never allowed women to observe his sacrificial offerings, and Grandfather Isaac had been too ill to offer sacrifices by the time Dinah arrived in his camp. "Why would you include us in your sacrifice?" The cry of Dinah's heart escaped, but she managed to restrain the words that would expose her true feelings, her deepest fear. She would never ask Job when he expected them to leave.

Job's features softened, lighted only by the dim rays of his flickering lamp flame. "Because you are a part of my family now. You and Nogahla are my responsibility before Yahweh."

Emotion strangled Dinah, and only one word escaped. "Wait." She slammed the door and leaned against it, pressing her fists to her eyes and holding in silent sobs. He couldn't have meant she and Nogahla could *remain* as part of his family. It was too much to hope for.

"Mistress, what's wrong?" Nogahla tried to hold her, comfort her. "Tell him you don't want to go to the sacrifice." The poor girl was grasping at consolation, but Dinah held up a silencing hand. Trying to explain would only make controlling her tears more difficult.

Breathe. Breathe. Silently coaching herself into calm, Dinah forced the mask back into place and offered a half explanation to Nogahla. "It's a great honor to be included in another time of worship with Master Job."

132

Nogahla's expression showed her utter confusion. "I thought he shaved everything last night."

Dinah laughed in spite of herself and brushed the girl's cheek. A stab of regret pierced her that she hadn't confided in Nogahla the significance of the burnt sacrifice during their journey from Hebron. How much did the girl know of El Shaddai? Had her Cushite maid ever witnessed a burnt offering in Grandfather Isaac's camp? With Job waiting in the hallway, there was no time for Nogahla's lesson.

The creak of the opening door alerted Job. "Please forgive us for making you wait," Dinah said. "We would be honored to join you in worship." She bowed slightly, and Nogahla followed her example.

"I'm pleased." Job bowed in return, the slight curve of a smile on his face.

"Can you wait just a moment while we get our sandals?" Nogahla was hurrying to gather them even as Dinah asked the question.

"All the preparations have been made, so dress quickly." He offered a kind smile and closed the door. The women cinched their robes and flung open the door, scooting their sandals onto their feet as they walked.

With eyebrows raised and an approving nod, Job chuckled. "My, my! That was quick indeed." Leading them down the dimly lit hallway, he explained, "Elihu, Shobal, and Lotan will join us at the altar."

"Will Sitis and Nada be coming too?" Nogahla asked. Dinah issued a chastising glance. The girl had not yet learned to apply a winnowing fork to her questions and comments, separating the timely from the intrusive.

Job stopped abruptly, and Dinah wondered if her maid's

words would reap his anger. Instead, the weariness that had marked his features last night returned, his tears glistening in the lamplight. "No. Sitis and Nada have refused to come." He paused as if he wanted to say more, but then turned and continued down the hallway. Nogahla mouthed a soundless *I'm sorry*, and Dinah hoped the girl would learn to be more sensitive.

Job led the two women up one flight of stone stairs and through a corridor of what appeared to be guest chambers. Like a grand monument, a beautifully carved cedar door at the end of the fourth-story hall marked the farthest boundary of this rock-hewn palace. As he opened the door, Job's lamp illumined only the first few steps upward. Far above them, Dinah could see a small orb of red light. As they climbed the countless stairs, the light beyond grew larger and changed hue, and Dinah realized the glow was the morning sky shining through an entryway at the top of a towering stairway. Her legs burned after hundreds of steps, and they finally emerged through a rectangular opening in the rock. Her breath caught. They stood atop the center mountain ridge of Uz.

"Look around you," Job said, stretching his arms wide, "and see the glory of God."

"Ohh." Dinah and Nogahla spoke in unison, both turning in circles, taking in the scope and breadth of Job's sandstone city with its emerald plains. Dinah saw the first sector's marketplace, still quiet before the day's trading began. Her eyes traveled to the narrow siq that split the great red cliffs through which their caravan had passed. In the second sector, dawn's light shone on the grand fountain and over the grasses of the great plain that stretched north and south between the mountain ranges. Little specks, most likely servants, scurried to begin the day's tasks around the opulent rock-hewn palaces and tent homes. And for the first time, Dinah saw the rubble of Ennon's once beautiful home, where Job's children lay entombed. Her stomach rolled.

"It was my custom to come here after my children had enjoyed a time of feasting," Job was saying, and when Dinah turned, she found him looking at her. "I would send servants to summon them, asking if they were willing to offer a sacrifice—much like I asked you and Nogahla this morning." Turning his attention to the men waiting by the altar, he added, "Just as I asked Elihu, Shobal, and Lotan to come this morning." Elihu knelt near the sacred altar, cradling the goat's neck under his arm.

"You can see why I brought my children here early in the morning," Job said, pointing to the pink and lavender hues cast over the sandstone altar where the men waited. The round pile of rocks, flattened on top, was surrounded by a trench and a carved bench in a perfect circle.

"Dinah, you and Nogahla kneel by Elihu and place your hands on the animal." Dinah noticed a silent exchange between Elihu and Job. The younger man seemed to challenge his teacher but finally acquiesced. Job ignored the subtlety and knelt on the other side of the goat, mirroring Elihu's grasp on the animal. "Shobal and Lotan, please kneel beside me and place your hands on the sacrifice." The two herdsmen knelt directly across from Dinah but avoided her gaze. She had the sickening feeling that all the men knew her identity this morning. Last night she'd been an anonymous face united in grief. This morning she was the shamed Dinah of Shechem.

Job spoke softly now to the little group. "It was my practice to offer a separate lamb for each of my children—" His voice broke. "Ennon, Epher, Letush, Leum, Jokshan, Jetur, Zimran, Manathah, Alathah, and Uzahmah. But since we have only one animal, I believe El Shaddai will know our hearts and accept the one sacrifice for us all." Elihu placed a supportive hand on his shoulder. Job returned an appreciative nod. "Just as I feared my children might have cursed God in their hearts, I offer this sacrifice now if any of you cursed God in your hearts last night. It would be understandable, after hearing my wife's open curses against El Shaddai." He bowed his head as if pondering his next words, and when he looked up, tears streamed down his face. "I cannot make this sacrifice for my wife or her maid. They have refused its atoning power."

Elihu wept aloud. Shobal and Lotan exchanged pained expressions. Sitis's rebellion had shocked Dinah, but she had assumed it was the restatement of a longtime conviction. Judging from the sorrow on these men's faces, Sitis's and Nada's refusal to participate this morning was as surprising and devastating as the deaths and blasphemy had been last night.

Job used his free hand to wipe the tears from his face before continuing. "I praise El Shaddai that the rest of you have agreed to come for cleansing through the offering of blood." Turning his face toward heaven, Job cried out, "El Shaddai, please hear from heaven and forgive these in my household if we have secretly blamed You or cursed You in our hearts." Gazing intently at each of those present, Job said, "If any sin weighs on your heart, confess it now to El Elyon, silently."

Job lifted the goat's chin and drew his flint knife across its neck. Nogahla gasped, and Dinah looked into her maidservant's eyes just in time to see horror bubble up. "No, Master Job!" the girl cried, burying her head in Dinah's chest.

The men looked up in surprise, but Job spoke with compassion. "Nogahla, my little friend, this is the way El Shaddai allows His people, who deserve death, to be forgiven for sin." Job's hands deftly pressed the animal's neck over the stone-carved drainage trough.

Nogahla lifted her head, her face stricken. "The goat had to die because I hated your mean old steward, Atif?"

Shobal hid a grin behind his big, callused hand, while the others worked hard to maintain reverence in the face of such unabashed innocence.

"The goat had to die," Job said with tenderness, "because each one of us has sinned in some way and needs to be forgiven."

Dinah listened in rapt wonder while the greatest man in the East, the priest of his household, explained El Shaddai's plan of redemption to a young Cushite slave. Dinah regretted that she'd neglected to share her own forgiveness experience at Elath, the joy she'd felt and her fleeting moments without shame.

Why were they fleeting? she asked herself, still listening to Job's confident words of restoration. Glancing at Elihu, Shobal, and Lotan, she wondered, *Why do I reclaim the shame of Shechem each time a man averts his gaze or looks at me scornfully?*

Job lightly touched her hand, and instinctively she jerked away, startling everyone. Her cheeks aflame, she lowered her chin. "I'm sorry," she whispered.

Again, she heard only compassion in the gentle voice carried on the morning breeze. "It's all right," Job said. "I think we're all a little anxious this morning."

She looked up then and noted the shepherd and herdsman walking away and Elihu's hands skillfully completing the tasks of the offering. Job had taught him well. Her gaze wandered to Job himself, who was watching her intently.

"I would like you and Nogahla to remain as members of my household," he said. She started to protest, but he held up his hand. "I know all the reasons Jacob's daughter will say she must leave." He paused, seemingly searching for words. "You have a purpose in my household, Dinah. Will you try to discover what it might be?"

Elihu's hands momentarily stopped mid-motion, and his quick, sharp glance stabbed her like a bronze-tipped arrow. Job noticed it too and expelled a disapproving sigh, but returned his gaze to her, awaiting her answer. She could continue to run, keep hiding in tents beneath a mantle of shame, or she could step into the dawn of a new life in Uz.

Dinah looked down at Nogahla. "Shall we make a life here in Master Job's household, my friend?"

The smile began in the Cushite's eyes before creasing her lips. "Yes, and I'll try not to kill any more goats with my sinful thoughts."

9

~*Genesis 12:1–3*~

The LORD *had said to Abram, ". . . I will make
your name great . . . and all peoples on earth
will be blessed through you."*

Job smelled the crisp morning breeze and felt the sun's rays
on his back, watching the flames lick up the fat portions of
the offering. The grisly task of returning his servants' bodies to their families lay before him. In honor of their loyal
service, he would retrieve their bodies before unearthing his
own children from the rubble of Ennon's home tomorrow.
Breathing deeply, Job absorbed the aroma of obedience from
Yahweh's altar as dawn gave way to morning. Though his
world had been shattered, he knew God remained steadfast.
Peace guarded Job's heart.

Elihu, however, was the antithesis of Job's peace. The
young man sat sullen, jaw flexing, hands restlessly kneading together. Elihu's agitation had begun early this morning

when he, Shobal, and Lotan inquired about the woman who had tended Lotan's wounds last night. Job noted their silent recognition of Dinah's name and how they spurned her during the sacrifice. The tension lingered after Dinah and Nogahla said their good-byes and returned to their chamber. A conversation needed to happen. What better time than amid the fragrance of God's forgiveness?

"You're going to wear away your skin if you keep rubbing your hands like that," Job said, trying to coax a grin.

Elihu looked down, taking Job's jest to heart, and then turned a scowl on his elder. "Abba Job, haven't you taught me that the Most High hates sin?"

Ah, so we're going to have a spiritual lesson to work through your anger, Job mused. "Yes, El Shaddai hates sin."

"Then why did you bring a sinful woman into your household?"

"She was to become Ennon's wife." Job offered the words with immeasurable calm but saw a fire ignite in Elihu's eyes. "It's a long story, my son, but I suspect you're not interested in the details." He watched Elihu struggle for control.

"You're mistaken, Abba. I desperately want to understand the reasons you would subject your son to such humiliation and then invite this woman to remain in your household when she no longer has a purpose." His voice became a schoolboy whine. "She is an adulteress, Abba!"

"Dinah is not an adulteress." Job worked to maintain his level tone.

"But she is a temptress."

Job eyed his student and would-be son. Had Dinah acted inappropriately somehow? Job had known her only a few days, but he'd immediately felt she was a woman of impeccable honesty and character. "Why do you say she is a temptress, Elihu?"

The young man fell silent, staring at his hands again, his jaw beginning its sulking dance.

"Oh no you don't," Job said, anger rising. "You started rolling this ball down the hill. Now you'll unravel the twine completely."

When Elihu lifted his yellow-brown eyes, Job expected the same flashing fervor with which he always argued for the Most High, but the fire was gone. The windows of his soul were empty, hollow. "Abba, I loved Uzahmah with my whole heart." Tears pooled, and the boy looked at the sky to keep drops from spilling over. He inhaled deeply and puffed his cheeks, exhaling emotion without words.

Job's heart ached at whatever battle raged in Elihu's heart, but a man's sorrow needn't disfigure the truth. "I know you loved my daughter, Elihu, but why does that make Dinah sinful?"

The vacant eyes blazed. "Dinah's sin has nothing to do with my love for Uzahmah!"

Job placed a calming hand on Elihu's shoulder. "Then why speak of the two as though they were related?"

"Ahh!" Elihu stood to pace. "I've heard about this *Dinah* from shepherds' gossip and traders' tales." His arms gestured widely, his long legs giving him the appearance of an ostrich attempting flight. "I've heard she wore rings on her fingers and toes. That she painted her eyes like the Egyptians and went into Shechem to ensnare the prince." He slapped both arms at his sides. "Abba, I never expected her to be wise. And compassionate. And *naturally* beautiful." Elihu grabbed at his head where the thinning brown hair used to be, seemingly tortured by his admission. "Oh, I can't believe I said such a thing about another woman, when my beloved Uzahmah lies under a pile of rubble . . ." He sat down hard on the carved stone bench, grieving quietly, his face buried in his hands.

"Elihu, you haven't betrayed Uzahmah by speaking the truth about a woman who was maligned and hated nearly all her life. In fact, I believe my spirited youngest daughter would've been proud of you for being sensitive enough to truly *see* Dinah."

Elihu lifted his head, lashes matted with tears. "I won't be looking in Dinah's direction again, Abba." He stared at the roasting sacrifice, no doubt pondering more deeply than his words revealed. "But she acted nobly last night, with courage and wisdom, when I was driven purely by emotion." He pressed the heel of his hand against his forehead. "Will I ever learn to respond to circumstances as you do? Will I ever turn to El Shaddai first? Or will my emotions always rule me?"

Job clamped a firm hand on Elihu's shoulder. "Tell me who you are, my son." It was a command Job often used, teacher to student, abba to son, reminding the boy of his worth and his purpose.

A submissive smile stretched across Elihu's face. "I am Elihu, son of Barakel. Of the tribe of Buz, second son of Nahor, Abraham's brother. I am of the faithful tribe who sent generations of representatives to the House of Shem until my father became ill unto death. He was the last Buzite disciple of Eber, Noah's great-great-grandson, and I am the first Buzite disciple of the great Edomite teacher, Job." Elihu's voice broke, and he looked up. In that cleanly shaven, ash-covered face, Job saw the boy of twelve he'd accepted from his friend Barakel. "Abba, may I remain in your household too?"

Job grabbed the young man's shoulders and pulled him into a ferocious embrace. "I would hobble any animal that tried to carry you away from Uz," he said through sobs. Laying his heart bare before the Lord, he held Elihu and silently prayed, *My household is broken before You, O God. Pour into it whom You will. Take out of it whom You wish.*

Quieting his mind and spirit, Job allowed his own grief to wash through him, when suddenly he remembered Abraham's covenant promise.

All peoples on earth will be blessed.

He was so startled by the thought, he jerked away from Elihu, scaring the poor boy.

"Abba, what's wrong?"

But Job was speechless. Had God just whispered to his spirit? Or was this Job's own idea? God's covenant promised blessing to *all people* through Abraham, not just to Abraham's seed. Could the fulfilling of the covenant begin with Elihu, a Buzite from Nahor's clan, marrying Jacob's daughter?

"You're frightening me, Abba." Elihu's features were now riddled with concern. "What's the matter? Why are you looking at me that way?"

Job breathed deeply, spoke evenly, trying a subtle approach with his surrogate son. "Perhaps the Most High has called you and Dinah to my household for a greater purpose than we realized."

❖❖❖❖❖

"Nada, you must go to Sayyid now, this morning." Sitis spoke in hushed tones as they began their kitchen inventory. "Tell him I have something important to discuss, and he must come later this morning while Job is checking the fields with

Elihu." She pushed two large baskets of freshly harvested barley into the corner, fighting more tears.

Nada peeked inside a few glazed clay crocks, wincing at the fermenting contents. "What was Cook thinking? Who could ever eat this many pickled olives?" Nada crinkled her nose and glanced at Sitis.

"They were Leum's favorite." Sitis felt her face twist in sorrow.

"Why do you fight your tears, mistress? Let them flow." Nada reached out, but Sitis held up her hand in warning.

"Don't come near me. I can't keep from crying if you hug me." She picked up a polished bronze serving tray and peered at her reflection. "I'm all puffy, and I must look my best for Job." But the tears won the battle and crept down Sitis's cheeks. "Oh, Nada. I'm getting old, losing the woman's red moon. What if I can never bear more children for Job? I saw the way he looked at Dinah. What if he takes her for his wife now that our Ennon is gone?" A sob escaped. She wavered between confiding fully in her maid and keeping the intimate details to herself. But in whom else could she confide? "Job would not lie with me last night, Nada. I must get pregnant quickly if I am to bear more children." She melted into the soft, warm arms that had been her haven since her earliest memory.

"Your husband adores you, my little Sitis." Nada smoothed her hair and kissed her head. "He is mourning as his God commands, but he will never take another wife. He promised it on your wedding day."

"I know what he promised, Nada, but that was long ago, and now our children are gone. A man is nothing if he leaves no children on this earth." She struggled out of her maid's arms and held up the mirror again, trying desperately to repair the damage done by new tears. "Now a young and beautiful seductress sleeps a few chambers away from my husband. She can bear him children, and he cares for her." She slammed the bronze tray against her leg and stomped her foot. "I will not be Job's first wife but second best!"

The maid removed the tray from her mistress's hands and piled it with a few other items they had separated out for trade. "My little Sitis, you must calm down. If my master thought she was good enough for Ennon, he will simply find another honorable man in Uz to marry her."

"Who would marry a woman with Dinah's reputation? Every man east of Egypt is afraid of waking with his throat cut—or should I say not waking!" Sitis's voice was shrill and frantic.

"Shh, hush now!" Nada whispered. "Master Job and Elihu could come down any moment from the sacred altar, and that woman is in her chamber. Your husband must never know your true feelings about her because he obviously has feelings for the girl."

Nada's observation renewed Sitis's tears, and the lady fell into her nursemaid's cushioned embrace.

Patting Sitis gently, Nada cooed, "All right, all right. What can I do to help my Sitis?"

"Please, Nada. Just go to Sayyid and tell him I must speak with him today."

Nada's hands stopped their slow and steady comfort on Sitis's back, and she grasped Sitis's shoulders, wrinkle lines of suspicion on her brown forehead. "What plans are spinning in your head, my girl? How can Sayyid possibly help?"

"He will marry Dinah." Sitis spoke so matter-of-factly,

she left no room for debate or explanation. "Now go!" At Nada's slight hesitation, Sitis stomped her foot once more and pointed at the doorway, reminding her protective nursemaid who commanded whom.

⁂⁂⁂⁂⁂

Dinah and Nogahla peeked through the red tapestry kitchen door, watching the mistress and her failed attempts at grinding barley. Dinah hid a grin as kernels skittered over the sides of the trough. "Sitis looks as skilled grinding grain as a shepherd herding cats."

Nogahla's giggle drew the mistress's attention, forcing them to come out of hiding.

"Good morning." Sitis greeted them stiffly, returning quickly to her task.

Dinah and Nogahla entered the airy kitchen. Sitis stood at the farthest of three large stone tables, near a tall archway that led to the kitchen courtyard. "Good morning, mistress," Dinah replied, nodding her head in a respectful bow. "Nogahla and I have come to serve in whatever way might be most beneficial."

Herbs and drying flowers hung from the ceiling in bundles, filling the air with the scent of coriander, garlic, and cloves. Grain baskets of every size lined one wall, with shelves above them bearing kitchen utensils and dishes of varying shapes and sizes. Copper pots hung on another wall.

Sitis lifted her gaze, her eyes welcoming though not warm. Dinah had hoped to ask about retrieving her midwife supplies from the Hebron caravan, thinking perhaps Job could refer her services to a few wealthier women in Uz. At least then she would feel of some value to his family for the protection

146

he'd provided. However, the mistress had returned full concentration to her grinding. She poured another mounding cup of barley into the circular furrow and shoved the heavy stone wheel over the kernels.

"Ahh!" A frustrated Sitis slammed the table with her fist, sending barley—ground and unground—into the air.

Dinah cast a cautionary glance at Nogahla and stepped farther into the kitchen. "May we be of help?" Dinah offered, bowing slightly.

"I was just grinding a little grain before making dough to bake in the public ovens." Sitis smoothed her robe and calmly gathered the scattered kernels into the grinding trough. It was a poor attempt at appearing casual. "Job's cousin Zophar has ovens in his own kitchen, but I'm afraid the merchants in Uz have not progressed to such conveniences." Dinah noticed a slight quiver in the woman's voice. "Does your maid know how to cook and run a household?"

Dinah placed her arm around Nogahla's shoulder to bolster her confidence.

"I know some about cooking," the Cushite said quietly, "but I cannot manage a household."

"We're here to help, mistress." Dinah winked at her maid, offering her approval. "I'm sure you and Nada can give us direction."

Nogahla turned and mumbled, "I'm sure bossy Nada will tell everyone what to do."

Dinah's breath caught. Feeling the blood rush from her face, she measured Sitis's response. The woman glanced between her two guests and then released a good-natured chuckle, snapping the thread of tension. "Yes, Nada will no doubt give us all her opinion, little Cushite, but I fear she knows little more about this kitchen than I do." Wiping a bead of sweat and a tear with the back of her hand, she exhaled and let her shoulders sag. "Do either of you know how to work this awful mill?"

Nogahla's big, questioning eyes sought Dinah's permission, and a quick nod sent the girl to retrieve a basket of grain from the corner. Relief washed over Sitis's features, and all three women pulled stools near the central basket. Nogahla and Dinah each lifted a hand mill from the shelf, and Sitis carried hers from the table. Nogahla adeptly leveled her mill on the stool and knelt beside it, while Dinah and Sitis sat on the stool balancing the mills in their laps, gawking as if the contraptions were two-headed camels.

Nogahla stifled a giggle and shoveled a small cupful of grain into the trough. As she pushed the heavy wheel steadily around the groove, the tender kernels slowly and evenly yielded to the crushing.

Dinah smiled and silently followed Nogahla's example, kneeling and leveling the mill on her stool. She caught Sitis's eye, and the mistress seemed equally moved by the Cushite's gentle instruction. Soon all three women worked together, lulled by the sounds of grinding wheels and the swoosh of finely ground flour emptied into the jug. The peaceful rhythm surrounded them, lifted them, soothed them.

"Sitis, I spoke with—" Nada burst through the tapestry, her face turning gray when she spotted Dinah.

"Nada!" Sitis leapt from her knees, spilling half the barley from her mill. "I'm so glad you're back from the market!" Her voice was shrill and unnatural.

Dinah had no idea what errands had occupied Nada's morning, but these women were poor liars. Dinah had grown up in a camp of four imas—a blood mother, her ima's sister, and two jealous handmaids—where a complex web of deceit was daily bread. She had no intention of becoming ensnared by treachery in Job's house and therefore had no desire to know where the nursemaid had been.

Nada grasped Sitis's hands and inspected her palms. "Mistress! You have blisters! What are you doing?" Her eyes narrowed accusingly at Dinah. "How dare you ask the lady of this house to help you grind grain!"

Dinah opened her mouth to explain, but Sitis intervened. "Nada, we must all work since our servants are gone."

Nada set balled fists on her hips. "But mistress, you shouldn't—" Her protest was once again cut short, this time by Dinah.

"Mistress Sitis, I have gum-yamin in my midwife supplies to soothe your blisters." She glanced from Nada to Sitis and hoped she sounded more confident than she felt. "I haven't had a chance to unload my things from the Hebron caravan in the stable. Would you like me to get them now?"

The kitchen fell awkwardly silent. Sitis tilted her head, assessing Dinah as if deciding whether to keep or discard an old blanket. "Yes, Dinah," she finally said, her voice controlled and calculating. "Now would be the perfect time for you to unpack your things from the caravan. I'll send Nada to your chamber when we need further help in the kitchen." She smiled, and gooseflesh rose on Dinah's arms. In the few moments since Nada's arrival, Sitis had changed into something sinister, like a snake emerging from its skin.

Grasping Nogahla's arm, Dinah nearly dragged the girl from the kitchen.

The Cushite's eyes reflected the dread Dinah had felt in

the pit of her stomach. "The mistress looked like she would eat you with the midday meal."

Dinah motioned Nogahla to be quiet, and they proceeded through a grand banquet hall filled with intricately carved wooden tables and benches. Dried flowers decorated each table, and the pungent aroma of frankincense filled the air.

"I don't know why Mistress Sitis wanted us out of that kitchen, Nogahla," Dinah said, hurrying toward the stables, "but I've never been so happy to unpack a camel."

❈❈❈❈❈

"Come in, Sayyid. My mistress is waiting for you." Nada met him at the canopied courtyard gate. Sayyid inspected the workmanship of the Hittite iron bars, a gift from Job's merchant cousin, Zophar. Eyeing Job's trinkets and calculating their value, he thought, *I must tell the bandits to enter through this gate. The bars are iron but have no locks.*

"Nada," he began casually, "how can you feel safe when one of the gates remains unlocked?"

The old woman waved away the question as they passed through the beggars' dining room and then into the grand banquet hall. "Master Job never locks any of the gates, so the servants—" She stopped as if suddenly reminded of the awful truth. "Our servants used to remain alert through the night to offer bread to beggars in need. All Master Job's doors remained open." Her sadness slowly turned to resolve. "Master Job is a good man, Sayyid, but you would be better for our Sitis." A curt nod, and she continued guiding Sayyid through Job's palace while he pondered the revelation of his new ally. The old woman could be of great help in his quest for Sitis's affection.

Nada led him into a private courtyard teeming with life.

A small fountain bubbled merrily and a vegetable garden boasted ripe melons and lentils. Surrounded by a high sandstone wall with olive trees and flowering shrubs lining the perimeter, a lone figure reclined in the center of the lush garden on a red-cushioned stone bench. Sayyid could see only the shapely silhouette of a woman's left side—her shoulder, waist, and hip, shaking as she wept. Nada cleared her throat loudly to unsettle the resting form.

Sayyid quietly approached the stone lounge. "Good afternoon, my Sitis-girl."

Hearing his voice, she sat up immediately but kept her back to him. "Sayyid, you shouldn't call me that. Someone might hear you." She wiped her face, and he watched the contours of her shoulder blades through her gray linen robe.

Closing the distance between them, he placed his hands on her shoulders. "There's no one here except Nada, and she knows that I love you—that I've always loved you."

Sitis leapt from the bench and away from his touch, staring toward a climbing vine on the wall. "Others are here who might tell Job. Please, Sayyid, you must be careful."

Who could be here? He'd seen Job and his men leave this morning. They'd trotted off on camels and donkeys toward Job's death fields. Then he remembered. *Ah, the tall beauty and the Cushite I saw in the dining room last night.*

"All right, Sitis. I'm sorry." He moved around the bench and sat down. "Come. Sit. Tell me why you've summoned me."

She turned, and his heart shattered. Her eyes, ringed by dark shadows, were nearly swollen shut from weeping.

"Oh, Sitis." His shock came out in a whisper. She raised her hands to calm him, and the bleeding blisters on her palms sent him into a rage. "By the gods, I'll kill Job!"

"They're only blisters, Sayyid." Sitis pressed her hands against his chest but winced and drew back. "I've been grinding grain. Please, just listen to me." She sat timidly beside him.

He cradled her hands gently, turning them, examining them, caressing them. He could think only of destroying Job. He would protect Sitis, provide for her, give her the life she deserved.

"Tell me everything." He paused and kissed her palm. She drew back and glanced nervously at the doorway. Sayyid blew gently on her neck, and she gaped at him, startled. Smiling at her renewed attention, he said, "I will do anything you ask of me, my Sitis, but you must listen carefully to what I have to say." He saw his reflection in her ebony eyes and wondered if she truly saw him. Would she see the wealthy, respected grain merchant of Uz, or would she still see the poor farmer's son from their childhood village?

"Would you finally take a wife if I asked it of you?" She whispered the question.

Sayyid chuckled, thinking at first she was teasing, but her expression remained an enigma, her emotions undecipherable. Was it regret? Was it hope? What could cause the determined set of her jaw but the hesitant furrow of her brow?

"I suppose it depends if that wife is you," he said finally. "I vowed never to marry any other woman, my Sitis-girl."

"I told you not to call me that!" she shouted. "Why do you torture me with our past, Sayyid? I have been Job's wife for forty years. That will never change."

Now Sayyid's anger flared. "Did I mention that Bela has convinced the city elders that Job is cursed by the gods?" He paused, letting his words hit their mark. "And were you aware that this morning, at Bela's suggestion, the elders rescinded Job's position as chief judge?"

All Sitis's bluster faded, and Sayyid easily read the new emotion on her features. Etched into the fine lines around her eyes, fear transformed her into workable clay.

A smile played at the corners of his lips. "I have been named Uz's newest city elder, filling Job's open position."

"They gave you Job's seat?" Sitis's voice held the slightest glimmer of hope. "Could you not refuse it if I asked you?"

Sayyid rested his elbow on the back of the bench and brushed her cheek with his hand.

"Please, Sayyid," she said, moving closer. "You said you would do anything for me."

Sayyid studied the woman he'd loved most of his life. He was forging new territory in their relationship, and a strange satisfaction settled in. Sitis had always been the one in control. She was the prince's daughter and he the lowly farmer's son. She had condescended to love him when they were children, deigned to befriend him when he arrived in Uz as a young grain trader.

He moved closer and placed his arm around her shoulders, whispering in her ear, "I said I would do anything for you, and I will, my Sitis-girl." Sayyid waited for a protest to his nearness. None came. "But what are you willing to do for me in return?"

She leaned into his nearness and gently cupped his cheek with her hand. "I am willing to be your loving friend and offer you a beautiful wife named Dinah."

Her intoxicating touch softened the sting of her denial. But why did she deny him, and who was this Dinah? With every fiber of restraint, he quelled his anger. Reaching up to cover her delicate hand, he locked it in place. "What if your husband never regains his wealth and power, Sitis-girl? Will you be satisfied to live as a beggar or become my *second* wife?"

153

Sitis jerked her hand away and glared daggers at him. She drew a breath to speak but hesitated, quaking as an evident inner storm gathered strength. When words finally came, she spoke eloquently, as expected from a prince's daughter, her back as straight as the measuring rod Sayyid used for his grain.

"My husband *will* regain his wealth and power, and it is to your benefit to curry his favor now, Sayyid. Heal old wounds, and show him kindness during our time of need." She leaned close, her sweet breath warm on his neck. "Someday men will bow to Job again as they would a king, and when that day comes, he can crush you or bless you." With a wicked grin, she kissed Sayyid's cheek. "Offering a dowry for Dinah will bring you into Job's good graces." Drawing a finger seductively from his cheek to his shoulder and down his left arm, she added, "And I assure you, my friend, I will never be anyone's second wife."

"Ahh!" The fire of her touch drove him mad. Sayyid grabbed her and kissed her firmly.

She struggled out of his embrace, slapping him. "Stop it!" She looked breathless, shaken.

He smiled and waited for more words. She was silent, breathing heavily now. Did he see pleasure on her face? "I will wait a little longer for you, my Sitis-girl, but I will not wait forever."

"Excuse me, Mistress Sitis and Master Sayyid." Nada appeared at the doorway with a beautiful blonde woman. "We didn't realize we were interrupting."

Sayyid saw the maid's disapproving glare the moment she glimpsed their kiss. Nada's squinty eyes and puckered frown still made him feel like a naughty child. But why should he wait for divorce to reap the harvest of Sitis's sweet lips?

"I've come to introduce Mistress Dinah to Master Sayyid," the old maid said, tugging the tall, elegant woman toward the stone bench.

The stunning blonde was as red as a pomegranate. Sayyid stood and bowed, inspecting the woman as she walked stiffly behind Nada. She must have seen or overheard some of his interchange with Sitis.

Sitis also rose from the bench and stepped toward the young woman, extending her hand. "Dinah, I'd like you to meet my friend Sayyid. The last time you saw Sayyid in this house, it was under similar misleading circumstances." The mistress coaxed the beauty to sit on the bench beside her, but Dinah looked as if she'd rather kiss a camel than meet Sayyid. "Please, Dinah," Sitis nearly begged. "Look at me."

The woman hesitated, as if not bound by the dictates of the lady of the house.

Hmm, Sayyid mused. *She does not obey like a servant.*

Dinah boldly met Sitis's gaze. Another clear indicator that this woman was not a handmaid. "I will meet your friend, mistress, but you have no obligation to explain your actions to me."

Sayyid raised an eyebrow, studying this suddenly interesting creature as the woman turned her azure eyes on him. *Dinah*, he thought, *where have I heard your name? You are exquisite.* Perhaps he would take her as a concubine when he claimed the rest of Job's possessions. He paused at the thought. Why was Sitis so anxious that he marry Dinah? Why would the marriage curry Job's favor? *Does this Dinah hold a special place in Job's heart, or is my Sitis-girl simply trying to get rid of her?* The flush of Dinah's face dimmed, but her cheeks still budded like roses.

"Dinah, Sayyid is a childhood friend," Sitis said. "He is like a brother to me."

A brother, Sayyid fumed inwardly, casting a chastising glance at Sitis. He returned his gaze to Dinah, noting her sneer. *You're reading my thoughts, Mistress Dinah.* She was perceptive, this one. He chuckled inadvertently as Sitis chattered on.

"Sayyid, this is Dinah. She is the daughter of Jacob, Great-Abba Esau's brother. Job brought her to Uz to marry—"

"Well, *Dinah*!" Sayyid heard nothing beyond "daughter of Jacob." He was too mesmerized by the presence of the infamous Dinah, the poor raped girl of Jacob's clan, the murderess of Shechem—whichever story one chose to believe. No wonder merchants had wagged their tongues for twenty years about her. She was extraordinary.

Sayyid bowed with exaggerated formality. "A pleasure to meet you," he said smoothly to his newest challenge.

"As I was saying, Sayyid . . ." Sitis enunciated as though interpreting for a slow student. "Job brought Dinah to Uz to marry our Ennon as the patriarch Isaac commanded."

This time Sayyid heard clearly, and the information sweetened Dinah's mystery. Sayyid casually returned his gaze to Sitis, but her fresh tears startled him. Suddenly his wolfish game lost its luster. "Sitis-gi—" Coughing, he tried to recover before finishing the familiar name. His heart broke as he watched a single tear slide down Sitis's face and sadness seize her lips. "Mistress Sitis," he said, working to portray a formality that might please her, "I can't imagine your pain at the loss of your children. I'm sorry." And he meant it with every fiber of his being.

Sayyid's breath caught when Sitis reached out and tenderly touched his cheek. "Thank you, my friend," she said. "I know you will do all you can to help us."

10

~*Job 2:1, 3–7*~

On another day . . . the LORD *said to Satan,*
"Have you considered my servant Job? . . .
He still maintains his integrity, though you
incited me against him to ruin him without
any reason." "Skin for skin!" Satan replied.
". . . Stretch out your hand and strike his flesh
and bones, and he will surely curse you to your
face." The LORD *said to Satan, "Very well, then,*
he is in your hands; but you must spare his life."
So Satan went out from the presence of the
LORD *and afflicted Job with painful sores from*
the soles of his feet to the top of his head.

Afternoon stretched into evening, and Dinah's patience wore thin. Surveying the kitchen, she wondered again what she and Nogahla might find to occupy their time. After Dinah's disturbing encounter with Sayyid, she'd fled to the kitchen and found Nogahla kneading mounds of bread dough. Remembering Sitis's mention of the public ovens, the two escaped the house with baskets of dough to explore Uz. When they returned with their warm brown bread, the house was as quiet as a tomb. They'd baked as much bread as was prudent and had ground all the wheat and barley. Without further direction, they were at the end of their usefulness.

"Mistress, why did those women at the ovens run away when they discovered we lived in Master Job's household?" Nogahla's eyes were distant, her thoughts obviously reliving the scene of their afternoon.

"Well, my friend, the Ishmaelites believe Master Job is cursed by their goddesses, and the Edomites believe he is cursed by Yahweh or their mountain god, Kaus. And they all believe that whichever god is punishing Job will attack anyone who associates with him or his household."

Nogahla seemed to absorb the words like a soft woolen cloth. She bent over one of the stone tables, her elbow balancing on a pomegranate, chin resting on her hand. Plucking a grape from a platter of fruit with her free hand, she placed it between her lips and sucked it into her mouth. Dinah chuckled at the entertaining way Nogahla chewed on the little fruit, much like she must have been chewing on the afternoon's events.

"Why do you think Widow Orma didn't run away? Doesn't she believe in the gods?"

Dinah too took a grape from the fruit tray and considered her answer. She and Nogahla had approached the serving women who encircled the cone-shaped clay ovens, each heated cylinder as high as a ram's head. Heat waves rose from the top and side openings, while idle gossip and busy hands bound the women in a common bond. When they discovered Dinah and Nogahla belonged to Job's household, however, the docile scene erupted.

Amid shrieking and confusion, Widow Orma remained rooted to her reed mat, a look of consternation on her face. "What foolishness!" she had said, and then motioned Nogahla and Dinah to move closer so she didn't have to shout her welcome. "Master Job has always made room for me at his widows' tables. I can at least help his guests learn to bake bread." She spent the remainder of the afternoon demonstrating the art of plastering bread circlets against the sides of the ovens and retrieving the golden brown loaves with a stick and clay platter.

Dinah sighed deeply at the memory and was brought back to the moment by Nogahla's slurping noise. Another grape met its destruction as she spoke. "So, what do you think, mistress? Why did the widow help us today?"

Eyeing her friend, Dinah saw a spark of challenge in those ebony pools. "Why do you think Widow Orma helped us, Nogahla?" This little Cushite had proved to be a deep well of wisdom.

"I think it's easier to know why people do bad things than to understand the true meaning of kind acts." Before Dinah could comment on Nogahla's newest insight, the girl asked, "Do you think Nada will be angry that we gave some of Master Job's bread to Widow Orma? I could sacrifice my portion if you think that old crow will be mad." Nogahla's furrowed brow indicated she'd given the matter special consideration. While waiting for Dinah's answer, she rearranged the grapes to hide the bare spots.

Dinah tried to restrain her laughter by pressing her lips into a stern line. She felt the same animosity toward Nada but mustn't show it. "Nogahla, we must be respectful to Sitis's nursemaid." But after spending such a lovely afternoon with the kindhearted widow, she didn't care if Nada begrudged a few loaves of bread either.

Widow Orma had regaled them with touching stories of Job's family, and with disgust she had confirmed the wretched news: "After all the good things Master Job has done, not a single person in Uz is willing to help him."

Glancing at the eight bread loaves stacked in a neat row on the table, Dinah tipped Nogahla's chin to meet her gaze. "You will not give up a single bite of your portion, my friend. Perhaps the aroma of this warm brown bread will warm Nada's heart."

Nogahla's eyes sparked with mischief. "No, mistress. I think Nada will be mad, but I'm glad we gave the bread to Widow Orma anyway."

Chuckling, Dinah nodded her agreement and again studied every nook and cranny of the kitchen, hoping for some inspiration that might busy their hands and minds. "At least we've unloaded my herbs and ointments from the caravan. I can dress Mistress Sitis's blistered hands if she ever summons me, as she promised."

"So what do we do until then?" Nogahla sat on the low wooden stool, resting her elbow in her lap, chin in hand again.

Dinah peered into the kitchen courtyard. There were no goats to milk, no vegetables to clean, no meat to prepare. She glanced at the pile of ashes with a mingling of sorrow and praise. In the corner, beyond the waste heap, she noticed a broken spindle. "Nogahla!" she said, clapping her hands and startling the girl. "Let's go exploring! We'll go through every room until we find the servants' stores of wool and spindles." Her wide-eyed enthusiasm was met with Nogahla's eager nod.

The evening light cast orange-tinged shadows against the courtyard walls. "Come, Nogahla, it's getting dark. Master Job, Elihu, and the other two men will be hungry when they return from inspecting the fields. We'll set out the fruit and some cheese and olives in the dining hall for them." She handed the tray to Nogahla and gathered a pitcher of honeyed wine with four glazed clay cups. "After that, we'll find something to keep us busy."

✤✤✤✤✤

The dusk breeze stirred the linen sea in Sitis's bedchamber. Nada's embrace felt as warm and safe as when Sitis was a child. "I haven't had nightmares like this since Ima died, when I was five years old." Sitis shut her eyes against the memory.

"It was just a dream, mistress." Nada stroked her hair, quieting her. "Just a dream."

"Will we ever wake up from *this* dream, Nada? Will Al-Lat restore Job's wealth? Will Al-Uzza open my womb? Will my husband and I ever be happy again?"

"You will awaken, my Sitis." Nada stopped rocking and laid her chubby hand against Sitis's cheek, tilting her head and searching her expression. "What else is troubling you?"

A fresh wave of tears overtook her. "Oh, Nada. I thought Sayyid would do anything for me," she moaned. "He has always been so kind and generous, but I didn't even recognize the man who visited me today." Sniffing loudly, she used her maid's apron as a handkerchief. "He actually said that if I forced him to marry Dinah, and then Job didn't regain his wealth, he would make me his *second* wife." Sitis's sorrow turned to fury at the thought. "Ohh! Can you imagine, Nada? Me, a second wife?" She drove balled fists into the soft woolen mattress and sat upright, daring Nada to disagree.

"No, my Sitis, I cannot imagine you as a second wife."

Sitis thought she glimpsed a smile before Nada ducked her head. "Don't you dare laugh, old woman!" Hurt and angry tears erupted. How could Nada laugh when her whole world had crumbled in a day's time?

"No, no, no, my girl," Nada said, reaching up with her apron to wipe the new tears from Sitis's cheeks. "You misunderstand. You know I love you more than life itself." The maidservant hugged her tightly. "Listen, if Master Job does not regain his wealth, Sayyid's proposal of marriage *is* a kind and generous offer. He would be saving you from a life of shame, Sitis-girl."

"How can you still feel that way after how he acted today? I've never seen that wicked, selfish side of Sayyid's character."

Nada released Sitis and challenged her with a stern gaze. "You hurt our Sayyid today. He came here in hopes of winning your heart and making you his wife."

"What?" Sitis couldn't breathe. "Did he actually tell you this when you relayed my message earlier?" The blood rushed from her face, and her heart felt as though it would pound out of her chest. "Nada, why didn't you warn me? Why didn't you tell him I love Job?"

Nada was suddenly immovable, her expression firm, her gaze steady. "Do you truly *love* Job?" She lifted one dark eyebrow as if knowing the answer and daring Sitis to tell the truth.

"Nada! Of course I love Job. He's my husband!" The lingering silence drained the power from her statement, and Nada's unwavering gaze unnerved Sitis.

Do I love Job? She knew she was incapable of Job's standard of love, but no one was as selfless as her husband. *But have I ever truly loved someone sacrificially?* She loved her children, of course. But it had been Nada who cared for their sicknesses, and Job's wise and kind discipline that had guided them through life. When she quarreled with her loved ones, Sitis withdrew her affection until they complied, or she ignored the dispute, pretending all was well. Had she ever truly loved someone through difficult times without turning away?

She could feel tears welling again, and no matter how hard she tried, Sitis couldn't outstare Nada. "I don't know if I'm capable of love," she cried, melting into her maid's embrace once more. "My heart feels like an old grain sack with too many holes to be of any use. What if I can't love, Nada?"

The old woman held her tightly. "You will learn to love again, my Sitis. Every child is born with the ability." Sitis could feel Nada's tears now dampening her hair. "Sometimes our hearts forget as we grow older, and we must relearn the lessons of love we knew as a child."

"But how do I relearn, Nada? What if Al-Uzza, the mighty goddess, doesn't open my womb? What if Al-Lat never restores Job's fortune? What if Manat has already decided my fate and refuses to relent?"

"Enough. Enough of this 'what if' talk, my Sitis-girl." Nada sat up and grasped Sitis's cheeks, her hands warm and scratchy like a woolen scarf. "You listen to me. We are going to pray right now to our goddesses." Scooting off the bed, she hurried toward the curtain-draped closet carved into the stone wall. "You know our prayers are most powerful if we glimpse the evening star of Al-Lat before the last shadows of sunset dim." Reaching into the closet, she retrieved the precious basket containing the sacred cube and idols and placed it on the bed.

The two women began their familiar ritual. Nada carefully unwrapped each of the images and filled a shallow copper brazier with incense and sweet-smelling herbs. Sitis gathered a small pitcher of oil and a jar of grain kept hidden under her bed. Collecting the offerings and goddesses, Sitis and Nada marched to the balcony, where the pleasing aroma of incense would ascend with their prayers. With a final glance across the inlet to ensure Job's absence, the women began their secret ceremony.

"Mistress?" Nada motioned for Sitis to kneel on the customary cushion. The nursemaid knelt beside her on a small fleece and led the chanting. "Al-Uzza, goddess of life and wealth and power, we offer to you—"

Suddenly there was a knock on the door, followed immediately by a young woman's voice in the bedchamber behind them. "Hello? Is anyone in here?"

Sitis was on her feet, arms stretched wide like the feathers on an arrow shot from a bow. "What are you doing in my private chamb—"

It was too late to hide. Dinah and Nogahla stood wide-eyed and open-mouthed, staring at the ritual components before them. Job's face flashed in Sitis's mind. The shock and horror on these women's faces was a dim reflection of what her husband's reaction would be.

"I'm sorry," Dinah said. "We thought it was just another empty chamber."

Sitis's arms fell to her sides, and her head lolled forward in shame.

Nada labored to her feet and flailed her arms like an angry hen. "Get out! Get out of Mistress Sitis's chamber! How dare you!"

Sitis lifted her head and saw them walking out through her linen dream. "No, wait." She hadn't the strength to match Nada's zeal, but the pair somehow heard her. "Come back, Dinah. I want to explain."

The beautiful blonde turned, and her expression surprised Sitis. Instead of judgment and hatred, she saw compassion, even pity, in Dinah's eyes.

"As was true this morning in the courtyard, mistress, you owe me no explanation." Dinah bowed gracefully. "Please forgive us. We had no idea this was your chamber. Nogahla and I were looking for something to busy our idle hands."

"You were spying!" Nada's voice was shrill and accusing. "How dare you. Master Job opens his home to you, and the minute he leaves, you rummage through his house."

Dinah's anger flared. "We were looking for something to occupy our time since Mistress Sitis hadn't summoned me to her chamber, nor did her *maid* offer any instructions for managing this household!"

"Well, let me instruct you now, you ungrateful—"

"Nada! That's enough!" Sitis had never seen her nursemaid act so disrespectfully, but come to think of it, she'd never seen anyone challenge Nada as Dinah did. "Job would not approve of your disrespect to a guest in his home." Turning once again to Dinah, she said, "However, it seems your position in this household is a bit of an enigma. You are neither guest nor servant, so . . ." Her voice broke and her mind reeled. How could she explain to this beauty that Nada was simply protecting her?

Just then she noticed a welcome diversion, a small basket hanging on Dinah's arm. "May I ask what you have in your basket?" She would try hard to offer peace, though she wasn't sure why or if she truly desired it.

Dinah took a tentative step forward, her expression hopeful. "I've brought some of my supplies from the caravan to bandage your hands." Casting an uneasy glance at Nada, she confessed, "We had hoped to find your chamber at some point in our search."

So you weren't spying, but you were looking for me. Sitis vacillated between being offended and being pleased. Stepping outside her world of grief and tragedy for a moment, she tried to imagine Dinah's predicament. She realized this young woman was nearly the same age as her son Ennon—alone in a strange land, her future uncertain, surrounded by unfriendly people. For the first time, Sitis's heart was moved by the girl, and she wondered if her kind and loving friend Sayyid might truly be happy with this beautiful young wife. Dinah needed a home, and Sayyid needed a good woman. Sitis was suddenly more determined than ever to see Sayyid marry Dinah, not because it fit her plan, but because it was best for Dinah and Sayyid.

"Come, sit with me on the bed, dear." Sitis patted the soft mattress, and Nada stepped aside, frowning as Dinah passed. The Cushite maid looked like a frightened fawn, and Sitis chuckled, wondering if the girl would bolt from the room. "You can have your maid go back to her chamber or wait in my anteroom if she'd be more comfortable there."

Before Dinah could voice her preference, Nada issued the command. "The girl should wait outside, mistress." Nada grunted and sniffed, folding her arms across her chest like a sentry.

"Why don't you go back to our chamber, Nogahla," Dinah said. "You'll be more comfortable there." Dinah grinned victoriously when the Cushite scampered past Nada.

Sitis watched, fascinated, at the interchange between her lifelong friend and Jacob's daughter. The two seemed locked in a competition of sorts, and Sitis realized she must expose it in order to gain any lasting peace in their household. Gently touching Dinah's arm, she said, "You really love your little maid, don't you?"

The young woman met her gaze, smiling easily. "I suppose it's similar to how you feel about Nada. She's more than just my maid. She's my friend." Taking a roll of bandages out of the basket, Dinah paused and glanced at Nada. "And I expect Nogahla to be treated with respect."

Nada raised her chin, and Sitis leveled a chastising glance at her. "As I want Nada to be treated with respect." Sitis offered her hand to Dinah, waiting for the spirited young woman to meet her gaze again. She did, and Sitis let her eyes communicate a silent reprimand.

"Agreed," Dinah said, a penitent smile stretching across her perfect red lips. She grasped Sitis's blistered hand, and Nada stepped forward, her wagging finger poised to command. Sitis issued a warning glare, deflating the maid's bluster, and the young beauty continued her ministrations.

"Now, mistress, place your hand on my lap, palm up, like this," Dinah said, "and I'll apply a little gum-yamin before wrapping it—"

Nogahla burst through the door. "I heard Master Job in the dining hall! He's coming up the stairs."

Sitis's heart leapt to her throat as she exchanged a panicked glance with Nada. "Gather the goddesses." She paused. "No, wait! It's too late." They'd never be able to hide them if he came directly to her chamber.

Dinah grabbed Sitis's shoulders. "Have Nada take Nogahla to the anteroom and tell Job he can't come in until I'm finished bandaging your hands." Turning to Nada, Dinah barked instructions. "Tell him Sitis's hands are blistered from grinding grain, and I need privacy to concentrate on tending her wounds."

Nada hesitated, looking to Sitis for approval.

"Go! Do as she says," Sitis said.

The two maids scurried from the room, closing the heavy door behind them. Sitis once again tried to rush to the balcony to retrieve the goddesses, but Dinah's grip held her firmly to the bed.

"Mistress," Dinah said, "isn't it time to stop deceiving your husband?"

Sitis started to pull away, but the girl's eyes, brimming with tears, beseeched her to do the right thing. Sitis looked away, breaking the honorable spell cast by Dinah's pleading. "I can't. He will disown me." She pulled her head covering off, dragging her fingers through her hair. "What do I do, Dinah?"

"Job will never disown you, mistress. We both know that."

She looked up, startled that this beautiful woman would speak with such intimate certainty about her life. "How can you be sure? You don't know us. You don't know our lives." She wanted to be angry at the girl's presumption, but the kindness in Dinah's eyes cut her to the heart.

"I know that your husband believes in a God who forgives everyone for everything if they simply ask it of Him."

Sitis turned away. *Why would I believe in any god at all? None of them have saved me from this pain.* "Dinah, don't ask me to trust El Shaddai. You don't know what I've suffered at His hands."

Sitis felt a trembling hand on her cheek and met Dinah's tender gaze. "I don't know what you've suffered at His hands, but I know what you've endured without His comfort. And I'm sorry for you, mistress." Both women straightened at the sound of Job's voice just outside the door.

"I want to see my wife, Nada." He sounded weary but resolute.

"I won't help you deceive Job," Dinah whispered to Sitis. "If you want to hide the idols, you must do the work yourself. But I won't tell him what I've seen either."

Relief washed over Sitis as she scooted off the bed and ran to the balcony to retrieve the goddesses. She hastily covered them and cast them into the stone cube and basket, shuffling it under the bed. Out of breath and short on time, she leapt onto the cushioned mattress and held up her hands for Dinah to bandage. "Hurry, please. He's becoming impatient."

"Hold still," Dinah commanded, beads of sweat forming on her brow. Sitis grimaced but decided to allow the woman's impertinence after all her other kindnesses this evening.

"I said I'm going to see my wife, Nada!" Job barged in, slapping the linen scarves aside just as Dinah finished tying the last bandage. Looking as shocked as the rest of those in the room, Job stammered, "Oh, Dinah. You're bandaging my wife's hands."

"Just as I said." Nada, hands on hips, didn't have to feign her frustration.

"Job! You smell like death!" Sitis said as she and Dinah instinctively covered their noses. The moment she said it, his face looked stricken, and a stab of regret pierced Sitis's heart.

I should have considered what he's seen today, the death he encountered in the fields, instead of criticizing him the moment he entered the room. And just as suddenly, Sitis realized she wouldn't normally have considered her husband's feelings. Shocked and inspired by her own burgeoning sensitivity, she addressed the other women. "Will you excuse us? My husband and I need some time alone to talk about his difficult day."

"Of course." Dinah bowed and guided Nogahla out of the room. Nada closed the door behind her with an authoritative sneer at Job. Their epic battle would no doubt continue.

Job stood at Sitis's bedside, gazing down at her. He was dirty, smelly, and forlorn. Everything within her wanted to banish him until he bathed. She'd never endured odors well. Even when she was a child, Atif and Nada had filled her tent with frankincense on the days the wind carried the stable stench in her direction. Perhaps her sacrificial love began with a smelly husband who honored the edict of no bathing during the seven days of mourning.

She swallowed the extra saliva gathering in her mouth. "Tell me, husband, were the fields as awful as you feared?" She patted the bed, indicating a nice fluffy spot beside her.

Job lifted an eyebrow. "Though I didn't touch the bodies, Sitis, my clothes are saturated with the smell of death. Are you sure you will allow me on your bed?" He leaned over, placing a tentative hand on her beautifully woven covering.

"No," she said, watching his smile fade. She patted the bed again. "I'm *inviting* you onto my bed." The relief in his features made the odor tolerable. He fell onto the bed beside her, exhausted. Her ensuing nausea made her thankful she hadn't eaten anything since breakfast. Swallowing again, she concentrated on his eyes. "Tell me what you found in the fields."

He affectionately laid his hand on her leg, and she instinctively flinched. The dirt on his hands and around his fingernails would most certainly stain her fine linen robe. "Sorry," he said, starting to pull away.

Suddenly realizing the great gulf her elegance had carved between them, she enfolded his soiled hand and wiped it with her robe. His eyes misted, and he gazed at her longingly. *I do love you*, she thought, *I just haven't been very good at showing you.*

"It was worse than we'd expected, Sitis. Hundreds of our servants—men, women, children. Their families are refusing to touch the dead bodies for fear of retribution from the gods. Elihu, Shobal, Lotan, and I tried to just heap dirt over the bodies, but we couldn't even begin to bury them all. We'll unearth Ennon's home and take our children's bodies to the family tomb tomorrow, my love."

Sitis listened long into the night while Job described the horrors he'd seen. He held her, and they wept for all the children lost to Uz. At some point, they fell asleep in each other's arms—the filth, the stench, all part of their shared experience now.

❋❋❋❋❋

Sitis turned in her sleep, vaguely aware of the birds' morning chatter. Eyes still closed, she sensed darkness jealously yielding to dawn's first rays, and at the same moment Job gasped and wheezed beside her. A lazy grin stretched across her lips as she wondered why her husband would begin snoring after forty years of slumbering bliss. She rolled toward him and let her arm fall across his strong, broad chest.

Her bloodcurdling scream split the morning silence.

171

Sitis bolted upright, staring at her husband—the man she thought was her husband—now lying paralyzed in pain, covered on every visible surface with seeping sores.

"By the gods, Job! What has happened to you?"

The first rays of sunrise streamed in from her balcony, the light breeze mingling the putrid odor of the death field with a new rotting stench from his sores. Sitis turned away and retched on the floor. Wiping her face, she stared at Job. He was shaking uncontrollably. Unable to speak, he began to grunt and gasp for air.

Revulsion stepped aside and fear seized her. Remembering Sayyid's words that the city elders had spurned them, she wondered who in Uz would treat Job's wounds. No physician would come near them. She covered her mouth, silencing the panic that threatened to overtake her.

And then she smelled it. The gum-yamin ointment on her bandaged hand.

"Dinah!" Sitis screamed. "Dinah!" She slid off the bed and ran down the hallway, uncertain which chamber housed the blonde beauty and her maid. "Dinah, get your medicines! Come quickly! My husband is dying!"

11

They succeed in destroying me. . . . They
advance as through a gaping breach; amid the
ruins they come rolling in. Terrors overwhelm
me; my dignity is driven away as by the wind,
my safety vanishes like a cloud.

Elihu sat atop the middle mountain ridge by Job's sacred altar in the early glow of pre-dawn stillness. Crystal-clear nights sharpened the desert chill, and his chattering teeth sang a remorseful tune to the lonely blanket still in his bedchamber. When Elihu had first arrived at Job's home as a boy of twelve, he dreaded the pre-dawn climb from his fourth-floor bedchamber each morning. Abba Job's chamber had been next to Elihu's, and they'd often made the climb together, counting every step in the tower passageway. Four hundred thirty-two rock-hewn, steep-grade, narrow-walled stairs led to an immense porthole in the mountaintop. As an adolescent, he'd found the tower climb to be a nuisance. As an adult, he saw it as a wonder, the gateway to Elihu's most holy place—the only place on earth he felt Yahweh truly heard his prayers.

This morning, they could bring no animal for sacrifice, but Abba Job would undoubtedly arrive at dawn for morning prayers. The two herdsmen would most likely join him. Would Dinah come too? Rubbing his bald head, he gazed at the amethyst sky, trying to focus on the miracle of God's wonders rather than the mystery of God's plan.

Last night sleep wouldn't come, and Elihu couldn't eat after arriving home from the death fields. Even more unsettling than the smell clinging to his robes were Abba Job's words churning in his mind. *Perhaps the Most High has called you and Dinah to my household for a greater purpose than we realized.*

Elihu smacked his forehead with the palm of his hand. "For what purpose, Abba?" he had asked. Like a camel with its bridle and tail knotted, Elihu's naïveté had marched him in a senseless circle. He was mortified when Abba Job bounced his eyebrows, giving his slow-witted student a moment to absorb the implications.

El Shaddai, if it's truly Your will for me to marry Dinah, why didn't the thought occur to me? Why do I still love Uzahmah?

Elihu fought tears. His emotions had gotten the better of him the night of the tragedies. He couldn't let it happen again. He needed to be strong for Abba Job and Ima Sitis.

But is it weak to mourn Uzahmah? Is it weak to doubt that I could ever love a woman like Dinah?

Of course, she was stunningly beautiful, and her devotion to El Shaddai seemed genuine. But her past would forever stain the man who married her. Could Elihu live with the questions for the rest of his life? Was he as certain as Abba Job of her innocence? He felt like a jackal for even admitting his doubts, but could he defend Dinah publicly when so many for so long had accused her?

He was suddenly distracted by movement in the canyon below. Elihu crouched, hurrying to the edge of the cliff. In the infancy of dawn, he watched several men leading pack animals near Job's kitchen courtyard. Startled, he realized dozens more hammered at the courtyard wall, creating a gaping breach through which more men filed into the house! His heart slammed against his chest. Who would break down the wall when the gates were unlocked? What evil were they plotting, and how could he stop them?

If he hurried down the sharp eastern cliffs, where the mountains met and the canyon ended, he might reach the sleeping Shobal and Lotan in the stables. Surely they could find swords still packed in the Hebron caravan. But how could three men fight fifty, and what about Abba Job and the others still in the house? He must take them to safety first!

He saw a shadowy figure standing at Job's main courtyard gate, positioning guards at every exit of the home. *Who are you?* Elihu thought. The man turned slightly, and dawn's early rays revealed the chiseled features of Sayyid's captain. Elihu's mind raced with devastating possibilities. Uzahmah had once mentioned the tension between Sayyid and her abba, but Elihu couldn't imagine Ima Sitis's old friend organizing an attack on his neighbor.

Regardless of Elihu's doubts, the fact lay before him. Sayyid didn't even sneeze without his captain offering up his sleeve to wipe his nose. Elihu must act quickly to stop whatever Sayyid had planned.

Running toward the hole in the mountaintop, Elihu jumped down the tower stairs two and three at a time. His heart pounded in his ears, his breathing hard and fast. "I must get to the women in time. They'll attack the women first," he whispered, coaching his feet to move faster.

Finally reaching the bottom step, he burst through the heavy wooden door and was suddenly aware of a woman screaming. *Am I too late?* He ran faster and stumbled through the fourth-story hall, nearly tumbling headlong down the remaining stairs. Then he saw her—Ima Sitis hysterically screeching as she ran down the hallway in her night robe.

"Dinah, where are you?" She was running from door to door.

"Ima Sitis, quiet!" Elihu half-whispered, half-shouted. She turned, having obviously heard him, but then bolted in the opposite direction. "Ima, what are you doing? You must come—"

Nada burst from an adjoining third-story chamber, knocking Elihu's wiry frame into the wall. "What's wrong, my Sitis?" she asked, her eyes wild. Elihu recovered from the jolt and motioned her to be quiet, but she ignored him and chased after her lady instead.

At the sound of Nada's voice, Sitis turned. "I must find Dinah! Job has sores. He can't speak, his pain is so great. Help me find Dinah."

"This way," Nada said. The two continued down the hallway, Elihu pleading behind them.

"Ima Sitis, Nada, come back!" Exasperated, he wondered if he had become invisible.

"Mistress?" Dinah emerged from a veiled doorway down the hall, her small Cushite maid peeking out beside her.

"We have no time for this!" Elihu exploded, his whispering forgotten. By now, the bandits had no doubt heard the women's screeching. "Ima Sitis, all of you, don't ask questions. Just follow me. Now!" His deep, resonant voice echoed against the sandstone walls.

"Don't talk to me that way, young man. My husband is ill!" Sitis said, stomping her foot.

Nada placed a balled fist on her hip, no doubt preparing to scold someone, but seemingly confused at where to start.

"Ahh!" Elihu hoisted Sitis into his arms, surprising everyone, including himself. "I said *now*!" Whirling toward the stairway, he said, "We'll collect Abba Job on the way."

"Elihu, put me down!" Sitis kicked her legs in protest. "I'm too heavy for you to carry. Put me down! Job needs Dinah's medicines!"

Elihu gritted his teeth, partly from frustration and partly from the strain of carrying someone matching his own weight. "Ima, we can tend Abba Job's wounds later," he whispered. "Right now men are entering your house and sealing off the exits. We must get to the mountaintop altar." Sitis stopped kicking, and her face finally registered the concern Elihu had tried to convey. "We have to go up the tower stairs and escape across the mountain path," he said, more gently now that fear scarred her features.

"But Job's pain is too great," she said. "He won't make it." Sitis glanced over Elihu's shoulder and began flailing again. "Stop! Dinah is going back to her chamber. Put me down, Elihu." He nearly dropped her but managed to land her gently on the tiled floor. "Nada and I will go to my chamber and get Job on his feet," she said, "but you must get Dinah or Job will die."

✵✵✵✵✵

"Nogahla, hurry," Dinah said, grabbing the two baskets of herbs and potions they'd unloaded from the caravan earlier. "Take this basket, and I'll gather the linen bedcover for bandages. I heard Mistress Sitis say Job has sores and needs medicine, so we'll take everything we have and hope for the best."

Nogahla was already moving toward the door, basket in hand, when Elihu arrived with panic in his voice. "Hurry!" he said, and then suddenly stilled. Dinah heard raucous laughter and sounds of breaking pottery coming from the floors below. Elihu whispered, "There's no time to bring the supplies!" He motioned them down the long hallway toward Sitis's chamber.

"I'm bringing my medicines," Dinah whispered adamantly, encouraging Nogahla in front of her. Elihu either chose to ignore her or didn't hear. He flattened his narrow body against the wall, snuffing the oil lamps as he passed them, leaving Nogahla and Dinah to follow in a trail of near darkness.

Nogahla began to whimper, and Dinah nudged her from behind. "No crying!" The words registered familiarity between the women, locking their gaze, prompting tremulous grins. Dinah had given the same stern warning when they'd ridden the camel through the narrow siq.

Nogahla had been brave then, but this time she added a little humor. "Well, we certainly didn't stay long at Master Job's house, mistress. It's a good thing we didn't unpack." Dinah grinned and nudged her a second time. Nogahla rewarded her with a brilliant white smile that lit the darkened hallway.

"Shh!" Elihu scolded and glanced behind them.

Dinah lifted an eyebrow, convinced Elihu's hissing-snake impression made more noise than their quiet whispers. Tensions were high, but he acted much too serious for his age. His newly shaved head, slender nose, and close-set eyes gave him the look of a man approaching forty, but Sitis said he would have turned thirty just before marrying Uzahmah.

Nogahla reached back, needing a little comfort, and Dinah took her hand. "It's all right. We're almost to Mistress Sitis's chamber."

Elihu sighed, and before Dinah had time to wonder what new frustration vexed him, he turned, stepped around Nogahla, and faced Dinah. "I asked you to be quiet because I'm trying to get us out of here alive. If you're going to be my wife, you must learn to heed my words." Without so much as a nod, he slipped through the billowing linen veils of Sitis's doorway.

Dinah froze. Nogahla turned slowly to face her, and in the darkened hallway, Dinah saw only Nogahla's wide eyes, glowing like eclipsed full moons. "Mistress, did he say you were going to be his wife? When did he find time to like you?"

Dinah could barely breathe, and as usual, Nogahla's innocent words encapsulated the bold truth. She had last seen Elihu when he'd shunned her at the altar yesterday. Their only words had been angry, their only glances awkward. What had happened to make him think . . .

"Nogahla, go inside. We must check on Master Job." Dinah peeked once more into the dark hall behind her. She didn't know if her heart was thudding wildly at the threat of danger or the thought of marrying a mere boy who obviously disliked her. Seeing no glimmer of light approaching in the darkened hallway, she turned to enter the chamber but was met with a ghastly sight.

Job's body writhed in pain, his face and hands covered in sores.

✤✤✤✤✤

The torturous searing of his flesh was relentless, surreal. Caught in the hellish divide between consciousness and sweet oblivion, Job prayed for death. He was thrust in and out of miserable awareness like a dirty garment plunged into the river and scrubbed against a rock. First came Sitis's scream, and then he was alone. His next recollections were tinged with the distorted perceptions of darkness, agony, and terror.

"Abba, can you hear me? Abba Job?"

He gazed into Elihu's frightened face, the bright blue sky above him. Job tried to move his head, to take in his surroundings, but the pain cut through him like a dull-edged dagger. Every movement, every point of contact—flesh to flesh, flesh to cloth, flesh to air—burned like the fires of Sheol. Eyes wide, hands clutching his robe, he felt the cold stone altar bench lying beneath him. They were on the mountaintop. How? Why?

"Sitis?" His voice emerged a mere croak, and the effort scraped his throat like a blade.

"Nada is tending to Ima Sitis." Elihu leaned down, whispering, glancing nervously toward the porthole of the tower stairs.

Panic rose in Job's chest. The memories were returning slowly. Elihu and Dinah carrying him up endless stairs. Men's ribald laughter echoing in the darkened hallway below them. Crashing pottery. Women crying. "Dinah?"

"I'm here, Job." A soft voice. The smell of frankincense and myrrh. "I've wrapped some of your wounds with herbs," she said. The warmth of her whispered words burned the sores on his cheek. "They should give you some relief from the pain."

A tear slid from the corner of Job's eye, the salty drop

like lava on his tender flesh. Unconsciousness threatened to claim him again, but he heard Sitis's wailing intensify and Elihu's frustrated sigh. "Dinah, stay here with Abba Job," the boy was saying. "I must keep Ima quiet. We still don't know what Sayyid's men are doing in the house or if they'll try to attack us up here."

Job's eyebrows rose at the mention of his enemy. "What? Sayyid?" More words wouldn't come. His tongue moved painfully over open wounds. *El Shaddai, what is happening to my life? Why have You allowed this? What sin have I committed? What sacrifice have I neglected?*

Dinah's face appeared before him, her golden hair pulled over one shoulder, the sun aglow around her. "Try not to talk, Job. I know you're frightened. We all are." She smiled and reached out to touch his face but stopped short. Was it because of his wounds or because he was a married man? Both were good reasons. "It seems you have sores in your throat. Blink if that's true."

Job blinked and marveled at the simple but effective communication she devised.

"All right," she said, "I'll brew mint tea as soon as possible. It should help."

She moved away to sit down, and Job grunted. The only sound he could make. He needed to know what had happened, but he couldn't ask. He couldn't reach out for her—the pain of touching another human being would blind him. So he grunted. Like a baby. Like an animal.

"What is it, Job?" The pity in Dinah's expression shamed him. He had promised this poor young woman a new life, but what did she have now? What did *he* have now?

"Sayyid?" he croaked again.

Dinah cast a hesitant glance in Sitis's direction. Job tried to glimpse the spot, only a stone's throw away, where Elihu was working to quiet Sitis and Nada. "Elihu saw Sayyid's captain leading a raid on your house this morning," Dinah began. "They've broken down the courtyard wall near the ash pile, where we worshiped on the night of the tragedies. We escaped up the tower stairs before the bandits arrived on the fourth story. We're praying they don't come up to the altar." Dinah covered her trembling lips, and for the first time, Job realized they were still in very real danger.

"Send Sitis."

Dinah snapped to attention. "What? Do you mean send her to speak with Sayyid?"

Job blinked hard, deliberately.

"Elihu!" Dinah called out in a shouted whisper. "Bring Sitis over here."

Job heard the scuffle of feet and a mournful cry. From the corner of his eye, he saw Sitis's reticence, and then Dinah approached her with some sort of pouch and mask. Sitis calmed as Elihu led her to Job's side, her face covered by the linen mask, the pouch of herbs held tightly under her nose. Job smiled, though the action caused searing pain through his cheeks and lips. His Ishmaelite princess could never suffer a stench, and his seeping wounds would sorely test her senses.

"By the gods, Job, there you are smiling again," she said, frustration and relief mingling in the fine lines around her eyes. "I know I look ridiculous, but—"

"I love—" Job swallowed with difficulty. "You."

Sitis's tears wet the mask she wore. "I love you too, my husband."

"Sayyid?" Job watched his wife's features turn to stone at the mention of his name.

Glaring accusingly at Dinah, she asked, "What lies did you tell my husband?"

"Mistress Sitis," Dinah said calmly, "I said only what Elihu told us all."

"Go." Though Job's voice was barely a whisper, the single word resounded like a shout.

Nada and Elihu leaned in closer, while Sitis stared in disbelief. "Job, you want me to go to Sayyid?" Her eyes were wary, like a mouse stealing cheese from a trap. "And ask for help?"

Job blinked, and Dinah explained his silent sign of assent. A sudden flush overtook his wife, her eyes questioning those around her. She looked frightened, unsure. And in that moment, Job knew. If Sitis thought Sayyid innocent, she would have leapt at the chance to redeem him, but her reaction spoke louder than a thousand denials. Even Sitis believed Sayyid had initiated the raid.

"Don't go," he croaked, a tear sliding down his face again. "Stay."

In the same instant, Sitis glanced away, and Job watched horror dawn on her features. "Nooo!" she cried, suddenly on her feet and running toward the mountaintop entry. Elihu jumped up, reaching for Sitis's arm, and Nada clutched at her garments.

Job's breaths came in gasps, fear and confusion wrestling for dominion. "What?" he asked Dinah. She and Nogahla had remained at his side, both shaking their heads, tears flowing down their cheeks like rain.

Covering her mouth, Dinah refused to explain. Job felt

helpless, completely at the mercy of this young woman who now watched his family suffer unknown agony.

"What?" he roared, tearing the raw flesh of his throat until the pain almost sent him into oblivion.

Dinah released the words through her sobs. "Smoke, Job. Black smoke is rolling out of the tower stairway and rising from the balconies and windows of your home."

12

~*Job 18:12–15*~

*Calamity is hungry for him. . . . It eats away
parts of his skin. . . . He is torn from the
security of his tent and marched off to the king
of terrors. Fire resides in his tent; burning sulfur
is scattered over his dwelling.*

Sayyid watched from the safety of his balcony while the
Nameless Ones fled Job's blazing home and pack animals
escaped the canyon with the stolen household treasures. As
flames licked the sandstone shell of Job's grand palace, Sayyid
envisioned every shred of fine linen, every bauble the bandits
left behind, swallowed up in the destruction.

Through the rising plumes of smoke, faint shadows of
Job and his newly made beggars huddled together on the
ridgetop of his home. Without wealth, food, or shelter, Sitis
would have no other choice. Tonight the object of Sayyid's
obsession would finally rest in his arms.

185

A slow, wry smile creased his lips. "Or perhaps I will teach you a lesson, Sitis-girl," he whispered to no one. "Perhaps the lovely Dinah will share my bed on the first night of my victory, while Job sleeps in the ashes of his charred home."

"Master Sayyid." Aban's voice broke into his reverie, startling him.

"What is it, Aban?" He turned, staring daggers at the captain. "Is there a problem with the bounty? Are the Nameless Ones demanding more than their agreed portion?" In Sayyid's experience, beggars were an unscrupulous lot, without even the honor common among thieves.

"No, my lord." Aban had stopped at the balcony threshold and appeared pale as a ghost. "Mistress Sitis is in your courtyard and demands an audience with you." He pressed his lips together tightly as if more words were like wild horses pawing at the gate.

Hmm. Stops short in his approach and his report. Something is terribly wrong. His captain hadn't demurred like this since his childhood training, when Sayyid was honing this strong and disciplined warrior. "Tell me now what you've done, and perhaps it will go better for you." Sayyid placed his hand on his leather belt and watched Aban note the action. His captain hadn't felt the sting of his strap for years, but the familiar movement evoked the intended obedience.

The big man squared his shoulders and raised his chin. "Mistress Sitis has accused me of leading the raid. She said Job's student Elihu reported seeing me in the canyon at dawn, placing the bandits at the exits of their home." The corner of Aban's mouth twitched nervously.

Sayyid allowed silence to torture his young captain. Removing his hand from his belt, Sayyid clasped his hands behind his back and began a slow, reflective stroll around the anxious captain. After completing two rounds, Aban's muscles looked as tight as lyre strings.

Sayyid rose to his toes but still stood a head shorter than this giant man. "Go now and tell Sitis I require her presence in my chamber." He watched a bead of sweat roll down the captain's forehead and into his eye. Still the well-trained soldier didn't flinch. "You will say nothing in your own defense, Aban. Nothing."

The captain's face was plagued with questions, but his intelligence silenced him. "Yes, master," he said, offering a curt bow. Aban strode from the room, his black robes fluttering in the wind of his hurried retreat.

Sayyid chuckled. He could think of no better punishment for Aban than to face Sitis's wrath. A full-fledged belly laugh escaped at the thought of Aban herding Sitis up four flights of stairs and into Sayyid's bedchamber while enduring her threats and accusations. If Elihu saw Aban in the canyon, Sitis would certainly know that Sayyid had plotted her husband's latest demise. Considering the likelihood that Elihu would accuse Aban publicly before the elders, Sayyid would have Aban deal with Job's young student promptly. But he would handle his Sitis-girl personally.

❈ ❈ ❈ ❈ ❈

"Mistress, please sit down." Nada's consoling arms guided Sitis to a bejeweled bench under an olive tree in Sayyid's courtyard. Sitis offered a weak smile, but standing, sitting, or lying flat on her back wouldn't change her true position. She was destitute, and Sayyid had arranged it.

"How could I have been blind for so long?" she asked

Nada, not really seeking an answer. Job had tried to warn her of Sayyid's deceitfulness.

Even moments ago, when she and Nada had left the sacred altar, Job's eyes begged her to be cautious. "Shobal, Lotan." He had croaked the names of the herdsmen who had arrived at the altar frightened but unharmed. Elihu asked to accompany her and take the herdsmen along as an escort, but she knew her best chance at success lay in meeting Sayyid alone.

The nursemaid hugged Sitis's head to her shoulder and stroked her hair. "We don't know why Sayyid's captain was in the canyon this morning. Save your judgment until you talk with him, my Sitis."

Serving maids passed by, a few at first, and then as the wait grew longer, more servants walked casually through the courtyard. No doubt they were awed that the first time the great lady of Uz visited Sayyid's home, she would arrive in such a disheveled state.

An older maid shyly approached and knelt before Sitis. "Mistress, may I bring you some sweet wine?"

Sitis looked into the woman's face, and it was as though she had raised a bronze mirror. Her stomach lurched. The startling truth of Sayyid's obsession knelt before her. Panicked, Sitis stood, running to each serving maid, studying her hair, her eyes, her lips. "Nada, they are me!" she cried, fresh horror gripping her.

Nada dropped her gaze, seemingly unable to reply.

"You knew?" Sitis said. "In forty years I've never visited Sayyid's home, but you have come many times at my bidding. You've seen these women, Nada." She let her unspoken betrayal linger in the silence.

Finally, Nada looked up, lips quivering with emotion.

"Sayyid has loved you since you were children, my girl. I thought his love was pure, incapable of harm. Please, just listen to what he has to say."

"Mistress Sitis." Sayyid's captain stood on the bottom stair. How long had he been there? How much had he heard? "My master requests your presence in his chamber." The young man she knew as Aban bowed slightly, keeping his gaze averted.

"Nada, come," Sitis said, motioning the old woman to her feet. By the gods, she would not go to Sayyid's bedchamber by herself.

"I'm sorry, mistress, but Master Sayyid requests your presence alone." Aban's imposing form blocked the stairway as the women approached.

Sitis grasped Nada's hand and thrust out her chin, her resolve as unyielding as the captain's Hittite sword. "I know you are mighty enough to force my obedience, Aban," she said, using the young man's name to prompt recollections of the times he'd accompanied Sayyid to her home. "You may guide me up those stairs, alive and *with* my maid, or carry my dead carcass *without* my maid to your master's bedchamber. You decide which Sayyid would prefer."

The young captain shifted nervously, eyeing Nada's wide stance and clenched jaw. "All right, but she remains silent," he said, casting a menacing glance at Nada before turning to ascend the stairs.

Sitis sighed with relief and began the long climb. Aban snatched a wall lamp from a niche and handed it to her. "You'll need this." Their eyes met for just a moment, and she caught just a hint of . . . was it compassion? Remorse? Guilt? Just as suddenly, he turned and continued his march up the stairs.

Sitis's anger reignited. "How dare you raid and pillage my home."

Silence. He continued the march.

"And then burn everything we own!" Her voice disintegrated into a whine, her legs burning from the climb, her throat burning with emotion.

The giant, black-robed figure stalked up the stairs in front of her without comment.

"Stop!"

He continued to ignore her.

Desperate for a response, she lunged at his foot and pulled hard, sending the hulking man to his hands and knees. A rush of dread choked Sitis. She sat back against the wall, bracing herself for his heated retaliation.

Aban's smooth, brown face turned slowly, but the anger Sitis expected was absent. His hand came toward her, and she flinched, thinking he would strike her. The blow didn't come.

She looked up and found his outstretched hand waiting to help her stand. "Please come, Mistress Sitis." His voice was gentle. "My master will answer your questions."

✦ ✦ ✦ ✦ ✦

The mountaintop altar had proven a clever escape from the bandits and a safe harbor from the fire, but as the sun brightened, their future dimmed. The rejoicing when Shobal and Lotan returned changed to mourning at their departure.

"We smeared ourselves with mud and soot and escaped on Master Job's camels among the Nameless Ones," Shobal had reported when they arrived earlier. "When the filthy bandits began arguing over their share of bounty, we slipped away.

We knew you would come to the altar, Master Job." Shobal hesitated, making his next words resound like a trumpet. "But none of us have anything left to sacrifice."

Lotan nodded and then stepped forward. "If Sayyid is involved in all this, Master Job, we must consider the safety of our families." His voice was choked. "Shobal and me—well, we're sorry to leave you like this . . ." He trailed off like a breathless flute player.

Now Dinah watched the silhouettes of Job's herdsmen fade through the waves of heat. *Will we all fade away, El Shaddai—like words, like silhouettes, like breath?* She felt the oppressive rays beating down on her head and felt the stone bench warming beneath her.

Lifting a linen sheet from the pile beside her, she handed Nogahla a coverlet from the pile of bed linens they'd brought out of their chamber. "We must tear this cloth into bandages a handbreadth in width."

Elihu was pacing nearby, and Dinah tilted her head, shielding her eyes from the sun. "Do you have a job, or would you like me to give you one?" She half smiled, but Elihu's brow furrowed as if considering a troublesome child.

He rushed over, and his thin frame cast a slender shadow. "My job, if you must know—and it seems you must—is to challenge the most conniving, deceitful man in Uz. I need to prove Sayyid's guilt to the city elders, but I have no witnesses, no resources, and no support from Abba Job's friends or family." His face had grown redder as he'd ticked off the impossibilities, but Dinah refused to be cowed.

"Well, while you're at it," she said, standing to match his fervor, "you can also find us shelter. And soon." She punctuated the last two words with a nod and returned to her seat beside Job. "He can't withstand this sun much longer, and I need your help dressing his wounds."

She began lifting Job's robe from his chest, thinking he was unconscious. He moaned, as some of the weeping sores had already started to adhere to the cloth under the sun's scorching heat. "I'm sorry, Job." Emotion strangled her throat. Prayer was her only hope. *El Shaddai, please carry Job into sweet unconsciousness, where he'll feel no pain, while we tend these wounds.*

"Why?" Job's labored voice broke through her silent petition.

Elihu hurriedly knelt beside Job. "What do you mean, Abba? Why what?"

"Sores because I sin . . . sinned?" Job's words seemed more pained than his deepest wounds. Dinah knew that kind of heartache. She had asked herself the same question a thousand times, when her life had turned to dust after Shechem.

"No, Abba. Your sores aren't because of your sins." Elihu's eyes welled with tears. "Remember, we offered the sacrifice yesterday morning. You are forgiven."

Job opened his eyes, and Elihu leaned close to meet his gaze. The teacher seemed to be searching, testing, begging his student. "Certain? No offering . . . today." Tears began cascading from Job's eyes, following the deep, uneven patterns of freshly opened flesh.

"Abba, remember the teachings of Shem. While they were on the ark, Noah couldn't offer burnt sacrifices, but he was obedient in his heart and gathered clean animals for the offerings he would make when the journey ended." Elihu's voice broke, and he wiped his face. "Abba, you will offer sacrifices again someday. El Shaddai knows your heart." Sobs overtook him, and he buried his face in his hands.

"Tears burn." Job's tortured expression revealed more than mere physical pain. He was devastated to have nothing to offer the God he loved and served wholeheartedly.

Like a dove settling on its nest, the object of Job's offering settled into Dinah's heart. "Your tears are your burnt offering, Job." She had not learned this teaching as Elihu had learned of Noah's story in the House of Shem, but El Shaddai had testified to its truth in this moment. The finality in her spirit surprised her, and the relief on Job's face thrilled her.

Elihu looked up, startled. "What did you say?" His face was an unmarked grave, no trace of his opinion there.

"Job's tears burn like fire," Dinah explained, a little less confident now that a learned student might challenge her. "He offers them to El Shaddai in sorrow and repentance. Aren't his burning tears more costly than the burning of an animal that bears him no personal pain?" She gazed down and watched Job's eyes close, the faintest smile crease his blistered lips. One of her tears dropped onto his face, mingling with his in a deep wound on his cheek. She cringed, hating the thought of adding to his pain. Wiping her eyes, she said, "I have no doubt that Job will sacrifice a hundred lambs when this journey is ended. But for now, his tears are enough." Dinah remained focused on Job, suddenly caring nothing about Elihu's reaction. She knew in her spirit that Yahweh was pleased.

"I think I'd rather face a hundred bandits than contend with you." Elihu's quiet voice interrupted her peace. Dinah gazed into his close-set eyes, now compassionate and tender-hearted. His gentle smile unnerved her. "I loved Uzahmah, but you have earned my admiration." He looked down at Job as if bolstering his courage. "Perhaps El Shaddai has brought us to Abba Job's household for His greater purpose."

Job's brow furrowed, causing him to gasp.

"Job, what is it?" Dinah was thankful for the distraction. If Elihu considered his last remark the prelude to a betrothal, he needed serious counsel on the ways of men with women.

"Elihu . . . accuse Sayyid . . . now." Job swallowed with great difficulty.

Nogahla appeared with a mint tea leaf. "Here, Master Job. Put this on your tongue."

After sucking on the leaf for a few moments, Job's eyes opened with more clarity, and Nogahla offered a satisfied smile. "Elihu, you must accuse Sayyid at the city gate *now*." His words were slurred from the tea leaf, but he grew more adamant. "When Sitis tells Sayyid that you know he's responsible, he'll try to kill you."

Dinah's mind reeled at the dreadful possibility that their nightmare wasn't over but merely beginning a new scroll in an ongoing story.

"But what about Ima Sitis?" Elihu's voice was shrill, panic setting in.

"If you go to the elders now, they'll summon Sayyid immediately and interrupt whatever he plans for Sitis." Job swallowed again and focused hard on his would-be son. "Elihu, you must leave Uz immediately after the trial. You cannot return here after you accuse Sayyid. Take one of the camels the herdsmen brought back, and ride quickly to find Sitis's brother, Bildad, and Uncle Eliphaz. They're the only people who can help us."

✳ ✳ ✳ ✳ ✳

Sayyid tightened his belt and smoothed his robe. Ridiculous. He was as nervous as a virgin bride. The clicking of sandals on the stone floor outside his chamber left his mouth parched, and just as he reached for his cup of wine, Aban appeared at the door with Sitis and Nada.

"Master Sayyid, Mistress Sitis and her maid have arrived." His captain bowed, and Sayyid inhaled both wine and breath, causing him to spray and sputter like a disgruntled camel. Not the noble impression he'd envisioned for Sitis's first visit to his bedchamber. Aban rushed to his side while Sitis and Nada watched wide-eyed from the doorway.

"I'm fine. I'm fine." Clearing his throat and wiping the choked tears, Sayyid shoved away his captain's awkward attempts at concern. Replacing his cup on the tray, he strode toward his beloved and cupped her face in his hands. "By the gods, Sitis, you look like death!"

The woman's stony black gaze would have crushed a weaker man, but it was precisely Sitis's regal air that drew him. "Perhaps my death was your intention when you sent your captain to burn my house this morning, Sayyid."

Stroking her cheek with his thumb, he noted a crack in her stately wall of control, a slight trembling of her chin. "You know I would never harm you, my love."

She tried to pull away, and in the tussle, Sayyid's fingers became ensnared in her hair. She tossed her head and whimpered when his gemstone rings tangled around her black tresses. "Sitis, wait!" Frustration driving him, he grabbed her head and shook it like a melon. "Stop fighting me!"

Eyes wide with fear, his Ishmaelite princess was struck dumb. A frightened dove in the fowler's snare.

The old nursemaid raised tremulous fingers to untangle her mistress's hair from his rings. "Master Sayyid, my mistress has come seeking your help." Nada's hand rested on his forearm, a chastising glare reminding him that Sitis preferred honeyed promises to prickly threats.

Slowly, gently, he released Sitis's face, and she stepped back into Nada's waiting arms. Sayyid studied his beloved from head to toe. Her feet were dust-covered and bleeding. No doubt the past two days had been more perilous than anything she could have imagined.

"My Sitis-girl, how could you think I would ever intend harm against you?" Reaching for her hands, he studied every feature of her lovely face. "My heart is broken at the hardships I see written all over your body." His eyes roamed every curve, every contour of her shape. He'd waited forty years for this day. He mustn't ruin his long efforts with a short temper.

Ever so slowly, she removed her hands from his grasp. "If you had nothing to do with the fire in my home this morning, Sayyid, explain why your captain was positioning bandits at every exit."

He watched a single tear slide down her cheek and dangle precariously from the point of her perfect jaw. Sayyid longed to catch the lonesome drop on his finger, taste its salty sweetness.

"Sayyid, did you hear me?" Her slight stomp cleared his distraction and sent the tear cascading down her slender neck.

"Of course I'm listening, Sitis-girl. I'm just stunned you didn't know." Sayyid gave his best impression of confusion. "But how could you know? You would have been sound asleep in your chamber at dawn." Motioning Aban to join their conversation, he began his fantastic falsehood. "You see, Aban was the first to witness the same divine lightning that killed your sheep. It revisited the skies of Uz this morning just as dawn was breaking." He eyed the young man, and Aban quickly registered halfhearted agreement. "My captain wasn't positioning bandits at the exits of your home, my love. He was trying to force men into your house to save you from another divine tragedy."

A lovely *v* formed between Sitis's brows. "Divine tragedy?"

Sayyid realized the story sounded absurd, but hadn't Job's day of tragedy been just as astounding? Certainly Sayyid would tell this tale to all of Uz with as much believability as the rest of Job's destruction. "Yes, the fire of the gods reached into your balconies and windows, setting your house ablaze. Those *bandits*, as you called them, were my hired men that Aban tried to force *into* the entrances of your home to save you." He reached up, squeezing Aban's shoulder with an authoritative hand. "My captain and twenty witnesses saw a shaft of lightning split the sky and ignite an inferno in your home, Sitis. I fear this is just more divine retribution for your husband's sins against the gods."

"You liar!" She flew at him in a rage, fists flailing, but Aban rushed to subdue her. The mighty captain held Sitis draped over one arm, thrashing and kicking until her strength was spent and sobbing settled in.

Nada stood like a statue, seething as her mistress lost all dignity. "My Sitis has endured enough without adding your lies, Sayyid." She stepped forward, asserting her lifelong influence over a farmer's son who was now a mighty merchant. "Order your captain to release her. My mistress has come to request your help."

Sitis stilled at Nada's voice, and Aban responded, gently steadying Sitis's feet on the floor. His hands cradled her, large and awkward on her back. "Are you all right, Mistress Sitis?" he whispered. A strange air of unease surrounded the young man.

Sayyid's eyes narrowed. *How dare Aban obey Nada's command without my approval? He owes loyalty to his master alone.* "Sitis will be fine when she bows to my will." Sayyid kept his voice low but leveled a deadly glare at his captain.

Cupping Sitis's chin, Sayyid grabbed the back of her neck and bent low, his whisper almost touching her lips. "Nada says you come for help, but all I've heard are accusations." He could smell the fear in her warm breath. "If you want my help, ask. But remember my terms, Sitis-girl." He felt her chin tremble beneath his grasp. He released her and stepped back, her brokenness creeping up his arm and into his heart.

"Nada is right. I *have* come to ask your help." She wiped her tears, smearing the soot on her face. "Job awoke this morning with seeping, smelly sores from head to foot. He'll die if we don't have bandages, shelter, and food, Sayyid." Like a child working a ball of clay, she forced up the corners of her lips in a pained smile. "Can you help us until I can get word to our families?"

Sayyid's heart sang at the words "he'll die," but his world suddenly grew dim when Sitis mentioned their families. When Sayyid and Bela hired the Chaldeans to ruin Job's camel trade, Sayyid's only considerations had been winning Sitis's love. Bela's aim was to diminish Job's wealth and secure Esau's favor as successor to the Edomite kingdom. But if Sitis sent messengers to her Ishmaelite brother, Prince Bildad, or to Job's great-abba Esau, Sayyid and Bela could both be destroyed by a unified Ishmaelite-Edomite army.

"I can't believe Job would dishonor himself and beg help from your families." Sayyid's sneer of disgust was genuine. "Didn't you say your husband was dying, Sitis? Why shame the man among your families? Let him die an Edomite with some dignity."

"He won't die if you help us," she said, lifting her chin, her Ishmaelite streak of stubbornness returning.

Sayyid studied her, considering the ramifications of his own heritage. If Esau heard rumblings that Sayyid—an Ishmaelite—had dealt wickedly with his favorite great-grandson, the Edomite father might call for all-out war against the Ishmaelites and break the treaty established by Job and Sitis's marriage.

He must post guards to be sure Sitis sent no messengers to either the Ishmaelites or the Edomites. Just to be safe, however, he must continue some semblance of goodwill.

"Ah, Sitis-girl," Sayyid cooed, "I will most certainly help you." He watched her face brighten, relief softening her features. He saw his advantage and held out one hand. *Let her step back to me if she wants my favor.*

Sitis cautiously planted her hand in his.

"I will hire men to begin restoration of your home today, but it will take many full moons, my love." He raised her hand to his lips, locking his eyes in a hungry gaze. She didn't pull away but allowed him to taste the sweetness of her skin. "And I will provide a place for Job to recuperate from his illness if . . ."

The fragile clay corners of her smile chipped away. "Sayyid, I will never marry you." Her lips trembled, tears began anew. "I love my husband. I will always love Job."

Sayyid's hand tightened around hers, and he nuzzled her hand, working his way up her arm, pulling her closer as his lips found her neck. *Why must you defy me?* Suddenly without concern for the Edomites and Ishmaelites, he tasted the salt and soot mingled on her throat. "So you would rather your husband starve than marry me, Sitis-girl?"

She pulled away as though bitten by a serpent. "I don't understand. What are you saying?" Sitis retreated, taking refuge behind Nada—as though the old woman could somehow protect her.

"I'm saying if you continue to refuse me, I will not only deny Job food and shelter, I will make all of you wish for death." He circled his childhood obsession like a vulture and leaned in to shred the vestiges of her tattered dignity. "Elihu will be banished from Uz, disgraced and humiliated. Dinah and her little maid will starve, no one to marry and no one to serve. And you, princess, will spend your days cleaning slop jars and scrubbing floors like a common servant." He laughed, expecting her to crumble under the weight of his new threat.

Instead, her eyes probed his soul. Seeming to have found some inner strength despite her piteous existence, she whispered, "Sayyid, why are you doing this? You've been my best friend all my life. You opened my heart to Al-Uzza after El Shaddai closed my womb. If it hadn't been for your kindness, I might have gone mad." She reached up and gently placed her hand on his cheek. "This villain before me is not the companion who supported me through all manner of hardship." She stepped toward Sayyid, boldly moving him back a step. "Please, my friend, do not ask me to dishonor my family by denouncing my husband in the city given to me as a dowry."

Sayyid's heart melted at her touch. For forty years he had waited for her love. His heart warred with his mind. Could he wait a little longer? Find another way to woo her, to win her?

No. He was finished waiting. He would simply possess

Sitis—with or without her love. He dare not kill Job and risk Edomite revenge. The death of Esau's favorite great-grandson would come naturally, as Sitis said. And if his plans continued to prosper, Sayyid might just rival Bela in wealth when all was said and done.

Covering Sitis's hand on his cheek, he turned it over and kissed her palm. She didn't pull away. "Sitis, please forgive me if I seemed uncaring. I'd like to speak with you alone."

Panic-stricken, she reached for Nada's comforting embrace.

Sayyid stepped between them, his focus remaining on Sitis while he spoke to her maid. "Nada, my captain will direct you to the kitchen. You'll be working for me now." He sensed the old woman's hesitation behind him, saw Sitis's stricken face. "Sitis, tell Nada that you are grateful for my kindness."

Sitis glanced from Nada to Sayyid, lingering between an iron will and willing submission. The stunning wild mare was tamed by Sayyid's bit and bridle. "Go, Nada." She bowed her head. "We must be thankful for Sayyid's help."

A slow, satisfied smile crept across Sayyid's face. *The first of many victories*, he gloated.

Just as Aban and Nada reached the chamber doorway, a messenger appeared, breathless. "Master Sayyid?"

"Yes, who are you?" Sayyid demanded. He would find the maid who had allowed this stranger into his private chamber and have her whipped. Just then two guards, swords drawn, appeared at the messenger's side. "And who are they?"

"You and your captain have been summoned to the city gate to answer charges, Master Sayyid." The messenger stepped back, his gaze measuring Aban's height and breadth.

Sayyid laughed and grasped Sitis's arm. "There's been a

terrible mistake. I'll go to the elders and clear up the confusion, but my captain has duties elsewhere. Job is ill and will be sheltered in his kitchen courtyard until his wounds heal, and Aban is preparing to escort Mistress Sitis to her new home."

The messenger looked as befuddled as the guards who accompanied him.

"Yes, Mistress Sitis is the new serving maid for Master Bela's wife." Sayyid heard Sitis gasp and shoved her into Aban's arms. "The two women with Job are beggars and should be treated as such." Leaning close to his captain, he whispered, "I will take care of these charges. You take care of Elihu after the hearing, when he leaves the city gate."

PART

13

~From Job 19~

*Though I cry, "I've been wronged!" I get no
response; though I call for help, there is no
justice. . . . He has stripped me of my honor and
. . . tears me down on every side. . . . His troops
advance in force . . . and encamp around my
tent. He has alienated my brothers from me. . . .
My kinsmen have gone away; my friends have
forgotten me. . . . My breath is offensive to my
wife. . . . All my intimate friends detest me;
those I love have turned against me.*

Dinah lay awake, listening to Nogahla's slow, steady
breathing, waiting for dawn's glow to seep through
the tattered curtain covering Widow Orma's cave entrance.
The long winter had passed without life-giving rains, but the
summer sun cast its consistent rays of dawn. The widow's
small cave in the cliffs of Uz's impoverished first sector was

a crowded little nest for three women, but with each passing moon and changing season, their hearts had melded together into a loving family.

Nogahla slept along the back wall because she was the shortest. Dinah laid her fleece-scrap pillow next to Nogahla's head and stretched her long limbs beside the eastern wall. The widow slept across from Dinah, her head at Nogahla's feet—much to the little Cushite's dismay, until the widow assured her no feet had ever smelled more like henna blossoms. A crackling fire lay between the three, warming them through the cold desert nights and offering light throughout their days.

"Nogahla." Dinah nudged her shoulder, and the girl stirred reluctantly. "Come, we should go early today and change Job's bandages before Sitis arrives."

"It's not even dawn yet." The Cushite turned her back to Dinah and held her small patch of fleece over her ears. The wool-stuffed mattresses of days past lay in ever-growing mounds of ash and waste in Job's kitchen courtyard. During the renovation of Job's home, the Nameless Ones had created many ash piles, heaping insults and fine, gray ash into Job's wounds. Sayyid compounded the disgrace by adding ash from his braziers and dung from his stables to the piles in Job's canopied courtyard. The city elders, acting on Sayyid's suggestion, sequestered Job on his own property, threatening him with death should he try to leave. Dinah wondered which fear dominated Uz more—Job's skin disease or Sayyid's threats of divine retribution if they helped the once great man.

"Come on, Nogahla. Sitis plans a morning visit today, and we must try to finish our care before she arrives."

Nogahla didn't move.

"You know if she returns to work after Bela's wife wakes,

206

she'll feel the woman's whip." Dinah pulled the fleece from her maid's hands. "Nogahla, wake up!"

The girl bolted upright, her frustration evident before she spoke her first word. "Why must we go so early? Bela's wife sleeps until midday."

Dinah met her friend's fury in silence. The little Cushite knew Sitis couldn't bear watching Job's pain when they moved him to a new ash pile. Each morning, they settled him atop the most sun-dried mound in hopes of averting infection and finding the most absorbent ash for his weeping sores.

"Mistress, it's embarrassing to bandage Master Job's wounds without Mistress Sitis present." Nogahla's frustration was fleeting, but Dinah could see that more concerns lay beneath the surface.

"You know Sitis doesn't have the stomach to tend Job's wounds," Dinah explained quietly, "especially since his sores have become worm-infested." The supplies of frankincense and myrrh that Aban had secured from Sayyid's physician lasted only the first six moons. Now their bandage supply was running low, so many of Job's wounds were left uncovered.

"Sayyid's guards make rude comments because Master Job is dressed only in a loincloth." Nogahla looked into the fire, avoiding Dinah's gaze. "I don't want Aban to think ill of me."

"You what? Aban?" Dinah could feel the blood rush to her cheeks. She had noticed Sayyid's captain inspecting Nogahla with his gaze. "Since when do you call Sayyid's captain 'Aban'? And why do you care what such a man thinks?"

"Good morning, my lovely daughters," came an airy voice from the darkness.

Dinah turned and saw the bent silhouette, hawk-beaked nose, and tousled gray hair of the ima their hearts adored. "I'm sorry we woke you, Orma."

"Old women never sleep, my precious girl. We simply study the insides of our eyelids until we can stand it no longer." The widow moved slowly in the morning, so Dinah waited patiently while she stood and took the six steps around the fire. Cupping Nogahla's chin in her palm, she said, "Listen, my beautiful Cushite, I would consider it an honor to tend Master Job in your place. He's like a son to me, and those guards would shame themselves if they spoke coarsely to an old woman."

"No, no!" Nogahla's voice held a note of panic. "I want to go." Dawn's light peeked through the curtain holes, revealing the girl's intense dark eyes.

"Well, you two finish your haggling because I must gather what little herbs and bandages we have left and be on my way."

Dinah regretted her sternness toward Orma but didn't have time to waste while Nogahla made up her mind. Casting a backward glance, Dinah opened the curtain and watched Nogahla kiss Widow Orma's cheek.

"Thank you, but I'm not ashamed to help Master Job," Nogahla said. "I just wish Mistress Sitis could help us."

She waved at the old woman, and Dinah's heart squeezed. She too wished Sitis could help, but Sitis couldn't endure the heartache. The mistress often could visit Job only in the evening, after she finished her serving duties. By then, both Job and Sitis were exhausted from their daily battles. Job against the Nameless Ones, shielding himself from their cruel taunts and shovels of ash and dung. Sitis against Bela's wife, trying to guess what would keep her from the whipping post.

"I'm sorry my heart cares about Sayyid's captain, mistress." Nogahla's soft voice intruded on Dinah's brooding. "I can try to hate him if you'll tell me why I should."

The words pierced Dinah's heart. Were Nogahla's emotions as simple as her wisdom? "Isn't the fact that he destroyed Job's home enough reason to hate him?" she asked, stepping carefully down the steep mountain path. The two always chose the hidden trail leading from Orma's cave to the siq rather than the main road through the market.

"Mistress, Aban is a soldier who follows the commands of his master, just as any servant must. However, he has told me he regrets the suffering Master Job and Mistress Sitis are enduring, and he is trying to find a way to help."

Dinah rolled her eyes, safe in her snide reaction since Nogahla followed behind and couldn't see. "Aban lives in Sayyid's household, Nogahla, and is probably just as deceitful as his master. Come to think of it, you've barely spoken to Aban. He stands with the four guards at the wall of Job's kitchen courtyard. How can you care about him, Nogahla? This is ridiculous." Stepping onto level ground, Dinah hurried her pace, and Nogahla rushed behind.

"My heart doesn't care about his household, mistress. It cares about the man." Dinah heard Nogahla's footsteps lag. "I see the way he gently leads Mistress Sitis to the top of the ash pile to visit Master Job. And have you watched him protect Master Job when the bandits try to throw ashes and dung on him?"

Dinah stopped in mid-stride and felt Nogahla's nose bump her shoulder blade. She must have been daydreaming again. The girl's giggle echoed against the red siq walls around them. Turning, Dinah fell silent and studied her friend's innocence in the dim glow of dawn. *How can you see others so clearly when I barely even see myself?* she thought.

"I'm sorry, Nogahla," Dinah said. "Forgiveness seems to be a lesson I must learn again and again." Reaching out to brush the girl's cheek, she said, "I still don't trust this Aban, but I must admit he has treated Job and Sitis with kindness—under the circumstances."

The two began their trek to the ash pile again, Nogahla's brow knit together in thought. "Forgiveness is like an olive tree, mistress. Once it takes root, it will grow, and it's hard to kill. You have learned to forgive once, and you will forgive Aban someday."

Her friend's words always seemed to blossom at just the right moment. Today they had revealed bitterness taking root in Dinah's heart, but oftentimes her wit and wisdom were the soothing balm Job needed as Dinah's herb supplies dwindled.

"I will try to see Sayyid's captain through your eyes, my friend." Reaching for the girl's hand, Dinah added, "In fact, I'll try to see the whole world through your eyes." They walked side by side, emerging from the narrow siq into dawn's light.

Nogahla gazed longingly at the spring-fed central fountain and cascading waterfall in Uz's lavish second sector. "Mistress, perhaps forgiveness is more like taking a bath. We must be washed by it over and over." Bouncing her eyebrows, she tilted her head toward the inviting pool.

Dinah chuckled at the sly plea. "Perhaps on the way back we can wash ourselves." She too longed to feel clean again—inside and out. Both women were wearing the only robes they owned, having used every stitch of cloth and clothing for Job's bandages. And it had been over a year since their inner cleansing of the morning sacrifice on Job's mountaintop altar. *Your tears are your sacrifice*, she'd told Job. *God knows your heart*. But did the same apply to her? Did El Shaddai know her heart longed to be forgiven and to forgive, that she would offer a thousand lambs if she had them?

Servants walked quickly past the beautiful gardens and courtyards of the merchants' homes, scurrying about their morning chores. Dinah averted her gaze from the rubble of Ennon's home. The smell of decay had finally faded, but the wreckage was a reminder of Sayyid's unrelenting wickedness. He had convinced the elders to leave the ruins untouched for fear of retribution from the gods, but Dinah was convinced he simply wanted to punish Job.

His relationship with Sitis still puzzled her. When Sitis had introduced them that day in the courtyard, Dinah thought she'd noted Sayyid's deep affection for Job's wife. But a man in love did not make his beloved a slave in another man's home.

Dinah and Nogahla rounded the jagged corner of the private canyon, where Job's and Sayyid's homes were carved into opposing cliffs like soldiers arrayed for battle. "Mistress," Nogahla whispered, "when will Elihu return with Master Job's relatives? He's getting sicker every day, and I'm not sure how much longer Mistress Sitis can work as a servant. She wasn't born to it like we—I mean, like I was."

Dinah smiled down at the girl. "Mistress Sitis has done remarkably well for a woman born to privilege, but you're right, Nogahla." Dinah placed a comforting arm around her friend's shoulders. "I hope Elihu comes soon."

At the sight of black-cloaked guards surrounding Sayyid's home, Dinah remembered her relief a few days after Elihu's departure, when she'd overheard a guard's reported failure to capture the young man. "El Elyon is faithful!" she had told Job excitedly. "We must tell Sitis that Elihu escaped safely and that he will surely return soon with your relatives." Job had tried to nod his head, tried to smile. But both elicited his now familiar face of pain—a quick breath, gritting teeth, and welling tears. She couldn't remember him smiling since.

"Dinah!" A shrill voice echoed against the canyon walls, and both women turned to find Sitis running behind them. "Wait, I want to talk to you before you see Job." The mistress arrived huffing and trembling, her eyes sunken and shadowed.

Dinah reached out to steady her. "Mistress Sitis, you are not well. Sit down." Guiding her to a low-lying rock, Dinah wished she had some cool water to offer the woman. "Your face is pale and clammy. When was the last time you ate?" The woman had lost so much weight that her robe folded almost twice around her.

Sitis glanced at Nogahla, seemingly uncomfortable at the maid's presence. Dinah winked at the girl, and the little Cushite smiled knowingly. "I believe I'll go back to the waterfall for a quick bath."

Relief washed over Sitis's face when Nogahla walked away, but she seemed self-conscious, picking at a callus on one of her trembling hands. "I haven't eaten a full meal since I began working for Bela."

"What?" Dinah laid a steadying hand on Sitis's shoulder and tried to peer into her lowered gaze. "Mistress Sitis, doesn't he feed his servants?"

Tears sprang up immediately. "Please don't call me mistress, and yes, of course he feeds his servants. He just doesn't feed *me*." She wiped her eyes before they overflowed. "He gives me only one piece of bread and a bowl of gruel each day. When I asked him why the other servants ate two meals a day, he said he was following Sayyid's strict orders, and if I had any complaints, I should take them to Sayyid."

Sitis pulled away and stared into the distance, her posture

as straight as an arrow in a warrior's quiver. Dinah wondered if this woman would open her heart to anyone ever again.

"Sitis, I want to be your friend." Dinah understood the need to keep people at a distance. Sitis had lost her children, home, and social standing, and then Sayyid took Nada from her. "Tell me how I can help you."

Sitis's lips trembled as she spoke, every fiber of her being seemingly focused on maintaining the little dignity she had left. "I've been eating my portion of gruel, but I pilfer my piece of bread for Job."

Dinah started to question, to ask why she must steal her own bread. But before the words were formed, Sitis suddenly fell into her arms, heaving giant sobs, bathing Dinah's shoulder with her tears. Restraint was finally gone, the walls tumbling down. Dinah was so shocked, she said nothing for a long while, simply letting the woman release her seemingly endless sorrow.

When Sitis's crying slowed, she sat back, and this time reached out for Dinah's hands. "Sayyid has ordered the guards to give Job only broth because I've refused his repeated marriage proposals." Sitis glanced over Dinah's shoulder, whispering because of the echo in the canyon. Desperation set in. "Bela discovered I've been bringing my bread to Job, and now he's cut my ration to only gruel. It probably won't matter anyway. Job hasn't been eating the bread." She slammed her fist on her leg. "He can't chew, Dinah. His gums are swollen, and he's in so much pain. I don't know what else to do!"

Dinah hugged her fiercely and whispered in her ear, "Job needs to eat, but so do you. Widow Orma has been very generous to Nogahla and me. Yahweh provided the widow with a servant's position, and she shares her two meals with us. Nogahla and I can bring part of our portions to Job."

"No!" Sitis pulled away, her voice echoing against the canyon walls.

"Shh," Dinah cautioned. "Why not?"

"If you're caught, Sayyid will harm the widow or you or Nogahla, or . . ." Sitis's crying made the rest of her reasoning unintelligible, but Dinah understood. Sayyid's power seemed absolute in Uz. He'd blocked any opportunity for Dinah to use her midwife skills. He'd also hired the Nameless Ones to restore Job's home, paying the bandits with the wealth he confiscated from Job's Hebron caravan and what little he could scavenge from the shell of Job's palace. The Nameless Ones had lingered for over a year, their only progress being the height of the ash pile that added to Job's torment and soaked up the seeping of his sores.

Where are You, El Shaddai? Dinah prayed. The only sign of God's intervention was Job's grueling survival amid unspeakable suffering. *But Yahweh must have some great plan for Job if He has sustained him this long.*

Dinah held Sitis until the sun peeked over the eastern cliffs. The woman cried so many tears, she could have filled the central fountain three times over, but Dinah felt honored to be the pool that caught them. "Sitis, I will pray for your wisdom," she said finally. "I believe El Shaddai will direct you in the days to come, and surely Elihu will return soon with your brother and Job's uncle."

Sitis's features grew hard, her chin suddenly set in a defiant tilt. "Bildad and Eliphaz are powerful men, but they live their own lives. Bildad never had time for me as a child. I don't expect his comfort as an adult. And as for your El Shaddai—He would never direct me after I've committed such blasphemy against Him." Shrugging her shoulders, she added, "Besides,

I've given up on all the gods. What good have they ever done me?" She stood and wiped her face, erasing all evidence of emotion. Dinah recognized the familiar mask of indifference she had once worn, now fixed firmly on Sitis's face.

Oh, El Shaddai, please give me wisdom to show her Your love and forgiveness as Job showed it to me. Dinah didn't correct or reprove. Sitis simply needed to be loved.

When the woman turned to walk out of the canyon, Dinah's heart plummeted. "Aren't you going to see Job?"

"Please tell my husband I hope to visit him later today." Sitis looked toward Sayyid's home and then set out toward the siq. "I may have found a way to make the elders listen to my demands."

※※※※※

Job watched Sitis walk out of the canyon, away from Dinah, and disappointment stabbed him. He watched Nogahla pass his wife and crane her neck, probably wondering, like him, why she was leaving so soon. Walking toward his dung heap, Dinah looked worried and drawn. *El Shaddai, if Your plan was to humble me, You've done it.* He'd brought this beautiful young woman to Uz to redeem her future, to give her a life after she'd experienced nothing but death and tragedy. Instead, she had saved both him and Sitis, offering friendship and a keen knowledge of herbal medicine after Sayyid had banned everyone in the city from helping them.

"Good morning!" Dinah called from beyond Sayyid's guards, four men posted at the perimeter of Job's canopied courtyard. She nodded curtly in their direction but walked past them as if she wore Philistine armor.

How I wish I could shout back my answer, Job thought, his

throat raw with sores. He studied her features, the painted-on smile, the sad eyes, the quaking cheeks. She'd been crying. What had she and Sitis discussed?

"How are you this morning? Any change?" Dinah slipped off her sandals at the edge of the ash heap and climbed to the peak where Job was seated. He noticed Aban approach quickly and little Nogahla offer a tentative smile. Dinah must have noticed as well, and she stood like a sentinel between them until Nogahla's sandals were removed and the girl was halfway up the ash heap.

Job silently applauded Dinah's maternal protection. Aban seemed too good to be true, apparently a compassionate mountain of a man, yet subservient to Sayyid's wickedness. The captain slowed at Dinah's challenge, pretending some issue with one of his guards but maintaining his boyish gander at Nogahla.

"No change," Job croaked to Dinah, his voice rougher than usual with its first use of the day. The women sat on his right and left, no sign of disgust on their features, no revulsion or recoiling, though the worms in Job's wounds still nauseated him.

"The worms aren't all bad," Dinah had said after using the last of the frankincense and myrrh several moons ago. "The worms will eat away the infection." But Job appreciated their unplanned benefit. Before the grotesque infestation, Sayyid's children by his concubines often crossed the canyon and braved the ash piles to throw dust or spit on him. Though not Sayyid's legal heirs, they had certainly inherited his wicked character. The worms may not have eaten away all the infection, but they certainly scared away the heartless little children and even gave the taunting Nameless Ones pause.

216

"Good morning, Master Job." Nogahla's brilliant smile lifted his heart. He winked at her, their secret greeting.

"All right," Dinah said, reaching for the bandage on his left hand. "It's time for you to tell me about Bildad and Eliphaz while Nogahla and I change your bandages."

"It hurts to speak," he croaked, hoping the excuse would save him the emotional pain.

"I know, and I'm sorry we didn't bring the mint tea to soothe your throat." Dinah's voice was weary with sadness. "But Sitis is hurting too, Job, and I need to know her history in order to help."

Job nodded. Perhaps talking would distract him from the pain of the bandaging process, but where did one begin a life story?

While Dinah tenderly untied the first knot, he realized he should start with their connection to her abba. "Both Bildad and Eliphaz were disciples with your abba Jacob in the House of Shem. All three were my teachers." He winced as Dinah pulled away the bandage, expecting overwhelming pain but relieved when it was manageable.

"Oh, Job," Dinah said, gasping. Tears welled in her eyes. Nogahla staggered back.

Job looked at his hand and found the tips of his fingers gone. His fingernails had fallen away last week, and he'd felt no pain in his fingertips since then. Now he knew why. "Perhaps we'll leave the bandages off my hands and feet," he said, awed at the surreal sight. "That way I can at least say good-bye to them when they leave."

Dinah wasn't easily shaken, but she seemed unable to speak. Nodding her head, she continued to unbind his wounds, and Job was suddenly struck with an unusual wave of thanksgiv-

217

ing. For weeks he'd fought bitterness and despair as effectively as eating soup with two fingers. Now he prayed aloud, hoping to spill encouragement to his caregivers. "El Shaddai, thank You for my pain. At least my flesh is alive when I feel the pain."

Tears threatened, and in an effort to keep the fiery drops from his fleshy cheeks, he continued with his story. "As I was saying, Uncle Eliphaz, Bildad, and Jacob taught both Zophar and me at the House of Shem. Uncle Eliphaz is Great-Abba Esau's firstborn son, and Zophar is Uncle Eliphaz's third-born son."

Nogahla grinned, wiping a tear and unwrapping the large bandage from Job's torso. "You're making my head hurt, Master Job—thirdborn, firstborn, abba, uncle."

Job tried to smile but simply managed to clench his teeth and draw in a quick breath against the pain. "Just remember this," he said, when he could speak again. "Uncle Eliphaz was like a father to me when Great-Abba Esau killed my father."

"What?" Dinah straightened, hands on hips, a single tear still lingering on one cheek.

Job gazed at the woman whose sapphire blue eyes could rain compassion one moment and cast daggers the next. "Uncle Eliphaz was to lead my abba and several others to kill your abba Jacob after he stole Esau's covenant blessing. When Eliphaz spared Jacob's life, my abba told Esau the news. The Edomites say Esau simply shoved Abba, who then struck his head on a rock—but we all know it isn't true."

Her hands fell limp, resting at her sides, eyes soft and compassionate again. "I have seen you with Esau, Job. How do you show him love and respect after such a wrong?"

"Because El Shaddai forgives me for the wrongs I commit, Dinah, I can then forgive others." Job watched his words settle into her heart, her features change from granite to workable clay.

"Master Job takes lots of baths." Nogahla exchanged a knowing grin with Dinah.

"Baths?" Job glanced at the women, waiting with anticipation for another of Nogahla's simple treasures of wisdom.

"Ugh!" Dinah expressed her good-natured frustration. "I have found it difficult to forgive someone." She cast a sidelong glance at Sayyid's big captain still hovering at the base of the pile. "Nogahla explained to me this morning that forgiveness is like taking a bath. We do it over and over to stay clean."

Again Job winked at the wise young girl and offered an approving nod to Dinah. Jacob's daughter had proven fertile soil, a soul hungry for Yahweh.

"All right," she said in feigned reproach, "continue with your story."

"After my abba died, Uncle Eliphaz raised me as his own son, continually teaching me the ways of El Shaddai. That's why his son Zophar and I are like brothers."

He noticed Dinah's discomfort at Zophar's name. "So tell me about Bildad," she said, searching through her basket, not so subtly changing the subject.

Job's heart squeezed a little. How much should he say about Sitis's older brother? He respected the man without question, but Bildad had hurt Sitis deeply and repeatedly, and she still carried the scars. "Bildad is the son of Shuah, but neither are truly Ishmaelites."

Dinah set down her basket and herb pots, staring at Job in disbelief. "What do you mean? I've never heard this. Shuah is a great prince of Ishmael, and Bildad, a prince after him."

"Yes, but Ishmael *adopted* Shuah. The two are actually

brothers by blood. Ishmael is Abraham's son by Hagar, just as Shuah is Abraham's son by Keturah. When Abraham died, Isaac received all his father's wealth, so Keturah was left without provision. Ishmael married the young slave-widow and adopted her sons as his own."

Dinah blinked in astonishment. Job wished he could smile at the innocent shock on her face, but the stretch of his mouth would cost him too much. "Bildad views his disheveled heritage as a reason to prove himself. His heart is committed to teaching El Shaddai's truths to the Ishmaelites though he acknowledges Isaac's line holds the covenant blessing." Job's heart ached at the thought. "Just as my heart was committed to teaching El Shaddai's truths to my family—the Edomites—though I acknowledge your abba's line holds the blessing."

Lost in grief at the mission that had died with his sons, Job didn't realize Dinah had drawn close enough to whisper in his ear. "Why does Sitis feel Bildad betrayed her?" she asked.

Job squeezed his eyes closed and let salty tears and the excruciating stretching of his sores overwhelm the pain in his heart. "I don't want to talk about that."

Dinah paused. She seemed to respect his pain, but her intruding voice demanded an answer. "I need to know, Job. If Bildad doesn't return with Elihu, I must try to mend Sitis's broken heart."

Opening his eyes, Job saw both Dinah and Nogahla waiting, concern etched on their faces. "Bildad studied at the House of Shem from the time he was eleven, instructed by Noah's great-grandson Eber, of the priestly line of Shem. Bildad, Eliphaz, Zophar, your abba, and I are the only living disciples of Noah's direct descendants. Bildad was forty when his and Sitis's mother died, and their father died soon after.

Bildad chose to continue his training at the House of Shem instead of returning home to be a father to Sitis. She blames Bildad *and* El Shaddai that she was raised by servants. She loved Atif and Nada but always felt neglected by her brother." Job bowed his head. "But the second betrayal was worse. Bildad forced her to marry a disciple of the House of Shem rather than the man she loved." He couldn't voice the names aloud. *El Shaddai, please let Dinah and Nogahla understand.*

"She loves that man from the House of Shem now, Master Job," Nogahla said, tears glistening. "And she will see the wisdom of El Shaddai soon."

Dinah spoke in barely a whisper. "How could you allow Sayyid to live across this canyon all these years? This was *your* city. You could have banished him." Her voice rose, every word feeling more like an accusation. Still, he was glad the women had guessed who the men were without an explanation.

"At first I didn't know who my young bride mourned. By the time I discovered it was Sayyid, he'd become an established merchant in Uz, and I thought I'd won my wife's heart." His lips trembled. "Dinah, true love must be chosen, not forced. If I had imprisoned my wife or removed her choice, would I ever have been certain of her love? Even this morning, when I watched Sitis walk away without visiting me, I didn't question her love. I only feared for her soul."

He watched a spark of angst ignite in Dinah's eyes. "We must pray for Sitis, Job."

A writhing dread burned in Job's belly at the words.

"I don't know what her plans entail, but I fear for more than her soul right now."

14

~*Job 2:8–10*~

*Then Job took a piece of broken pottery
and scraped himself with it as he sat among
the ashes. His wife said to him, "Are you still
holding on to your integrity? Curse God and
die!" He replied, "You are talking like a foolish
woman. Shall we accept good from God, and
not trouble?" In all this, Job did not sin in what
he said.*

Sitis walked through the busy marketplace, parting the
citizens of Uz like the bow of a ship in the Great Sea.
Most stared in silence, but some pointed and mocked the
disheveled, dethroned queen of Uz.

"Where is your master?" Sitis asked one of the bread vendors,
her stomach rumbling at the aroma of the warm, brown loaves.

"Master Sayyid is at the city gate with the other elders," the
loathsome man answered, his teeth the color of desert sand,

his breath like camel droppings. "Mistress Sitis is looking a little worse for wear these days. Hard work is hard, eh, mistress?" He threw his head back, laughing. The open ridicule seemed to empower the crowd, who no longer made way for Sitis's passage. She was jostled from side to side as others in the unforgiving crowd joined the mockery.

Were these the same people she and Job had served in their home at the beggars' tables? Hadn't she been kind to them? Hadn't Job taken food from his own children's mouths to feed these ungrateful slugs? She struggled like a donkey in deep sand, wading through the throng toward the ornately carved pillars at the city gate, where Sayyid stood screaming at a caravan merchant.

"My barley and wheat are the best-quality grain in any city from Egypt to Damascus. You're a fool to buy your grain in Egypt and try to transport it all the way up to your northern cities."

"I'm sorry, Master Sayyid," said the man, red-faced, "but Egypt's vizier has been stockpiling grain for seven years. He can offer his grain at a lower price, and we can trade twice as much by the time we reach Uz."

"Who is this imbecile? Doesn't he understand the complexities of trading, bartering, and caravanning for all the cities along the trade routes? Egypt's grain can't last forever, you know, and when the Nile basin shrinks to a withered brown hole, that arrogant vizier will have to get on a camel and curry the favor of merchants like me." Sayyid's composure looked badly chipped and nearly broken.

Sitis smiled for the first time in several full moons.

The merchant bowed but remained silent. Sayyid sat down sullenly and let Bela present his merchandise.

"Now, my gems are not so dependent on Egypt's weather, good man," Bela began smoothly.

Sitis rolled her eyes, nauseated at Bela's hypocrisy. He was a fat cow who starved his servants. A man who spoiled his wife to gain more concubines. Because he was an Edomite, and therefore a kinsman to Job, Sitis had been compelled in her previous prosperity to invite Bela and his wife to annual celebrations. Bela had eaten at their feasts, drank their wine, played with their children. Now he treated her as if she were lower than a slave, less than a woman. It was clear he'd helped Sayyid ruin Job, and by the gods, Sitis would repay him today.

"I have a complaint to bring before the elders!" Sitis lifted her chin and gathered her tattered dignity.

The visiting merchant trying to haggle for Bela's gems sneered as though she was rotting fruit on the refuse pile, but Bela's expression grew fearful.

Sayyid rose from his marble elder's throne, standing beside his portly Edomite friend. "I'm sorry, sir," he said to the disgruntled trader, "but this woman once held a position of some importance in this town, and we must be patient with her." Offering a forbearing smile, he nodded to Sitis and resumed his seat.

The commotion had drawn the attention of the bustling market, which had fallen as quiet as a tomb. Villagers hurried to the city gate, every voice hushed, every eye focused on the once great lady of Uz.

Sitis straightened her posture and held her head high, reminding herself she was an Ishmaelite princess, daughter of Shuah, sister of Bildad. "Elders of Uz, I have been wronged by my current employer." Worry lines deepened on Bela's forehead, and she delighted in his obvious discomfort. "Bela

224

has chosen to obey Sayyid's instruction to give me only one bowl of gruel each day in order to keep me from sharing bread with my husband."

Sitis had chosen her words carefully, pregnant with insinuation, yet veiled enough to save Sayyid's reputation if he wished to recant. She hated Bela with all her heart, but a part of her still wanted to believe Sayyid was capable of kindness—if he was forced into it.

Bela's mouth opened and closed several times, emitting no sound. He was as awkward as a newborn camel, and Sitis smelled victory in the silence. But Sayyid stepped forward again, brushing aside the flustered elder.

"Citizens and visitors of Uz, if you would gather round, please." Sayyid spread his arms grandly, like a father welcoming his children to a feast.

A terrible sense of foreboding wrapped Sitis like a shroud.

"Let me restate Mistress Sitis's complaint for all to hear. She's offended that I have limited her daily ration to one bowl of gruel. How many of you eat only one bowl of gruel a day? Come on, let me see your hands."

Several in the crowd lifted their hands, and Sitis could feel her cheeks warm. "Sayyid, you know that's not my point."

He held up his hand to silence her. "Mistress Sitis has forgotten that a petitioner remains silent when an elder begins his judgment." Offering her a denigrating smile, he continued. "But the mistress has neglected to inform the elders of the reason for her small ration. Out of respect for Sitis's *past* position in this city, Bela has remained silent about her laziness."

"What? I am not lazy!"

Disapproving stares shot at Sitis like darts.

"The woman takes off at all times of day and night—as she

has done today—to visit her husband and rest in the sun." Sayyid allowed his words to further unsettle the grumbling crowd. He pierced Sitis with raven black eyes, and she was finally convinced they reflected the complete evil of his heart.

She bowed her head, listening to the dying rumble of the crowd. When she looked up again, Sayyid had descended the platform and was standing before her.

"Mistress Sitis, I would be happy to *sell* you some bread. For a price. As we speak, my vendors' booths are full of warm loaves." The crowd was now hushed, seeming to relish her humiliation. When she hesitated, Sayyid feigned shock. "Surely you don't expect me to simply *give* you bread."

Sitis bowed her head. "I cannot pay you for bread, Sayyid. You know this."

"I'm sorry, Mistress Sitis. I couldn't hear you. What was that?"

She looked up, expecting some mercy, some relenting from this torture. "Sayyid, please." Tears began spilling down her cheeks. She couldn't lose control in front of these people.

"Truly, Sitis, the bread is just waiting for you if you'd like to purchase it."

Feeling her lips quiver, she tried to speak. She closed her eyes, fighting for composure. "I don't have any gold or silver kesitahs, Sayyid, and you know it!" she screamed at him, and began beating his chest.

He grabbed her wrists and held them with as little effort as a child's toy. "Come now, Sitis. We both know you can buy bread with something other than gold or silver." His voice mocked her, and when she stopped struggling, she gazed into the face of evil personified.

"You wouldn't ask it of me, not in front of all these people."

Sayyid bent to whisper in her ear. "Don't worry, Sitis-girl. I wouldn't marry you now if you begged me."

"Ohh!" She began kicking and fighting, but he was too strong. His laughter rang out, and the crowd joined his mocking.

When all her energy was spent, she collapsed, sobbing. Sayyid slipped one arm around her waist and carried her, lying limp over his arm, to the same bread vendor she'd visited on her way to the gate. "Come, Sitis, let me show you my price."

Sitis glanced up at what seemed to be the whole town behind them. Too beaten to care, she leaned against the one she had leaned on all her life. "What do you want from me, Sayyid? We need bread." His arm tightened around her waist, and he drew her chin back against his chest. She could feel his heavy breathing, but he said nothing.

He glanced at the vendor and said, "Give her your stool."

While the man hurriedly placed the stool in front of his booth, Sayyid set her down roughly. The bread vendor shielded them momentarily from the approaching crowd, and Sayyid stood behind her. As he loomed over her, his hand, hidden from the crowd, found its way inside her robe.

She was too weak to fight but whispered, "Please, Sayyid, stop." Her sobs were a muffled whimper, choked by shame.

"Do you want bread?" he whispered.

Her head rested against him. As she looked up through her tears, his face no longer appeared as her handsome friend but as the fiendish mask of an enemy. "Yes. We need bread."

"Then I will never stop." Removing his hand, he stood and held her head roughly between both hands. To the crowd, he announced, "Mistress Sitis has agreed to trade her hair for three loaves of bread." At the first tug, her headpiece fell to the ground, and Sayyid combed his fingers through her loosely braided hair.

"Sayyid, what are you doing?" It was Bela's voice. "Women are shielding their children's eyes and turning away."

"The woman and I have struck a bargain," Sayyid replied. "Her hair for bread." His rough hands continued their probing, meticulously unweaving Sitis's long braid. Each stroke became bolder. "I am inspecting my payment." Sayyid's voice was dreamy, distracted.

Sitis squeezed her eyes shut, her heart beating faster as he clutched great fistfuls of her hair and caressed her throat. Tears flowed amid moaning sobs. If she had been stripped naked, she wouldn't have felt more exposed.

A presence stood in front of her, blocking the afternoon sunlight. "Sayyid, you must stop this." Bela's voice again. Urgent now. "People are leaving. They're offended at this spectacle."

Sitis reached for her head covering to hide her shame, but Sayyid used her hair like a bit and bridle, pulling her back into submission. When she cried out under the force of his iron grip, he laughed.

"Let the women take their children home," he said. "The men will enjoy it more if their wives are gone."

Sitis began to tremble, a soft whine threatening to overtake her. She felt her sanity slipping away—until she heard the sing of Sayyid's dagger unsheathing. The cold blade rested against her cheek, focusing her senses.

"You're mine now, Sitis-girl," he said, leaning in so only she could hear. "You may take this bread to Job and tell him good-bye. Then you will enter my household—not as the wife you could have been, but as the concubine you will become."

In what seemed a dream, she nodded her consent and heard a sickening *swoosh!* Sitis felt Sayyid's blade slice off fifty-six years of luxuriant hair. The few stragglers drew a collective gasp. Her heart slammed against her chest, and she longed to cry for help—but what god would hear her? She fell forward, burying her face in her hands, hiding at least the windows of her soul from those in the public square.

"I will have no further part in this," she heard Bela whisper to Sayyid.

"I have no further need of your services," Sayyid said. "I have finally broken her. Sitis is mine now."

✾ ✾ ✾ ✾ ✾

Job had spent most of the morning gazing at his unbandaged hands, trying to determine which fingers—if any—would recover fingernails. *El Elyon, if I live through this, will You restore my flesh?*

Dinah had suggested leaving most of his sores uncovered today in hopes that fresh air would speed his healing process. They had moved him to the farthest ash pile in hopes that the Nameless Ones wouldn't spray him with ash or dung, and Nogahla had spoken to Sayyid's captain, asking for special protection while the wounds were completely exposed. After his caregivers left, Job wondered if Dinah's suggestion was motivated by medical genius or the inevitable shortage of bandages. She said she would return this evening to check on his progress, and when she did, she would get an earful of complaints. He itched terribly! And without fingernails to scratch himself, he had resorted to shattering one of her discarded pots and scraping the wounds with the shards.

He was in the midst of a frenzied scratching fit when Sitis's voice split the afternoon sounds. "By the gods, Job, look at you."

He jumped as if a shofar had sounded in his left ear. "Oh! Sitis, you startled me." His voice was still raspy and painful, but he was pleased she had drawn so near to him this afternoon. Usually she stood several paces away because of the odor. "What's this?" For the first time, he noticed three loaves of bread in her arms. Her headpiece looked odd, and she'd been crying. "What happened, my love?"

"What happened? You ask me what happened? I'll tell you what happened, Job." Her cheeks flamed, and she threw the loaves—one at a time—on the dung heap. "Your God has abandoned you. That's what happened. Are you still holding on to your integrity? Are you still saying He will defend you, restore you someday?"

"Sitis, tell me what has happened so I can help you."

"You can't help me, Job!" She tore off her headpiece, revealing patchy, cropped hair. "The only way you can help me is to curse your God and die. Die! Release me from this marriage and let Sayyid do with me as he wishes." She picked up a handful of ashes and threw them with such force, she fell to the ground. "Let me go to the man I deserve!" She lay there swimming in ash and dung.

Job's breaths came in giant gulps, his mind spinning, the pain in his heart now greater than the excruciating sores on his body. *El Shaddai, help me! What has happened to her hair, her dignity, her strength?*

"Sitis, look at me!" he shouted as best he could. The woman at the edge of the dung heap was writhing in sorrow. "Sitis, you're not making sense. Tell me what's happened."

He choked out the words, horrified at the thought. "I will never let Sayyid do with you as he wishes."

She grew still and gazed at him with bleary eyes. "I want to sleep on a wool-stuffed mattress again, Job. I want to drink honeyed wine in the shade. I'm tired of cleaning slop jars and being whipped by a lazy witch." She began to beat her fists into the dung pile. "Please, Job. Please. Curse your God and die. I beg you. And release me from this torment." She buried her face again, her shoulders heaving with great sobs.

Job searched the tattered woman he'd called wife for so many years. "My precious Sitis, how can we accept good from God and not trouble? This will pass, my love, but my commitment to you and to my God will endure forever."

"Nooo!" she cried. "Please, Job. Please, stop." She lifted her face.

"Sitis, come to me." He spoke softly now, barely over a whisper. "Come to me, my wife."

She lay still, staring at him in silence. He wondered for a moment if she'd even heard his plea. Finally, she began to crawl on hands and knees toward the pinnacle of Job's ashes. She'd never come this close without covering her face against the stench, and Job saw her gag several times before reaching the top. Judging from her frail frame and dry heaves, it could have been days since she'd eaten anything.

She sat beside him and refused to meet his gaze, staring instead across the canyon at Sayyid's grand palace. "Please curse your God, Job. Please do *something* dishonorable so I can stop loving you."

"I will not curse God, Sitis."

"Sayyid cut my hair in the public market today as payment for that bread." She motioned to the three cold loaves lying in the ashes and began to cry again. "I'm not strong like you, Job. I don't deserve your love. Part of me enjoyed Sayyid's touch. It's been so long since I've felt a man's contact . . ." She covered her face and fell silent. "Curse your God, Job," she breathed, "and release us both from this misery. I deserve a man like Sayyid, and you deserve a good woman like . . . like Dinah."

The words were like a searing blade piercing Job's soul. "I will not curse El Shaddai, Sitis." Tears burned the sores on his cheeks. "I love you, my wife. I will always love you."

He reached for her, but she pulled away, crying out when she saw the deformity of his hands. "How can you keep faith with a God who does this to you—to us?"

And then her face registered a horror that surpassed even the night of the tragedies.

"El Shaddai has done this because of my blasphemy, because of my idolatry!" She scrambled to her feet, crouching over Job, then backing away slowly. "This is my fault, Job. My children are dead because of me. Our home destroyed because of me. You've lost your fingers because of—" Hysterical, she ran down the ash heap.

"Sitis, no, wait!" Job's weak voice was swallowed up in the immense canyon, but to his utter amazement—and relief—his wife ran headlong into Dinah.

✤✤✤✤✤

Sayyid waited in his bedchamber for Sitis, sipping sweet wine as a serving girl fanned him with an ostrich plume. *How long does it take to deliver three loaves of bread to a leprous husband?* Of course, the maids would need time to bathe her—especially after visiting Job on that dung heap.

But after forty-one years of waiting, Sayyid would finally taste the forbidden fruit of his Sitis-girl. He swished a mouthful of wine through his teeth and eyed his chambermaid. She kept her gaze averted, using the black-and-white feathers to stir warm afternoon air with deep, rhythmic stabs.

"Come here, girl." Sayyid studied his newest young Sitis, her glossy raven hair and full lips. Though he would soon possess his one true obsession, he would always need the young replicas—especially since Sitis had become disheveled and gaunt in the past year.

Setting aside the ostrich plume, the maid's hands trembled, and she smoothed her sky blue linen robe.

Just as he pulled her into his arms, a violent knocking resounded on his chamber door. "Master Sayyid! I have urgent news of utmost importance."

"Aban, someone had better be dying or *you* are dead, my friend!" Sayyid leapt from his seat, and the girl jumped back like a skittish mare. He clutched the collar of her robe, drawing her close enough to smell the frankincense he insisted all his girls wear. It was the scent of royalty, the scent Sitis had worn since they were children. "Pick up your fan. We are not finished yet." By the time he'd released her, Aban had entered the chamber.

"Master, our scouts have just returned with word of a great army approaching Uz." His chest was heaving, beads of sweat rolling down his forehead.

"What? Uz has never been at war." Sayyid felt the blood drain from his face. "What *great army* would dare attack our town? Job has a family treaty with the Edomites and Sitis with the Ishmaelites."

"Sitis's brother Bildad and Job's uncle Eliphaz lead the

army. Our scouts say that Bildad commands at least a thousand men and Eliphaz over seven hundred. The merchant Zophar travels with them, his caravan loaded with supplies, presumably to restock Job's household."

"How long before they arrive?" Sayyid choked out the words, considering possible strategies.

"Just before dark." Aban paused. "It seems the young man Elihu was successful in his mission." The captain bowed as if his words sealed Sayyid's tomb.

A terrible premonition washed over Sayyid, and his feet felt rooted to his bedchamber floor. As if lifting two boulders, he commanded his legs to carry him to the balcony. Desperately, he searched the canyon below. There on the dung pile were three discarded loaves of bread—his bread—and Sitis lying next to her leprous husband.

Something inside him snapped.

"Aban," he said barely above a whisper. When his captain didn't respond, Sayyid turned calmly and beckoned the man to the balcony railing. Aban obeyed, but reluctantly. Sayyid placed one hand on the large man's shoulder as if consulting a close friend. "Aban, are the Nameless Ones still refurbishing Job's home?"

"Yes, my lord," the guard said warily.

"Speak to their leader. I want him to kill Sitis. Now, this instant. He can name his price."

Though Aban was young, he was already a hardened warrior, nearly unshakable. However, this command slackened his jaw like a corpse.

Sayyid patted his cheek to draw a little blood to the surface. "Do you have a better idea, my friend? Shall we let Sitis show brother Bildad her hair, cry about her home, complain that

234

I let her children's flesh rot from their bones? Or will you join me in accusing the Nameless Ones of her murder and ascribing Job's ranting to a mind demented by the gods?"

Aban shoved away Sayyid's hand, his gaze hard and unwavering. "I will issue your command, but it will be the last time I obey you. I have wronged too many for too long with too little in return." His face twisted, disgust seeming to war with a burgeoning streak of greed. "From this moment on I will name *my* price for keeping your secrets. I will no longer call you master. You will show me respect, *Father*." The big man strode out of the chamber, his retreating footsteps echoing down the stairs.

Sayyid stood aghast. Silent. Stunned at Aban's sudden fury and insolence. His heart raced, and he struggled for control. No child of his concubines had ever dared assert their position as his offspring.

Only a moment passed, however, before a slow, wry smile replaced his shock. *Perhaps he is more like his father than I realized.*

An echoing chuckle rumbled from deep in his belly. Yes, Aban might someday be worthy of Sayyid's bequest. "But today you will obey me," he said aloud.

"Come, girl, you can fan me on my balcony," he said to his chambermaid. Turning toward the canyon, Sayyid watched Job's ash pile, ready to witness the end of his lifelong obsession.

15

~Job 2:11~

When Job's three friends, Eliphaz the Temanite,
Bildad the Shuhite and Zophar the Naamathite,
heard about all the troubles that had come upon
him, they set out from their homes and met
together by agreement to go and sympathize
with him and comfort him.

Dinah gathered Sitis in her arms, comforting the once proud Ishmaelite princess who was now stripped of her hair and dignity. "Sitis, I have no doubt it was Sayyid who did this to you." Bile rose in Dinah's throat at the thought of a man who could inflict such humiliation.

Nogahla deftly wrapped Sitis's headpiece around her short scalp of hair, and Dinah mouthed a silent "thank you."

"You're not going back to serve in Bela's household," she said as Sitis wept quietly. "Sayyid will find you there and mistreat you again." She bent down to meet the woman's gaze. "You'll come back to Widow Orma's cave and stay with Nogahla and me."

"No! I can't. I won't!" Sitis's eyes were suddenly wild, panicked, mirroring the confusion around them. The canyon echoed with children's playful songs, tambourines, and trilling flutes.

Dinah wanted to calm Sitis or at least ask why she reacted so vehemently, but a few paces away, the desert tribe pounded and scraped the walls of Job's home and shouted taunts at his pain. Job's wife began her march away from the dung heap.

"Sitis, wait!" Dinah cast a questioning glance at Nogahla. Perhaps she could guess at Sitis's hesitation. The girl just shrugged, so Dinah tried again. "I know it's only a cave, Sitis. It's not what you're used to, but—"

"No!" Sitis shouted as she turned. "I can't bring disaster on the widow, on you and Nogahla!" She whirled around and took another step. "Stay away from me. I'll bring a curse on you too!"

Dinah grabbed Sitis tightly, feeling every bone in her skeletal frame. Sitis flailed valiantly, but her strength was diminished by hunger and fatigue.

"Shh," Dinah soothed, "tell me what has happened. Tell me why you're so frightened." Dinah motioned Nogahla to ascend the ash heap, where Job was gesturing wildly and crying. Sitis finally sagged to the ground in Dinah's arms.

"I'm afraid of El Shaddai, Dinah," the woman said between hysterical hiccups. "All our tragedy is El Shaddai's punishment of *my* blasphemy, *my* idolatry. It's because El Shaddai is angry with *me*." She was limp, lying against Dinah like an infant in its mother's lap.

Dinah allowed a lingering silence to prepare the woman's

heart and then set her upright to look into her eyes. "And who has convinced you that this is Yahweh's punishment? Did El Shaddai reveal it to you?"

"I don't know." Sitis looked away, unable to hide her discomfort. "Not exactly."

"Did Job, the priest of your household, tell you the tragedies were judgment because of *your* sins?" Dinah waited, noting a slight spark of hope in the woman's dull stare.

"I think Job might have been trying to tell me my fears were unfounded, when I rushed away crying." Dinah watched the release of life-giving tears roll down Sitis's cheeks. "But Dinah, what other reason could there be for this punishment? Job certainly doesn't deserve this. It must be me. *I'm* the bad one. *I'm* unworthy. Don't you see?"

Dinah held Sitis's face tenderly between her hands. "I see more clearly than you know, my friend."

Sitis offered a furrowed brow and a puzzled tilt of her head.

Dinah chuckled at the irony. "Can you honestly say that I—Dinah of Shechem—don't understand feeling unworthy?"

Sitis tried to look away.

"No, don't turn away. Look at my face, Sitis. It bears no shame. Not anymore."

Sitis's eyes held new emotion. Compassion now mingled with sorrow. "Those stories can't be true, Dinah. I've seen who you really are. You couldn't have lured Prince Shechem into a false marriage or had any part in your brothers' murderous plot."

Dinah's heart stopped. There it was in an almond shell. The tale merchants and shepherds had told for twenty-one years. "No, Sitis. I did not lure Prince Shechem, and there was no plot. However, I sinned in my relationship with the prince, and my brothers' bloodstained hands carried me to

Canaan on Shechemite plunder. For these sins I bore shame for twenty years, but El Shaddai forgave me. He removed my shame and made me better than before."

Sitis's tears stopped, replaced by red-hot flames. "El Shaddai will never forgive me, and my life will never be better than before, Dinah. My children are gone. My home is destroyed. My—"

"I'm talking about *you*, Sitis," Dinah interrupted. "You will be better. Not your children or your possessions. You. Yahweh can wipe away your shame, and you can become cleaner, more complete, than ever before."

"El Shaddai might forgive others, but not one like me, who has blasphemed and cursed Him."

"El Shaddai forgives everyone who asks it of Him." Dinah locked Sitis in an unyielding stare, knowing intimately that secret turmoil between doubt and yearning. The silence stretched into discomfort, but neither woman was willing to look away—until something in the dust captured their attention.

Oop-oop-oop. The preening pink-and-black-crested hoopoe speared the dirt with its long beak, tossing dust into the air for a gritty bath. The beautiful little creature had no inkling of its significance, but Yahweh knew. And Dinah knew she should share her special treasure.

"Did you know that the hoopoe has recently become a sign of God's presence in my life, Mistress Sitis?" she confided. "Not an idol to be worshiped or an embodiment of El Shaddai Himself, but a reminder of His watchful care of even the most insignificant creatures." Dinah reached for Sitis's hands. "If Yahweh calls a hoopoe to encourage the brokenhearted, wouldn't that same caring God eagerly forgive anyone—no matter how undeserving—when they ask Him?"

A tentative glow rose in Sitis's features, and her voice rang with new clarity. "How do I ask Him to forgive me?" Her trembling returned, but it was accompanied by the hoopoe's trilling and her gentle gasp. "If Yahweh has the power to command the flight of a hoopoe, He could easily strike me dead. Are you sure He'll forgive me if I ask?"

Dinah watched the little bird run across the dusty canyon floor, and she shivered too—but from sheer joy at the prospect of Job's restored wife and marriage. "Yahweh won't strike you dead, my friend, and He will forgive you." Her words sounded more certain than she felt. Regardless, Job had helped her believe El Shaddai's mercy extended to any forlorn woman with a truly penitent heart. "Let's go tell your husband, and he can help you with the next step."

Just as the women turned toward Job's ash heap, they heard the thunderous pounding of a camel's swift approach.

"It's Elihu!" Sitis cried, looking over Dinah's shoulder and waving both hands wildly. Dinah saw joy light the woman's features, but just as suddenly watched disappointment strangle her hopes. She cupped her hands over her mouth and whispered, "He's alone, Dinah. Job's uncle Eliphaz and my brother have refused to help us." Letting her hands fall to her sides, she walked toward the dung heap. "Perhaps El Shaddai is the only one who can save us now."

✾✾✾✾✾

Aban stood inside Job's kitchen, peering around the archway at the approaching camel and rider. The scrawny, unkempt leader of the Nameless Ones gawked and prodded, trying to see past him. "Who's on that camel?"

Aban reminded himself to breathe through his mouth to

avoid the stench of the old man's breath. It could melt the skin off a snake. How could one so vile have risen to leadership over hundreds of men? Aban examined the desert bandit. The little man certainly couldn't overpower any of his ragtag crew, but perhaps he was as wily as he was repulsive.

Shrugging the old thief back, Aban returned his attention to the courtyard and canyon beyond. "The man on the camel is no one you know, but someone we should both fear."

The Nameless One straightened and smiled, a gaping hole where his front teeth used to dwell. "I fear no one, Captain, not even you."

Quicker than a cobra's strike, Aban clutched the man's throat and lifted his feet off the floor. "Then you are a fool, old man." The bandit sputtered and groveled, grasping Aban's forearm with both hands, gulping pleas for mercy. Aban released him and he stumbled, steadying himself with one hand against the wall. "Our plans must change." Aban spoke absently, returning his attention to Elihu, who was now dismounting his camel just outside the breached courtyard wall.

"Good. I have no patience for kidnapping." The little scoundrel sucked air between his back teeth. Probably dislodging some of the roast lamb Sayyid had provided for the bandits' midday meal. Aban turned toward the sound and noticed the man studying him. "I had hoped Master Sayyid would order me to kill Mistress Sitis, not *kidnap* her."

"No!" Aban roared, and the Nameless One staggered back. "The plan remains kidnapping. You are not to harm Mistress Sitis, do you understand?"

"All right. All right." Both sooty hands went up in mock surrender. "What do you suppose Master Sayyid wants us to

do with the woman now that our new visitor has arrived?"
The bandit's beady eyes and self-assured smile danced with
suspicion.

Had he somehow guessed Aban's double cross of Sayyid's
murderous command? Regardless, Aban refused to let any
harm come to Sitis. The woman looked just as he remembered
his mother—before Sayyid sold her to Egyptian traders. The
same fiery spirit that sustained Mistress Sitis through Sayyid's
abuse had also dwelt in his mother, giving her the needed
strength to serve such a man.

"I will take care of making plans, old man. You take care
of following my orders." Aban leaned down to meet his gaze.
"Now get back to work until I call for you again."

A chill skittered down Aban's spine at the wildness in the
man's eyes. This wilderness lunatic was unpredictable enough
to ignore both him and Sayyid. The only reason the Nameless
Ones had obeyed them at all was because of Sayyid's constant
supply of food and the roof over their heads. Thankfully, they
seemed in no hurry to return to their desolate wasteland to
eat salt herbs and broom tree roots.

⁜⁜⁜⁜⁜

Job's heart raced at the sight of Elihu's bouncing form on
the galloping camel. If he'd not been overcome with grief for
his wife's humiliation, he might have even felt some hope at
the young man's return.

"Nogahla, you must go and persuade Sitis to come up
here so I can talk with her." Job's voice was barely a whisper
now. His attempts at shouting must have torn open the sores
in his throat. He was now spitting blood into the only clean
bandage Nogahla had rationed for the day.

"Master Job, I'm sure Mistress Dinah is coaxing her to do that very thing, but you must trust El Shaddai to do His work." The girl sat close beside him, as comfortable as his own daughter.

Job watched Dinah's ministrations, silently praying for her wisdom and for Sitis's receptive heart. *El Shaddai, I would bear ten times the pain of my sores if You would just heal my precious wife. Please, Yahweh, know her despair and heal her inner wounds!*

When Sitis turned toward the ash pile and gazed up at Job, something had changed in her countenance. Job cast a questioning glance at Dinah, who stood at the base of the heap with glistening eyes and a glorious smile. Her hands were pressed together at her lips as though in grateful prayer. And Job knew. Sitis was indeed healed—from the inside out.

He began to cry. Silent weeping shook his whole frame.

Nogahla panicked and stood, motioning wildly. "Mistress, mistress! Something is terribly wrong with Master Job! Come quickly!"

He smiled and shushed Nogahla, trying to assuage his adorable Cushite daughter. Then he held out his arms to his wife, who began to weep and smile and then to laugh. How long had it been since he'd seen Sitis laugh?

She pumped her legs, trying to run up the dung pile, but the faster she churned, the deeper her feet dug into the mire. Sitis stumbled again and again, making the moments linger. The dawning realization changed Nogahla's cries into a happy jig atop the heap. Dinah was suddenly beside Sitis, lending a hand to aid her ascent, but Sitis stopped short of falling into Job's arms.

"I want to cling to you, my husband," she said through

243

tears. "I want to hold you close and whisper in your ear." She looked at Dinah and then reached out to take Nogahla's hand, touching the Cushite for the first time in Job's memory. "Or perhaps I feel more like shouting it from the mountaintop altar." She searched her husband's face, her voice quivering. "Dinah said if I ask El Shaddai to forgive me, He will do it."

Job ached to caress her cheek, but he dare not move lest he wake from the dream. His dream reached out to touch his cheek instead.

"Job," she said, "will your Yahweh forgive me?"

"Yes!" came the confident squeak from Nogahla's lips, quickly reined in by both hands tightly clasped over her lips. Her penitent glance darted from one face to another, while Job reveled in her true and simple faith.

"Our friend is correct as usual," Job agreed with a twinkle in his eye. Tentatively he covered his wife's hand on his cheek and marveled at two miracles. First, the pain did not overwhelm him, and second, Sitis did not recoil. "Normally I would sacrifice a lamb on the altar for your sins, but El Shaddai knows the intentions of our hearts, my love."

Just then a terrible wailing stole their attention, and everyone turned to see Elihu fall to his knees at the edge of the dung pile. "Nooo! This cannot be you, Abba." He began pulling out patches of his hair and beard. "My ima, you're starving to death!" He buried his face in his hands and wept as Sitis hurried down to comfort him. When she embraced him, her headpiece fell away, and he became inconsolable. "God of my fathers, God of Abraham, may El Shaddai repay one hundredfold the evil done to you!" He threw ashes into the air, bathing his hair and beard in the fine gray mist of mourning.

"Go to him, Dinah," Job whispered, new tears wetting the furrows where happy tears had been. "Perhaps your lovely face will cheer him."

"I don't think anything I can say will comfort him," Dinah said, hinting again at her answer to Elihu's possible proposal. Job had talked with Dinah often about the possibility, and she stubbornly held to her conviction that Elihu deserved a devout and kind young woman.

"Are you firm in your decision then? You've decided to decline Elihu's marriage proposal?"

Dinah nodded and whispered, "This moment is for you and Sitis to share with Elihu. But when the time is right, and if he should ask me to be his wife, I will insist he marry a pure and deserving bride." She lowered her eyes, and Job accepted her decision, though he believed Elihu would be blessed with such a woman as Dinah.

"Oh, Abba, I'm sorry I took so long." Elihu finally started his climb, ash and dung clinging to his tear-dampened beard and hands. Sitis followed closely behind, head bowed. Her motherly instincts seemed to respect Elihu's need to mourn, and she set aside her own good news for now.

"You needn't be sorry for lingering, Elihu," Job said. "I know the sight of us must have been a shock." Job exchanged a strengthening glance with Dinah while Elihu made his silent ascent. He could only hope Elihu gracefully accepted Dinah's decision.

"Abba Job, they wanted to meet together before coming to Uz," the young man began, breathless as he reached the peak. "And I couldn't find Bildad. He'd gone to pasture his flocks in the far Eastern Desert because of the drought. We also had to wait on Zophar's caravan to return from Gaza.

The Sabeans stole his horses in Elath, but thanks be to El Shaddai, his caravan traveled on to Gaza unharmed."

Job suddenly realized Elihu's apology had nothing to do with lingering at the bottom of the ash pile. He'd apologized for lingering a year on his journey, and it sounded as if . . .

Sitis stopped her climb and shouted, "Bildad? Did you say Bildad? My brother is coming? And Eliphaz and Zophar?"

Like winnowing grain from chaff, Job's mind discarded everything but the names—Eliphaz, Bildad, Zophar. Elihu turned, glancing back and forth between Job and Sitis.

The height and depth of their surprise must have registered completely then. "Oh, I'm sorry I didn't tell you right away!" In the muck he dropped to his knees at Job's feet. "Eliphaz and Bildad bring a great army to defend you, and Zophar's caravan bears herbs for your wounds. They'll arrive before sunset."

Sitis shrieked for joy, and Elihu reached for Job's hands. It was then that he noticed the disease-rotted gaps. "Abba, where are your fingers?" The horror on his face turned to rage aimed at Dinah. "You! You've done this to him."

Before Job could come to her defense, Nogahla stood beside Dinah and shouted, "Master Elihu, don't talk to my mistress that way!"

"Stay away from Abba Job." Elihu turned on Dinah, who stood by Job like a wilted flower. "You're barely a trained midwife, and you've nearly killed him with your herbs and potions."

"Elihu, that's enough." Job's heart was in his throat, making his voice even weaker. "Sayyid has made certain no physician in Uz will touch me. If it weren't for Dinah, I would be dead by now."

Elihu turned, and Job was startled at the blazing hatred in his expression. "If it weren't for Dinah, none of these tragedies would have assailed your household in the first place."

Stunned silence settled over the ashen hill as Dinah's face crumpled like a stone wall under siege. After regaining some control, she stepped forward. "Come, Nogahla—"

"No, I said stay away from him!" Elihu moved between Dinah and Job, causing her to stumble backward and topple headlong down the ash heap. Her lovely form settled motionless at the bottom.

Job was aware only of a swift black blur, and suddenly a gasp, a pop, another tumble—and Elihu lay at the base of the pile beside Dinah, rubbing his jaw and cursing loudly.

Aban stood by Job, his hand extended in compassion. "Master Job, are you all right? Did he hurt you?"

"No, of course not." Job was flustered, befuddled. Sayyid's captain had been kind during the past months—even apologetic. *But why would he protect Dinah—and why is he concerned about me?*

Nogahla was at the base of the hill by Dinah, crying and cradling her mistress. Sitis had slid down the ashes to tend to Elihu's quickly swelling jaw.

"What has come over you, Aban?" Job's voice was merely a whisper, but it didn't matter. The big man was already retreating to the bottom of the ash heap.

Elihu recoiled and Sitis shielded him in her arms like a child. Aban stood menacingly over them, issuing his promise with a warning. "I won't hit him again, Mistress Sitis, as long as he treats Mistress Dinah with respect."

"Aban, help Dinah," Nogahla gasped between sobs. "I need to take her home, to Widow Orma's cave."

Job watched as the big man tenderly placed his giant hand on Nogahla's cheek. "She'll be all right, little Cushite. You see, she's coming around." Aban knelt and scooped Dinah into his arms as though she weighed no more than a sack of barley. Job's heart squeezed at the captain's tenderness. The big man's heart had softened considerably during their lonely midnight discussions on the ash heap.

"Show me this cave you call home." Aban took his first steps away.

Elihu aimed venomous words at his back. "Oh, so you've fallen under the spell of *both* Dinah and her Cushite. Have they both shared your bed as well?"

The captain's backward glance promised future retribution, and Job feared for his brilliant student who had spoken so impudently.

"Elihu!" Job's reprimand was no more than a whispered peep.

Sitis's slap found its mark, silencing the young man. She pushed him out of her arms and stood over him. "You have lost all good sense in your absence, my son. I pray that by the time I return, you will realize that Dinah deserves both your respect and your gratitude." Sitis hurried to catch up with Aban, who carried Dinah in his arms and tenderly reassured Nogahla.

Job's heart had been broken into pieces before, but watching Elihu pound the ashes with raging fists shattered his spirit. Elihu's desire for knowledge was fertile ground, and Zophar was the only gardener who could have yielded such rotten fruit to throw at Dinah. Job wept anew that Jacob's daughter had once again endured wicked accusations. *El Shaddai, will her accusers ever cease?*

His prayer was abruptly curtailed by the cold, sharp claws

of fear. Two Nameless Ones crept like desert scavengers behind Aban and the women, following the unsuspecting band to the widow's hidden cave. He tried to shout his warning, but no one could hear over the noise of Elihu's hatred.

✣✣✣✣✣

Dinah felt strong arms lifting her, carrying her. A light breeze flowed beneath her head covering, her head and hair dangling over a strong-armed pillow. She didn't have the strength to move or speak. Opening her eyes, she saw white, puffy clouds in an afternoon sky and heard hoopoe birds in the distance. And Nogahla's chatter.

"Aban, is she all right? There, her eyes are open. Mistress? Are you all right?"

Sitis's calming voice soothed the anxious girl. "Nogahla, she'll be fine. We must get her to Orma's cave, where we can tend to her head wound. She fell on a pottery shard."

Dinah became vaguely aware of a wet, sticky warmth at the back of her neck and looked up at her human conveyance. "Aban?" She tried to escape his arms, but he tightened his grip, rolling her toward his chest and whispering, "Be at ease, lovely Dinah. I won't hurt you." She could feel her throat tighten with emotion. Who had held her or spoken so kindly since Shechem? Only Job.

Someone removed her head covering and stroked her forehead. "Rest, Dinah. Nogahla and I are with you." Sitis's serene face hovered over her, bouncing in step with the big man's strides.

Dinah could hear Nogahla's sobs and felt the girl's hand caressing her feet. "Up this path," the Cushite directed. "Be careful of your footing. Don't drop her, Aban!"

Dinah felt the deep rumble of laughter in Aban's chest and noted the familiarity with which Nogahla spoke his name. The Cushite had recognized goodness in this man long ago, and Aban's attentions had been drawn to Nogahla for weeks. Oh, her head hurt too much to think of how complicated their relationship would be.

"Here we are." The Cushite rushed into the cave while Aban and Sitis waited outside with Dinah.

"Mistress Sitis," Aban began haltingly, "I know my fath—I mean, Master Sayyid has kept—"

"What?" Sitis and Dinah shouted and gasped the word simultaneously, interrupting whatever the captain had planned to say.

After closing his eyes briefly and expelling a long sigh, Aban seemed to search Sitis's face for approval. "Mistress Sitis, my mother was Sayyid's concubine for many years. She was his favorite because everything about her resembled—well, *you*."

Dinah remembered Sitis telling her about the serving girls in Sayyid's home, their uniform resemblance to his obsession.

"Where is your mother now, Captain?" Sitis asked flatly.

Dinah felt Aban's subtle incline toward Sitis as he spoke, his breath choppy, anxious. "Sayyid sold her to Egyptian traders when I was twelve because it was time for my military training to begin. He feared her coddling would interfere with my journey into manhood." A sigh lifted Dinah up and down in his arms. "Sayyid has been my only guiding force. I have obeyed him unquestioningly—until today. What I saw on his face this afternoon made me regret my role in your pain."

Dinah watched a battle rage in Sitis's eyes. Could she forgive her enemy's most lethal weapon?

After only a moment's hesitation, Sitis reached up to cup

his cheek, her voice full of emotion. "Oh, Aban, I'm sorry you grew up without a mother's love."

Dinah felt Aban's arms tense. "It matters not. I declared my position as Sayyid's heir today." He stood taller, a slight grin bending his lips. "Let us say he did not disagree, and we are currently in negotiations."

Dinah tried to lift her head, but the pain restricted her movement. Still, she had to caution him. "Aban, you cannot negotiate with a snake. It strikes without reason or provocation." The effort of speaking caused the clouds to spin.

Sitis continued when Dinah's strength was spent. "If Sayyid has any idea you've helped me or Job, he'll kill you, Aban—son or not. He has no loyalty to anyone but himself." Sitis removed her own head covering then, revealing her shorn hair, and Dinah felt Aban's chest swell with his gasp.

"Mistress Sitis, I had no idea." For the first time in all this misery, Dinah saw Aban's eyes glisten. "I give you my word," he said as Nogahla emerged from the cave with Widow Orma, "you will have food and supplies in this cave by sunset."

"Well, young man," the widow said, her pink gums beaming a smile, "we won't refuse a loaf of bread."

Everyone chuckled at her modest thanks.

"You will see more bread than you've eaten in a year, widow." Aban's expression softened again as he turned to Sitis. "And you, mistress, will see the nursemaid you haven't seen in over a year."

"Oh, Aban!" Sitis threw her arms around the big man's neck, crushing Dinah between them.

Trying not to squirm, Dinah was just about to protest when another voice came to her rescue. "Enough! Enough! You're squishing my mistress!" Nogahla squeezed between

Aban and Sitis, exchanging a furtive glance with the man who had seemingly captured her heart.

A deep, resonant chuckle erupted from Aban's chest and vibrated Dinah's shoulder. "All right, little Cushite. Where shall I put this mistress of yours?"

Nogahla chattered on about Widow Orma's hospitality and their sleeping arrangements. Dinah glanced over Aban's shoulder, and there at the bottom of the stony path were two filthy vagabonds crouched behind boulders. When Aban stooped to enter the cave, Dinah looked once more, but the beggars were gone.

Perhaps my eyes are playing tricks on me, she thought. *A head wound can do that sometimes.* Thinking no more of it, she allowed loving hands to minister to her weakness and praised El Shaddai for Sitis's safety among them.

16

When they saw him from a distance, they could
hardly recognize him; they began to weep aloud,
and they tore their robes and sprinkled dust on
their heads.

Widow Orma's cave was cool and dark, every patch of dirt covered by a sleeping mat, a woman, or a basket filled with Nada's food. Smudge-faced children peeked through the tattered curtain. Some even scooted a finger or toe under the obstacle to snitch a cake or date from the piles. Giggles and gasps erupted from the little residents of Uz's first sector vying for a glimpse of the widow's newest guest. Sitis pretended not to notice, but it was hard to ignore in a space only slightly bigger than the sleeping room she had occupied at Bela's palace.

"Shoo! Get away from there!" Nada patted at the curtain, chasing away prying little eyes. "Mistress, how can I leave you here in this . . . this . . . *cave*?" Tears brimmed as she embraced Sitis for the hundredth time.

Sitis soaked up the love of Nada's soft arms. "Aban says this is the safest place for me now. Sayyid may still try to kill me if I show myself publicly, and then he'll shift blame to the Nameless Ones."

"Are you afraid?" Dinah whispered. The question seemed to capture everyone's attention. The widow, Nogahla, and Nada leaned in close to hear.

"I suppose I'm a little afraid," Sitis said, "but I'm so relieved, I can feel little else."

"Relieved?" Nada laid the back of her hand against Sitis's forehead and guided her to a mat to sit down. "I think you must be ill, my Sitis. No one can feel relief in your situation."

Sitis nudged away Nada's hand, and the others chuckled as they nestled beside her. "I am relieved that Sayyid's anger has finally turned away from Job—even though I'm now his target. I'm relieved to see my precious Nada again." She cupped the woman's cheek and held her gaze. "I'm immeasurably relieved to be at peace with God, and I would be even more relieved . . ." She paused, her fingers now brushing the feathery wrinkles of Nada's brown face. "If my friend and nursemaid would discover the true God as well." Nada's gaze fell to the red dirt floor, and the other women grew uncomfortably silent.

Aban's large brown hand drew back the curtain. "I'm sorry to interrupt, but I must return with Nada before Sayyid realizes we're gone. Bildad and Eliphaz's army will arrive soon, and I must accompany Sayyid with our troops."

Sitis let her hand fall from Nada's cheek, but the woman clasped it tightly and kissed it. "On my next visit, I'll bring your favorite fruit gruel, my Sitis-girl."

"On your next visit," Sitis said, "we'll talk more of El Shaddai."

Nada grinned and labored to her feet. After one last embrace, Sitis pulled the curtain aside and ushered her lifelong friend into the dusky shadows of the day's end.

When Sitis tried to follow a few steps, Aban halted her gently. "Please, mistress. Remain inside as much as possible." He pointed to the surrounding caves carved into the mountain face. "I can't tell if these beggars belong to the first-sector caves or if the Nameless Ones have discovered your location. I'll send a few of my trusted guards to stand watch."

Sitis trusted Aban's judgment and his caution. His warm smile reminded her of one of her own sons. "Thank you, Aban. I don't know why you've chosen to be so kind, but I'm grateful."

✳✳✳✳✳

Astride his new Egyptian stallion, Sayyid cast a long evening shadow against the vacant merchant booths, and Aban's sleek dapple gray mount stepped in flawless cadence alongside. One hundred of Sayyid's guards, dressed in fine black cloaks, emerged from the siq on camels draped with red-and-yellow braided mantles. Sayyid was determined to impress the opposing army, even if his hopes of victory were slim. If Bildad the Ishmaelite and Eliphaz the Edomite could not be bribed or duped, Uz would be bathed in blood tonight.

The worn and weary inhabitants of Uz's first sector watched as Sayyid's entourage paraded through their midst. Women gathered children into their small tents and caves, and men stood guard with roughly hewn weapons. Sayyid sneered. *A lot of good those silly spears will do if Bildad's troops have come for retribution.* The first sector lay exposed on the eastern side of the narrow siq and therefore unprotected by its natural fortification.

Signaling his men to a halt just outside the city gate, Sayyid rehearsed the plan with Aban a final time. "Remember, if Bildad and Eliphaz have come in peace, we'll lead a small contingent through the siq tonight. However, at the first sign of aggression, we must begin our defense plan. If an enemy sword is drawn or an arrow flies, I'll circle to the rear while you and the men make an initial surge. Then you must retreat through the siq into the second sector. When their army pursues us through the siq, I'll signal our waiting troops on top of the mountain to rain down boulders on their men below. When the last of our guards have safely exited the siq, we'll seal off the opening with a rockslide and escape through the western mountain range."

Aban's suspicions kept his voice low. "How do I know you won't seal off the siq before *all* of our men are safely through it—*Father*?"

Sayyid smiled. "I suppose we'll have to trust each other, *Son*." Aban's graying complexion was just the response Sayyid expected. "Like I trusted you to order the Nameless Ones to kill Sitis this afternoon." Clucking his tongue, he dug his heels into his stallion's side and proceeded toward the oncoming army.

"Wait!" Aban followed on his dapple gray. "What would you have had me do?" he whispered when his horse pulled alongside Sayyid's stallion. "Elihu arrived just as the men would have slaughtered her. Even the Nameless Ones aren't foolish enough to murder the great lady of Uz in front of a reputable witness."

Sayyid responded with one lifted eyebrow. He would let his captain squirm. Aban need not know that while he'd been playing hero to the three women this afternoon, the leader of the bandits had come to Sayyid with the details of Aban's betrayal and had suggested a delightful alternative plan.

"Come, Aban. We have guests to welcome. Or perhaps a battle to fight. Hi-yah!"

Sayyid's horse tried to bolt, but he calmed the beast to a noble gait. As they approached the oncoming sea of animals and riders, Sayyid wished his heartbeat was as easily controlled. The enemy's army of camels stretched as far as the eye could see, walking three abreast along the winding mountain paths. A smaller caravan of donkeys, carrying supplies and a few riders, meandered at the rear.

"Have you ever seen anything like it?" Sayyid breathed more to himself than to Aban, who had ridden up beside him.

"No, and I wish I weren't seeing it now."

Sayyid and his captain rode in silence until no more than ten paces separated the opposing leadership. Sayyid stayed his courage, determined to impress Sitis's brother. "Greetings, Prince Bildad."

The setting sun and forty years had only heightened the Ishmaelite prince's nobility. His robe of sky blue linen and the deep purple sash distinguished him as a son of Shuah. His beard was longer, grayer, but he was still handsome. Beauty also seemed an inheritance of Sitis's family.

As a boy, Sayyid had been forced to bow with his nose to the ground each time Bildad visited their village. Not anymore. He sat a little taller in his Egyptian saddle. "It is an honor to welcome you after all these years."

"We are here to rescue my sister from your abuse, Sayyid." Bildad's obsidian eyes stared through Sayyid, not at him.

"And my nephew!" The old man on Bildad's right erupted with a thunderous voice like Esau's. No doubt this was Eliphaz, Esau's firstborn. He displayed none of Zophar's or Bela's ruddy Edomite coloring. Rather, his face resembled a dark raisin with a long white beard. "El Shaddai will rain down His vengeance for your violence against Job," Eliphaz shouted, shaking his gnarled fist.

He certainly has Esau's temper, Sayyid thought, wishing he could hoist a javelin into all their bellies. Instead, he inclined his head and spoke somberly. "I understand your concerns, brothers. However, I fear you have sorely misjudged your family's circumstance and my participation." Before any of the men could draw breath, he pressed his defense. "Your sister is not well, Bildad. She has lost all her children—even her three precious daughters, named after the Ishmaelite goddesses."

Sayyid saw his first arrow hit its mark. Bildad blanched at the truth of his sister's idolatrous penchant.

While the others shifted uncomfortably on their saddles, Sayyid continued. "In a single day, Eliphaz, all of Job's wealth was destroyed either by raiding parties attacking from opposing ends of the earth or by the fire of God. The following day your nephew was struck by wasting boils." Hesitating only slightly, Sayyid leaned closer, as if sharing a secret. "I can assure you, I am a powerful man in Uz, but I can neither rain down fire nor inflict boils on a man's flesh."

Sayyid's gaze fell on Zophar, Job's favorite cousin-brother, the great spice trader. "Even as Job draws his last breaths, he casts aside your advice, Zophar, and clings to the harlot of which you warned him."

Shock shattered each man's stony expression at the pronouncement, and then Sayyid added his final blow. "Elihu, student of the Most High's teachings, your ima Sitis sold her hair today in the marketplace for three loaves of bread." He held up the long, ebony locks he'd sheared off Sitis's head earlier. "She asked me to take it to the temple of Al-Uzza in Moab as an offering."

"You are a liar!" Elihu shrieked, eyes wild, spittle spilling onto his beard. "Ima would never—"

"That is enough, Elihu." Bildad spoke with the regal calm of a man accustomed to being obeyed, and Elihu fell silent immediately. "Elihu's passions carry him away, but I trust his integrity completely. He has accused you of falsehood, Sayyid." Bildad pierced Sayyid with his gaze. "Which of your statements would he have judged false?"

Sayyid smiled but felt the left side of his mouth twitch nervously. He inwardly cursed his weakness.

"My father lied about Mistress Sitis's desire to make her hair an offering at the temple." Every eye darted to Aban, the source of the confession, but the captain's gaze was fixed on Bildad. Sayyid glared so hotly, he was certain Aban's face would burst into flames. Alas, it did not.

Bildad lifted one gray eyebrow. "Sayyid is your father?"

"By the gods, Aban . . ." Sayyid's voice was low, menacing, daring him to continue.

"Yes, from an Egyptian handmaid. Much like our forefather Ishmael was the son of Abram's Egyptian woman, Hagar." Sayyid noted Aban's respectful, intense expression and felt a stab of envy. How could Aban hold Bildad's gaze without flinching?

"How do you know Sayyid lied?" Bildad asked.

"I am Sayyid's captain, and we have issued a detachment of guards to protect Job. Those guards reported to me a conversation between Mistress Sitis and Master Job that would preclude your sister from requesting such an offering." For the first time, Aban looked away from Bildad and glanced in Sayyid's direction. "My father didn't want to tell you the truth because . . ."

Sayyid glared at Aban, forbidding him to speak. Begging him to keep silent.

"Sayyid—my father—well, he is a liar. It's what he does."

The four visitors couldn't have looked more shocked if they'd swallowed their camels' cud. Sayyid's face blazed like an inferno, humiliation kindling fury.

Bildad laughed so hard, he nearly fell off his camel. "Well, Captain, at least you don't seem to have inherited your father's treachery."

Sayyid considered running his sword through Aban's heart then and there, but his personal humiliation seemed to be placating the leaders of this great army. "My son paints a dreadful picture of a grain merchant's life," Sayyid said, shrugging his shoulders good-naturedly while glaring daggers at his son. "Aban has the luxury of a soldier's life, black-and-white, right and wrong." Looking at Zophar, Sayyid included the spice trader in his generalization. "We merchants understand that in order to survive, one must sometimes sculpt the truth to accommodate the situation."

"And what situation confronts us that you felt the need to sculpt such a lie, Sayyid?"

Though Sayyid was growing weary of Bildad's incessant hammering, he noted the prince's hardening features and decided humility was the best approach for the final negotiation. "I thought if you believed Sitis to have embraced idolatry, you might accept hospitality from an idolater." Sayyid bowed his head and opened his arms wide. "My home is open to you and to as many of your troops as you deem worthy." Sayyid's stallion pranced nervously, but its master maintained his penitent pose, waiting.

During the long silence, Sayyid watched Aban's hands on his reins, clenching and unclenching, twice, three times. His captain was nervous, but still he'd proven himself a fine negotiator. He obviously couldn't be trusted in matters related to Sitis, but even in that circumstance he'd proven useful to unwittingly lead the bandits to where she was hiding. The Nameless One's visit had been timely and his predictions as insightful as a sorcerer. He had assured Sayyid that half-truths and lavish hospitality would win these men's favor. And so far . . .

"Lead us into the city, and we will camp on the plains," Eliphaz commanded as though ordering his own troops. "You are clearly not a man to be trusted, Sayyid, and I intend to speak with Job before any agreements are struck."

Sayyid's head snapped to attention, and he drew breath to match the venomous tone of Esau's firstborn. But Aban interrupted, showing infuriating tact and diplomacy. "My father would be happy to lead you and a *detachment* of your men into the city, Master Eliphaz, with an equal number of Prince Bildad's soldiers. Our cooks have already begun preparing a meal for one hundred extra mouths." Aban started to turn away but snapped his fingers as if remembering something at the last moment. "Master Zophar?"

The merchant looked startled to be addressed directly. "Yes?" he said, glancing cautiously at his father and his teacher.

"I wouldn't presume to instruct you on tending to Job, but if your caravan holds herbs that might help him, you should bring them when my father escorts you." Aban nodded respectfully to the three elders and then shot a hostile glance at Elihu before turning his dapple gray stallion in the direction of the city gate. He then issued the retreat signal to the first two rows of guards, and the ornately adorned camels and riders returned to the city with their captain.

"Well, Sayyid," Bildad said, reminding him that nearly two thousand men awaited his instruction. "I hope your fine son is a testament to your changed character. I remember you as a scheming peasant boy, but perhaps you have improved, as you say, to a conniving grain merchant." Bildad and his three friends sniggered.

Annoyed, Sayyid returned his attention to the siq entrance. The guards on camels had disappeared through the siq, but Aban's dapple gray stallion was tethered at the base of a rocky mountain path. *Where have you gone, my son? And why are you in such a hurry to get there?*

✸✸✸✸✸

The night sky gulped away light, and every heart throbbed with tension, waiting for the cries of battle or some word of aid from Job's and Sitis's relatives. Around the soft glow of firelight, the four women chatted quietly until the cave exploded with a muscular figure dressed in black. After reflexive gasps, the ladies stood to welcome Aban—three offering smiles of relief. One, not so relieved.

"What brings you back here when it's almost dark?" Dinah said, hands balled on her hips. "And you could have been followed by any number of Sayyid's men or Nameless Ones."

262

The words tumbled out much harsher than she'd intended, but this man was still untried. Granted, he'd proven a godsend earlier today, but what would he prove tomorrow and the next day and the next?

Aban looked as if he'd been slapped, and Sitis gently placed a hand on Dinah's shoulder. "I think she's asking if you've come with news about Sayyid's meeting with my brother and Job's uncle."

Dinah crossed her arms and set her feet like a commander waiting to hear a scout's report. She sensed Sitis's disapproving frown and was certain Nogahla and Widow Orma shared the woman's adoration of their new champion.

Aban suppressed a grin, which only stoked Dinah's fire. "Sayyid is leading a hundred of the visiting army through the siq, where they will make camp in our canyon and see Job for the first time." He sobered and turned to Sitis with concern. "My father's words dripped with honey. I'm sure he plans to smother them with hospitality and win them over to his version of the truth."

"I must go! Job's throat is too raw to speak," Sitis said, grabbing a cloak to throw around her shoulders. "We can't let Sayyid interpret the last year's events. You know his silver tongue twists the truth."

"No!" The cave resounded with the answer.

Dinah pulled Sitis into a fierce embrace. "Please, Aban, remind her of the dangers. Tell us what Sayyid is planning."

She watched a cloud of sadness darken his features. "I'm sorry, Mistress Sitis. I don't know what Sayyid is planning anymore."

Dinah glared, silently accusing him of lying.

He raised his hands, pleading his case. "My father discovered that I tricked him earlier and has now changed his plans with the Nameless Ones. I've positioned my most trusted guards around this cave, but I cannot protect you, mistress, if you leave here."

A stream of tears flowed down Sitis's cheeks. "But who will speak for Job?"

"Elihu is among them, Sitis." Dinah gently grasped the woman's shoulders and faced her. "Elihu knows Sayyid's treachery. He will recognize it and speak out."

Aban spoke softly but firmly. "I'm sorry, Dinah, but I believe Eliphaz, Bildad, and Zophar see Elihu as an impetuous, emotional boy. His opinions seem to matter very little among them."

Anger rose inside Dinah. She knew Sitis was hanging on by a thin thread of hope. How dare Aban cut it off so carelessly! "Well, Aban, do you have a better idea?"

"I will speak for Master Job and Mistress Sitis," he said simply.

Silence reigned.

Dinah's heart nearly stopped when she saw the inner battle raging on Sitis's features. *Surely you won't place your life in the hands of this stranger*, she thought. Trying to spare Sitis from a dire mistake, she turned to the captain and said, "Please, Aban, don't take offense, but . . ."

"You don't trust me to speak the truth because I'm Sayyid's son." His voice bore a tinge of anger mingled with defeat. "Why do you allow my past to eliminate the possibility that I have become a man of integrity?"

Dinah felt the blood rush from her face. Had she become like those who judged her? Unwilling to forgive? Unable to see beyond her past? Yet something about this man held her back. His integrity had not been tested over time.

"I'm truly sorry for the way I've treated you, Aban, but please understand. My friends' lives depend on this moment. I would even go myself if it would help." She chuckled at the thought. *Wouldn't that cause a stir, if Dinah appeared beside Job at the ash heap?*

"But who will go if Aban doesn't?" Sitis whispered in Dinah's ear as the two women clung to each other.

"May I go, mistress?" Nogahla's quiet voice came from the darkness of the cave, and Dinah turned to see her beautiful round eyes.

"Nogahla, my friend, they will not listen to you." Dinah exchanged a knowing glance with Sitis. "Though we know you are a kind Cushite girl with great wisdom, those men would not hear your words."

"No, I don't intend to talk to Master Job's relatives. I mean to go with Master Aban to set your mind at rest that he is being truthful on Master Job's behalf." Nogahla blinked several times, punctuating her request, and Aban raised pleading eyebrows. Dinah thought he resembled a wolf ready to devour her little lamb.

"I don't think it's proper for a young girl to be traipsing alone with a soldier after dark." Dinah sounded like her ima—scolding, nagging, chiding. But if she'd listened to Ima Leah, she might not have landed in Shechem's bed.

"Nogahla can tend Job's wounds with the supplies Zophar is bringing," Aban said a little too quickly. But Aban's mention of medicinal provisions sent Dinah's mind humming with hope, and now Sitis also pleaded silently with her. Only Widow Orma remained neutral, warming herself by the fire.

Dinah's heart squeezed at the thought of sending her precious friend with a man she didn't fully trust, but what else could she do? "All right, Nogahla, you'll need to take this basket of supplies with you for the first visit." Dinah began filling it with some of Nada's food provisions and the few small jars of herbs they had left.

Widow Orma handed Nogahla a rock-hewn pitcher insulated with woven mesh. "I'm sending the last of our mint tea. Have Master Job drink it while it's still hot," the widow said. "It will help soothe his throat and stomach so he can tell his own truth soon."

Nogahla nodded, but Dinah wondered if she truly comprehended any of their instructions. The girl was smitten—deeply, completely, undeniably.

Dinah held Aban's gaze, and to the man's credit, he didn't flinch. "She's ready, Aban. Nogahla is my most treasured friend. You will keep her safe." It was a command, not a question, and the big man nodded. "I will join Nogahla and Job at the ash heap when the moon is at its peak. By then the visitors should be sleeping, and I can sort through the new supplies to find the best herbs for Job's sores. I'll tend his wounds and move him to a dry pile at night so as not to offend . . . anyone." Dinah's voice broke, and she looked away. Why did she have to sneak like a thief to tend the wounds of her dear friend, and why did Zophar still frighten and shame her?

"We will be waiting for you there, Mistress Dinah." Aban's voice was gentle.

She nodded, emotion strangling her voice. Nogahla kissed her cheek and scooted down the incline of rock toward the path. Dinah watched Aban hoist Nogahla onto his sleek stallion and then disappear into the siq.

✾✾✾✾✾

Nogahla felt like a queen. Never had she dreamed she would ride a stallion as beautiful as Aban's dapple gray. "My first childhood memories are of my father's stables," she said, hoping Aban would speak freely about the new revelation of his father. Nogahla hadn't heard Aban's first declaration to Mistress Dinah and Mistress Sitis, but the women had told her later while tending Dinah's head wound.

"You mean, you remember horses when your father worked in a master's stables?" Aban's tone was easy, conversational, as if they were strolling through a quiet meadow rather than emerging from the great siq toward a visiting army.

"No, my father was the master of a grand Egyptian estate, one of Pharaoh's officials, and my mother was a Cushite slave in his household. My father's wife hated my mother and sold me to Ishmaelite slave traders when I was five winters old—just to be mean."

Aban walked beside the horse, loosely holding its bridle in hand. "I'm sorry, Nogahla."

"It's all right." Nogahla looked up at the moon and stars. "The last words my mother said to me were, 'My little princess, the night sky will always unite us.'"

Without altering his stride, Aban turned and offered up a smile. "So I was wrong before when I called you 'little Cushite.' I should have said 'Egyptian princess.'" His eyes sparkled even in the dim shadows of dusk, and Nogahla thought her heart might burst.

He resumed his forward gaze and reached a brawny arm under his stallion's powerful neck, patting the other side. Bowing his head, he spoke in soothing tones to the beast, and Nogahla wondered what secrets they shared. Suddenly mesmerized by the sinewy muscles of his back, she noted the proportions of his shoulders and waist like a finely shaped funnel. *Oh my!* She clapped her hands on her burning cheeks.

"Nogahla, are you all right?" Aban turned, stopping in a warrior's stance, his eyes darting in every direction.

Nogahla squeezed her eyes shut and tried to calm herself. Now she really felt foolish. "Yes, Aban. I'm just a little frightened." It was the truth—though he didn't need to know why. What if Dinah was right and Aban could not be trusted? What if her heart was leading them all astray?

Nogahla met Aban's gaze and saw only tenderness and sincerity there. *Please, El Shaddai, let me return with a good report to Dinah and Mistress Sitis about this man. Let his words be true and his heart pure.*

As the final words of her prayer ascended heavenward, Nogahla heard terrible wailing echoing from the canyon.

"Hold on to the riding blanket!" Aban shouted to Nogahla as the stallion broke into a trot to keep pace with the soldier's long stride. They weaved through the visiting army, whose shmaghs and keffiyehs were pulled over their faces. Some of the soldiers within sight of Job were even coughing and retching.

Nogahla soon spotted the source of the keening. Three exquisitely garbed older men tore at their robes and threw dust on their heads, while Elihu faced Job's ash pile, his head bowed.

"Are those his relatives?" Nogahla asked, leaning across the horse's neck. Aban slowed his pace as they drew near the display, walking now between the front lines of soldiers. "Why are they remaining so far from Master Job?" she whispered. "They're not even as close as your four perimeter guards."

Aban hesitated, and Nogahla wondered if he was winded from his run or searching for polite words. He leaned close so she could hear him over the wailing. "I'm guessing they're not accustomed to the odor."

Nogahla nodded her understanding. Torchbearers dotted the perimeter of Job's ash heap, but the visitors remained at least one hundred paces away. Like an invisible barrier, the sight and stench of Job's suffering warded off any true comfort his friends might have attempted.

Nogahla slid off the stallion easily, remembering the long-ago days in her father's stable, and Aban was there to catch her. When she and Aban passed Eliphaz, Bildad, and Zophar, the men barely paused their cries long enough to notice a lowly servant girl and a guard.

Elihu nodded a silent greeting to Nogahla, and she returned it coolly. She would tell him later exactly what she thought of him. Nogahla felt Aban's grip tighten on her arm and noticed the fiery stare pass between the two men. She wondered how Elihu, whom she had thought so kind and benevolent, could become so angry, while Aban, trained to fight and kill, could be so kind.

Then she saw Job, and every other thought was lost to the depth of his suffering. If one could stare into the abyss and continue breathing, Job was doing it tonight. If one could eat and sleep and speak while a wild beast tore at his flesh, Job was living that too. If one could love after his heart had been ripped from his chest, Job had surely achieved that ability.

He smiled when Nogahla began her trek up the dung pile. She poured mint tea into his mouth to soothe his wounded throat and spoke her simple wisdom to lift his weary soul. And when the fervent pitch of keening clouded Job's face in lonely torment, Nogahla sang melodies from her heart, drowning out his distant friends.

17

~Job 2:13~

*Then they sat on the ground with him for seven
days and seven nights. No one said a word to
him, because they saw how great his suffering
was.*

Sayyid watched from his moonlit perch as Job's friends
dissolved into sniveling mounds of grief. Their spectacle
had been more pathetic than he could have imagined. Sayyid
loved the poetic justice of it. Job, who had mourned and
touched so many in their times of need, endured his relatives'
mourning without a single encouraging word or—gods forbid
it—tender touch. A lingering smile stretched Sayyid's lips.

His only grating concern was Aban. Was he friend or foe?
Casting another glance over the balcony, Sayyid stayed in the
shadows but saw Aban's tall, imposing form stationed at Job's
breached courtyard wall. *What are you about, Aban, my son?*
He'd remained there since escorting the little Cushite early

in the festivities. He left only long enough to accompany the servants to deliver the guests' meal, and then he joined Sayyid in offering sympathetic drivel about Job's circumstances. After a sufficiently hospitable show, Sayyid had returned to his balcony and assumed his captain would follow for their nightly debriefing. But Aban lingered in Sayyid's kitchen and then resumed his place near the dung piles. *What keeps you so close to Job's stinking heaps?*

Sayyid noticed Aban making his way to the peak of Job's current perch. "Now this is something new," he said aloud. He'd never noticed his captain join the wasting figure at the pinnacle of mire.

The full moon offered enough light to see another figure, this one a woman, with Job and the Cushite on the heap. Sayyid's heart slammed against his chest. *Is it Sitis? Aban, you could prove your allegiance to me now by strangling her with your bare hands.*

But even as the thought raced through his mind, he knew Aban would never harm Sitis. He had winced when Sayyid issued the order to kill her. Something about Sitis had pierced the big man's heart. Sayyid smiled. *Of course it has. He must have inherited that vulnerability to her charms from me.*

"Now who is this woman on Job's dung pile," he whispered to no one, "and what will you do with her?" Sayyid waited patiently, watching the woman's gestures, the tilt of her head, the way she moved her hands. It was Dinah. He could tell by the soft curls that fell over her shoulders when she bent toward the Cushite.

Sayyid chuckled and fingered the soft locks of Sitis's hair still reverently held in the folds of his robe. *Job will never run his fingers through his wife's hair again. He has no fingers,*

271

and Sitis has no hair! Oh, how he wished he could laugh without waking the whole canyon. Perhaps tomorrow he would summon the Nameless One and share his wicked delight. Certainly Aban wouldn't appreciate his humor. He'd become too friendly with the enemy.

Sayyid noticed the tall, dark figure descending the ash heap. At the bottom, Aban hesitated.

"Yes, think carefully, my son. Consider your options."

His captain seemed to be weighing some great decision, leaning one direction and then the other.

Sayyid smiled, amused at the moments in life that defined fate, destiny, survival. "Choose wisely. Your life depends on your allegiance."

Though Sayyid's voice was but a whisper, Aban's foot took its step the moment the last word was spoken.

In less time than Aban's mother had required for wooing, Aban was knocking at Sayyid's bedchamber door. He burst in without waiting for an invitation and spoke without a greeting. "Father, I have a request." A slight bow was his only attempt at fealty.

Sayyid feigned a yawn. "How dare you storm in, waking me at this hour, demanding—"

Aban straightened, waving off his father's protests. "We both know you've been watching from your balcony all night."

Sayyid's battle between indignation and amusement was quickly nullified by Aban's urgency.

"I believe the best way to win the favor of Job's relatives is to make a grand show of gifts—to both his relatives and to Job himself." Before Sayyid could comment, Aban rushed on. "I think we should begin with offering medicinal supplies for Job—immediately."

272

Medicinal supplies. Aban's motives were becoming clearer. He was a man in love, trying to impress the woman of his heart. Dinah. "And what will we tell Job's relatives when they ask why we haven't provided medical care for Job previously?"

"I don't know, Father. Lying is your expertise. I'm simply trying to keep peace with an army that triples our manpower and makes our weapons look like toys."

Sayyid held up his hands in mock surrender. "I know we've established that I'm the liar and you're the truth teller." He smiled mischievously. "So tell the truth, my *son*. Is it peace you hope to gain with this benevolence, or the love of Job's blonde nursemaid?"

The shock on Aban's face was priceless. "I am your captain, acting on your behalf, Sayyid. The request has nothing to do with Dinah." He straightened into a rigid military pose. "My job is to convey your explanation of previously forestalling Job's medical care."

"Well, oh truthful one," Sayyid said, chuckling, "why don't you take a stab at this lying business. Evidently I'm quite good at it, but you need a little practice."

Aban's eyes hardened at the mocking, but Sayyid was determined to mete out some retribution for his son's divided public loyalty.

"Perhaps we could say that your physician refused to treat Job for fear of the gods." Aban lifted one questioning black eyebrow.

"Yes, I believe we could say that. But what if they ask why we didn't provide more herbs for your beloved Dinah to treat Job?" Sayyid delighted when Aban's nostrils flared at the mention of his attachment to Dinah and watched with a measure of satisfaction as his son crushed his weak emotions and stiffened his back with purpose.

"We will play on their disdain for Dinah," Aban said flatly, "and tell them we refused to provide supplies for her blood-stained hands. We'll leave it up to them, now that they are here, to employ another physician or let her continue his care."

Sayyid's chest barreled with pride. At the outset, Aban had seemed torn at the thought of the deceit and disgrace that would shadow lovely Dinah, but he had seemingly overcome his rudimentary quibbles with integrity and sacrificed them on the altar of success. Sayyid slapped Aban on the shoulder. "My boy, you might just make a suitable heir someday."

"Where will I get the herbs at this hour?" Aban said, turning toward the door without any appreciation for Sayyid's esteem. "The moon is three-quarters past, and the whole town sleeps."

Sayyid stood still and let his words halt his captain. "You can demand anything at anytime, Aban. You are my son." His captain turned as expected, meeting his father's gaze. However, something in the man's eyes sobered Sayyid.

"I will demand no more than what is fair and right, Father. Just what is fair and right."

Sayyid felt Aban's self-righteous undertone as if Sheol had opened the earth and swallowed him. *How dare this boy censure me!* Sayyid narrowed his eyes in warning. "You will go to the Edomite Bela and have a detachment of guards escort him here to me. Then march your troops to my physician's home and seize every jar of herbs and potions he owns." Sayyid approached his captain with the slow, steady prowl of a lion on the hunt. "It is *fair and right*, Captain, for Bela to share my dread when his kinsmen arrive with an army. And isn't it also *fair and right* for my physician to offer up whatever supplies my grain has purchased for his livelihood?"

Aban stood stately and stiff, staring into the distance.

Sayyid's anger simmered in the face of his son's impeccable military calm. "Go," Sayyid said after a long silence. "Get Job's precious supplies and bring Bela to me so I can keep us all out of burial clothes."

✵✵✵✵✵

"I can't stand it, Dinah. Why don't they come closer?" Job raised his arm so Dinah could wrap the linen bandage around his chest. "It's been six days, and still my so-called friends, my relatives, can't stand the sight or smell of me. Ahh!" The night sky echoed his cry.

"Job, I'm sorry!" Dinah eased the bandage away from the tender area, her tears immediate.

Job hated himself for crying out, hated that he made this compassionate woman cry, hated that his wife had to hide in a cave like a caged animal. But none of it was Dinah's fault. "I'm sorry for shouting, and I'm sorry you have to come here like a thief in the night to bandage my wounds. And I'm sorry I cry out like a child." Would this humiliation never end?

Nogahla ducked her head to meet Job's gaze. "Master Job, you are much quieter than a child."

His temper deflated at the sincerity in her eyes.

Matter-of-factly, she picked up a worm that had fallen from one of the sores on his shoulder and returned it to its festering home. "There you go, little worm. You can't leave until Mistress Dinah's myrrh kills you dead, dead, dead."

Job and Dinah shared a glance, transforming their tears

to wonder. Dinah's lilting laughter was met with a cautious grin from Job, the joy of the moment worth the pain of his upturned lips.

"Thank you, faithful assistant," Dinah said and then looked at Job. "The worms are managing your infection, and the myrrh has reduced some sores to scabs in less than a week. That's reason to hope, Job."

He swallowed hard and nodded. Anything else would have sent more tears searing through the open furrows on his cheeks.

"Though your voice is still a whisper," she said, "it's becoming stronger, and you're able to eat broth and egg whites now."

Dinah seemed as intent as the Cushite to battle his despair. She pulled away the strips of cloth from the tender flesh under his arm. His whole body trembled at the pain while a low, guttural moan escaped between chattering teeth. Tears flowed down Dinah's cheeks as she worked. "If you would allow Aban to accept the qat leaves Zophar brought from Saba," she said, anger rising in her tone, "we could manage your pain better. Now that the sores in your mouth have healed, you could chew the leaves or use Zophar's pipe to smoke them." It was the second night in a row she had broached the subject.

"I told you before," Job said, gritting his teeth against the pain, "I need a clear mind when Eliphaz, Bildad, and Zophar find the courage to finally come up here. I can't be dazed and witless, chewing on a wad of qat, while they argue away my home and land."

Dinah's hands grew still, her voice kind but disbelieving. "Do you really think that's why they came, Job? Do you think they brought their army to take your home and your land?"

Job could feel his chin quiver. *Please, El Shaddai, hold back my tears. The pain is too great.* He breathed deeply and forced out the words that had been churning inside for six days. "I think their original intention was to protect my home and land, Dinah. But every day they come to the edge of the dung pile, Bela and Sayyid leading the two elders by the hand, Zophar walking beside them. They listen to Sayyid's lies, eat Sayyid's food, and enjoy Sayyid's entertainment. When I try to call out, they hear only my whisper, and Sayyid coos in their ears, saying, 'Look at how the poor man suffers.'

"Bela remains silent, but he fawns over Uncle Eliphaz shamelessly, and I know he presses his own agenda. He wants to see me ruined so he can rise to power as the first Edomite king. My three relatives seem oblivious to everything but their distant mourning, content to be well fed and deceived by my enemies." Job's tears finally overflowed, and he inhaled through clenched teeth.

"Master Job." Nogahla's quiet voice broke through his shroud of pain. "I want you to know that Aban has told your relatives everything truthfully, just as it happened." Her eyes glistened in the moonlight, and Job knew she bore a great weight of responsibility.

He brushed the girl's cheek with his bandaged hand, thankful for the numbing herbs and a friend who did not recoil. "I know your heart holds great hope in the captain's ability to sway my relatives, little one. But I know Eliphaz, Bildad, and Zophar better than their imas and wives. I have lived with them, prayed with them, studied with them, and even learned to think like them in the House of Shem."

His voice became gravelly, so Nogahla lifted a cup of mint tea to his lips, enabling him to continue. "From the conversations you've reported to me, Bildad is especially convinced of some hidden evil in my life that has brought judgment on my household. And he sees Sitis's idolatry as a weakness in my leadership."

He looked at Dinah then, trying to convey his level of certainty. "I *know* Eliphaz, Bildad, and Zophar have been swayed by Sayyid's deception, and they will judge me harshly. But even worse . . ." His throat tightened, and he could barely utter the words. "I believe Bildad will take Sitis away from me unless Yahweh intervenes." He bowed his head so the tears would fall into the ashes rather than onto his cheeks.

✶✶✶✶✶

Sitis heard the familiar crunch of footsteps on the rocky path leading to the widow's cave and pulled back the lovely new curtain Aban had brought them. The early rays of dawn no longer peeked through tattered holes, and the linen cloth created a barrier against daytime summer heat and nighttime desert chill. Sitis saw Dinah and Nogahla returning from their nightly ministrations to Job, but this morning Aban escorted them. All three looked as somber as shepherds without sheep.

Sitis let the curtain fall and glanced at Orma's sleeping form. In only a week's time, the precious widow had provided a home and family in this small cave that meant more to Sitis than she could have imagined. She missed Job and could think of a thousand questions she wanted to ask about El Shaddai, but her heart was more peaceful than it had ever been. *Thank You for my life*, she prayed, waiting for her friends to arrive.

When Dinah and Nogahla quietly pulled the curtain aside and gazed into the cave, Sitis whispered, "I'm awake." Usually Dinah offered news of Job's progress while Nogahla went directly to her sleeping mat for a few hours' rest before returning to observe Sayyid's and Bela's interaction with the relatives. But this morning, Dinah silently waved Sitis to the cave entrance to join them.

"Sitis, Job wants us to prepare you for the worst but pray for God's best." Her friend spoke without preface, her gaze intense. Sitis nodded but didn't speak, appreciating Dinah's directness. "What we know is this: Nogahla has listened carefully at the meetings and Aban has spoken truthfully of Job's character and the events of the past year."

Sitis smiled down at Nogahla, brushing her cheek with her thumb. She must certainly be pleased that the man who held her heart had proved faithful.

But the little Cushite's eyes welled with tears. "I'm so sorry, mistress. It doesn't seem to matter. Your relatives seem bent on believing Master Sayyid's lies."

Sitis nodded, and her own throat tightened as she studied Dinah's worn features. "So is that the worst of it?"

"I'm afraid not." Dinah hesitated.

Sitis's heart plummeted, and she lifted her shaky hand to her throat. "What then?"

"Job believes Bildad will try to take you away from here—away from your husband."

A small sob escaped before Sitis could master her emotions. Struggling for control, she reached out to steady herself against a boulder. *El Shaddai, give me strength. Give me wisdom.* "Why would Bildad take me away from Job?"

Dinah opened her mouth to speak, but Aban blurted out the ugly truth. "Your brother and Job's relatives believe he has committed some hidden sin, and he refuses to repent. Bildad will not leave you in the care of a wicked husband."

"Which is ridiculous!" Dinah's eyes flashed. "If Aban had taken the time to know Job instead of spending his whole life taking orders from that leviathan father of his, perhaps he could have mounted a better defense." She grabbed Nogahla's arm. "Come, Nogahla. You must get some rest before you return to the camp today." The girl cast an apologetic glance over her shoulder before disappearing into the cave with Dinah.

Aban was left wide-eyed and wounded, shoulders drooping. "Why is she angry with me? Mistress Sitis, please know I've done my best. Nogahla has heard my testimony. She knows—"

Sitis reached up and cupped the young man's cheek, silencing him. The feel of his taut skin and cropped, oiled beard reminded her of her own sons, who would have been about Aban's age. "I believe you," she said, not entirely sure why. But the relief on his face bolstered her confidence. "Dinah is frustrated that she can't do more, and she's probably feeling a little hopeless, like the rest of us." Patting his cheek, she added, "She also feels responsible to protect Nogahla from this handsome, charming, and utterly perfect captain until she is certain of his intentions." Aban took her hand, turned it over, and kissed the back of it—like her boys used to do when they were practicing to be grown-ups.

The memory pierced her heart, and unexpected grief nearly strangled her. In that moment, however, the answer to her dilemma struck like a bolt of lightning.

"Aban!" She snatched her hand from his grasp, and he jumped like a child. "You're not going to like what I'm about to say, but I believe all our futures depend on it." She stepped away from the cave entrance so the others wouldn't hear. "I'm going to see Job this morning." When he started to protest, she held up a hand to silence him. "Hear me out. Before I see Job, I'm going to meet with Eliphaz, Bildad, and Zophar. I want them to see my hair, to hear my side of what happened last week in the market. And most importantly, I want them to retrieve my children's bones from the rubble of Ennon's home." She watched shock and admiration slowly spread across Aban's face, and she wished Dinah could have seen it too. *I'm sure the victory in Aban's eyes would convince you of his loyalty, my friend.*

"I wish you didn't have to leave the cave, but I think your plan is brilliant. The undeniable cruelty Sayyid showed in refusing your children's burial will overrule his flimsy excuses—especially when your relatives witness the depth of your humiliation and grief."

Sitis studied Aban's expression and saw glimpses of his father's handsome features. "I'm about to place my life in your hands, Aban. I must ask you a question."

His eyes remained clear and unmasked. "And I will answer you truthfully, mistress."

"Why are you doing this? I've wanted to ask before, but I didn't want Dinah or Nogahla to hear your answer. I want the truth, Aban, whatever it is." Deep within, Sitis feared Aban's answer. But she had to know, and something beyond reason convinced her that he'd be honest.

The young man leaned against a nearby boulder, his features remaining open and relaxed. "When my father issued the order to kill you, I knew he'd lost his northern star. The one person he'd always cherished, his singular passion, was no longer guiding him. When an evil man loses his guiding force, he becomes a madman. And a madman destroys everything in his life."

His words were so matter-of-fact, so detached. For the first time, Sitis realized the depth of this warrior's training. Life and death were as common as bread and air. A spear and arrows were as much a part of his daily routine as spoons and figs.

Feeling a strange mixture of relief and concern, she asked, "What is your guiding force, Aban?" Words escaped her lips before they'd formed in her mind. "Do you follow a god, a moral code, or your heart?"

Aban kicked at a few pebbles on the path, again reminding Sitis of her sons when they struggled with a hard question. The silence forced Sitis to kick a few pebbles of her own while waiting for Aban's answer.

"I don't know this El Shaddai of whom you and Master Job speak. My mother was sent away before she could teach me of Egypt's gods, and Sayyid never taught me to worship the Ishmaelite gods." He paused, looking at the sunrise. "I suppose I'm following my heart for now. But perhaps someday I'll have a better answer for you."

She reached up, held his face between her hands, and drew his gaze to hers. "Someday my husband will teach you of the Most High, Aban. I have found Yahweh to be the only answer any of us needs." Sitis punctuated her words with a little pat. "Now, let's go see my brother."

※ ※ ※ ※ ※

The shouting roused Job from a fitful morning nap. Through bleary eyes, he saw Aban running toward the dung pile in the early rays of dawn.

"What? What is it?" Job tried to shout, his voice still weak. The big guard held up his hands to assure calm was in order, but the gesture did little to slow Job's racing heart. After all that had happened, any sort of screaming—even children's play—instilled immediate panic.

Job noticed a sudden commotion near Bildad's tent and saw Eliphaz and Zophar running half-dazed to Bildad's domain. More wailing commenced. "Aban!" Job yelled with all his might and felt something give way in his throat.

The guard reached the edge of his ash heap. "Don't be alarmed," he said, marching up the ever-growing pile of ash and waste. "Sitis has gone to visit her brother, and he's just seen her hair."

Job couldn't decide whether to laugh or cry. Aban's phrasing sounded as if a maid had just plaited Sitis's hair horrendously, and the Ishmaelite prince was displeased. "Well, I pray he not injure himself over her hair."

Job's sarcasm earned a chuckle from Aban, who sat beside him like an old friend in the stinking mess. They lingered in amiable silence until the sun rose into morning.

"I didn't want to bring your wife here, Master Job," Aban said finally. "It's dangerous. Both Sayyid and the Nameless Ones want her dead, but I promise I'll do all I can to protect her." He continued looking straight ahead. "Sayyid watches you from his balcony day and night, watches this canyon, your visitors, everything."

"Thank you, Aban." Job wanted to say more, but his throat had started to bleed. He longed to beg Aban to guard Sitis carefully, but the man said he would. He hoped Aban was telling the truth and would remain loyal, but the man had already confided a hidden truth. Yes, "thank you" was enough.

"Look, Sitis is coming out of Bildad's tent." Aban was on his feet and halfway to greet her before Job realized he was escorting her to the dung pile.

Job's heart nearly leapt from his chest at the sight of his wife. Though it had been only a week since he'd seen her, she was like air to him. "Sitis, my love." His voice was a scratchy whisper again.

"Job." She'd been crying. Aban held her hand as she stumbled up the ash heap, tears streaming down her face, her eyes red and swollen.

"Sitis, what happened? What did they say to you?"

She fell before him, her face so near the filth that he reached out to catch her. The pain of her head against his hands nearly blinded him.

"I asked them to bury our children's bones, Job, and Bildad agreed, if I would . . . if I would return with him to live the rest of my days in seclusion."

Her words sent rage through his fingertips, replacing the pain.

She looked up, searching his eyes for a response, but then looked down quickly as if afraid of his answer. "He said I have shamed my family, but if I return willingly, you can keep the lands he gave you as my dowry."

"No." It was only a whisper, but the single word lifted Sitis's head.

She smiled then, breathing deeply, a single tear working its way down her perfect cheek. But like a storm cloud on a sunny day, her countenance changed. Haltingly, she said, "Eliphaz stands in agreement. If I do not willingly go with Bildad, Eliphaz will forcibly take all Edomite lands from you and give them to Bela. You will have nothing, and Bela will become the wealthiest man in the East. We will be wanderers, Job, and Bela will most likely rule the Edomites when Esau dies."

Job longed to shelter her in his arms. Instead, he held her with his eyes. "Jehovah-Jireh, Sitis. God is my provider. I have wronged no one. If they wrong us, God will defend us. If it is my choice, you will not go with Bildad, my love. I have everything if I have Yahweh and you. But you must choose where your heart finds contentment."

Job had never seen the light in his wife's countenance shine so brightly. "I choose Yahweh and you, husband. As long as I know nothing can separate me from God or you, I am content."

Sitis, his Ishmaelite princess, her hair two finger-widths long, face smudged with ash and dung—the most beautiful woman he'd ever seen.

She called to Aban, who waited at the edge of the dung pile. "You may take me home now, my friend. I'm staying in Uz." She tentatively kissed Job's blistered lips. "I'll return tonight with Dinah to help her bandage your wounds." She turned and started to slide down the mire.

Oh, how he longed to hold her, to kiss her and love her thoroughly. "Someday you'll lie in my arms again, wife, and I will never let you go." She giggled like a shy maiden and batted her lovely lashes as if she were trying to win his heart.

Job watched Aban lead her away. He reveled in the sway of her hips, the slender curves of her form. Sitis turned back to wave, and Job's heart melted as it had the first time he saw her on their wedding day.

18

~*Job 3:1*~

After this, Job opened his mouth and cursed the day of his birth.

Dinah slowly became aware of a woman shouting her name. *Am I dreaming?* "Oh!" She bolted upright on her sleeping mat and realized from the light streaming in through the curtain that she must have been asleep for a good portion of the morning.

"Mistress Dinah, are you in there?" came the voice from just outside the cave. "I've come with a gift." The screech was loud enough to wake the dead. But it didn't rouse Nogahla, who was sprawled like a hide for tanning. Widow Orma lay trapped beneath Nogahla's right arm, a smile on her wrinkled face. Her twinkling eyes stared up at Dinah.

"Hellooooo!" the persistent voice called once more.

"All right!" Dinah crawled toward the door, yanked back the curtain, and stepped outside. She didn't recognize the smudged face that met her there. The woman displayed only two teeth in a peculiar smile, and her left eyelid—half closed—almost hid the crevice where an eye used to be. Dinah's heart softened immediately. "What gift could you have for us, dear woman? I don't know you."

"I bring a gift for Mistress Sitis from her maid, Nada." The poor thing stretched out a small pot of cold gruel and then chuckled at Dinah's furrowed brow. "Nada said only Mistress Sitis would appreciate the concoction. It's a mixture of slow-cooked fruit, seasoned with cinnamon, saffron, and honey. Here, my child. Take it."

Dinah received the small pot, and the aroma instantly made her mouth water. "It smells delightful."

"Yes, but Nada said this gift was for Sitis alone. If *she* wants to share it with you, that is her choice."

The woman's one stern eye forced Dinah into a compliant nod. "Of course. Sitis should be returning from her visit with Job anytime now. I'll be sure she gets it. Please tell Nada thank you." The woman patted Dinah's cheek as if they were old friends and began her climb down the rocky mountain path.

"Who was that, dear?" Orma had dislodged herself from Nogahla's grasp and curled up with a blanket in her corner of the cave. "What's that in your hand?" The widow had become nearly invisible during the past few days. Dinah sensed she wasn't well, but Orma would never admit to it.

Quiet curiosity must have screamed louder than the woman's greeting because Nogahla's bleary voice said, "What's that?" She sat up and smacked her lips, clearing her mouth.

Dinah chuckled. "Well, I've never seen such a stir over a little pot of gruel." Offering the precious vessel to the widow for safekeeping, Dinah knelt in the cozy space beside Nogahla and recounted the old woman's instructions. "Nada said its contents are for her lady alone." Orma lifted the lid, and the pungent aroma permeated the small cave. Dinah lifted one eyebrow at Nogahla. "A special gift for Sitis *alone*."

The Cushite was no longer sleepy. "Oh, that bossy Nada . . ."

"Now, Nogahla, we must be patient. Perhaps she will share."

Sitis slipped past the curtain, her face alight. "Oh!" Dinah gasped. "We didn't hear you come in." She hoped the woman hadn't heard their frivolous coveting.

Falling to her knees, Sitis joined Dinah on Nogahla's sleeping mat. "Aban is waiting outside to take you and Nogahla to Job." Her voice was intense, her manner urgent. "Bildad, Eliphaz, Zophar, and Elihu have agreed to talk with Job today. I need both of you to be there."

Dinah's heart leapt to her throat. "Sitis, I can't. I . . . Why must I go? My presence would only enrage Zophar and Elihu, and by now Bildad and Eliphaz probably feel the same."

Before Sitis could explain, Dinah felt Nogahla's hands gently curl around hers. "Mistress, I know you are afraid, and I know you battle shame each time those men say bad things to you." The girl's face now shone with a woman's tender expression, and Dinah wondered how she'd grown up without her permission. "You once told me that El Shaddai removed your shame, and no man could ever make you carry it again. Do you still believe that, mistress?"

Dinah's throat tightened, and a sob broke through before words could come. How could she deny Nogahla's simple faith?

Widow Orma set aside the little pot of gruel and crawled on

feeble knees to join them. "Perhaps we should ask Yahweh's blessing on the day to come."

Their heart-knit family of four joined hands and bowed their heads. "El Shaddai," Dinah began, "I don't know the right words. I don't have a goat or lamb to sacrifice, but I believe You will hear our cries and see our tears."

When emotion strangled Dinah's words, Sitis continued. "*We* are the offering, Yahweh. We lay ourselves on the altar of sacrifice today." Sitis lifted her head, paused, and when the others nodded in agreement, they joined together. "Amen."

Dinah cupped Sitis's chin. "Nogahla and I will go. What would you like us to do?"

"Job will need extra care while presenting our case to the relatives." Sitis began reaching for items to put in a basket. "Take plenty of mint tea for his throat and enough herbs and bandages to keep his pain at tolerable levels." She reached up to rake a callused thumb across Dinah's cheek. "Just your presence will mean the most."

Orma had moved into the corner and wrapped herself in her blanket again. "What about Nada's gift?" Her voice was weak but full of mischief.

"Oh, Sitis! I almost forgot." Dinah turned in time to see Orma offer up the little pot of gruel.

Dinah received it and transferred the aromatic mixture to Sitis's hands, watching the woman inhale with utter delight. "Nada hasn't made this for me since my children were toddlers!" she squealed. "Orma and I will save some for you to try when you return." Dinah and Nogahla shared a grateful grin and said their good-byes as Sitis and Orma dipped portions of Nada's heavenly gift.

Job watched them assemble like an invading army. Sayyid emerged with Bildad from the cluster of Ishmaelite tents on the western side of the canyon, and Elihu fell in step behind them. Eliphaz and Zophar were waiting by the center path at the edge of the Edomite encampment, ready to confront their wayward relative. He searched for Bela but didn't see the conniver. *At least one of my enemies has decided to stay home.*

Scanning the canyon dotted with visitors' tents, Job saw no sign of Aban or any of his friends. He would fight this battle alone. Job's heart slammed against his ribs with such force, he thought his chest would burst. As the men drew nearer, bitterness rose like a flood and threatened to drown him.

Elihu pressed ahead of the elders, leading the other four men toward Job's stinking courtyard. Several of Sayyid's guards had come earlier this morning to spread fresh ashes where the elders' mats would be placed—a safe distance from Job's seeping stench. Elihu led the march, as solemn as a burial procession, everyone except the young man wearing a fresh sachet of herbs over his nose and mouth. Job's student must have remembered Dinah's remedy for Sitis and suggested it to the elders.

Before the others reached their mats on the freshly strewn ash, Elihu raced to the pinnacle of Job's heap. Bowing formally, he made a proper show for those arriving. "Abba, your relatives have hesitated to come earlier because of your great suffering. Eliphaz, Prince Bildad, and Zophar . . . they wanted to wait until—"

But the dam of Job's resentment burst. "I curse the day of my birth," he said, ignoring Elihu's excuses. "Why didn't I die as I came from the womb? At least now I would be lying down in peace. God has all but disappeared!"

A few paces away, the elders had just removed their sandals at the edge of their ash pile and stood wide-eyed at Job's outburst. They turned toward Sayyid, as if waiting for his direction before being seated.

As if Job didn't exist, Sayyid extended his hand toward the top of the ash heap, speaking quietly, distracting them from Job's cries. "Please, sit down," he said, playing the gracious host—even on a dung pile.

Job's blood boiled, but he held his tongue until all five men sat on his mountain of filth.

Uncle Eliphaz was the first to venture a word. "If I speak, will you be impatient with me?" He didn't wait for Job's answer but plowed ahead like a wild ox tilling soil. "How could I keep from speaking? Think of how many young men you've instructed." He nodded in Elihu's direction, his voice a muffled singsong under the herb sachet his shmagh held in place. "You've supported those who stumbled and strengthened my own son's faltering faith. Now trouble comes to you, and you're discouraged and dismayed, but shouldn't your blameless life be your confidence and hope? Consider carefully, my son, for you are like my own son, you know. What man being *truly* innocent has ever been destroyed? If you have not hidden away secret sin in your heart, you will not perish."

Tears formed on the old man's lashes, and Job's heart cracked a little. Eliphaz had always been full of bluster, but Job knew the man loved him. "Listen, Job." Eliphaz tented his fingers and rested his gray-bearded chin on them. "A word was secretly brought to me last night amid disquieting dreams. Fear and trembling seized me and made my old bones shake. A spirit glided past my face, and the hair on my body stood on end. It stopped, but I could not see its form. It stood before me, and I heard a hushed voice say, 'Can a man be more righteous than God? Can a man be more pure than his Maker?'"

Eliphaz peered out from beneath his wiry gray eyebrows, his raisin-brown face a mask of awe for El Shaddai. The first-born of Esau was the undisputed and impassioned spiritual leader of the Edomite clan and had been known to have these nighttime visitations from the spirit world before.

"If God charges His angels with error, casting them from His presence, how much more willing is He to crush those who live in houses of clay?" He shook his head, his white beard swishing across his belly like an old woman's broom on a dusty floor. "You can cry out your innocence to El Shaddai, but it seems you are sitting atop His judgment and your children have been crushed in His court without a defender. Men are born to trouble as surely as sparks fly upward. If it were me, I would appeal to God's mercy. Blessed is the man whom God corrects, so don't despise His discipline, my son. He wounds, but He also heals." Nodding to Bildad and Zophar, Eliphaz secured their smug agreement. "We three have examined your plight and find these things to be true. So hear our words and apply them to yourself."

Job gasped for air, feeling utterly robbed. Robbed of breath, life, dignity, and his right to be heard. Eliphaz did not intend his questions to be answered or his answers to be questioned. But how could anyone know the immeasurable depths of Job's suffering? "If only my pain could be weighed on a scale, it would outweigh the sand of the seas, Uncle." Indignation strengthened Job's feeble voice. "No wonder my words seem impetuous to you! God's terror has seized me. I can't eat, can't sleep. My only prayer is that God would let me die before I deny the words of the Holy One!"

The elders seemed unmoved, but Elihu's face was stricken. "Abba, you don't mean that."

"I do mean it! What hope do I have left? Even if a despairing man forsakes El Shaddai, he should still have the devotion of his friends! But you have all turned out to be as unreliable as a wadi—rushing with water one minute, dry as desert bones the next. You came here to comfort me but then saw something horrifying that frightened you. Look at me. Remember who we are to each other. Have I ever lied to you?"

They watched the dung beetles crawling on their mats.

"I said look at me!"

Reluctantly, their eyes raked over his sores.

"Have I asked for a scrap of bread or that you replenish my household?" He waited, but they gave no reply. "No! Yet you accept my enemy's gifts while I am allotted nights of misery and days without hope."

Bildad's handsome features, so similar to his sister's, remained impenetrable. Zophar shifted his bulk and was distracted by a pesky fly buzzing around his head. Eliphaz, to his credit, was attentive, though continued to offer a sympathetic tilt of the head that Job could tolerate no longer.

"Remember, O God, that my life is but a breath," Job cried, voice and hands lifted high. "If I have sinned, what have I done to You, O Watcher of Men? Why have You made me Your target? Why don't You forgive my sins by sacrifice as You promised?"

Bildad's face blazed crimson. "Is that the way you were taught to approach the Most High? To just shout at Him, accuse Him, question Him? How long will you be allowed to speak and act as you wish? Does God pervert justice? Your children sinned against Him, and Yahweh judged them for it. Even Elihu understands this. He told us that you had to make morning sacrifices each time one of their celebrations ran its course."

Job stared at Elihu, astonished that the young man he'd trained and loved would betray him.

Elihu shook his head in denial but said nothing, and Bildad bristled at Job's silent reprimand. "It's not Elihu's fault that your children were raised in an indulgent household by an idolatrous mother."

Job felt as if he'd been slapped. His breath left him. And something in Bildad's expression changed. Perhaps even he realized he'd gone too far.

"Listen, Job," Bildad said, his voice showing a measure of remorse, "if you will look to the Most High and plead with Him, if you are pure and upright, He will restore you to your rightful place. Eliphaz and I have lived a long time, and the older generations have much to teach you. Tradition is a valuable guide, and we can assure you that God does not reject a blameless man or strengthen the hands of evildoers."

Job looked at the line of his once dear friends—Elihu, Zophar, Eliphaz, and Bildad—and then noted the smug grin on Sayyid's face. Job released a deep sigh. He was spent. Weary and miserable, he longed for death.

As he glanced beyond the relatives' tents to the canyon's entry, the sun's rays illuminated the approach of three silhouettes. The sight of them was like cool water to a thirsty soul. Aban, Nogahla, and . . . yes, even Dinah, were marching toward him. He suddenly recalled Sitis's promise. "I'll return tonight," she had said. He must be able to tell her he fought well.

Job met Bildad's commanding stare. "I have witnessed the truth of your statement, 'God does not reject the blameless or strengthen the hands of evildoers.' However, what of Eliphaz's miraculous revelation? How can a man be blameless before God? By that argument, isn't every man evil?" Job delighted in the consternation on Bildad's face as he caught the old man in Eliphaz's web of logic. "You say, 'Plead with El Shaddai,' but how can I? He is too powerful, invisible, and has set His purpose that will not be moved. If the Most High granted me a hearing and found all my actions to be right and good, I'm sure my words would condemn me, Bildad. So it seems to me that God toys with us, mocking when tragedy befalls the poor and lowly. If God does not harm the lowly, who does? Is there another force at work in the universe?"

Job watched Sayyid's smile widen and the veins in Bildad's neck bulge. Eliphaz placed a calming hand on Bildad's leg and cowed him with a subtle nod. No doubt they would let Job condemn himself, but his next line of argument was for Sayyid's benefit.

"Of course there are other forces in the universe," Job continued, answering his own question. "The Ishmaelites in Uz believe in the power of their three goddesses, and many of my own Edomite clan accept the mountain god, Kaus. What about you, Sayyid? Don't you worship idols?" Sayyid glanced at the hardened expressions on his guests' faces, and Job felt a moment of triumph. "And yet the idolater Sayyid seems to be quite prosperous. Wouldn't you say, Uncle Eliphaz?" Job leaned forward and spoke quietly to the most sympathetic of his visitors.

Turning his face toward heaven, Job cried out again to El Shaddai. "Does it please You to hurt me, while You smile on the schemes of the wicked? Do You have eyes of flesh? Do You see like a mortal man? Do You enjoy probing me for sin—though You know I am not guilty and that no one else can rescue me from Your hand?"

"Job!" Eliphaz tried to silence him, but Job would not be stilled.

"Your hands shaped me and made me. You knit me together and gave me life, showed me kindness. Will You now destroy me? I can't understand it. I've tried to smile and pretend that everything will turn out for my good, but I cannot mask my despair any longer. Please, Yahweh, I am just a man! I need an arbitrator. Otherwise, just let me go down to the grave in peace." At these words, Job fell silent and allowed his tears to flow.

He felt a gentle hand touch his bandaged shoulder, and when he looked up, Dinah held out a warm cup of mint tea. She and Nogahla had slipped through the charred shell of his home and discreetly ascended his ash heap. With their quiet presence behind him, he felt empowered, warmed by their friendship. Aban stood like a sentry at the front edge of the courtyard wall, a safe distance from both sides of the battle. Job noticed a shared glance between Sayyid and his captain, but Job also received a smile and wink from Aban. *Can you be trusted, my young friend?*

Job's momentary distraction was interrupted by a low, feral growl. Zophar had spotted Dinah.

✿✿✿✿✿

Every time Dinah saw him, the hate in Zophar's eyes startled her. She tried to steady her shaking hand so as not to spill Job's tea. *I stand innocent before El Shaddai. No man can shame me. Innocent before El Shaddai. No shame.* She played the words over and over in her mind, trying to knead the truth into her heart like yeast into bread dough. So far it wasn't working.

"Are all Job's words to go unanswered?" Zophar shouted, and Dinah jumped like a spooked donkey, spilling tea on Job's bandaged hands.

"I'm sorry," she whispered. He indicated with a nod that she should sit behind him, and she gladly tucked herself behind his shoulder.

"You imply that your beliefs are flawless and you are pure in God's sight. I wish God would speak against you and disclose the secrets of His wisdom, for true wisdom has two sides. Know this, Job: God has even forgotten some of your sins."

Job shook his head and threw his hands in the air. "What does that mean, Zophar? When you don't know what to say, you spew forth this intellectual gibberish with many words and little meaning."

Zophar's lips pressed tight, his face red and trembling like a rumbling cooking pot ready to explode. "Can you fathom the mysteries of God?" he said. "If God has put you in prison, who can oppose Him? No one! God recognized a deceitful man and acted appropriately. If you put away the sin that you clutch in your hand . . ." Zophar pointed his chubby finger directly at Dinah, and she wished she could dig a hole in the dung pile and crawl into it. "If you put this evil away, then you'll be able to show your face without shame and stand firm in your rightful place without fear." He moved his accusing finger to Job. "But the wicked man fails, and escape eludes him. His hope becomes a dying gasp."

Dinah peered over Job's right shoulder and noticed his whole body beginning to tremble. "I'm sure you three are the keepers of all God's wisdom and perfect understanding will die with you!" Job's shout resulted in a coughing fit, and the clean cloth Nogahla offered was quickly smeared with blood.

Job's pompous relatives stared, horrified.

"You live in your finery and ease," he said through coughs, "and you show contempt for my misfortune. It's easier to convince yourselves it's my fault than to believe this could happen to you." Job raised his hand in Sayyid's direction. "But how do you explain the prosperity of those who provoke God—those who carry their gods in their hands?" Sayyid shifted uneasily on his mat, and Dinah felt an immense sense of pride at the case Job was making.

The poor man barely paused for breath. "To God belong wisdom and power. Counsel and understanding are His. He makes nations great and destroys them. All the things you have learned, I have also been taught. I am not inferior in knowledge."

Job wiped his mouth, his coughing settling some, and he held up his hand when Eliphaz tried to interrupt. "Would it turn out well if God examined you as you are examining me? Would not His splendor terrify you as His arrows have terrified me? All your maxims are ashes and your proverbs shatter like clay. I speak to God plainly as I would speak if He stood here before me. Why? Because though He might slay me, He is still my God, my only hope of deliverance."

He wiped his mouth again and handed the dirty rag to Dinah. "Consider this. Would a godless man dare speak so boldly? Would a godless man ask these two things of God—that He would withdraw these frightening terrors and that

He would meet me face-to-face? Do these sound like requests from a godless man?"

Dinah wanted to clap, to rejoice, to cheer for this man who had suffered so violently and yet held so firmly to his faith. But no one cheered. The lengthening silence throbbed with tension until eerie laughter rose from behind the dung heap. Dinah's eyes darted to the shadowy, burned-out remains of Job's home, where she spotted the Nameless One cavorting with some of his men. She glanced at Elihu. He too had noticed the ominous presence. Foreboding crept up her neck, raised the fine hairs on her arms.

Sayyid cleared his throat, drawing attention to his satisfied smile. "Job appears to need a rest, and all this talk has made me hungry. I'll instruct my cooks to serve the midday meal, and we can reconvene when the heat of the day has passed." He clapped his hands and rubbed them together as if trying to start a fire with two sticks. Standing on Bildad's left, he was able to appear as though he was speaking to Job, but his eyes shot cunning arrows in Dinah's direction. "Our dessert will be a special fruit gruel that will be especially pleasing to Job and Bildad."

When Sitis's brother tilted his head in silent question, Sayyid laughed melodiously. "Bildad, do you remember Nada, Sitis's old nursemaid? She has prepared a honeyed fruit gruel." He paused and then stared at Dinah. "It was Sitis's favorite."

Dinah thought it strange that Sayyid rehearsed Nada's menu, and even stranger that he spoke of Sitis as though she had gone away . . .

The Nameless One released another eerie chuckle that wriggled up her spine, and as she turned to issue a scathing glance, her blood turned to ice in her veins. Standing next to the leader, enjoying his lecherous pawing, was the one-eyed old woman who had delivered Sitis's fruit gruel to the cave earlier that morning.

"Nooo!" Dinah was instantly on her feet but was paralyzed with indecision.

Every upturned face questioned her silently, but it was Job who whispered, "Dinah?"

"Job, I must go." She motioned to Nogahla to follow, and the girl obeyed without question.

"Dinah, won't you stay and try some of Sitis's favorite dish?" Sayyid's singsong voice called after her as she slid down the ash heap toward the courtyard wall, where Aban had been standing. He would know what to do.

"Mistress, why can't we stay for the meal?" Nogahla asked, trying to catch up with Dinah's quick pace.

Tears began to cascade down Dinah's cheeks. No one else had pieced together the awful truth yet, and she couldn't bring herself to say the words aloud. *They've poisoned Sitis with Nada's gruel.* She had to get to Aban. But as she rounded the jagged corner of broken red bricks, Sayyid's captain was already halfway across the canyon, presumably to deliver instructions for the midday meal.

Dinah broke into a run and Nogahla followed. "Aban, wait! I must speak with you!"

He turned, his features showing his annoyance at first, but Dinah's tears stopped him in mid-stride. "Dinah, what is it? What happened up there?"

"It's Sitis, Aban," she whispered, careful not to let the echo of the canyon carry the news to Job or betray Aban's allegiance. "They've poisoned her with Nada's fruit gruel." Dinah saw the horrified realization on Nogahla's face.

Aban grabbed Dinah's shoulders. "How do you know this?"

"Did you hear the Nameless One laughing?" Aban nodded, and Dinah continued, breathless, tears now blurring her vision and slurring her words. "The one-eyed old woman who stood beside him delivered a pot of Nada's fruit gruel this morning before you returned to the cave with Sitis. The old woman was adamant that Sitis eat the concoction alone—as a gift from Nada." Dinah gasped at a new horror. "El Shaddai, no! Widow Orma ate it too!" She glanced at Nogahla, and the girl darted away before Dinah could stop her.

Aban panicked. "She can't go by herself." He started to chase Nogahla, but Dinah clutched at his massive arm to stop him.

"Aban, stop! Think about who is watching," she whispered. "Be wise." Dinah tugged at his robe with all her might. "You must finish your responsibilities for Sayyid, Aban. You cannot risk further your tentative position with your master."

Aban relented, his expression like granite. Turning abruptly, he held Dinah's face between his hands and drew her close enough to kiss her. He whispered violently, urgently, "You get to the cave! Get there before Nogahla finds two lifeless bodies and has to remember that image for the rest of her life. I care too much for her to let that happen." He bent and kissed Dinah roughly. "Sayyid believes I want you. That should convince him and create an excuse for me to slip away to the cave later. Now go!"

19

If only you would hide me in the grave and
conceal me till your anger has passed! If only
you would set me a time and then remember
me!

The afternoon sun burned through Sayyid's black robe, but he lingered outside the courtyard entry to his kitchen. He found Nada precisely where he'd left her earlier—standing over a steaming pot of fruit gruel, weeping. She'd been understandably distraught when one of the serving maids told her of Sitis's death. Nada's whole life had been devoted to her mistress. She needed Sitis like a fire needs dung chips.

The left side of his lips turned up in a wicked grin. *I've cleaned out the dung from both our lives, Nada.*

Quietly studying the maid, Sayyid wondered, *Will she try to return to Bildad's camp now that Sitis is gone?* Sayyid

302

clenched his teeth, working his jaw muscles. *I will never allow Bildad to take anyone from me again.*

Nada glanced in his direction but quickly returned her attention to the pot. Could he trust her? Before he ate confidently from her hands, he must be certain she believed him innocent of any involvement in Sitis's death. She was no fool and knew his love for Sitis had skidded into dark hatred.

"Still crying, Nada?" he said, stepping into the doorway. "Surely you realize that Sitis is in paradise with her goddesses, and you need not feel guilty." He kept his distance, realizing that the old girl could turn her boiling pot of stew into a weapon. "How could you know our new cook would put Apple of Sodom in your fruit gruel? She was a bad woman who used your helpful purgative remedy to poison our friend."

"But I shouldn't have left the Sodom gourds anywhere in the kitchen, Sayyid." Nada wiped her nose across the sleeve of her robe from elbow to wrist, and Sayyid felt a fleeting disgust at what else might have dripped into the fruit stew. "I didn't know the woman, and I shouldn't have trusted her."

"Nada, as I explained this morning, no one could have anticipated her hatred for Sitis. She kept it a well-guarded secret all these years." Sayyid took two careful steps toward the old woman, but Nada raised her wooden spoon in warning. He halted and spoke soothingly. "When one of my guards saw the old crone coming from Widow Orma's cave this morning, he questioned her and found out she'd held a grudge against Mistress Sitis all these years for the loss of her eye."

While Nada used her already dampened sleeve to wipe her tears, Sayyid wiped perspiration from his own brow, hoping the story had fooled her. Nada need not know the betraying cook was the Nameless One's wife, who had lost her eye

303

twenty years ago in a drunken clash with a woman from her own tribe.

Nada finally looked up from her cooking pot. "Sayyid, you look hungry. Would you like some of my special gruel?"

Something in the woman's eyes gave him pause. Could she know he had ordered the Nameless Ones to find Sitis and kill her? "I had a fine meal with our guests, Nada. I don't think I need any gruel."

"All right," she said, "but I know how you loved Sitis's favorite dish when you were a scruffy farm boy visiting Master Bildad's camp. It's a shame to let this gruel fill your maids' stomachs when you could enjoy it yourself."

The woman removed the pot from the fire and started ladling it into bowls. Sayyid watched her work, the aroma of cinnamon and saffron breaking down his resolve. *She seems convinced that the old hag alone poisoned the gruel. Even if Nada suspected I was involved, she wouldn't dare try to poison me.*

As a final effort to safeguard his stomach, he said, "Nada, if you'll join me in a bowl of stew, I'll have some."

She hesitated, and again Sayyid wondered if perhaps she was conniving. "Master Sayyid, I feel awkward eating alone with the master of the house. Should I call some of the other servants to join us?"

Sayyid chafed at the idea of allowing his servants to lounge at midday. "Why should you feel awkward, Nada? We're old friends. Let's pretend this is Bildad's kitchen and I'm that scruffy young farm boy."

Motioning to the reed mat beside the low table, he sat down. The woman carried over two bowls of the aromatic gruel, placing one in front of Sayyid and the other before herself. Sayyid studied his portion and then switched the bowls. "Ladies first," he said, lifting the curved and hollowed wooden spoon she offered.

A flicker of understanding registered in the old woman's expression. "Oh, Sayyid, I would never do such a thing." She scooped the first taste into her mouth. "Now eat! Eat!"

No further encouragement was needed, and Sayyid shoveled in mouthful after mouthful of the sweet and savory mix. "Nada, this is heavenly!" He was so busy enjoying his portion that he overlooked the fact that Nada's bowl remained untouched after her initial bite.

"Nooo!" The sickening realization was followed almost immediately by a ripping pain in his bowels.

The poisonous Apple of Sodom served in small doses was a mild purgative. But as Sayyid curled into a tight ball on his side, he realized Nada had most likely used enough to purge his bowels from his body. Delirium set in quickly, and Sayyid could only recall the rags stuffed in his mouth to silence his cries and the wrinkled brown face of a woman he'd once thought kind.

⁂

Job awakened to the sound of a hoopoe bird's *oop-oop-oop*, and watched its preening dust bath at the edge of his dung pile. The sun was well past midday, and the canyon remained eerily quiet after his relatives' feast on Sayyid's provisions. The aroma of cinnamon and saffron lingered, bringing a wave of grief. Bildad and Elihu had taken second portions of Sitis's favorite dish, the fruit gruel his children had savored as little ones bouncing on his knee. Zophar had even joined the reminiscing, telling stories of Ennon's boyhood schemes to steal his sister's special dessert.

Job's stomach twisted now as it had at midday. He couldn't endure their conversation or the fruit gruel that reminded him of happier days. How could his friends laugh and pretend all was well when his whole life was dust? How could these men, who called themselves family, go on living when Job died more every day?

Movement at the far end of the canyon arrested his attention, and he recognized Aban's mountainous physique winding through the tents of the visiting army. Two willowy figures walked beside him, and Job sighed, relieved that his friends would soon return to offer their silent support. He wished Sitis could join them too, but Job had agreed it best she not hear their relatives' detailed accusations. Forgiveness was hard for Sitis, and words once spoken were not easily forgotten. It was best she not come until after the relatives returned to their tents for the evening. Perhaps tonight Job and his wife could enjoy a few moments alone. Sitis still thrilled him, even when all else was heartbreak.

Aban and Dinah drew nearer with Nogahla close behind. Job sensed a heaviness in their countenance. Their shoulders sagged, faces drawn and gray. A terrible sense of foreboding crept into his bones. The hoopoe bird flew away, taking its bright feathers and lovely song with it. The canyon was quiet—too quiet. Where was Sayyid, and why hadn't he roused his guests to begin the afternoon meeting? It wasn't like him to wait patiently to see Job tortured further by his friends.

Dinah spoke momentarily to Aban and then left him in front of Bildad's tent while she and Nogahla continued toward Job. Dinah's odd behavior and quick departure before the midday meal had been cause for concern, and Aban's shocking kiss seemed completely out of character for both of them. *I'm sure there's a reasonable explanation.*

As Dinah and Nogahla slogged through the ash and dung, Job saw that their eyes were swollen and their cheeks streaked with tears. Dinah wrung her hands, a habit she acted out unwittingly when she was nervous or afraid. *Why would she be afraid now? I'm the only one here.* But when he looked into her eyes, he became afraid too.

"Job, I need you to listen to everything I say before you ask me any questions. Please." Dinah's voice broke, and she nearly wrung her hands off her wrists. "Sayyid is dead."

Job didn't know how to respond. His lifelong enemy was gone. He wanted to rejoice. *But the Most High says I mustn't gloat over my enemy's misfortune.*

Before he could form another thought, Dinah continued. "Nada killed him in retribution."

What? Job's head spun at Dinah's stream of words.

"An old woman took Nada's fruit gruel to Sitis at the cave this morning, but the woman was working with Sayyid and had poisoned the gruel. Sitis and Widow Orma ate it while we were here at the meeting." She reached out to hold his bandaged hands, but he couldn't feel anything. "Job, can you hear me?" He nodded. "Sitis and Orma are dead too."

Dinah's face twisted into a tortured mask of grief, and something inside Job splintered. He thrust himself backward into the muck and clawed at his wounds, wailing and keening. "No, Yahweh! Nooo!"

Could one die of pain? Of grief? He would try. Let the agony of his sores drown him in sweet blackness.

"Ahh! Yahweh, You have destroyed all hope! All I am is gone. I am nothing."

Hands were on him. "Job, please. You're tearing open your wounds."

"Master Job, you must listen to me now. You must believe. Master Job, it's Nogahla. Remember to trust."

Hands tried to restrain him, tried to hold and comfort the tempest raging inside and out. He ripped at his flesh. The searing fire that consumed his body gave relief to the mortal wound of his soul. He fought with all his might, blinded by rage and grief and doubt, until strong hands restrained him, held him, carried him back to his place at the pinnacle of the mire.

"Job."

At first he refused to respond, refused to acknowledge that life and breath still held him. When he finally opened his eyes, Aban's face met him, and the big man's tears revealed his heart.

"I'm so sorry. I failed you." The simple words soothed Job more than herbs. "You must let Dinah and Nogahla tend your wounds. Your relatives will come to you in a few moments to make plans for Sitis's burial."

Job realized that he was lying in Aban's arms like a child. How long had it been since he'd been held in a caring embrace? "Thank you," he whispered. Tears still falling, he was spent.

Aban laid him on the visitors' reed mats. "Your so-called friends can find their own mats." The guard's face clouded. "Dinah, when you and Nogahla are finished, I'll go to the relatives' tents and tell them they cannot talk to Job until I return from the city gate."

Job heard Dinah speak as if she were at the bottom of a pit. "Why must you be the one to speak in Nada's defense, Aban?"

"Because I was the one who found her and my father's serving maids wrapping his body for burial."

Job closed his eyes, wishing he could join Sitis. When would the madness of this world end? *El Shaddai, if only You would hide me in the grave until Your anger has passed.*

A troubling thought crossed his mind as Dinah began the arduous process of tending his broken body. *If a man dies, will he live again?* The question had never been answered in his days at the House of Shem, and now that his children and Sitis were gone—would he ever see them again? He heard himself cry out. And then the darkness he yearned for overtook him.

❖❖❖❖❖

The moment Aban entered Bildad's tent and reported Ima Sitis's death, Elihu wanted to run to Abba Job, to hold him and comfort him. When he heard Job's wailing and saw Aban dart away, he had no idea the guard would treat Job so gently. Elihu followed at a distance and watched the guard cradle Job in his arms and speak soft words of encouragement. *I should be caring for Abba Job*, he thought.

Elihu realized he should never have left Uz. He'd been so certain that by gathering the influential Edomite and powerful Ishmaelite prince, Sayyid's treachery would be exposed. Instead, Elihu's departure left Abba and Ima more vulnerable to Sayyid's torture and brought nothing but condemnation from the visiting elders.

He walked the last two steps into the mire and sat on a reed mat atop a nearby mound, five paces from his unconscious

Abba Job. Working feverishly to rebandage Job's wounds and stop the bleeding, Dinah and Nogahla were like a perfectly fitted jar and lid, two pieces of one unit. Dinah breathed in, Nogahla breathed out. Even Aban worked well with the women.

Elihu covertly wiped a tear, listening to Dinah command Sayyid's captain. "Aban, lift Job's arm so I can wrap his torso while he's still unconscious."

That woman could lead an army. His heart squeezed in his chest, and something inside snapped like a bent stick finally broken. Dinah wasn't the monster Zophar described. How could Elihu have let himself be poisoned by hatred, forgetting all Abba Job had taught him about Yahweh's forgiveness? The woman before him was a compassionate healer, who cared deeply—and purely—for Abba.

Dinah glanced up and caught him studying her. He didn't turn away this time, nor did he glare. "I'd like to help if I can," he said quietly, expecting Dinah to curse him or throw one of her herb jars at his head. Instead, she turned away, and he didn't blame her. *El Shaddai, please forgive my hate and unforgiveness. I want to be right with You, even if no one else accepts my efforts at peace.*

Nogahla's voice interrupted his prayer. "You can come over here and lift Master Job's other arm—if you promise to behave yourself." The Cushite's round, dark eyes nearly burned a hole through him.

Rising from his mat, he crossed the chasm of emotion between the two piles. He gave the large guard a wide berth, standing next to the little maid and across from Dinah. "I will do more than behave, Nogahla," he said. "I will apologize to Dinah."

The beautiful healer lifted her sky blue eyes. Elihu thought for the first time he might one day be Dinah's friend but knew she would never be his wife. Not because she was unworthy as Zophar had said, but because he knew in his spirit that El Shaddai would lead them on different paths.

Still Dinah remained silent, and Elihu voiced his tortured repentance. "I'm sorry I allowed Zophar's hatred to infect me and hurt you, but I don't know if I can stand in your defense against the elders as Job does." He felt weak and pathetic, less than a man. But all his life he'd been taught to keep silent in the presence of his teachers. How could he stand against them now?

Aban glared at him. The sight of the captain's massive arms and the clanking of the bronze-tipped arrows in his quiver nearly sent Elihu fleeing down the ash heap in terror. The mountainous guard opened his mouth, but before he uttered a sound, Nogahla's smooth, dark hand rested on his cheek. The man was transformed into a lamb. He turned an adoring gaze on the Cushite maid, and Elihu watched—utterly thunderstruck—as the two exchanged silent affection.

Elihu expected to see the jealousy of a woman scorned on Dinah's features. Instead, her expression was that of a patient teacher with a slow student. "Things aren't always as they appear, Elihu. When Aban kissed me, it was to distract Sayyid, giving the appearance of possessing me and then returning to his duties." Her hands continued coating Abba Job's bandages with frankincense and myrrh. "In reality, Aban slipped away to help us prepare Sitis's and Orma's bodies for burial." Tears gathered on her lashes and dripped into the myrrh pot. "Sayyid was Aban's father, Elihu."

Aban bowed his head and expelled a long sigh. Elihu felt

as if daggers had been thrust into his belly. *Will my misjudgments and assumptions never cease?* Elihu had misjudged Aban and Dinah's relationship and assumed that a powerful captain would have no emotional attachment to his master.

"I'm truly sorry, Aban," he said, glancing at the ash and dung between his feet. "I too lost my father, and it is a moment that changes a son's life." Elihu looked up, meeting Aban's gaze for the first time. "Though I won't pretend that I cared for Sayyid, I know the loss of a father is difficult to bear—no matter the relationship." In the silence, a common cord of understanding entwined the men's hearts.

Finally, Aban straightened to full height, dwarfing all those around Job's still form. His outward struggle to maintain a soldier's composure was evident. "I mourn in the secret place of a boy who did not know his father well," he said. "But as a man, I had hopes for the father Sayyid could have become."

Elihu wiped another tear. This time he didn't hide it. "You are a worthy son, Aban, and you have risen above the weaknesses of the man who gave you life."

The captain bowed, and Nogahla laid her hand on his arm. Aban's large hand covered hers, and Elihu marveled at their tenderness, deepened by the extreme hardships they'd faced together.

Nogahla tilted her head toward the big man, her concern evident. "Perhaps Elihu would testify for you when you speak on Nada's behalf. He could defend your rights as Sayyid's heir to the city elders this afternoon." She glanced between the two men.

A rush of dread washed over Elihu. Who was he to appear before the elders of Uz? No one listened to him.

He studied the dung between his feet again. "I can't attest to Nada's actions, but I heard Sayyid call you 'my son' when Eliphaz and Bildad arrived with their armies. I would be honored to testify to your parentage, Aban, but I'm not sure my words hold much sway."

Aban hesitated only a moment. "Thank you, Elihu." He drew a deep breath. "I hope the elders will relent on Nada's sentence when I tell them it was a blood-for-blood killing."

"And then will you keep Nada as your cook?" Nogahla asked quickly. Then, just as quickly, her face looked stricken. "Oh my. I don't suppose you would keep a cook who poisoned your own father."

Aban reached out to touch her cheek, regret shadowing his features. "If I had better protected Mistress Sitis, Nada would never have killed my father." His hand fell to his side.

"Ima Sitis wouldn't want you to blame yourself, Aban." Elihu's voice was gentle, holding no malice.

The big man inhaled again, seeming to use every seah of strength to maintain his composure. "And I must not blame myself. My energy must be spent seeking the Nameless One and his wife—those truly responsible for the deaths. My guards have gone into the desert to find them." Sniffing and looking to the heavens, he wiped his hand down the full length of his face. "And I will concentrate on freeing Nada."

Turning to Elihu, he said, "Though you think your words hold little importance, your testimony regarding my inheritance could still be beneficial. I don't care about myself, but . . ." He lowered his voice, casting his gaze toward Eliphaz's tent. "Bela the Edomite holds most of the land surrounding Uz, and he believes Eliphaz will award Job's land to him. Job's land is valuable because it consists of both Edomite and Ishmaelite properties. Adding Job's estate to his own holdings will almost certainly ensure Bela as the first king of Edom. But some of my soldiers overheard Bela conspiring with Eliphaz to seize my father's property—which is *Ishmaelite* land—if I can't prove that Sayyid was my father. If Bela is successful, the Edomites would control all the land in Uz, and the Ishmaelite treaty, established by Mistress Sitis and Job's marriage, would end."

Dinah spoke up then, her cheeks flushed. "You mean a war could begin if the Edomites gain too much control of Uz?"

The big man nodded. "The city of Uz sits squarely on the Ishmaelite-Edomite border. So it's a bit more complicated than that, but I suppose when the stew boils all day, that's the truth left in the pot."

Elihu heard Nogahla whimper and watched Aban place a comforting hand on her cheek. "Perhaps I make too dire a prediction," he said and then turned to Elihu. "Still, I ask that you testify for a practical reason as well. As a soldier, I could sleep in a stable or the open field, but if Bela takes Sayyid's home, Dinah and Nogahla will have no place to stay, and Nada will have no master to serve. Since Prince Bildad ordered Mistress Sitis to remain entombed in Widow Orma's cave, they can hardly return . . ."

Aban continued speaking, but Elihu felt as if all breath left his body. *Ima Sitis in a beggar's cave? Why not in the family tomb?*

"What!" he shouted. "How dare Bildad show such disrespect to my ima! Her Ishmaelite nobility alone should merit burial in a tomb, not a cave."

Everyone gawked at him as if he'd sprouted horns, but Aban recovered and spoke first. "I'm sorry, Elihu. I thought you knew of Prince Bildad's decision." He glanced down at his callused hands and spoke slowly. "The Ishmaelite prince said he would not allow an idolatress to be buried according to Yahweh's teachings." Aban's features stilled. Stepping forward, he landed a strong hand on Elihu's shoulder. "I understand your grief, my friend. Please don't feel you need to accompany me to the city gate. Take time to visit your ima Sitis at the widow's cave. Perhaps you'll feel better then."

Aban turned and began a slow, weary slide down the dung pile. "Wait!" Elihu said, his voice choked with emotion. "I believe the city gate is on the way to the widow's cave. I can grieve best by helping a friend." Wiping his face, he took a step to leave but was stilled by a tender touch on his shoulder.

"Thank you, Elihu." Dinah's azure eyes pooled with tears, her lips curved into a tentative smile. "Thank you for being here when we need you most."

His throat tight with emotion, he nodded a silent goodbye and hurried to catch up with Aban. "We must stop at Bildad's tent on the way," he said, when he'd swallowed his heart back into place.

"Would you like me to wait outside?" Aban spoke quietly, respectfully, and Elihu marveled that this gentle man lurked inside the beast he'd imagined.

"No, Aban. I'd like you to come inside and explain to Prince Bildad what will happen to Ishmaelites in Uz if Bela gains control of your inheritance. Surely Bildad, an Ishmaelite prince, who also heard Sayyid's parental declaration, will provide testimony to tip the scales of justice that have been broken too long."

20

*I know that my Redeemer lives, and that in the
end he will stand upon the earth. And after my
skin has been destroyed, yet in my flesh I will
see God. . . . How my heart yearns within me!*

Job woke to a searing pain in his back. He groaned and tried
to open his eyes, but his eyelids felt as if they were on fire.
He wept, and the salt in his tears burned like coals rolling
down his cheeks. And then he remembered Sitis. "Nooo!"
He tried to sit up, and his constricting muscles scraped the
bandages, sending a shudder through him.

Dinah rushed to one side, Aban to the other, and Nogahla
supported his back. Their hands, pressing on the bandages,
felt like blades against his flesh. He sat. They steadied him.
Breathe. Breathe. Black spots obscured his vision, but gaug-
ing the sun's western haunt, he guessed his unconsciousness
had given him several hours of blissful relief. He saw Bildad,

Eliphaz, Zophar, Elihu, and now Bela sitting opposite him on reed mats, faces ashen.

"Where is my Sitis?" Job sobbed. "Will she live again?" *Breathe. Breathe. Perhaps this is a nightmare.* But this was no dream, and his pleas turned to bile in his throat. "At least a tree buds again. At least a dry riverbed runs with water again." Shaking his fist at heaven, Job shrieked, "The days I have left are few, O God. You've already determined their number, so let me put in my time and leave me alone!"

"Job! You blow empty words like the hot east wind!" Eliphaz shouted in a voice so much like Esau's, Job had to look twice to be sure his great-abba had not arrived. "Do you think you're the only one suffering here? Your own words condemn you, my son."

"My son," Job seethed silently. *How can you call me "my son" when instead of comforting me, you sat and listened to the lies of my enemy for seven days?* The realization struck Job anew. *Sayyid is also dead!* He turned to Aban, who was as gray and immovable as Elath granite.

Before Job could offer any words of comfort, Eliphaz's thunder turned toward Aban. "You spoke with a silver tongue, Captain, when we met your father, but a guard at your rank thrives on treachery. Mark my words." He laid a protective arm over Bela's shoulder. "Fire will consume your wealth because you bribed those elders today. You have stolen Sayyid's estate from my kinsman Bela, but Yahweh will repay your wickedness."

Even through his grief, Job felt his cheeks flush, ashamed at his uncle's venom. Why would Eliphaz think Bela deserved Sayyid's property, and by what evidence would he accuse Aban of bribery? Had he no respect for a grieving man?

Job's heart squeezed at the depravity of the man he had once respected as an abba. His elders had proven their cruelty, heaping on abuse at a person's weakest moment.

Suddenly Eliphaz released Bela and bounced his gnarled finger at Dinah. "And you, Jacob's daughter! The godless conceive only trouble and give birth to evil. Their wombs fashion only conceit." He sputtered as if he wanted to say more but had used up all the vile words in his basket.

Once again Job found himself cringing on behalf of a friend. He offered silent apologies to Aban and Dinah, both of whom smiled their forbearance. Mustering what little life he had left, Job met Eliphaz's fiery gaze. "Uncle, if I were sitting in a fine robe at your ripe old age, I could utter long-winded speeches too—but I would hope my words could be encouraging, not disparaging."

Eliphaz shifted uncomfortably. Job's uncle prided himself on holiness, Bildad on tradition, and Zophar on intellect. Job could debate each man's shortcomings, but what purpose would that serve?

Job turned his face heavenward again, crying out against those truly responsible for his pain. "El Shaddai, why have You blessed the efforts of evil men and turned me over to be mocked by wicked people? All was well with me, but You crushed me! You pierced my kidneys and spilled gall on the ground. Now I wear sackcloth and my eyes are ringed with death's shadow."

He fell silent, watching the startled faces around him. Pondering his venomous prayer, he searched his heart. Did he regret it? *No!* He felt betrayed by God. Alone. Abandoned.

And then came a subtle call. *Oop-oop-oop.* He looked to the front edge of the ash heap and saw the hoopoe bird.

The stony edges of his heart chipped away as he watched the instrument of Yahweh's reassurance bathe in the dust. Yes, God had allowed his pain, but the Creator had also sent the hoopoe bird to comfort Job.

"Yet even now, my Lord, You are my only advocate." Fresh tears came as sweet words rolled like honey on his tongue. "Who else but You can save me, restore me? You alone are my deliverer." He opened his eyes and saw the hoopoe bird fly away. Fresh despair shot through him like a flaming arrow.

Turning to his uncle, he pleaded with Eliphaz—dared him—to end the confusion warring within. "God has made me a byword, Uncle. People spit in my face as they walk by me. Please, try again with your words. See if you can tell me something I don't already know."

"How can you speak to us as if we were stupid cattle when you're the one who is completely insane?" Bildad interrupted, shaking a balled fist in the air. His words escaped through tightly clenched teeth. "You've lost all ability to reason. You tear yourself to pieces and then expect everyone to disregard God's truths for your sake. The wicked man perishes from the earth, and he leaves no descendants among his people. Such is the place of one who—knows—not—God." The old man punctuated his last words by poking the air, each jab like a dagger into Job's heart.

"How long will you crush me with your words?" Job cried. *Does he truly believe that now I don't even know El Shaddai?* Weeping overtook him. Could this be the same man who had rejoiced at Job's wedding? The same beloved teacher who had doted on him in the House of Shem, calling him the star student, chosen by God to teach the clans of Esau?

"If I have gone astray," he choked out between sobs, "it's

my concern, not yours. But know this . . . God has wronged me."

Dinah placed her hand on his shoulder, and pain radiated through him. "Job, please choose your words carefully."

"Though I have cried out for justice," he shouted into her pleading expression, "I get no justice from on high. My servants have abandoned me, my friends detest me, my breath is—was—offensive to my wife."

Job noted Dinah's troubled expression, and the reflection of her doubts glistened in Nogahla's eyes. But Job fought his own inner battle. He suddenly realized he could argue either aspect of God's grandeur—His power to destroy *and* His power to revive.

"In the depths of my spirit, I *know* life cannot end here. I know my Redeemer lives." Though never taught this in the House of Shem, still he knew it to be true. "After my flesh is destroyed, God will stand on the earth, and I will see Him face-to-face. Oh, how my heart yearns for that day."

Zophar sneered. "You talk out of both sides of your face. You say we die and there is no rising, yet you say you will die and then see God. I think Bildad is right. You are lost in sin, and your ability to reason has left you."

Job glared at his onetime best friend and brother. "If you think you can draw me into a debate and reveal some deep, dark sin, perhaps you should search your own heart because someday you too will meet God face-to-face."

Zophar rocked back and forth in his fury, trying to stand, but his bulk made the task a difficult one. "You have dishonored your elders and me long enough!" On the third try, he rolled to his knees and straightened his robe, then marched to Job's ash heap, towering over him. "You think you're clever, but your pride has always been your downfall. Evil tasted sweet, didn't *she*?" Zophar aimed his finger at Dinah, less than a handbreadth from her nose. "But judgment fell on your house because of her! God has made you vomit up the riches you gained through oppressing the poor and your deceitful trading."

Zophar folded his arms across his puffed-up chest, releasing longtime resentment Job had no idea existed. His hatred of Dinah was a tired repetition of the same drumbeat, but his bitterness toward Job rent their relationship like a shofar splitting the silence.

Aban jumped to his feet, the sudden motion causing Zophar to stumble back. "You will not speak of Dinah with such blatant disrespect, my lord." Aban's humble bow accompanied his authoritative command. "She is neither a harlot nor a criminal, and I will use every weapon at my disposal to defend her honor."

Zophar drew himself up to his full height, tilting his head back to meet Aban's gaze. "I hope your men are willing to die for a murderess." Glancing over at Bela, he sneered. "My kinsman would have made better use of his household guard. It's a shame your father left his troops in a fool's hands."

Elihu slapped his knees and unfolded his wiry frame. "Why must we involve Dinah at all?" Exchanging a comrade's glance with Aban, he descended the elders' ash pile and stood in the neutral space, leveling his question at Zophar. "Your hatred toward Dinah has colored your opinion of Job's circumstances, and you made sure Bildad, Eliphaz, and I shared that hatred before we arrived."

Job glanced from Zophar to the elders to Dinah and couldn't decide which face was most shocked by Elihu's defense. *What happened to unite Aban and Elihu during my afternoon of darkness, and what has given my brilliant student such courage in the presence of these elders?* Job felt an overwhelming pride in the young man and wished Sitis could have seen his confident air and noble bearing.

Zophar's face turned as red as the cliffs around them, but before he could slice Elihu with his sharp tongue, Aban came to the rescue. "Won't you return to your mat, my lord?" Aban extended his hand toward the elders' ash pile, his words a request but his eyes a command.

Silence stretched as tight as a bowstring.

"Zophar," Job said softly, "please sit and listen carefully." The round, red-haired man maintained his wide stance next to Aban, and Job continued staring into unrelenting eyes. "Is my complaint directed at any of you elders? Take a good look at me and be afraid, Zophar. Why do wicked men grow old and prosper, their flocks and herds flourishing? You have seen it in your travels from Damascus to Egypt—evil men spared from calamity. So how can you console me with this nonsense about only the wicked receiving punishment?"

"That's enough!" Eliphaz shouted, the little sensitivity he had previously displayed now completely cast aside. "You declare your righteousness before God. Fine! Does God take this much notice of a righteous man? Is it for your holiness that He rebukes you? No! It's because you stripped the poor of their clothing. You gave neither water to the weary nor food to the hungry. You sent widows away empty-handed and broke the backs of the fatherless with endless days in your fields. Why not just admit your sins, submit to God's discipline, and be at peace with Him? Then your prosperity will return to you."

Job's mouth dropped open at his uncle's wild accusations,

marveling that his venom could match the earlier charges of bribery against Aban.

Just as the thought formed in Job's mind, Eliphaz extended his hand toward Dinah and the captain. "And if you remove the wickedness from your household, God will hear your prayers and deliver even those who are *not* innocent because of the cleanness of *your* hands."

Aban clapped his hands together, causing everyone to jump. "We're finished for today." Elihu followed his lead, the two men nodding agreement. "The sun is descending in the western sky," Aban continued, "and I must arrange lodging for my new guests." He extended his hand, inviting Dinah and Nogahla to exit the dung pile. Shyly, the women rose and exited before the esteemed elders, causing a fresh myriad of complaints.

"It's an insult for a woman and her slave to show her back to an Ishmaelite prince," Bildad sputtered as Elihu offered his hand to steady the old man, stepping down the pile of ashes.

"That ridiculous soldier has no concept of hospitality," Eliphaz roared. "His honored guests always leave first." Zophar cast a loathsome glance over his shoulder and stalked away while Bela supported Eliphaz on his extended elbow.

Weary, confused, and beleaguered, Job watched everyone disappear into the fading light. He wanted to cry out, to stop them. But what would he say? *Don't go. Please, someone stay with me tonight!* Ridiculous. He wasn't a child. He placed a steadying hand on his mat, turning toward the sunset. A ripple of blinding white pain shot through him—but even this seemed dull compared to the bottomless heartache.

Letting his head loll forward, he felt the deepest agony of his life. He was utterly, undeniably alone.

Something shifted in his spirit. Some glowing ember was finally snuffed out.

✸✸✸✸✸

The morning sun blazed with an already torturous heat. Elihu arrived early at the ash heap, hoping for a few quiet moments with Abba Job. But the air between them was as heavy as the haze that shrouded the canyon.

"Abba, did you hear? The city elders absolved Nada of any wrongdoing in Sayyid's death. They ruled her act as a blood-for-blood killing, and Aban asked her to serve in his kitchen."

Job offered no reply.

What happened to you during the night, Abba? When Elihu had left the ash heap with the elders at sunset, Abba had been responsive. Now he sat silently in slack-jawed despair. Elihu's eyes clouded with tears. His once robust abba and teacher slouched over folded legs, arms no thicker than twigs. Bandages hid protruding bones of starvation, and a loincloth hung loosely around blackened skin. The canopied courtyard protected Job from direct sunlight, but the wind and small animals nipped at his exposed flesh. Job's eyes were river pebbles, rubbed smooth by tears, set in a skeletal mask of pain.

"Abba, did Nada have the right to take Sayyid's life?" Elihu moved closer, hoping to draw his beloved teacher into conversation. "Aban's guards have given up hope to find the Nameless Ones in their familiar desert haunts. Do you believe justice has been served through Sayyid's death alone?"

Job issued a cold stare. "Justice?" The muscles in his face began an eerie dance. A twitch at the crest of his left cheek. A tic at one side of his mouth and left eyelid. "You should discuss justice with bored men on white thrones," he said in monotone, fixing his gaze on the visitors' tents.

Activity stirred across the canyon, and Elihu glanced toward Sayyid's palace. Today it was Aban's home. *Though Abba Job's suffering overshadows Aban's victory over Bela*, Elihu thought, *still we should celebrate Yahweh's provision and power.*

"Aban has acquired Sayyid's estate," he said, trying to impart some hope, "and Aban has promised to care for us all: Nada, Dinah, Nogahla, me—and you, Abba, when your wounds heal." He paused, unsure how Job felt about remaining on the ash pile. "He said you could live inside the house whenever you wish. El Shaddai is at work."

Wrapped inside an invisible shroud of his own making, Job remained aloof, offered no reply. Aban, Dinah, and Nogahla approached from across the canyon, waves of heat causing their silhouettes to dance in dreamlike steps.

Elihu leaned close and whispered, "They come because they love you, Abba. As I love you."

Job's facial tic intensified, and a leaden dread settled into Elihu's stomach. If Abba's countenance didn't brighten at the approach of Dinah and Nogahla, what hope remained for him? These two women had been his sun and moon.

As if summoned by the presence of Job's supporters, Bildad, Eliphaz, and Zophar emerged from a single tent, their expressions as hard as Hittite iron. Elihu sighed deeply, dreading the moments to come. He had spent the morning listening to the elders' plot. They would remain silent to frustrate Job into submission.

"Abba," he whispered, "remember the night of the tragedies, when you praised Yahweh."

Job's stare was as vacant as the charred shell of his home.

"Remember, Sayyid has met a wicked man's fate. His son, a good man, has received his inheritance. Righteousness has prevailed."

Again, no response.

Knowing his time to speak had ended, Elihu dutifully slid down the mound of ash and dung. He met the elders at the broken courtyard wall, extending his hand to assist them to their reed mats. The three relatives wore fresh herb sachets beneath their noses, ready to overcome the stench of Job's stubborn resistance. Bela, on the other hand, remained at home, no doubt contemplating his losses and considering alternate gains.

Elihu arranged the reed mats for the elders and heard the deep, resonant sound of Aban's greeting.

"Good morning, Job," the big guard said. He followed Dinah and Nogahla, ascending Job's ash pile. Wearing the same sandals and robe as yesterday, Aban was evidently more interested in supporting his friend than choosing a new wardrobe.

Job's face reddened and his agitation grew, but still he remained silent while everyone assumed their positions. Aban sat at Job's right side. Nogahla took her place directly behind her beloved captain. Dinah knelt at Job's left, her hands constantly tending his needs, offering mint tea, rolling bandages, preparing herbal remedies.

The three elders, barely settled on their mats, were greeted with Abba Job's voice. "Even today my complaint is bitter. If I had the chance to stand before El Shaddai as Nada stood before the elders, I would be acquitted of all wrongdoing just as she was!"

Elihu's heart pounded. He barely recognized his abba in this moment. Yes, his voice resounded like the Job of a year ago, but his expression was pinched and his words embittered.

"I have looked for God—north, south, east, and west—to do that very thing, to present my case before Him. He knows I have treasured His teachings and kept every one. Yet God does what He pleases, and who can oppose Him? I am terrified, but I will not be silent in the thick darkness that covers me." Abba paused as if waiting for the elders to confront him as they had yesterday.

Elihu bowed his head. Their plot of silence was deafening and awkward. Eliphaz, Bildad, and Zophar were determined not to answer until Job showed some sign of repentance.

"Why was Nada judged so quickly while the Nameless Ones continue in their wicked lives? Why doesn't God set times for *their* judgment?" Abba Job was relentless. "Men steal flocks and pasture them in someone else's field. Are they punished? No! And then we all die. Everyone! Without knowing when or why or how. If I've spoken anything that is untrue, go ahead and reduce my words to nothing!"

Bildad thrust his fist into the air. "Dominion and authority are God's alone, Job! How dare you presume to instruct El Shaddai? Man is less than a maggot in His sight! You say you are righteous, but how can a man be righteous, when even the moon is not bright and the stars are not pure in His eyes?"

His voice had shattered the relatives' earlier agreement, and Eliphaz placed his gnarled hand on Bildad's arm, silencing the Ishmaelite prince. Elihu watched the wordless exchange, no animosity or anger, simply a renewed pact of stubborn piety, and Bildad recoiled like a dayflower at dusk.

Elihu thought he might retch. The stench of the dung heap and Job's wounds were more palatable than the air of hypocrisy in these men.

"My, my, Bildad," Job said, his words dripping with scorn, "by whose spirit do you speak such wisdom?"

Elihu saw beyond the sores on Job's flesh and mourned the resentment disfiguring his character.

"Of course God has all dominion and authority," Job continued. "He spread out the skies over empty space and suspended the earth over nothing. He wraps the waters in the clouds and marks a boundary between light and darkness. And these are but a faint whisper we hear of Him. But as surely as God lives, He has denied me justice."

Elihu gasped and watched Dinah's hands still on the bandages she was rolling. But Job did not seem to notice. He was swallowed up in self-justification.

"I will never admit you three are right. I will maintain my righteousness as long as I have breath. I am innocent before El Shaddai, and no man can shame me."

Dinah turned to him and whispered something. Elihu watched her lips form the words, *Innocent before El Shaddai, and no man can shame me.* His heart skipped a beat. Yes, Abba Job had spoken that same truth to Dinah many times, encouraging her to embrace Yahweh's forgiveness and rebuff the shame others continually thrust upon her. Job was applying his teaching to himself—but wasn't he twisting this truth to accommodate his anger?

Elihu glanced down the row of elders. How many truths had they twisted in their anger toward Job? He saw Zophar's neck shade a deep crimson as he watched Dinah. Job's cousin-brother had believed his own twisted truths for so long that he'd made Dinah an idol of the world's evil. To stop loathing her would open a floodgate of tolerance he couldn't accept.

Abba Job seemed calmed after Dinah's counsel, his voice

quieter, his words more reasonable. "If I were a godless man, what hope would I have? I tell you, brothers, my hope lies in El Shaddai alone." Looking to his right, he smiled weakly at Aban before turning back to his relatives. "Let me tell you the fate God allots to the wicked, the heritage a ruthless man receives from the Almighty: however many his children, their fate is the sword. His offspring will never have enough to eat."

"Job!" Dinah's shocked outburst mirrored every expression. Nogahla's tears were immediate, and the pain on the big guard's face was inexpressible. Even the cynical line of elders offered sympathetic glances to the son of a wicked father, now betrayed by an ungrateful friend.

"Dinah, let me finish," Job said quietly.

Aban bowed his head, most certainly ashamed and embarrassed. Everything inside Elihu wished to shout the truths of El Shaddai. Why weren't the elders encouraging Abba with the teachings? They were the only source of life and hope to answer Job's despair. Instead, no one spoke, and Job went on.

"As I was saying, though a wicked man heaps up silver like dust and clothes like piles of clay, what he lays up the righteous will wear, and the innocent will divide his silver." He extended his hand to Aban. "El Shaddai has surely cut off a wicked man and all his *other* offspring. He has placed Sayyid's great wealth in your hands, Aban, and I pray you will learn the ways of the Most High and honor Him with the gifts He has given you." He shrugged his shoulders as if considering what figs to purchase at the market. "Perhaps it will go better with you than it has with me."

Silence prevailed, and Job's expression grew contemplative. "Wisdom is hidden, Aban. Men have searched in the deepest caverns of the earth and found iron and gold and silver, but wisdom was not there. It cannot be found in the deepest sea or bought with gold from Ophir or topaz from Nogahla's homeland of Cush." Turning to the three elders, he said, "Not even destruction and death know where to find wisdom. Only El Shaddai understands the path to it. 'The fear of the Lord—that is wisdom, and to shun evil is understanding.' Isn't that what we were taught?"

Dinah poured another cup of mint tea and held it out to him. "Please, Job." Her eyes implored him, and Elihu silently begged him to drink it and quiet his runaway tongue. Alas, he did not.

"Wouldn't it be nice if I could sit in my elder's seat again? Oh, for the days when I was in my prime. Dying men blessed me, and I made the widow's heart sing. I was eyes to the blind and feet to the lame. I was an abba to you, Elihu."

Dinah bowed her head and lowered the cup.

Job began to tremble and tears welled in his eyes. Lifting his three-fingered bandaged hand toward heaven, he screamed, "My life ebbs away, and I cry out to You, O God. But You do not hear me. You turn on me ruthlessly. My skin grows black and peels, my body burns with fever. I mourn and I wail, yet You do not relent. Why?"

He turned back to the elders, his expression wild and fierce. "Let Yahweh weigh me on honest scales, and He will know I am blameless! I made a covenant with my eyes not to look lustfully at a girl." He pointed to Dinah. "If my heart was enticed by this woman, *that* would have been a sin to be judged, a fire that burned to destruction. When dealing with servants and the poor, I feared God's judgment, so I kept myself from wicked things. If somehow I have concealed my sin, as men do, I would tell you now. I would put it in writing and sign it. But I tell you before God, I am blameless. El Shaddai has wronged me, and I want Him to appear before me and give me a fair hearing!"

"This is madness!" Elihu sprang to his feet, staring down at the three elders. "How can you sit there and say nothing to comfort your friend? He has lost everything, and yet you give him no hope, only judgment and condemnation." Bildad offered no remorse, and Eliphaz crossed his arms over his chest. Zophar locked his gaze on Dinah, whose tears had formed rivers down the front of her robe.

"And you, Abba." Elihu crossed the few paces of courtyard filth and saw the justification on Job's pocked face. "You defend yourself with declarations of righteousness and then accuse God of injustice." Elihu glanced at both camps of mentors. "I have kept silent, thinking my elders should teach wisdom. But it is the Spirit of God in a man, the breath of the Almighty, that gives understanding. So now I will have my say, and you will listen to me!"

Elihu watched Job's expression harden and felt as if a dagger twisted in his gut. "Abba, my words come from an upright heart." He ascended the ash pile and knelt before his teacher and abba. "You taught me everything I know about El Shaddai. I am just like you before Yahweh. I too have been made from clay. You need not fear condemnation from me, nor will I show partiality to the elders. It is God's Spirit that compels me to speak, no other motivation."

Elihu thought he noted the slightest crack in Job's defenses, and as he drew breath for his first word, a chilly breeze swept through the canyon, cooling the blistering sun.

21

~*Job 38:1–2*~

Then the LORD *answered Job out of the*
storm. . . . "Who is this that darkens my counsel
with words without knowledge?"

Dinah's heart broke at Elihu's confidence in Yahweh.
There are no answers, Elihu. Even the elders know it.
Elihu was like a man wandering in the desert, leading another
man to a mirage. Job's despair sounded raw and ugly, but
Dinah was beginning to believe his words were true. And the
gravest truth of all sat beside her. El Shaddai could heal Job
and make all things right in the world, but He chose not to.
Evil men like Sayyid gained power and left an inheritance to
a son, while good men like Job died on a dung hill without
a legacy. Greedy men like Bela prospered, and poor widows
like Orma died in a cave.

Dinah's cheeks burned under Zophar's judgmental gaze.

She would live out her days stooped under the weight of his hatred.

Elihu's grand speech began, more words in a sea of endless blither. Dinah was sick to death of men's prattle about a God they understood no more than a tree could grasp the ax that felled it.

"Abba Job, you have said in my hearing that God considers you His enemy, but in this you are not right, for God is greater than man and doesn't make war with him." Elihu's words were gentle but firm. "Why do you complain to Yahweh that He answers none of man's words? God does speak—now one way, now another—sometimes in dreams, sometimes by chastening a man on his sickbed, and at other times through an angel or mediator. But in all these ways, God is speaking to a man for his good, to keep him from wrongdoing, so that the light of life may shine on him."

A resounding clap of thunder shook the ground. Silence reigned for two heartbeats as every eye went wide with wonder. A storm in the middle of a desert summer was unimaginable.

Elihu's features glowed with wonder, his fervor stoked by the loud clap. "Abba, it is unthinkable for the Almighty to do wrong. Who appointed Him over the earth? If He withdrew His breath, all mankind would turn to dust. So why would the God who sustains you destroy you without provocation? Look at the heavens, Abba."

Job stubbornly glared at Elihu. When had he become so angry, so unreachable?

"Please, Abba." Elihu pointed to the rumbling heavens, and finally Job complied. Peering beyond the canopy, Dinah saw a black, rolling storm filling the skies from the east.

"Look at the clouds, Abba," Elihu said. "If you sin, how does that affect El Shaddai, the Creator of the heavens? Yet His eyes see each one of us. There is no dark place, no shadow where anyone can hide. Men cry out under a load of oppression, but when times are good, no one says, 'Where is God my Maker, who gave me a song in the night, who teaches more to me than to the beasts in the field?'"

Elihu turned his attention toward the elders. "You, Bildad, have accused the Most High of using His power as He pleases, without restraint or conscience. And you, Zophar, have harbored the kind of resentment in your heart that befits a godless man."

"Ha!" Job laughed aloud like a boy whose ima had just scolded his naughty friend.

"Yes, and resentment is eating you alive, Abba Job." Elihu turned on him, compassionate but firm. "Those who suffer, God delivers from their suffering. He speaks to them in their affliction. Even now, He is wooing you—longing to comfort you in your distress. But you are so quick to blame, beg, or barter to prove yourself righteous, you're missing the relationship Yahweh wants to build through your pain. El Shaddai has a higher call than the dung pile on which you sit."

Relationship? Dinah glanced at Job to measure his approval of Elihu's assertions. She had never heard anyone declare that El Shaddai sought a *relationship* with a human.

Slowly Job's anger seemed softened by a sad but hopeful expression. Another rumble filled the sky, its vibration shaking Dinah to her core. Job turned to her with a warm glance that fanned the dying embers of her hope.

"You were a good teacher, Abba," Elihu said. Lifting an

eyebrow, he pointed to the darkening skies. "But Yahweh's voice is louder and stronger."

Dinah shivered as another cold breeze swept away the summer heat. She nearly bolted for cover when lightning skittered across the sky.

But Elihu was like a child at play, dancing delightedly among the ashes as the first drops of rain splattered the red dust and drummed the canopy overhead. "Who can understand how El Shaddai spreads out the clouds or scatters lightning across the face of the earth?"

Another great peal of thunder rattled the foundations, and tiny beads of hail began to bounce off the canyon floor like pearls from heaven. Elihu's praise sank deeply into Dinah's soul like rain into the thirsty soil.

"Listen! God's voice rumbles in marvelous ways. His breath produces ice, and water freezes. He brings floods to punish men, but the same clouds water the earth and show His love." Elihu ran to the courtyard wall beyond the canopy, catching a handful of hail like evidence at a trial. "Tell me, Abba, can we, with our limited understanding, draw up a righteous defense for ourselves to the Most High?" Turning to the elders, he said, "You were right—all of you—when you told Abba Job that El Shaddai is beyond our reach. But you misrepresent God's power if you allow any shadow of oppression to fall from His hand. Fear Him, yes, but recognize His work as a loving expression to draw a man closer, not crush or repel him."

Dinah saw a golden light split the northern sky, brighter than the sun, shimmering like rushing water. It descended over the canyon and lingered, an indefinable, shapeless pattern. The roar accompanying it was rolling thunder and sea combined—not a voice, but an understanding, a knowing. She could not look away; she did not want to—ever. For the first time, she understood Job's words, "Though He might slay me—He is still my God, my only hope of deliverance."

Wind blew rain sideways and battered her face. Dinah drew Nogahla close, and they huddled together in awe of the shimmering light and darkening clouds around them. Rain mixed with snow and ice pelted them. Incredible. Dinah glanced aside to see if Job was all right.

The sight was as shocking as snow in a summer drought. Job was standing, arms lifted to the sky, displaying more strength than she'd seen in over a year.

✱✱✱✱✱

Every sore, every wound on Job's body, buzzed as though bees' wings enveloped him—not stinging, simply kissing his skin with their vibration. The rumble of God's voice quaked through his inner being.

Who is this that darkens My counsel with words without knowledge? Brace yourself like a man, and I will question you, and you will answer Me.

Job tried to bow his head, tried to close his eyes, but he could not. God willed his attention, and he could not look away. He wondered fleetingly about the others. Could they see El Shaddai? Could they hear His voice? Job was not the keeper of the covenant promise as Jacob was. How could Yahweh be speaking to him? But he had little time for trivial considerations before the God of the universe began His interrogation.

Where were you, Job, when I laid the earth's foundation? Tell Me if you understand who marked off its dimensions.

Surely you know! Have you journeyed to the springs of the sea? What is the way to the abode of light? Have you entered the storehouses of snow or seen the storehouses of hail, which I reserve for times of trouble? Who endowed the heart with wisdom or gave understanding to the mind?

Finally, Job felt released, and he fell forward in worship, his face in the ash and dung. He dared not answer, dared not utter a word.

Do you hunt the prey for the lioness and satisfy the hunger of the lions? Do you know when the mountain goats give birth? Do you watch when the doe bears her fawn? Will the wild ox consent to serve you? Does the eagle soar at your command?

Job lifted his head, felt the cold breeze against his tingling skin, and saw the shimmering light transformed into a column reaching to the heavens. The Voice in Job's spirit changed to a Voice his ears now perceived.

The elders fell on their faces, crying for mercy, their fine linen robes mired in the rain-covered slop.

"We are destroyed!" Bildad bellowed. "Yahweh has judged us!"

"We have spoken foolishly!" Zophar wept aloud.

Job peered out of the muck to see a smile on Elihu's face. "Elohim! Elohim! You show Your power through snow, ice, and rain on a desert summer day!"

The Voice rattled the red cliffs around them. "Will the one who contends with the Almighty correct Him? Let him who accuses God answer Him!"

"I have no defense, Yahweh, for the things I said," Job replied. "I am unworthy to speak another word in Your presence—I put my hand over my mouth."

Through tears, Job glanced at Dinah, Nogahla, and Aban, who knelt with their faces in the dirt. Dinah's faith was surely strong enough to have withstood his senseless blustering, but what of Nogahla and Aban? Had Job's faithless words damaged the budding devotion of those who knew little of El Shaddai? Heartbroken, he looked into the shimmering column.

The light swelled, and the rain beat out the rhythm of God's rebuke, His voice no longer an inner knowing but a resounding drum for all to hear. "Brace yourself, Job, and you will answer Me."

Job's heart withered, but at the same time, he exulted in God's presence.

"Would you discredit My justice to tout your righteousness? Would you condemn Me to justify yourself?" A horrendous peal of thunder shook the earth. "Can you make your voice thunder like Mine or reduce proud and wicked men to the grave? On the day you can do those things, I will admit you have the right to question Me."

The fluttering sensation on Job's skin ceased, and panic stirred in his belly. *Don't leave me!* he prayed, keeping his gaze focused on the shimmering column. Suddenly he felt as if a sword sliced through his heart. In agony, he screamed and rolled onto his back. When he looked up, Dinah hovered over him, her lips moving but uttering no sound. He glanced at the elders, shock and terror still etched on their faces, but only the Voice resounded in his ears.

"Consider the hippopotamus, Job, which I made along with you—except he feeds on grass like an ox." The absurdity of the comparison nearly made Job chuckle. Why would God speak of a hippopotamus at this most holy moment?

"I endowed him with physical power, bones like bronze, and limbs like iron. He ranks first among My works."

Job gripped his chest, feeling the definition of every rib. He had once been muscular and sinewy. Had he too been ranked first among God's works?

Lightning flashed, and the searing pain in Job's chest intensified.

"Yet his Maker can approach the mighty behemoth with His sword."

Why would God need a sword to approach anything in creation? Job's heart beat wildly—was it the pain or the unanswered questions?

"Wild animals play nearby while the mighty hippo sleeps in the shade of the lotus plants, and when the river rages, he is not alarmed. He is secure, Job." The last words came as a whisper. The rain and storm ceased completely. "Can anyone capture him or trap him?"

Job wanted to laugh at that. Of course no one could capture the behemoth, but when he gazed at Elihu and the elders, he understood God's message. Why hadn't Job, like the hippopotamus, rested in his Maker's ability to sustain him when the storms of life raged? Why had he instead raged against God and his friends so fiercely?

"Do you think you can snag the leviathan with a fishhook?" the Voice continued. "If you lay a hand on him, you will remember the struggle and never do it again! No one is fierce enough to rouse him, so who could stand against Me? Who dares file a claim that I must pay when everything under heaven belongs to Me?"

The searing pain in Job's chest eased, relief coming with a great sigh. In the presence of such wonder, he marveled at his foolish demands on the Most High. Had he been utterly mad?

"Who can strip off the leviathan's outer coat, his back with rows of shields tightly sealed together? Joined fast, they cling together and cannot be parted."

Job marveled as the snow began falling again, gently now. A chill surged through him as the Voice continued a description that felt too familiar.

"His snorting throws out flashes of light, and fire streams from his mouth."

In his misery, Job had become the leviathan. Donning an impenetrable outer shield, he had roared fiery accusations against his friends and God.

"The leviathan makes the depths churn like a boiling cauldron, and behind him he leaves a glistening wake. One would think the deep had white hair."

Silently now, Eliphaz, Bildad, and Zophar stared at him from across the dung pile, their faces wasted, withered, aged. They had entered Job's nightmare, but their pride couldn't compare to the leviathan.

"Nothing on earth is his equal," the Voice concluded. "He looks down on all that are haughty; he is king over all that are proud."

Job bowed his head, broken. "I know You can do all things, Yahweh," he whispered, his voice full of reverence. "All Your plans will be fulfilled. I spoke of things far beyond my ability to comprehend. My ears had heard of You, but now my eyes have seen You. I despise myself and repent in dust and ashes."

For the first time in over a year, Job felt no pain in his body, yet his spirit ached to be forgiven. He had been so certain of his righteousness. Now his only certainty lay in his desire to please the merciful God who had spared his life after he had spoken so recklessly. He placed his forehead into the ashes and waited for God's judgment. Whatever Yahweh decided, he was convinced the punishment would be just.

The relatives' whimpering had ceased in anticipation of Yahweh's imminent response, and the ragged breaths of eight awestruck believers kept rhythm as the snow ceased and the lively patter of raindrops returned. Job raised his head from the mire and heard the thunderous Voice. Surprisingly, Yahweh's rebuke shifted to the elders.

"Eliphaz the Temanite, I am angry with you and your two friends, because you have not spoken of Me what is right, as My servant Job has. So now take seven bulls and seven rams and go to My servant Job and sacrifice a burnt offering for yourselves. My servant Job will pray for you, and I will accept his prayer and not deal with you according to your folly."

The Voice imposed judgment, and the red cliffs resounded with finality as the shimmering light throbbed. Job was breathless. Had El Shaddai really said the elders had spoken wrongly and he had spoken what was right?

But El Shaddai, I challenged You carelessly. His heart squeezed in his chest. How could he be judged innocent and the others found guilty?

Looking up, Job saw Uncle Eliphaz ensconced in an ethereal glow, his face turned heavenward, tears like raindrops streaming down his white beard. But Zophar lay in a fetal coil, face covered, weeping incongruent vows of allegiance and defiance. Bildad wept like a child in Elihu's arms and then suddenly beat the sludge with his fists, crying, "Elohim, I have studied Your teachings. I spoke the truth!" Elihu, seemingly shocked and ashamed, tried to quiet the old man, but Bildad shoved him away and wept alone in the melting pile of dung.

El Shaddai, Job prayed, *Eliphaz shows a repentant heart, but Bildad and Zophar seem unchanged by Your rebuke.* Job watched the shimmering light for some response. Nothing. He waited for the stabbing pain in his chest or the buzzing sensation in his body—a second command or confirmation of Yahweh's forgiveness. None came.

My servant Job will pray for you, the Voice had said, *and I will accept his prayer and not deal with you according to your folly.*

Job glanced at Aban. The captain looked full of anticipation, the blowing rain creating rivers down his ash-and-dung-covered face. "I will summon a cart to carry you to the mountaintop altar, my friend," he said softly, as if coaxing Job's obedience.

Dinah must have heard Aban's offer over Bildad's and Zophar's din. "We could use some blankets to soften your ride, Job." Her words were pleading too.

Job turned to Nogahla. Gazing into those big, bold eyes was like looking into an obsidian mirror. In hesitating to forgive, he saw his reflection in those he resented. He was Zophar, allowing anger to soar into hatred. He was Bildad, carving his opinions as sacred rules into stone. He was Eliphaz, elevating his holiness to alienate those he loved.

Job will pray for you, and I will accept his prayer and not deal with you according to your folly.

It was only by Yahweh's mercy that *anyone* was forgiven. No one was worthy. No lamb or goat was a sufficient sacrifice. Only El Shaddai's loving favor made it possible for any human to come before Him.

"Do my brothers have the seven bulls and seven rams for their sacrifice?" Job shouted, his voice resounding in the canyon.

Elihu looked up, face alight. "Yes, Abba. They brought a small herd for offerings." Bildad and Zophar stilled. Eliphaz opened his eyes, awaiting his nephew's direction. The shimmering column of light remained, and the miraculous summer rain continued its steady drumming on the canopy. A crowd had gathered at the mouth of the canyon, and servants stood outside Aban's home in awe of the spectacular.

Job turned to Dinah, whose face was radiant. "I will pray for my relatives," he whispered, "but I ask that you pray for me, dear friend."

Tears flowed in rivers down her cheeks. Dinah nodded her understanding. Of all Job's friends, she knew best the lasting scars of inner battles. Dinah knew him best in every way.

22

~Job 42:10–11~

After Job had prayed for his friends . . . all his
brothers and sisters and everyone who had
known him before came and ate with him in his
house. They comforted and consoled him over
all the trouble the LORD *had brought upon him,*
and each one gave him a piece of silver and a
gold ring.

Dinah's sandals clicked on the tiled hallway of Aban's home. "Hurry, Nogahla. We mustn't be late for the sacrifice again this morning." Two of the last seven mornings, they'd arrived at Job's mountaintop altar after dawn's rays had peeked over the eastern cliffs. Walking from Aban's fourth-story halls, across the canyon, and up to Job's mountaintop altar was the equivalent of a morning's journey for some merchants.

The fact that she and Nogahla were sequestered alone in a

spacious bedroom on the fourth floor, while Aban's servants slept six in a chamber on the ground floor, irritated Dinah like a splinter under her fingernail. Aban's reasoning seemed sound—to create as little upheaval for his household as possible—but Dinah could hardly stomach the thought of her expansive rooms and woolen mattress while serving maids slept huddled on reed mats. Aban had reserved the second story for Job and the personal servants he intended to hire as soon as Job was sufficiently recovered. But Job's healing was slow, and the restoration of his wealth would take time.

"Mistress, your frown is back." Nogahla's concerned voice broke into Dinah's thoughts as they hurried down the stairway.

Dinah wished she didn't wear her heart on her face. "Here," she said, reaching into her pocket and offering a clove leaf to Nogahla. "Chew on this. It'll make your breath even sweeter than you are." Dinah winked and slipped one into her mouth as well, noting Nogahla's eyebrow lift in understanding.

"I still want to know why your frown is back," the girl said, crushing the leaf between her teeth.

The two women emerged from Aban's home and reverently skipped over the steady red stream flowing through the canyon floor. The miraculous summer rains had continued in Uz, though traveling merchants reported the drought had nearly crippled every neighboring region.

Dinah and Nogahla stepped into Job's home, which now showed distinguishable renovation progress since reputable craftsmen had replaced the Nameless Ones. On their way to Job's tower steps, Nogahla pressed her concern. "Mistress, are you going to tell me about your frown?"

But Dinah hurried through the curved hallway toward the

first stairs they must conquer. "Nogahla, if we use all our breath for talking, we'll never reach the mountaintop in time for the sacrifice." They fell into amiable silence, concentrating on their climb, and soon the small rectangle of lavender at the mountaintop entrance exploded into morning.

"430, 431, 432! Whew!" Dinah had adopted Elihu's childhood habit of counting the tower steps aloud, but when she lifted her eyes to the stares of Bildad, Eliphaz, and Zophar, she nearly swallowed the clove leaf she was chewing.

Elihu stepped forward, extending a friendly hand. "I'm glad to know the workmen haven't added an extra step."

Dinah felt her cheeks grow warm. Nogahla grabbed the back of her robe, following meekly behind, and the women settled on a bench beside Aban. Dinah allowed Nogahla to sit between them, casting a sidelong glance at the big man. *I suppose I must finally admit you are trustworthy.* And she couldn't deny Aban's unquenchable thirst for El Shaddai.

Elihu took his customary position, kneeling beside the lamb and making the initial cut. Then arranging the carcass on the altar, he waited while Job blessed the offering and patiently answered each of Aban's questions.

Dinah stole glances at the three elders, who sat directly across from her, but they never lifted their gaze. The visitors seemed changed somehow—Eliphaz older, Bildad weaker, Zophar thinner. In the week of God's miraculous rain, Aban had offered fine meals, though it was discovered that Sayyid's grain storehouses were badly depleted by the drought. The elders accepted only watered wine, however, and returned their food trays untouched—a fast of repentance, they said. Dinah wondered if it was meanness, but she asked forgiveness for that thought at the next morning's sacrifice.

"Uncle Eliphaz," Job said, "would you like to explain to Aban the reason we allow fire to completely consume the lamb?" The old Edomite smiled but declined, graciously listening to Job's explanation that the completeness of the offering illustrates the dedication of the worshiper to God and His teachings.

As Job's account unfolded, Dinah pondered the ways in which his life had imitated the lamb during the past seven days. As if preparing a clean altar for Job's sacrifice, Yahweh's summer rain had washed away the piles of ash and dung from the kitchen courtyard, leaving no traces of the pain that had seeped into it for so long. Then, displaying sacrificial grace, Job had dedicated himself completely to healing relationships with Eliphaz, Bildad, and Zophar. The four men spent hours under the new tent Aban provided as Job's temporary dwelling on the mountaintop. Amid tears and forgiveness, Dinah witnessed Job's inner healing manifest outwardly. Fresh, pink skin replaced over half the sores on his body, and worms died by the hundreds, rolling away with his soiled bandages.

Aban was anxious to welcome Job into his home, assuring his friend he cared nothing about the odor or remaining worm infestation. "Fleeting afflictions, my friend!" Aban raved. "Look how El Shaddai has healed you already! In no time you will be herding your own flocks and plowing fields with your own oxen." But after all the men had left the mountaintop tent, Dinah and Nogahla remained, drying Job's tears and bandaging his wounds.

"I have no right to mourn," he told Dinah one evening as the three watched the sky change from orange to red to purple. "Look at the miracles God has worked on my behalf."

His face stretched into a mask of false strength, fighting the tears that would aid his healing.

Dinah placed a single finger under his chin and turned his gaze toward her. It was the first time she'd touched him without a bandage or herb. "Remember your words, my friend." Her voice quivered as she spoke. "'Naked I came from my mother's womb, and naked I will depart. Yahweh gave and Yahweh has taken away; may the name of Yahweh be praised.' You mourned that night the tragedies struck, but your tears were shed in complete surrender." She looked deeply into his eyes. "I believe trusting Yahweh with our tears is our greatest offering."

The floodgates of his tears burst free, and Nogahla placed a comforting hand on his newly healed shoulder. But Dinah released his chin, and her hand fell limply to her lap. One of his tears wetted her wrist in the glimmering sunset.

And then she realized it. *I love you, Job.* Her cheeks burned at the thought. Her own tears fell, cool streams across fiery beds of self-doubt. Was she betraying Sitis? How would Nogahla feel about this—Elihu, Aban, Nada? Then Dinah remembered Sitis—her friend, Job's wife, whom they both loved with devotion. *No, Sitis, my friend. You know my feelings for your husband have always been pure.* Sitis wouldn't want to see her husband's heart broken by loneliness for the rest of his life.

Dinah looked into Job's grief-stricken face and ached to heal more than his outer wounds. Their eyes met for just a moment, and renewed weeping overtook him. This man had faced tragedy and death, yet Yahweh prevailed in his life. How could she ever love another man after loving a man like Job?

But the next realization stole her breath as if she had fallen with a thud from a runaway camel. *A man like Job could never love a woman like me.*

Dinah was summoned back to the morning's sacrifice by a familiar voice. "Mistress?" Nogahla leaned close, whispering. "Are you crying for the lamb?"

Dinah looked up and realized the lamb had almost completely burned away. She wiped tears without realizing she had shed them. *What is wrong with me today?*

"Abba, look!" Elihu rose to his feet, his hands still dripping with sacrificial blood. The first rays of dawn revealed a distant line of caravans converging on Uz from both north and south, extending as far as the eye could see.

The elders stood, as did Aban. "I don't think it's an army," Bildad said. "I see too many women and children on donkeys for a military attack, and I see a great number of flocks and herds."

"Then what could it be?" Elihu was breathless, fear evident in his voice.

"When Sayyid and Bela paid the Chaldeans to attack Job's camels and servants, they came disguised as a caravan." Aban glanced at his sandals, and Dinah recognized shame clawing at the integrity Yahweh was crafting in the man.

"Now is not the time to consider the past," Job said softly.

Offering a grateful nod, Aban turned to Bildad and Eliphaz. "Gather your armies, and I'll muster my troops. If the caravans have come for battle, we must stop them before they enter the siq." Elihu ran ahead of the elders to the tower stairs, offering help to each man as he descended.

Dinah heard a whine beside her and turned to find Nogahla's face a mask of terror. "No crying!" Dinah shouted, relying on her traditional command. It had worked before, but today the words carried no weight.

Aban nudged Dinah aside and knelt before his beloved Cushite. "Nogahla, listen to me. I'll return as quickly as I can, but you and Dinah must remain on the mountain with Job. I'll send servants by way of the mountain path with camels and a litter on which to carry him." Looking up at Dinah, he said, "You must promise that you'll escape at the first sign of battle. Do you understand?"

Dinah nodded soberly and then retreated to the carved stone bench alone, heart pounding, watching Aban comfort Nogahla. Her heart yearned to be comforted too. If she approached Job, would he hold her and speak reassuringly as Aban did to Nogahla? When her gaze met Job's, she found him staring at her. As if reading her thoughts, he turned away quickly, his neck flushing as red as the canyon's mud river.

The sting of rejection pierced her. *Why can't you love me?* she thought.

Dinah leapt to her feet. "I'm going with you, Aban!" she shouted, startling everyone including herself.

"You can't go with me." He grimaced as if she had suggested he swallow fish eyes.

She started toward the stairs, tears already brimming on her lashes. "I can ride a camel as well as any of your soldiers and lead two beasts on a bridle."

"Dinah! Come back here!" Aban's demands were soon drowned out by the dark, close walls of the tower stairway, but another more daunting voice followed.

"Mistress, you cannot run away from me. Tell me why your frown has now turned to tears."

* * *

Servants cleared away scraps and dirty dishes from the midday meal while Job sat idly in Aban's grand banquet hall, listening to another embellished story from one of his

Edomite cousins. The grandson of his uncle's firstborn had been gushing feats of valor since he'd arrived with the first caravans six weeks ago. "The lion rushed at me from behind the boulder, and . . ."

Smiling patiently at the windbag, Job scanned the men and women seated at the finely carved tables, hoping to find a genuine smile amid the milieu of forced merriment. Bildad and Zophar had left two weeks ago to tend business and household concerns, and Eliphaz, Elihu, and Aban often avoided larger gatherings. The steady patter of rain kept rhythm with the incessant drumming of his cousin's endless stories. Job nodded occasionally when the younger man drew a breath, but he used these moments to ponder all that weighed heavy on his heart.

When Job had first glimpsed the caravans, he too had been concerned about imminent danger. He had watched Aban soothe Nogahla's fears but became as awkward as a camel in sandals when Dinah looked in his direction. He wanted to comfort her, but he felt more than that. For the first time in his life, he yearned to hold a woman other than his Sitis. Without warning, passions rushed in like a flood. Guilt said that he was betraying Sitis's memory by yearning for another so soon. Humiliation told him that Dinah would be repulsed by his embrace. Grief reminded Job that he missed Sitis's voice, her touch, her laugh. Fear returned his thoughts to the invading caravans after Dinah fled down the tower stairs in tears.

When the caravans arrived, full of Job's Edomite family and friends, his life altered dramatically. Joyful descendants of Esau offered gifts of grain, silver kesitahs, and gold rings in celebration of God's miraculous works. Job knew he should rejoice at the encouragement and divine restoration of his wealth, but Dinah's hysterical flight from the altar haunted him.

The caravans continued their relentless arrivals and blessing, but Job's emotions raged just as insistently. When a full moon had passed and still bands of Edomites clogged the trading thoroughfares of Uz, Job asked Dinah and Nogahla to journey with him to Widow Orma's cave. "Master Job," the precious Cushite had said, "perhaps your body has healed enough to make this journey, but has your heart healed enough?"

Job wiped his face as if he could wipe away the memory and then was rudely jolted back to the present by his cousin's bawdy laughter. "What's the matter, Job? Can't you take a story with a little blood and guts?" The man slapped him on the shoulder. "Well, did I ever tell you about the time I went down to Egypt to hunt a behemoth . . ."

Job raised both eyebrows, feigning interest. As long as his blustering cousin spewed stories, Job didn't have to conjure polite conversation. Perhaps a few more hours of pondering could smooth the frayed edges of his heart.

His thoughts wandered back to Sitis's grave—the visit two weeks ago. His bumpy ride on the litter behind Aban's exquisite dapple gray stallion. The curious glances of onlookers as Dinah and Nogahla steered the beast onto the secret pathway through the siq. His first glimpse of the seemingly impregnable mountain path leading to Widow Orma's cave.

"Please, Job, be careful," Dinah had said to him, offering her hand as he conquered the final steps on the rocky path. "Though your strength is returning, this is still a hard climb."

But he had done it. The muscles in his legs were on fire and sweat dripped into his eyes. His arms shook and he could hear his heartbeat like a horse race in his ears, but it felt good. "I'm fine," he said, hoping she wouldn't notice his weakness.

"Master Job, listen to Mistress Dinah!" Nogahla stood at the cave entrance, her finger bobbing like a scolding ima. "Slow down. We did not bring burial herbs to wrap your body and lay you next to Mistress Sitis!"

"Nogahla!" Dinah's disapproving gaze and one-word censure was enough to silence their little friend.

Nogahla's features fell, but Job tried to lift her heart. "Not long ago, I would have willingly let you lay me in the cave beside Sitis," he said. Turning to Dinah, he tried to steady his breathing and bridle his emotions. "Now I believe Yahweh has something planned for each one of us." Jacob's beautiful daughter turned away, as had become her custom since that morning on the mountaintop, and Job's heart plummeted.

Stepping toward the cave entrance, he greeted two soldiers from Aban's household, stationed there to prevent grave robbery. The guards had already staved off one attempt by bandits who had mistakenly believed Sitis was buried with pagan offerings. Job glanced just above the curved doorway, noting a small fissure in the red cliff where a sheer scrap of purple linen swayed in the breeze. He tried to reach it, but one of the soldiers stopped him.

"Master Job, if you don't mind." The young man's cheeks colored as if he was embarrassed. "My partner and I have been watching the female hoopoe in her nest." He cleared his throat, straightened his spine, and adjusted his leather belt. Job hid a grin. The young man apparently needed a better-fitted uniform to hide his tenderness. "Watching the silly creature keeps us alert during our long hours on duty."

Oop-oop-oop. Job's heart stopped at the sight and sound of the lovely pink-and-black-crested bird fluttering to its cliff-side perch with another wisp of fine linen in its long beak. Could it be the same little hoopoe that had appeared on Sitis's balcony the night of the tragedies? Job's spirit sang at the thought.

Oop-oop-oop. Oop-oop-oop.

He bowed his head and allowed the grateful prayer to fill his soul. *Yahweh, heal my broken heart and fill it with a new life, a new love that is pleasing to You.*

Job heard a dainty sniff and glanced up at Dinah. Her head was bowed, but he saw tears streaked down the front of her ambrosia linen robe. Confused, he looked at Nogahla. "My mistress cries each time she sees the bird at the cave, Master Job."

For the first time in weeks, Dinah looked into Job's eyes. "Do you remember the lesson you taught me about the hoopoe just before our caravan arrived in Uz?"

A stab of irony jolted Job's senses. He'd forgotten. His silence answered Dinah's question, and the pain in her expression pierced him.

Dinah glanced away. "It's all right. I saw another hoopoe bird in Uz," she said, picking at a thread on her sleeve. "On the day Sitis ran into my arms at the base of your ash pile, a hoopoe bird landed beside us. It was El Shaddai's loving command of that little bird that convinced my friend to open her heart that day." Once again Dinah looked up at Job. "Would you like Nogahla and me to wait outside while you say good-bye to your precious wife?" Dinah's lips quivered as she awaited his answer.

It was the last time Dinah had spoken to Job except to answer a direct question or to ask how his wounds were healing.

Job's stomach twisted, and blood drained from his face. The sounds of Aban's crowded banquet room entered his consciousness again, and his memory of Sitis's grave faded. *It seems all the pondering in the world can't answer my persistent questions about Dinah.*

Job glanced at the raucous faces and felt weary to his bones. His patience with his Edomite kinsmen was growing thin. No doubt they had originally flocked to Uz to offer gifts and cheer; however, the drought made them linger in the well-watered city, and Job's newly renovated home made them too comfortable to return to their desolate lands. Aban had graciously welcomed Job into his home, offering a much-needed escape from the crowds whenever Job chose to withdraw to his second-story chamber.

Practical and life-giving, Elihu, Eliphaz, and Aban had been like bread and water to Job. Elihu had kept careful records of Job's quickly growing wealth. Uncle Eliphaz showed hospitality on Job's behalf to welcome fellow Edomites, and Aban provided boundaries of privacy for Job in his well-guarded palace.

"Abba Job!" Elihu wound his way between rows of guests and tables, dodging children with toys, avoiding men who'd enjoyed too much wine. "Your great-abba Esau has arrived in Uz!" Elihu continued his perilous march, breathless by the time he arrived at the head table.

Job's heart skipped a beat, and the crowd of friends and family quieted. "Where is Aban?" Job asked, hoping the big man hadn't ridden to a distant field to check on his grain stores.

"Aban has sent word to Eliphaz that Esau will enter the canyon momentarily." Elihu held out his hand. "Come, Abba! We must meet them at the grand courtyard gate!"

355

Job's hands began to tremble. The Great Red Mountain himself had come to visit his favorite great-grandson. "Elihu, does Dinah have my canes?" He cast a hopeful glance across the room. No Dinah. She had become dutiful but distant, tending his wounds but guarding her heart. As his body healed, she seemed to feel he needed her less, when everything within him cried out for her more.

"I have your canes, Master Job." A young serving maid lifted a cane to his three-fingered right hand, her features nearly identical to his Sitis of forty years ago. Wrapping his thumb and fingers around the handle, the girl began tying his one-fingered left hand to the second cane with a leather thong. "Mistress Dinah has asked me to care for you while Master Esau is in Uz."

How did Dinah find out so quickly that Great-Abba was in Uz? Job imagined Dinah hiding like a frightened rabbit the moment she heard of Esau's arrival. He remembered how harshly Esau had treated Dinah at Grandfather Isaac's camp, and he was incensed that these strangers around him celebrated the arrival of his brutish great-abba while his best friend and greatest support felt compelled to hide like a criminal.

"Do you know where I might find Dinah?" he asked the girl.

She glanced right and left as though guarding a secret. "Dinah is in the kitchen courtyard grinding grain, Master Job. Nada is working day and night to feed everyone, and Mistress Dinah insists on helping her."

Job squeezed the cypress cane handles, his frustration mounting. He could never hobble through the kitchen, retrieve Dinah from the courtyard, and wade back through the crowd in time to meet Esau. *If it weren't for all these people* . . . A deep sigh. A quiet prayer. These were the frank-incense and myrrh for his people-weary soul. *El Shaddai, remind me that the celebrants are not strangers. They are my brothers, sisters, aunts, uncles, and friends—blessings from You, not curses to bear.*

Job spoke calmly to the girl. "Please tell Dinah I'd like to speak with her after I greet Esau." She nodded and was quickly on her way.

Steadying himself, Job parted the crowd and walked as regally as his canes allowed. Elihu followed closely behind, his enthusiasm to meet the Great Red Mountain spurred by exuberant youth. Eliphaz appeared at Job's side, dutifully preparing to greet his abba, a relationship neither man pretended to cherish. And finally, Aban divided the crowd, his bronze arrows rhythmically clanging with each step.

The four men stood at Aban's courtyard gate, the Edomite throng pressing behind them, waiting in the gentle but steady rain. Job received every drop as a whispered promise of El Shaddai's assurance, watching expectantly for his great-abba's arrival.

23

~Genesis 36:32~

*Bela son of Beor became king of Edom. His city
was named Dinhabah.*

Elihu could barely keep his feet from dancing. In all his
years in Abba Job's household, he'd never met the great
Edomite lord, Esau. "I don't think I can wait much longer,"
Elihu whispered, leaning close to Job so no one else could
hear his childish eagerness.

"There may still be time for you to hurry inside and make
use of a chamber pot," Abba Job whispered, mischief bright-
ening his countenance.

"Abba! Stop it!" Elihu's outburst drew a raised eyebrow
from Eliphaz and a melodious chuckle from Job. *Music to
my ears*, Elihu thought, relishing the playful banter.

Shofars sounded, and all attention focused on the tall,
broad-shouldered form approaching on a gold-and-red-
draped camel at the canyon's entry. The man described as

the Great Red Mountain was easily distinguishable even three hundred paces from Aban's courtyard gate. Power and authority emanated from him, dwarfing the riders beside and behind. His attendants were impossible to identify in the reflecting rainbows of afternoon sun that shone through God's miraculous rain.

Elihu glanced at his abba and noted beads of sweat gathering below his patchy mustache. Why was he nervous? Then Elihu looked at Eliphaz, a chief elder among the Edomite clan, fidgeting with his sash, eyes shifting from Esau to Job and back to the approaching procession. Why were these men—great in Elihu's view—so anxious about meeting their abba and great-abba? He had often heard Job recount stories of his childhood, when Esau had taken him on hunting expeditions, training Job personally with spear and bow to be the best hunter/warrior of the Edomite clan. Elihu recalled the wash of sadness on Abba Job's face after he'd told Esau of his decision to devote his life to the teachings of the Most High. Job's heart seemed to break each time he spoke of his great-abba's indifference toward El Shaddai.

The shofars sounded once more, and Elihu returned his attention to the oncoming parade. Astonished, he heard himself gasp. The camel to Esau's right plodded under Bela's wide girth. Triumph mixed with rain on the Edomite's face, and his rounded red cheeks were as bright as the sun. Since Job's recovery and Eliphaz's renewed support of his favorite nephew, Bela had been conspicuously quiet. His sudden appearance at Esau's side settled like a dull blade in Elihu's stomach.

"Perhaps *I* should find a chamber pot." Abba Job leaned close to Elihu, the weary tilt of his brow betraying the fear beneath his humor.

Attendants on camels flanked Bela and Esau, each carrying red linen standards bearing the image of a god with a mountain in his hand. A great army followed them, and Elihu's joyous expectation wilted into muddy dread.

A distant rumble of thunder shook the ground beneath their feet, and the heavenly patter of rain dwindled to a fine mist. A nervous buzz settled over the Edomites in Aban's courtyard. Elihu glanced at the line of his friends, Aban on the end, Eliphaz, and then Abba Job at his side. Each of them was as wide-eyed and confused as the rest. Suddenly a clap of thunder and bolt of lightning split the skies and raised the hair on Elihu's arms.

"Take cover! We are doomed!" Shrieks of terror rose as the gathered crowd scattered. The thunder, like a living thing, reverberated through the earth beneath their feet. And then, as if someone had poured the last drop from a heavenly bucket, the wondrous summer rain ceased. All of Uz stilled, devoid of the miraculous for the first time in seven weeks.

Esau's procession, so brash and arrogant moments ago, now halted in eerie silence just a few paces from where Elihu and the others stood. Not even a camel dared spit and break the suspense.

"Kaus lives!" Esau's voice echoed against the red canyon. "The mountain god remains!" he said, pointing to the cliffs.

Job gulped for air. Elihu placed a steadying hand on his shoulder and watched Eliphaz drop his head, rubbing a furrowed brow. In that moment, Elihu realized that of the four men standing in a row, only Eliphaz's abba was alive; however, Esau's blasphemy seemed to grieve his son as deeply as mourning his death would.

An uneasy flutter spread through the waiting crowd as

servants helped Esau and Bela dismount their camels. "Job, you look like death!" Esau's resonant voice filled the canyon. His massive build caused Elihu to cower. Matching Aban's colossal build, the Great Red Mountain was larger than life itself, a legend, a ruler.

Bela remained at Esau's right hand. Gloating, to be sure, but they had yet to discover why.

"My life is being restored, Great-Abba," Job replied, emotion strangling his voice, "by the one true God, El Shaddai."

Elihu stood taller, proud of his abba's brave response.

Esau's eyes narrowed dangerously. "El Shaddai has rejected the Edomites, Job, and He has given my conniving brother, Jacob, the land of Canaan." Raising his voice and arms to the crowd, Esau's voice echoed against the canyon walls. "Therefore, the Edomites have established the Seir Mountains as our home and embraced Kaus as our god." He pointed to the red flags affixed to the attendants' camels. "As you can see by the disappearing rain, Yahweh is unreliable. He comes and goes at His whim, but Kaus, the god of these mountains, endures forever!" Like trained monkeys in an Egyptian market, the people of Uz burst into praise.

Job and Eliphaz exchanged a disillusioned glance while Esau and Bela lapped up the applause. After sufficient pandemonium, Esau raised his hands to quiet them. "Listen, my children. I have come to Uz to declare my successor and Edom's first king. He has lived among you, holding my principles and beliefs as law. He is an Edomite first, above all else."

Esau focused on Job, but his arm embraced Bela. Every muscle and tendon in Elihu's body was stretched taut, ready to step forward, to support any of his friends at the first sign of resistance.

"I give you Bela, your king!" Esau slapped Bela's shoulder, and the army initiated a cheer that rippled through the crowd.

Elihu leaned close to Abba Job and noted Eliphaz's and Aban's questioning glances. "What should we do?" Elihu asked.

Job's features were a scrap of gray parchment, his body as rigid as the cliffs around them. "We allow Yahweh to do His work." The gathering pools in Abba Job's eyes revealed the agonizing wound of yet another betrayal.

✳✳✳✳✳

Job left Great-Abba Esau in Aban's banquet hall and hurried to the kitchen courtyard to find Dinah. The earth had shifted beneath his feet with Esau's public declaration of idolatry, and he needed to tell Dinah before anyone else blurted the news. As Job squeezed past busy kitchen maids, his canes made clunking noises on the tiled floor, and Nada offered a kind nod.

When Job reached the doorway leading to the courtyard, the sight of Dinah in the afternoon sun jarred him to a halt. Her cheeks were flushed, and tears stained her saffron robe. Long, wheat-colored curls cascaded over her shoulders beneath a sheer white linen head covering. Was she a vision, or was she real? Could anyone be so lovely, so vulnerable?

Dinah looked up. "Oh, Job," she said, wiping tears. The mere sight of her sent a rush of warmth through his veins that he thought lost to adolescence. He was mesmerized, seeing only her pink lips, rounded when she said his name, perfect for a waiting kiss. How was it possible to love anyone but Sitis? *El Shaddai, do I dishonor my wife by loving another so soon?*

"Are you all right?" he asked, his feet and canes crunching on the red gravel courtyard path. She avoided his gaze again, examining her sandals. *Why won't you look at me anymore?* He couldn't take his eyes from her. The possibility that his appearance disgusted her had crossed his mind. He had noted his deeply pocked face and patchy beard in Aban's bronze mirror, but surely he was less repulsive without the worm infestation. He simply didn't understand her changes.

He stood over her, casting a long afternoon shadow. Dinah wiped her cheeks again but continued inspecting her feet. "I heard Esau's allegiance to Kaus echo in the canyon, and then the rain stopped." Finally, she looked up. "Has Yahweh abandoned us?"

"No, Dinah. No." Job eased down beside her on the bench, allowing his canes to rest against his leg. "El Shaddai doesn't do things the way we expect. Who could have imagined a shimmering presence or a miraculous summer rain?"

Dinah looked up briefly, her smile stiff and contrived. He used her attempt at decorum to stoke his courage.

"I never expected the caravans to shower me with silver kesitahs, gold rings, grain, and livestock." He paused, watching her pick at a piece of lint on her robe. "And I never expected Great-Abba Esau to declare Bela his successor and first king of the Edomites."

Silence reigned for two heartbeats. He had expected her to gasp, to rage, to show some sort of indignation at the obvious folly of Esau's choice. But when she spoke, her tone registered only sadness. "I'm sorry, Job. Bela is an evil man, and Yahweh will not bless the Edomites under his leadership." The quiver in her voice told him there was something she wasn't saying . . . but he had yet to reveal the full truth as well.

"Dinah, Great-Abba Esau has also proclaimed Uz the new capital of Edom and changed its name. He will honor the woman whose healing herbs sustained me."

Dinah sat like a stone, her expression as unreadable as granite. "What is the new name?"

Job reached into Dinah's basket of freshly ground grain and spelled out the letters of their new city. "D-i-n-h-a-b-a-h. Uz is now Dinhabah, and the capital city of Edom," he said apologetically.

A slow, wry grin lifted one side of her lips, and she looked at Job with a measure of mirth. "Grandfather Isaac taught me to read my name during the years I took care of him, but it appears your great-abba Esau is no better at spelling than choosing his gods." Both of them made weak attempts at a chuckle, but the air between them was tense and awkward. Dinah's eyes filled with fresh tears, and her voice betrayed long-held anger. "If Uncle Esau wishes to humiliate me, he'll have to be more creative than affixing my name to his new pagan city."

Tears escaped over her lashes, and without thinking, Job reached up and brushed them away with his three fingers.

She gasped and withdrew, turning her face away.

Job couldn't breathe. What had he done? "Dinah, I'm sorry. I didn't mean to—"

"Job, I must go." Her voice was so small, he barely heard the words, which made them more frightening than if she had screamed them.

"No, I'll leave. I'll just go back to the banquet hall." He tried to gather his canes, but he was trembling. Why had he touched her with his hideous hand?

"I mean, I must go back to Abba Jacob's camp."

The words stabbed him in the deepest place of his being. A

sound escaped his lips—not a word, not a cry, not a breath. The sound of death. A puff. A moan. A wearied gasp. When his wealth and children were destroyed, when his body was stricken, even when his precious Sitis died—all had left him breathless. But this . . .

"No." He couldn't say more for fear he'd lose his mind. "No."

"I must, Job. Esau's messenger said that Abba Jacob is sick and needs my help."

He tried to hide his face behind emasculated hands. This couldn't be happening. Not now. Not ever. "How can you even consider returning to Jacob's tents after the way he's treated you, Dinah?" The words were an accusation, a venomous hiss at the victim as if she were to blame for her pain.

"He's dying, Job. He needs my care."

Her compassion stoked his anger. "Is there no nursemaid with herbs in Canaan? Must he demand his daughter's return so he can mistreat her again before he dies?"

Dinah's eyes mirrored the dagger in Job's soul. He'd hurled his pain at her and hit his mark. Why did hurt people, hurt people?

"Dinah, I'm sorry," he said. Watching tears cascade down her cheeks, he longed to draw her into his arms. But how could half a man comfort such a woman?

"You speak the truth, Job. My abba is selfish, and because of it, no physician will endure his moods. But just as you love Esau and tolerate his ways, I love my abba and withstand his shortcomings to serve him." She smiled and tilted her head as if explaining to a child. "Besides, Esau made it easier to leave. I cannot live in a city that bears my name and is ruled by an idolatrous king."

"Please, Dinah. Please stay and fulfill God's purpose for your life." He had no idea what he was saying, just that he needed her as a fish needs water or a flower needs sun.

"I have no purpose to fulfill, Job." She placed her hand on his cheek, the sensation sending an exquisite fire through his body. "Grandfather Isaac commanded I marry an Edomite. Esau made it clear no Edomite would have me until you offered your son. Isaac's command was my purpose, and it died with Ennon."

"But I need you." The words escaped Job's lips like a wild donkey without bit or bridle.

Dinah's features lost all life, and the mask she'd worn at Grandfather Isaac's camp returned, brittle and immovable. "Why do you need me, Job?"

Finally she held his gaze, but now he wished she'd turn away. He felt vulnerable before her, every pockmark, every scar, exposed. How could such a repugnant man dare to love a beauty like Dinah?

"I need you to take care of me," he whispered. It was the only reason he could imagine she would stay. Compassion had always moved her.

Her lips trembled. The mask was crumbling, but instead of compassion came fury. "Are there no nursemaids with herbs in Dinhabah to care for you?" She hurled his words back at him, the betrayal in her voice landing in his stomach like a dull sword.

She stood, and he tried to capture her but drew back his hand before it touched her perfect arm. "Dinah, wait!" But she was gone, the sound of her weeping whispering through the juniper trees.

*****

Dinah ran no farther than the sweltering kitchen. "Why the tears, my girl?" Nada bustled to Dinah's side, crushing her in a motherly embrace. "Tell me how you could be upset on a day when the whole town celebrates your name?"

"Ahh!" Dinah uttered her frustration, and Nada released her like a hot coal. "Renaming Uz *Dinhabah* was simply a sting to ensure I leave here, Nada. Uncle Esau is a wicked, conniving brute, but he's my only transportation back to Abba Jacob's tents in Hebron."

The busy kitchen, humming with preparations for the evening meal, suddenly grew as quiet as a tomb.

"Who needs transportation to Jacob's tents in Hebron?" The old woman's eyes narrowed, daring Dinah to repeat herself.

"We cannot go!" Nogahla threw her bread dough on the stone table, crushing the heel of her hand into its center. Dinah thought the kindhearted Cushite might be imagining her face in the lump of dough. "We have a good home here with Master Job and Aban and Elihu and Nada. And your father is mean!"

"Nogahla!" Nada's chastising came at the same moment Nogahla's own conscience struck her.

"Oh, mistress!" Nogahla gasped, clapping her flour-covered hands over her mouth, leaving traces of white powder all over her dark brown face. "I should not have spoken of your father so disrespectfully." She lowered her hands and raised her chin. "But we still cannot leave our home."

Dinah couldn't keep from grinning. *Oh, how I will miss you, precious one.* "We will not leave here, Nogahla," Dinah said, tears beginning to betray her. "*I* will leave, and you will stay, my friend."

Every serving maid stilled her busy hands, eyes fastened on Nogahla.

"All right," Nada said, breaking the uneasy silence, "we'll finish meal preparations in the courtyard. Everyone out!" She gathered the girls like a mother hen with her chicks, and too quickly Dinah was left to face the shocked and betrayed expression of her best friend.

"Mistress, how could you even consider leaving me?" Her chin quivered and unshed tears threatened to overflow.

"Because I leave you with the man El Shaddai has chosen for your husband." It was a fact they both knew but had never spoken. Though Dinah claimed no legal rights over the girl, nor did the women share a familial bond, it was understood that Aban would someday ask Dinah's permission to marry Nogahla. Permission would be granted and a wedding celebrated—but without Dinah's presence.

Heavy footsteps and a booming voice interrupted the tense moment. "What's all the commotion?" Aban playfully yanked back the tapestry separating the banquet hall from the kitchen, but his smile quickly disappeared. Stepping into the kitchen, he allowed the tapestry to fall behind him and walked directly to Nogahla's side. Taking both her hands in one large paw, he lifted her chin with the other. "Tell me why these beautiful eyes are weeping."

She pulled away and turned her back on him, and Dinah watched the big man's heart break. He looked to Dinah for answers. "I'm returning to my abba's camp," she said without adornment, "and I'd like Nogahla to remain in your household—because I believe you care for her, Aban."

The big man sighed deeply and squeezed the back of his neck, as if doing so might release some deeply rooted wisdom to untangle the knotted emotions before him. "Dinah, I should have spoken to you before, but I am trained to lead men, not women." Another sigh. He glanced at Nogahla and let one hand fall gently down her arm as he spoke. "I love Nogahla, but I wanted to wait until I was worthy before making her my wife."

At this, Nogahla turned a questioning gaze on the mighty man. He smiled down at her. "I have my father's wealth, but I want the wealth of God's wisdom. I want to lead my family as Job led his—as a priest of the Most High." Turning back to Dinah, he bowed slightly. "That's why I've waited until now to offer Nogahla's bride-price and ask your permission to take her as my wife."

Dinah's heart was so full, it nearly burst. She grinned, cried, nodded, and drew a breath to give her hearty approval, but Nogahla shouted, "No!"

Both Aban's and Dinah's celebrations came to an immediate halt. "What do you mean, 'No'? You love Aban!" Dinah closed the gap between them, watching Aban's features harden against the rejection he now feared.

Nogahla turned pleading eyes toward Aban. "I do love you, but I don't want to choose between you and my friend." She reached up to cup his face in her hands. "I know I have no right to ask it of you, but may I return with Mistress Dinah to her father's camp and then come back to you, Aban, after her father leaves this world?"

Dinah interrupted. "Nogahla, we have no way of knowing how long my father will linger. I promise I'll return to Uz for a visit someday."

"No! No one ever comes back." Nogahla's temper flared, and she beat her fists on the table. "My mother promised she would find me, but she never did. You will wave good-bye, and I'll never see you again!"

Aban gathered Nogahla in his arms, lifting her like a babe, cradling her against his well-muscled chest. "All right, my love, it's all right," he whispered.

Dinah's heart was torn in two. She grieved for the pain she caused her friend, but she mourned for herself too. Oh, how she longed for a man's tender touch. She curled to the floor, weeping for a husband she once knew, for a betrothed who had died before they met, and for the love of a man who saw her only as a nursemaid.

"Dinah?"

Startled, she looked up into Job's frightened face.

"What's happening?" he asked, casting a worried glance at Nogahla in Aban's arms. "Nogahla, are you hurt?"

Feeling utterly foolish, Dinah stood and straightened her robe, but Aban spoke before she could offer an explanation. "Job, I'm going to escort Dinah and Nogahla to Jacob's camp with Esau's army. Will you watch over my home and holdings until I return?"

Dinah was too stunned to speak, and it seemed Job was too. Both of them glanced from face to face, silently asking a myriad of questions, but finally it all came to just one.

"When will you leave?" Job asked, his eyes penetrating Dinah's soul.

"Tomorrow." Dinah lowered her gaze and left the kitchen, entering a banquet hall full of celebrants chanting her name.

PART

24

~*From Genesis 46*~

Then Jacob left Beersheba, and Israel's sons
took their father Jacob and their children and
their wives in the carts that Pharaoh had sent to
transport him. . . .
  These are the names of the sons of Israel
(Jacob and his descendants) who went to Egypt
. . . Reuben . . . Simeon . . . Levi . . . Judah
. . . Issachar . . . Zebulun . . . besides [Jacob's]
daughter Dinah . . .Gad . . . Asher . . . Joseph
and Benjamin . . . Dan . . . Naphtali. . . . All
those who went to Egypt with Jacob—those
who were his direct descendants, not counting
his sons' wives—numbered sixty-six persons.

Job's legs were becoming stronger each day, and it felt good to return to his fields with Shobal and Lotan. His shepherd and herdsman had eagerly returned to their duties, leaving the nearby towns where they'd fled to keep their families safe from Sayyid's long and evil reach. In the six moons since Aban had left with Great-Abba Esau's army, Job had purchased flocks of sheep for wool and teams of oxen to plow his fields. The drought continued its stranglehold, denying every region life-giving winter rains. Merchants' gossip said the two-year dry spell would last five more years—this prophecy from Egypt's mystical vizier, a man who reigned over all but Pharaoh himself. *But a seven-year drought? Never have the ancients recorded such a judgment from You, El Shaddai.* Despite Egypt's dire prophecy, Job hoped for God's merciful spring rains and hired Dinhabah's first-sector beggars to prune his grapevines.

"Dinhabah," he said aloud. Only the sheep grazing on scrub heard him, but it was better than talking to himself. He swiped his hand over the scraggly beard growing in patches on his uneven skin. *Protect her, El Shaddai*, he prayed. Every moment of every day, he thought of Dinah. No matter his activity or location, something reminded him of her face, her voice, her laughter. She was a part of him.

"Ahh!" He crawled to his cane and pushed himself to his feet. He used only one cane in his three-fingered hand now, so the maids no longer tied him to a stick. "Come, Bildad!"

Job had named his new donkey Bildad after Sitis's brother. Uncle Eliphaz, who had stayed to help Elihu manage Job's quickly growing wealth and Aban's estate, laughed each time the stubborn mule refused to obey. *Dinah would have appreciated the humor too.* Job took a deep breath and fondly imagined that the beast hailed from Ishmaelite herds. For truly his stubborn Ishmaelite brother-in-law and Sitis shared the same fiery spirit. But he had loved his wife for it. He remembered the spark of joy in her eyes when she spoke of El Shaddai on the morning before she died. *Dinah saw the hoopoe bird and spoke to Sitis of Your love, Yahweh. Your ways are amazing.*

Job's thoughts kept cadence with Bildad's hoofbeats, and they soon reached the city gates. While the rest of Edom, Moab, and Canaan wilted in the hot, arid weather, Dinhabah was thriving. The market bustled and merchants hawked their wares. Starving pilgrims who couldn't travel to Egypt's Black Land traded richly for the grain, earning Dinhabah the nickname Little Egypt. Job's family and friends had unknowingly boosted the city's trade economy when they bestowed lavish gifts of grain, which Job had in turn freely given Dinhabah's new grain merchant, Aban. The city's growing prosperity earned recognition for both men among local and traveling tradesmen.

Four-legged Bildad, most likely hot and thirsty, plodded directly to Aban's stables. Job was thankful Elihu and Eliphaz remained with him in Aban's home. Together they had decided Job's newly renovated palace was perfect for lingering family members, widows, the homeless, and fatherless beggars in need of shelter. The drought had severely affected even Dinhabah's water supply, but the solution came in reconfiguring the spring-fed fountain to produce more drinking water. Even the animals were well satisfied. Bildad sidled up to his favorite stable boy, who waited with a bucket of water. Job landed a firm and grateful hand on the boy's shoulder and then turned toward the house.

Elihu stood at the courtyard gate, his face riddled with concern, a rolled parchment of their accounts in hand. "We've received no messenger from Aban again today. Should we send a small caravan to check on their whereabouts?"

"Elihu, perhaps you should come to the fields with me tomorrow. You have too much time to worry." Job winked at Uncle Eliphaz, who rested in what little shade the sparse-leafed eucalyptus tree provided. Laying a fatherly arm around Elihu's shoulders, Job steered him toward the banquet hall and tried to allay his fears. "Aban sent word that while traveling with Esau's troops, they intercepted Jacob and his family in Beersheba on their way to Egypt. I'm sure they've had to travel slowly because of Jacob's ill health, and they'll send word as soon as they find sufficient pasture for their flocks and herds."

Job tried to keep his own concern muted. Egypt was a dangerous place, its Pharaoh as unpredictable as blowing sand. And he'd heard endless merchant gossip about the vizier, an undoubtedly cunning schemer who rose to the second-highest throne in Egypt with one magical interpretation of Pharaoh's dreams.

Elihu took a deep breath and slapped the parchment against his hand. "Our journey will be much more difficult if we don't hear from Aban."

"What journey?" Their leisurely walk came to an abrupt halt just inside the banquet hall.

"Our journey to find Dinah." Elihu raised one eyebrow over his close-set eyes.

The words splashed Job like cold water from Bildad's bucket. "Elihu, I cannot search for Dinah."

"But Abba, you must! Your body is healing but your soul is wasting away." The son of Job's heart abandoned all attempts at subtlety. "You are a good and godly man, Abba, and Dinah loves you. Why do you let your shame keep you from the woman God has given you?"

Job looked at his hands, considered the twisted legs beneath his robe, the half man now called Job. "Yes, I love Dinah." He felt a rush of panic. Never before had the confession passed his lips. "But you are wrong, Elihu. She doesn't love me—not in the way a man needs to be loved by a wife. If you saw affection for me in her eyes, it was born of pity for a broken man." Even as the words rolled off his tongue, they tasted rancid and bitter.

"Abba, you taught Dinah that when she was forgiven by El Shaddai, no man could shame her. Perhaps you need to learn a similar lesson." Elihu drew close, whispering now. "When El Shaddai blesses you, no one can steal His blessing—except you." He turned and studied the parchment, calling over his shoulder, "Nada has prepared the evening meal. The servants could have a caravan ready to leave for Egypt by morning."

Elihu's words echoed in Aban's empty banquet hall. Job was alone again, and the sensation startled him. Alone. *It's not good for man to be alone"—isn't that what You said to Adam, Yahweh?*

Job's heart beat wildly. He hadn't allowed himself to willingly love Dinah. Or to believe it possible she could love him—truly love him the way a woman loves a man. What if Elihu was right?

"Ooh!" he groaned aloud. The thought of declaring his love to a beautiful woman like Dinah terrified him. What if she laughed? Or worse, what if she pitied him? *Oh, El Shaddai, I cannot do it!* But if rejection was his only stumbling block, then pride was his real problem.

"Job, it's you." Uncle Eliphaz appeared at the doorway. "I thought I heard a wounded sheepdog moaning." The mischievous sparkle in the old man's eyes told Job that compassion lurked in his motives.

"I think I'm going to find Dinah," Job said haltingly, hoping to measure his uncle's reaction. Eliphaz had offered a frail apology to Dinah and Aban after his outburst on the dung pile, but he had completely ignored Dinah in the days following.

"Why have you decided to go now?" His uncle's raisin-brown face betrayed no emotion, gave no inkling of his opinion.

"I think . . . no, I know I love her," Job said, the phrase becoming more familiar on his tongue. "And I've never told her. If El Shaddai has blessed me with this love, I must not steal it away and keep it to myself." Elihu's advice was nestling deeply into his soul.

Uncle Eliphaz lifted one bristly, gray eyebrow. "You and Elihu will leave in the morning. I've already prepared a list of provisions that should get you safely to Egypt. The chief steward will see that your caravan is ready by dawn. Yahweh told me weeks ago this day would come."

"Why did you . . . ? How did . . . ? When did . . . ?" Job's mind ran hopelessly ahead of his mouth.

"If you cannot finish a sentence, my son, how will you ever find Dinah in Egypt?" The old man chuckled, but Job was suddenly struck with the most glaring barrier to his departure.

"Uncle, I cannot take Elihu away and leave you with two busy households in the middle of a drought."

"Yes, my son, both you and Elihu will go." Uncle Eliphaz's voice was gentle but firm. "I am quite capable of managing Aban's interests and yours while you're gone, and I hope by doing so to atone for some of the wrongs I committed against you—and Aban." He placed both hands on Job's shoulders. "You are the son of my heart, Job. After your abba was killed, I have watched you honor El Shaddai in every circumstance of your life. God blessed you with your Sitis and you loved her well, but this Dinah you now pursue . . ." Eliphaz pursed his lips into a pale, thin line, and Job prepared his heart to repel the venom he felt sure would come. "She is a gift from the Most High, and she will bring you joy for the rest of your days. Go in peace, my son. Find her. She is your future."

✿✿✿✿✿

Dinah reclined on a cushioned couch, listening to the trickle of fountains in Joseph's garden ponds. Though she'd lived in her brother's household for nearly seven moons, the sights and sounds of Egypt still intrigued her. And the miracle of Joseph's life and position thrilled her.

She giggled, pinching herself. "Ouch!" No, this was not a dream. Her little brother, the firstborn son of Rachel who had been nursed beside Dinah at Leah's breast, was now second in power to the king of Egypt. But second in name only—for it was Joseph who led Egypt after the young Pharaoh's father had died two years ago. Advisors and servants alike lauded Joseph as the "father of Pharaoh" since Egypt's eight-year-old king relied on the vizier's wisdom to manage the unprecedented drought.

Dinah recalled the moment she had realized her brother's importance. When she'd floated down the drought-starved Nile River, hundreds of Joseph's admirers lined the banks of papyrus reeds to greet his luxurious felucca. Slogging through mud and avoiding crocodiles, Egyptians cried, "Hail, the mighty vizier, the judge of the high court! Grace and peace to the righteous gatherer of the king's taxes! Honor and health to the keeper of Pharaoh's granaries!" Dinah had marveled at the elaborate titles constructed for her little milk brother while she sat on the ship's cushioned dais, watching in wonder as sixteen oars slapped the water and pulled them toward Thebes.

Dinah inhaled the scent of poppies, water lilies, and early acacia blooms, enjoying her few quiet moments while servants scurried about their busy tasks. She treasured these afternoons when her rambunctious nephews, Manasseh and Ephraim, were with their tutor. She adored the boys but valued the time alone to adjust to her new life in Egypt.

Browsing the colorful murals on the garden walls, she re-lived the honored history of her ancestors' relations with the land of Egypt. Joseph had ordered his home decorated with paintings of Abraham's travels, Isaac's stories, and even some of Abba Jacob's life as it related to the vizier's own journey toward the Black Land.

Her heart stopped at a scene she'd never noticed before—an older girl and boy playing near a stream, with a pink-and-black-crested hoopoe bird perched on a branch, watching over them. Glancing at the scenes around it, Dinah realized the girl and boy were meant to be her and Joseph. *Why would he order a hoopoe bird?* She was suddenly dizzied by the overwhelming scent of lotus blossoms and the everyday reminders of Job.

"Ahh!" She pounded the cushion beside her. Would she live a day without thinking of Job's smile, his kind heart, his caring eyes? Could she look at a painting or see a sunrise and not remember his voice or his godly character? *I suppose trying not to think of someone means I'm thinking of him,* she reasoned, curling her hands into tight fists and pressing them against her temples.

"Not a very attractive pose for the vizier's sister."

Joseph's teasing imposed on her brooding, but she was grateful. Dinah looked up to find the brother she remembered as a youth gliding across the tiled path with his innate regal bearing. No kohl or malachite around his eyes. No red ocher mixed with gull resin on his cheeks and lips. On the rare occasion that Egypt's vizier rested after his midday meal, he traded his fine Egyptian kilt for the speckled woolen robe of Jacob's tribe.

Pulling an ivory stool close to Dinah's couch, Joseph tilted his head and offered his most disarming grin. "What causes my lovely sister to pinch her face like a dried fig?"

Dinah couldn't resist his charm. Without his royal wig or golden headpiece, his short-cropped hair curled handsomely at his temples. "I'm not just the vizier's sister, you know." She thrust out her chin with an air of superiority. "I'm now *nursemaid* to the vizier's children." Dinah chuckled at the irony of it. She had become neither Abba Jacob's nor Job's nursemaid but a caregiver to two young boys. But when she paused her pondering, she saw that her teasing had missed its mark and somehow pierced Joseph's heart.

"*Nursemaid* is a servant's position," he said, reaching for her hand. "You are not a servant in my home, Dinah. I want to honor you, not use you. I should never have agreed to let you tend Manasseh and Ephraim. You can see my sons anytime you wish, but you will not be their nursemaid."

Panic rose in her throat and nearly choked her. Dinah felt as if yet another purpose in her life was being eliminated. "No, Joseph, please. I was just teasing. Please." She gripped his hands as if he was a rope suspended over a chasm. "I'll never have children of my own, and the tenderness of their arms around my neck, the sound of my name on their lips . . ." She clutched his hand to her cheek and began to rock and weep.

"All right. All right, shh," he said, soothing her, brushing her hair back from her face. "We don't know what Yahweh has planned for your future." He gently drew his hand away and coaxed her head upright. "Look at me, Dinah."

Tentatively, she obeyed the only man who had never betrayed her trust.

"Our brothers threw me into a cistern, but El Shaddai lifted me to the second-highest throne in Egypt. We don't know Yahweh's plans for you, my dear sister." He paused, and then mischief crept into his eyes. Dinah's tension began to melt. "But you may only care for my boys as long as you never call yourself a nursemaid again."

Relief came then, washing over her like a wave of the Great Sea. "If you try to take your sons from me, Lord Vizier," she said, a little mischief of her own returning, "I'll have to wrestle you to the ground and make you say, 'Hairy Uncle Esau,' as I did when we were children."

Joseph's resonant laughter filled the garden and her heart. "Well, sister. If you do, you'll show a dozen Nubian warriors that they can overpower their master with a tickle fight."

The pair chuckled, and Dinah reached once again for her brother's hand. "You know, I almost didn't come to Egypt with Abba Jacob." Joseph's furrowed brow told her that Abba hadn't revealed his heartlessness or Dinah's most recent betrayal. "Do you remember I told you that Uncle Esau promised to escort Aban, Nogahla, and me to Abba Jacob's camp in

Hebron, but we encountered Abba's caravan in Beersheba on the way?"

Joseph nodded, his eyes narrowing.

"When Esau's scouts saw Pharaoh's grand carts transporting Abba Jacob's camp, our uncle grew jealous—and nervous. He sent gifts and messengers ahead of his troops, much like Abba Jacob sent gifts and the procession of his wives to greet Esau when we were children, returning from Haran."

Again Joseph nodded at the memory.

Dinah bit her lips hard, trying to stem the tide of tears that threatened to drown her. "Uncle Esau had lied about Abba's ill health in order to remove me from Job's presence. When the discovery of his deception loomed, Esau offered Abba Jacob servants and livestock to assuage his inevitable anger at having to reclaim his shamed daughter."

Joseph reached out and touched her cheek, and Dinah's next words escaped in a whimper. "When I saw Abba Jacob strutting out like a crowing rooster to greet Esau's troops, I flew into his arms, weeping. My joy at seeing Abba healthy outweighed my fury at Esau's betrayal. Abba pushed me away, and I was certain he was about to condemn Esau for his treachery, but . . ." She paused, her humiliation too raw to continue.

"What?" Joseph whispered. "What did Abba do?"

"He laughed, Joseph. He embraced the brother he's hated all his life and congratulated his improving skills of deception."

Egypt's vizier moved to his sister's side, wrapping his strong arms around her, letting her tears wet the front of his robe. When Dinah regained control of her voice, she said, "Aban and Nogahla immediately began preparations for our return to Dinhabah, but I couldn't. I didn't know where to go or what to do—until Abba Jacob told me about you, Joseph. When I heard you were alive, I asked Aban and Nogahla to continue with me to Egypt."

A long silence stretched between them, though not uncomfortable, for they had always been like one soul in two bodies. "I'm glad you came," he said, his warm brown eyes searching deeper than words could express. "But for six moons, I've watched your heart ache for this man named Job. Why couldn't you go back to Dinhabah with Aban and Nogahla? Even now, I hear Aban prepares to return within the next three moons. Why don't you plan to go back with them?"

Dinah wiped her cheeks and sat up, shrugging away his embrace. "Job wants nothing more than a *nursemaid*, Joseph." The bitterness rang in her ears like cymbals. She turned away, ashamed at the lingering pain. "At least in your household, no one expects me to be their nursemaid."

A mischievous grin played on Joseph's lips. "So, you didn't come to Egypt for me." He tilted her chin up with his finger. "You ran to Egypt to escape Job."

Dinah's heart squeezed a little. "I left Uz because Uncle Esau lied, and then I discovered my brother's resurrection." She lifted her hand to brush his cleanly shaven cheek. "When Abba Jacob's caravan arrived at Goshen and I saw you adorned in all the splendor of Egypt, I thought our brothers had made a terrible blunder. I couldn't see Joseph in the kohl-rimmed eyes and white linen kilt. I couldn't believe the man wearing that golden neck band and headpiece was my little milk brother!"

Joseph's laughter filled the air like the aroma of lotus blossoms, and Dinah's heart fluttered as if a bird had taken flight.

A bird. She glanced again at the wall, gazing at the hoopoe.

Casually, she pointed to the mural. "Joseph, does that scene on your wall represent you and me when we were younger, with a hoopoe bird watching over us? Did you ask your artist to paint it that way, or did he add the bird through his own creativity?"

Joseph turned on the couch, resting an elbow on his knee as he'd done when he was a boy. Sadness shadowed his expression. "You're perceptive as usual, and yes, that's you and me. I asked the artist to paint the day as I remembered it, and the hoopoe has always been a symbol of my sister's strength and the good fortune I knew Yahweh would bring—after the sorrow."

Dinah's breath caught. "What do you mean? What day was that, and how can you think me strong?"

"It was the day before Shechem took you."

Dinah's heart stopped.

"You've never been more beautiful than you were that day, Sister. Innocent. Unsuspecting of what the world—and men—were capable of."

Her throat constricted, but her silence was blessed by the most beautiful words she'd ever heard.

Tears welled in Joseph's eyes as he continued. "We played in the meadow that day, and I remember seeing a hoopoe. Its flight was awkward and undulating like a butterfly, just as you were beautiful yet uncertain in your youth. A falcon swooped in, threatening the little bird, but suddenly the hoopoe soared to heights that put the falcon to shame. Through the years, I've thought of you often, wondering what became of my lovely hoopoe sister after her falcon attack at Shechem. I've always believed Yahweh would give you unexpected strength through which you would soar."

"Oh, Joseph." Tears streamed down Dinah's cheeks. She

had no idea the hoopoe had been a symbol to him so many years ago. And Joseph could not have guessed that a simple bird held such meaning in her days with Job. How could Yahweh use a simple creature to weave a golden thread throughout her life?

"Dinah, I was only fourteen, but I remember what Levi and Simeon did to the Shechemites." Joseph gazed intently at her, and she was overwhelmed by his love. "My sister, I could not deliver you when our abba and brothers used your pain to satisfy their own ambition. But I can protect you now. No one will ever harm you again."

Dinah hugged him tightly, whispering through her emotions, "You cannot save me from everything, dear brother. Job thought he would save me from wicked men, but he broke my heart more than any other." Laying her head on Joseph's shoulder, she asked, "Why did El Shaddai waste two years of my life, letting me fall in love so another man could hurt me?"

Leaning back, Joseph held her shoulders. "It's like I told our brothers, Dinah. Yahweh's plans are greater than ours. What our brothers intended for evil by selling me into slavery, God worked for good by allowing me to interpret Pharaoh's dreams and prepare the world for this drought. I believe El Shaddai sent you to Uz much like He sent me to Egypt. You have suffered much at the hands of men, but in the process, much good has come. You sustained Job in his illness and restored Sitis with your testimony of forgiveness. Your friend Aban and I have established Egyptian trade routes through Dinhabah." Joseph scowled. "What a ridiculous name for a city. I'm thankful Aban has some influence with the Ishmaelite prince Bildad, and will work to restore that city's name to Uz."

Dinah laughed and pulled at his earlobe.

"Without you," he continued, "your friends Aban and Nogahla would never have met and married, nor would they have come to Egypt and found Nogahla's father, Potiphar, my old master."

He gazed into her eyes as if searching for hidden treasure. Suddenly he stood and took Dinah's hand, lifting her to her feet. "The Dinah I see before me is meek yet strong. She is compassionate and loving, yet bold and fiery." Holding her face tenderly between his hands, he said, "The sister I left when I was seventeen could not have grown into this woman without the experiences of Uz."

Dinah coiled her hands around Joseph's forearms, and they leaned their foreheads together as they had done a thousand times when Joseph's brothers had teased or tormented him. The bubbling water in the garden pond washed away Dinah's weary thoughts, and it must have masked the clatter of Manasseh's sandals on the tiled walkway.

"Auntie Dinah, a wealthy cripple has asked to see you!" he said.

She looked up but held tightly to Joseph's arms. There was Job under the acacia tree, supported by only one cane, dressed in a fine striped robe. But his expression looked as though he'd lost his best friend.

25

~Genesis 36:33~

*When Bela died, Jobab son of Zerah from
Bozrah succeeded him as king.*

Job stared, dumbstruck, at the sum of all his fears. Dinah
stood in the arms of a wealthy, handsome husband who
obviously adored her. Job was too late. Elihu nudged him
from behind, but he couldn't take another step. They'd come
at midday, hoping to avoid the enigmatic cousin Joseph. Instead, they'd interrupted a couple's intimate moments.

Job and Elihu had arrived in Goshen to discover that
Egypt's legendary vizier was Jacob's long-lost son. They'd
left in haste, knowing only that Dinah lived in the vizier's
palace. Now it was abundantly clear that Dinah *and* her beloved shared Joseph's home.

"Manasseh! You mustn't say such things." Dinah gathered
the little boy in her arms. "This is not a cripple. He's my
friend Job."

The muscular, bronzed man wrapped a possessive arm around her shoulder. Awkward silence lingered while Job took in every detail of Dinah's loveliness—one last glance. The mandrakes and narcissus paled in comparison, and the heady scent of lotus blossoms awakened Job's reality. *I cannot give her all she deserves.*

Job cleared his throat and turned to go. "I'm sorry I interrupted. It was wrong of me to come—"

"Job, wait!" Dinah wrenched away from the man's arm. "Don't go. I want you to meet my brother Joseph."

Job's legs nearly buckled with relief, but he was still bothered by the dashing young man's impudent smile. "Your brother? I thought your brother was Pharaoh's vizier." This man-child was no older than Job's sons had been. And where were his Egyptian face paints, his kilt and royal jewelry? How could he be the lauded "father of Pharaoh," the provision of Egypt, who had saved the world from famine?

"Elihu!" Dinah rushed past Job, seeming to have just realized her young friend lingered behind him. Job awkwardly hobbled aside, making room for their reunion. "When did you arrive?" she asked, nervous excitement in her voice. "Have you been to Potiphar's villa to visit Aban and Nogahla?"

Elihu glanced from Job to Dinah and back again, measuring his response. "We arrived at your abba Jacob's camp yesterday and have traveled all night to find you."

Job bowed his head under the weight of his fear. There it was. Elihu had revealed the singular purpose of their journey. *To find you . . . to find you . . .* He felt like a shy boy, too embarrassed to meet her gaze. Silence settled on the garden, the fountains pattering like spring rain.

"I can't believe you're here." Dinah stepped toward Job,

and when her hand rested on his arm, his eyes rested on her sweet face. "Joseph," she said, "please come and meet my friend Job."

Job sensed the vizier's movement, though he could not take his eyes off Dinah. "I think I'll talk with Job another time, sister," Joseph said, moving past them with little Manasseh reluctantly trailing behind him. "I believe I'll get acquainted with your friend Elihu here." Joseph slapped his guest on the back and ushered Elihu into the pink granite halls of his palace.

Joseph's departure stirred the air with the faint scent of almond oil, and Job wondered if Dinah could be content with a man whose skin didn't gleam with the extract. She was so beautiful, and as vizier, Joseph could introduce her to the most handsome and powerful men in Egypt. Dinah seemed happy here. *El Shaddai, should I even tell her of my love?*

"What are you thinking?" she asked, her eyes as blue as the lotus blossoms floating in the pond.

"I . . . I'm thinking . . ." How could he tell her the thousand thoughts that raged against each other? Like opposing breezes, they swirled into a whirlwind of confusion. On the dung pile, he and Dinah had talked for hours. In the ashes, words had come easily.

"Why did you come?" The softness in her voice was drying up like week-old cheese.

"I came because . . . because . . ." Job studied his hands, the three fingers on his right, the single finger on his left. And then he heard her sob. Startled, he looked up into the great droplets of diamonds falling from her eyes.

She swiped the gems away with the back of her hand. "Do you still seek a nursemaid?"

The words pierced him. "Is that what you think?" He dropped his cane and grabbed her shoulders. "I am a cripple, begging a beauty to love me!" Tears rolled down his own cheeks. "But I have no right to tell you I love you with all my heart, when my arms cannot carry you to a bridal chamber and my wealth cannot promise you a kingdom." The outburst left him feeling almost as startled as Dinah looked. Breathing hard, he didn't know whether to kiss her or grab his cane and join the next caravan to Dinhabah.

They stood silently, weeping, searching each other's gaze.

"Did I hear you say you love me?" Dinah finally whispered.

"Is that all you heard?" Job replied softly. He longed to catch a tear that dangled at the corner of her jaw. But he released her shoulders, staring at his contemptible hands and then trying to hide them behind the folds of his robe.

"I have loved you, Job," she said, "since the day I met you." She must have glimpsed his uncertainty because she quickly explained, "I didn't *fall in love* with you until after Sitis died, but I loved the ideal of you, the man of God you are." Her cheeks flushed a shade that would have put a sunset to shame. She reached for his left hand, lifted it to her cheek, and then turned and kissed his palm. "But I love you now as a woman loves a man, as a wife should love a husband."

She bowed her head, turning her eyes away for the first time. He cupped her face, beckoning her gaze, and felt like he could drown in those blue pools. "How could you know those were the words I needed to hear?" He kissed away her tears, so sweet, mingling with his own as their lips met for the first time.

❉❉❉❉❉

The days following Job's declaration of love felt like a dream to Dinah. Joseph assumed the role of abba and determined to pay Job a handsome bride-price and provide an abundant dowry. Dinah chose linen and gauze cloth for her robes in every color of the rainbow, some with gold threads woven throughout, others having gems sewn into the fabric. A jewel merchant fitted Dinah's bridal crown, creating it out of gold from Ophir with precious onyx, sapphires, jasper, rubies, and topaz from Cush.

"I feel like a queen," she whispered to Nogahla on the morning of her wedding.

Dinah, Job, Elihu, Aban, and Nogahla had sailed with Joseph's family and guards away from the docks at Thebes two days before. Pharaoh's musicians serenaded their departure, and dancers moved along the banks, whirling streamers and turning in place like a child's spinning top. Dinah grew dizzy just watching.

More musicians accompanied the wedding party on the ship, trilling flutes and lyres, strumming harps. The longboat sloshed through the dwindling Nile, draped with great spans of white Gaza linen, a new type of cloth woven by the Edomites near Zophar's home.

"Wouldn't Master Zophar turn as red as mean old Esau if he knew his gauze decorated your wedding felucca?" Mischief danced in Nogahla's dark eyes, and Dinah enjoyed a moment of naughty delight.

After two days and nights on the Nile, they had reached Avaris this morning, where the wedding party disembarked and now traveled by land to Abba Jacob's camp in Goshen. The black soil and green plains of Goshen resembled a jewel amid the world's dusty brown drought. Pairs of men rode in Pharaoh's fine chariots, and the women rode in ox-drawn carts. Dinah jostled beside Nogahla and three handmaids in the ornate bridal cart with golden wheels, its team of oxen draped in purple, their horns polished to a brilliant sheen.

"Mistress—" Nogahla began, but Dinah placed two gentle fingers on her lips.

"You are now the mistress of your own estate, Nogahla, with serving maids to tend you. You are married to a wealthy man who loves you and worships El Shaddai. It's time you called me Dinah."

Nogahla reached for Dinah's hand and entwined their fingers. "All right, Dinah, but don't forget. You are also about to marry a wealthy man who loves you and worships El Shaddai."

Dinah lowered her gaze. Perhaps a former Cushite servant considered the gifts Job received from his Edomite clan an abundant estate, but Dinah knew they would have to live carefully in order to sustain Job's large home and raise a family. "Nogahla, I am happy with the riches of my husband's love and the modest gifts from family and friends."

Her friend gasped and covered her mouth as if she'd swallowed one of the flies swarming the ox's tail. "You don't know!"

Dinah waited, but Nogahla didn't elaborate. "Know what?"

"No, I'm not going to spoil the surprise." She began shaking her head and pressed her lips together, forming an adorable pink ribbon.

"Well, now you have to tell me!" Dinah was suddenly quite interested in the meetings Job and Joseph had enjoyed while in Thebes, their growing camaraderie and easy banter. In fact, now that Nogahla was acting so coyly, she remembered Aban and Elihu had joined some of those secretive sessions. "Tell me, or I'll bribe Nada to live with me half the time when we return to Dinhabah!"

Nogahla chuckled. "All right, all right, I'll tell you," she said. "But I think Nada will want to share us anyway. Don't you?" Dinah brushed Nogahla's cheek before she divulged the truth. "Aban said that in the time we've been away, Yahweh has increased Master Job's wealth considerably. Uz—I mean Dinhabah—has become a major trading stop, and both Aban's wealth and Master Job's have been more than blessed." Nogahla's eyes twinkled. "See? I told you we would both be married to wealthy men."

Dinah stared in disbelief. How could this be true? She remembered Joseph's words, "Yahweh's plans are greater than ours," and moments later, Job had walked through the door.

She focused on the chariots in the wedding processional ahead of them and realized each of the men had his own amazing story of Yahweh's personal involvement and blessing. "Nogahla, could you ever have dreamed you'd see your father again?" The gruff soldier rode in the first chariot with Joseph, holding the reins for the vizier who had once been his slave.

The Cushite's tears brimmed on her lashes. "Though he told me the sad news of my mother's death, at least I've come to know the father I met only briefly as a child." She raised her slender fingers to her throat, her features that of a woman, not a girl. "And El Shaddai answered a prayer I never dared pray. Yahweh granted me a husband who can speak with my abba as an equal—a soldier and a man of property, a man who has shown the great Potiphar that El Shaddai is not just for the Hebrews." Tears spilled onto her mahogany cheeks, and Dinah hugged her close.

"Your husband is a good man, my friend." Dinah watched Aban's mastery of the twin-stallioned chariot, in which Job steadied himself against a special prop that Joseph had ordered built within the groom's chariot. "We are blessed women indeed." She marveled at Sayyid's righteous son and praised God for Job's miraculous testing, faith, and healing.

In the third chariot, Elihu wandered in zigzag patterns across the emerald green pastures of Goshen. He'd spent hours studying the horsemanship techniques but used little time for practice. Dinah couldn't hold back a giggle at the sight of Job's exemplary student regally balanced with one hand on the reins and one on the chariot gate, while the vizier's guards made every effort to dodge Elihu's meandering stallions. *El Shaddai, bless my friend with a pure and lovely bride. He deserves a woman who will love him as I love Job.*

Abba Jacob's camp came into view, and Dinah's heart skipped a beat. Goat's-hair tents dotted the land while flocks and herds roamed the pastures and gleaned the fallow fields. It smelled like home—sweaty shepherds and sheep dung, lentil stew and roasting lamb. Children squealed, pointing and waving at the vizier's chariot guards, only to be greeted by unflinching kohl-lined eyes.

"Why did I agree to come back here, Nogahla?" Dinah's stomach lurched at the thought of facing Abba Jacob after the way he'd ridiculed her gullible trust in Esau.

Her friend clasped her cheeks in an iron grip, aligning her face-to-face. "El Shaddai can work in every circumstance, mis—Dinah. If we have learned anything, you and me, we have learned this truth." Dinah could only nod as the young woman continued her lesson. "It's easy to remember this truth when life is easy, but we must remind each other when life gets hard." The two hugged fiercely, squeezing their eyes closed—as if every tensed muscle could somehow fight future fears.

When Dinah opened her eyes, she looked beyond the festive tents of Jacob's camp and saw the red standards of an approaching army. "No!" She straightened, startling Nogahla. The flags bore the symbol of a god holding a mountain in his hand. "It's Uncle Esau!"

"Oh, mistress! Who invited him to your wedding?" Nogahla's hand slammed against the wedding cart. "Maybe now is a good time to remind each other about El Shaddai's presence." On any day but today, Dinah would have appreciated her friend's faith. But on her wedding day, she could see only the sun glinting off the iron swords of Esau's army.

Joseph's chariots arrived on the southern edge of camp well before the oxcarts, and Dinah watched the men's distant silhouettes hurry toward the center fire, where Abba Jacob and his sons waited for the ceremony to begin.

"Driver, take my cart directly into camp!" Dinah said. "Don't tether it with the rest of the animals." She spoke in broken Egyptian, and the man seemed to understand, though he was hesitant to obey. "Hurry up, or I'll drive the oxen myself!"

His reins came down hard on the oxen, but the beasts' pace remained slow in comparison to Esau's camels. By the time the wedding cart arrived at the central campfire, Uncle Esau stood with three weary-eyed captains beside somber-looking wedding celebrants.

"What?" Dinah shouted, hurrying from the cart without waiting for a servant's aid. She marched toward the knot of men. "What is so important that you have to ruin my wedding day, Uncle Esau?" Dinah was huffing and panting while the coins dangling from her wedding crown jingled and danced. She pulled the jeweled veil aside and for the first time saw Job's sullen face. Regret and fear battled for dominion. "Job, what has happened?"

Silence. She looked at Joseph, who stood beside Abba Jacob. Both men bowed their heads, while the eleven other brothers waited reverently behind them. Nogahla approached Aban, and he gathered her in his arms. Elihu looked ashen.

"Someone tell me what's wrong!" Dinah said.

Grasping her shoulders, Job spoke without adornment. "Ishmaelite troops have attacked Dinhabah in rebellion to the Edomite claim and Bela's reign. Bela was killed."

Dinah remembered Aban's prediction of violence if the Edomites gained too much control of Uz. She let the words sink in as Job continued.

"The Ishmaelites invaded the city and have returned it to its original name—Uz."

Dinah sighed. Glancing from face to face, she felt selfish at her relief. "I'm sorry about your kinsman," she said, "but doesn't this mean we can return to Uz and live there as before?"

Aban stepped forward, placing Nogahla in Elihu's reassuring arms. "No, I'm afraid no Edomite is safe in Uz right now. When the Ishmaelites invaded, Prince Bildad accompanied the army because he knew Eliphaz was still in the city."

"Oh no!" Dinah turned to Job, cupping his cheek.

"It's all right, my love," Job said. "Uncle Eliphaz is safe. Bildad's troops escorted him back to his home in Teman, while Bildad remained in Uz to protect Aban's property and grain supplies." Looking from Nogahla to Dinah, he said apologetically, "Aban and Nogahla must return as soon as possible, but I can never go back to Uz again."

Dinah turned to Nogahla, and they exchanged silent sorrow. Then she met Job's gaze again. "Aban and Nogahla will simply have to visit us then." But she could see that his heartbreak went deeper than tribal loyalties, and the silence in the camp drained the blood from her face.

"Dinah, Yahweh restored much of my wealth after the tragedies." Job cupped her cheeks in his hands. "But it was seized by the Ishmaelites during the raid. I have no home to offer a wife now."

The whole world fell away, and Dinah could see only the tears of regret wetting Job's lashes. But of what concern was gold and silver to them? He had lived on a dung pile, and they had found love amid the ashes. Peace coursed through her veins, warm and life-giving. She drew a breath to share her heart.

"No!" Aban's voice thundered. "Bildad is a prince among his people, and I still have a household military presence in Uz to enforce my decisions." Aban turned toward Job. "I promise that you will have every kesitah and gold ring returned to you, my friend, and I will give you fair compensation for your land and palace." Aban extended his hand, rousing Job to embrace it and seal the pact.

"Thank you, Aban," he said, stepping forward to grasp the man's forearm.

"I still need a successor." Esau's raspy voice broke into the tender moment. "Job, you've always been too soft-hearted to rule," he said, scratching his scraggly red beard. "So I'm changing your name in hopes of changing your character. You will be called Jobab, and you must learn to build the kingdom of Edom with an iron hand."

Job lifted an eyebrow. "I have no property, Uncle. How can I build a kingdom when I cannot even build a home?" Dinah wondered if he was gently refusing Esau's appointment.

"Might I suggest Bozrah?" Every eye turned toward Joseph, who had remained silent until now. "It's a small town but has great potential, located near two major trade routes and protected on all sides by steep cliffs."

Esau's eyes narrowed at his Egyptian-looking nephew. "And how do you know so much about a city in my country, *Vizier*?"

Joseph's kind face turned to quarried stone, the kohl and malachite lengthening his eyes into catlike weapons. "In the first two years of this drought, all of Egypt and Canaan traded their shekels and deben for Pharaoh's food. Now, in the third year, they trade their livestock for a cup of grain." He leaned forward. "But what if I'm not content to just build Pharaoh's kingdom?" His gold neck band and headpiece gleamed in the sun, causing Esau to squint at the reflection. "You see, *Uncle*, I have sent scouts into Edom to prepare for the day when your people come to Pharaoh begging bread."

"How dare you!" The red man matched the flags of his standard-bearers.

"I dare because I am the vizier of the most powerful kingdom on earth, and you would do well to curry my favor." Without waiting for an answer, Joseph wrapped his arm around Job's shoulder. "King *Jobab* will soon be the beloved husband of my favorite sister, and he is mistaken when he says he has no home. He will soon enjoy great prosperity. Aban has promised to return his wealth from Uz, and I am providing an enormous bride-price." Turning to Abba Jacob, Joseph said, "And I'm sure my abba wants to add to the bounty."

For the first time since Joseph began his discourse, Esau's

crimson began to fade. "So, Jacob, do you agree? Will you add to Joseph's bride-price for your daughter?"

Dinah watched her abba wilt under Joseph's scrutiny. She knew he would rather die than disappoint his favorite son. "Of course, yes," Jacob grumbled. "I plan to offer Job a bride-price as well."

Esau's satisfied grin nearly ruined the victory for Dinah, but Job's humble voice interrupted the outpouring of generosity. "I'm deeply grateful for your gifts, but one question remains." Turning to Dinah, he grasped both hands and gazed into her eyes. "We found our love amid the ashes," he said. "Can you now love a king?"

In the distance, a trilling sound anointed the moment. *Oop-oop-oop.* They gasped in unison, and Dinah glanced up at every date palm tree in the camp, hoping to find the precious hoopoe.

Tenderly, Job caught her chin and kissed her gently. Suspended in the moment, she could barely breathe. The taste of his kiss. The beating of her heart. The reminder of God's lifelong presence.

"Can you love a king?" he asked again.

"I love Job," she said.

Thunder gently rumbled through Egypt's Black Land, and a cool breeze stirred the trees. Dinah saw her reflection in Job's eyes—a woman loved. And her heart soared at Yahweh's pleasure.

EPILOGUE

~*Job 42:12–17*~

The LORD *blessed the latter part of Job's life more than the first. He had fourteen thousand sheep, six thousand camels, a thousand yoke of oxen and a thousand donkeys. And he also had seven sons and three daughters. The first daughter he named Jemimah, the second Keziah and the third Keren-Happuch. Nowhere in all the land were there found women as beautiful as Job's daughters, and their father granted them an inheritance along with their brothers. After this, Job lived a hundred and forty years; he saw his children and their children to the fourth generation. And so he died, old and full of years.*

AUTHOR'S NOTE

It has been my pleasure and privilege to search out hidden treasures and craft a story that confounds, thrills, and challenges you to open your Bible. Some people have asked how I can write biblical fiction when God's Word is truth. I hope that by sharing an illustration, I'll help you understand biblical fiction better.

Have you ever pulled your sweatpants out of the dryer and noticed the drawstring had slipped out of the waistband? Well, the tedious task of weaving that drawstring back into the waistband is a little like writing biblical fiction. The inerrant Word of God is like the waistband—fixed and unchanging. The elusive historical facts and flexible plotline are like the drawstring that a writer must weave through Scripture to pull the story together.

Some of the characters in *Love Amid the Ashes* are readily named in Scripture: Isaac, Jacob, Esau, Dinah, Job, etc. Other characters are named in historical texts outside of Scripture. For instance, in an ancient Jewish text called the *Testament of Job*, Job's wife is described as Arabian and given the name Sitis. In this mystical accounting of Job's life, I gleaned many plot ideas, using subtle variations to make the story more believable in the biblical context.

Dr. Karl Kutz, chairman of Multnomah University's biblical languages department, helped me immensely in my search for historical context. Although he was quick to point out the problems associated with trying to place the book of Job on a linear timeline, Dr. Kutz noted the connection inferred by the Hebrew term for Job's "servants" (Job 1:3), which occurs elsewhere only in the Genesis story of Isaac (Gen. 26:14). Similarly, the Hebrew term for the gift of silver kesitahs Job's family gives (Job 42:11) is found only in Genesis 33:19 and Joshua 24:32. Also, he agrees it is certainly feasible that Job lived during the patriarchal era since the Septuagint (a Greek translation of the Old Testament) records Job's death at 248 years old.

Dr. Kutz pointed out an addendum to the book of Job in the Septuagint that links Job to the historical character Jobab (mentioned in Gen. 36:33). It also says Job took an Arabian wife (which I present as Ishmaelite), and gives Job's first son the name Ennon. Although the data found in the appendix is of questionable historical value and reflects an attempt to historicize the character of Job, it does support a popular perception that Job was a contemporary of the patriarchs and provides a convenient setting for the story.

Mystery also surrounds the ancient city of Uz, causing some commentators to place it north of Canaan, near Aram, while others position it on southern borders between Edom and Arabia. The fact is, we don't know. This uncertainty makes my fiction drawstring possible and pliable. I chose to settle Uz on the border of Edom and Arabia and studied the mountains of Edom that skirted the Transjordan Highway. After realizing Petra was nearby, I created ancient Uz with amenities more congruent with Petra's Nabataean period but authenticated locations and descriptions of forests and natural springs with nasa.gov radar images. Unfortunately, I've never personally visited Petra, so I found myself thankful for an imagination and www.youtube.com.

Rabbinical tradition is a vital part of the Jewish faith, and two more texts formed my thinking on the permeating concept of the House of Shem. *The Book of Jasher* is a Hebrew text referenced in the Old Testament (Josh. 10:13; 2 Sam. 1:18); however, present-day copies of the original text have not been authenticated. In the faithful translations available, chapter 28 says, "Jacob is sent to the House of Shem . . . to learn the Way of the Lord, but Esau would not go." A later work by Rabbi Louis Ginzberg, *The Legends of the Jews*, refers repeatedly to the House of Shem. It attributes the godly educations of Abraham, Isaac, Jacob, and even Melchizedek (the priest of God Most High to whom Abraham paid a tithe in Genesis 14) to the teachings of Shem and his descendants. Though not biblical fact, the House of Shem is a rabbinical tradition that has survived millennia.

I began my research at the Multnomah University library with *A Commentary on the Book of Job* by Édouard Dhorme (Nelson, 1984). Like many women, I've wondered if commentators have an opinion about the identity of Job's unnamed wife. Seeing no mention of her name or lineage there, I thumbed to chapter 42 to search comments on Job's restitution and second-family blessing. And there it was—the first time I saw Jacob's daughter, Dinah, suggested as Job's second wife. My imagination exploded, and the seedling story was planted.

Rabbinic traditions such as the *Targum of Job* and *Pseudo-Philo* identified Dinah as Job's one and only wife, having borne all twenty children, and suffering his enduring trials and eventual restitution. As mentioned earlier, the Septuagint identifies Job's wife as Arabian. The author of the *Testament of Job* combines the two traditions, making Dinah Job's wife after Sitis dies during his suffering. I was thrilled at the prospect of Job's healing and Dinah's redemption; however, I then discovered Genesis 46, in which Dinah accompanied her father, Jacob, to Egypt. Suddenly my fiction "drawstring" was hung up in the biblical "waistband," and I had no idea how to pull it through. How could Dinah live in Egypt with her father if she married Job in Uz?

I continued to research. The Bible describes Esau's move from Canaan to the Seir Mountains and his Ishmaelite, Hivite, and Hittite wives. But the cultural and geographical significance of Edom's melting pot blossomed in my imagination after I read *Whence Came the Hyksos, Kings of Egypt?* by David J. Gibson. Though Mr. Gibson's theories are controversial, they added a dimension of Egypt's involvement with Edom that opened my mind to Esau's possible political role in history. Esau provided a believable caravan to transfer Dinah to Egypt and a despicable ploy to lure her. My drawstring broke free!

Finally, the little hoopoe bird ties a lovely drawstring bow, pulling together plot, history, and God's Word. Mentioned twice in Scripture (Lev. 11:19; Deut. 14:18), the hoopoe bird was chosen as Israel's first national bird on May 30, 2008. Though biblically categorized as unclean, the beautiful creature won Israel's heart above the red falcon, the white-chested kingfisher, the white barn owl, and other birds.[1] Once again, my little hoopoe sings its victory song.

Thank you, dear reader, for taking the time to weave the drawstring through God's Word with me. I hope you can see that biblical fiction is so much more than a fanciful imagining of how things might have been. It is truly my heart cry to know how biblical characters experienced the God I know today. Blessings and shalom to you.

1. Erez Erlichman, "Hoopoe Israel's New National Bird," Ynetnews.com, May 30, 2008, http://www.ynetnews.com/articles/0,7340,L-3549637,00.html.

ACKNOWLEDGMENTS

Philosophers say it takes a village to raise a child. Well, I've often felt like a child in my efforts to write this book, and have been so thankful to the village of friends, family, and colleagues who assisted, educated, and inspired me.

To my writers' group: Meg Wilson, for her long hours of phone edits, face-to-face encouragement, and late-night, last-minute counseling sessions. Velynn Brown, for seeing the overall picture and challenging me to feel more deeply on the page. Michele Nordquist, for her faithfulness to this project through email, though we've met only three times—she was at times the wind that propelled me forward. And to my sweet husband—the final detail man with his professor's red pen.

To my daughters, Trina and Emily, for being my best friends, brilliant young women, and cherished babies forever. To my parents, Charley and Mary Cooley, for blessing me with a godly heritage and a love of God's Word. To the parents of my heart, Pat and Sharie Johnson, for the tangible and intangible blessings your love brings into our lives. To my dear father-in-law, Bill Kidwell, who cooked many dinners for the family while I was sequestered at my computer.

To Vicki Crumpton: I had no idea an editor could be so kind and encouraging, a cheerleader from beginning to end. To Dan Thornberg for the gorgeous cover. To the rest of the Revell team, who led me like a babe through my first publishing maze. Michele Misiak, Jessica Miles, and Cheryl Van Andel: your patience resembles that of—well, Job.

To our Multnomah University family: Dr. Karl Kutz, who graciously spent lunches and many emails answering a myriad of Hebrew and cultural questions, and who has graciously accepted a fictional retelling of the precise historical data he spent years researching. To the Multnomah library crew: Suzanne Smith for her help in securing research materials, and Pam Middleton for her patience when I kept items well past the due dates.

To the incredible biblical fiction authors who have influenced my life by their expertise and well-researched novels: Francine Rivers's Mark of the Lion series for whetting my appetite and adding depth and dimension to the biblical era; Anita Diamant's *The Red Tent* for my first inspiration of a fascinating retelling of the patriarchal era from a Jewish perspective; and Angela Hunt's series on Joseph, Legacies of the Ancient River, for its vivid insights into Egyptian life.

To my friends in Israel, Marian and Veronika Brenner, for their help in Hebrew translation and wording. (Isn't God great to have arranged our dinner seating on that cruise?)

As mentioned briefly in the dedication, I have struggled for some time with chronic illness. I would be remiss if at the end of a book on suffering, I neglected to thank the professionals who helped ease my chronic pain. Many thanks to Dr. Marlene Dietrich, Dr. Richard Carroll, Dr. Donna Archer, and Ellen eAkins, LMP. Through their compassionate care, we have managed the pain and hopefully touched many hearts. In addition, I'd like to encourage those of you enduring chronic illness to visit www.restministries.com for great encouragement and resources.

No doubt I have forgotten to mention my heartfelt thanks to someone very important. To you, I ask for grace. Hopefully I'll have better record-keeping systems in place for the next book!

And to you, the reader, thanks for spending your valuable time with me here in these pages. My prayer is that you've seen God's Word fit together as an interwoven story that will, from this day forward, speak in a fresh new way.

Finally, most importantly, to my God—who speaks in whispers and rumblings when I open His Word. How can I ever express the depth of my love, my hunger, my joy, my thanks, to the Creator of all things creative?

Mesu Andrews is an active speaker who has devoted herself to passionate and intense study of Scripture. Harnessing her deep understanding and love for God's Word, Andrews brings the biblical world alive for her readers in this debut novel. She lives in Washington. Visit Mesu at www.mesuandrews. com or www.loveamidtheashes.com.

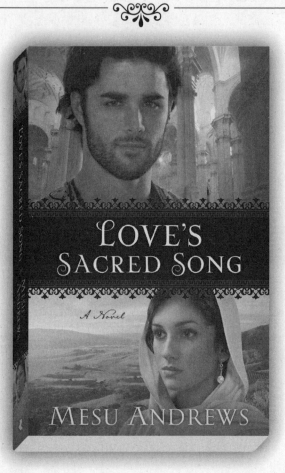